Taker of Lives

LESLIE WOLFE

 **ITALICS**

ITALICS PUBLISHING

II **ITALICS**

Italics Publishing Inc.
Cover and interior design by Sam Roman
Editor: Joni Wilson
ISBN: 1-945302-18-6
ISBN-13: 978-1-945302-18-3

Acknowledgment

The warmest thank you for my legal oracle and friend, Mark Freyberg of New York City. He has the talent to educate, formulate strategies and alternatives, and offer solutions to the most convoluted legal questions a crime novelist can come up with. I can't think of a smarter or more sophisticated lawyer, whether civil or criminal, business or real estate. Some say he's the best in New York; I believe he's the best, period.

1

Nightmare

She woke with a start, her heart instantly racing when the raw memory of strange, gloved hands on her body invaded her consciousness. She could still feel the cold latex on her skin, touching her, stripping her naked, manipulating her limbs, sending shivers of fear and aversion down her spine. She remembered feeling paralyzed, wanting to scream but staring powerlessly at the face of a monster hiding behind a mask, laughing in quiet, raspy gurgles that only she could hear, glaring at her with merciless, hateful eyes.

She rubbed her forehead with frozen, trembling fingers and forced herself to breathe, gasping in deep, long breaths of air to wash away the memory of the troublesome nightmare. Must've been a nightmare... she was in her own bed, wearing her favorite silk jammies, and she could hear her mother's rushed footfalls as she was getting ready for work. Nothing was out of place.

Just a night terror, that's all it was. The worst she could remember, a vivid one she won't be forgetting any time soon, still, just a nightmare. Her eyes fell on Pat's photo, framed on her night table, and she focused on his loving smile for a moment, imagining his strong arms wrapped around her body, making her feel safe again.

Better.

She stood, feeling a little weak at the knees, but pushed herself to walk out of the bedroom, heading toward the kitchen. Her throat was parched dry, as if she hadn't had a drink of water in ages. She filled a glass at the sink and gulped it down avidly, then breathed again.

"Good morning, sweetie," her mother greeted her, then grazed her cheek with a warm hand. "Feeling better?"

She frowned, a bit confused. What was her mother talking about?

Her mother stopped her morning get-ready rush and gave her a head-to-toe scrutiny, then a tiny smile stretched her lips.

"You were a little dizzy last night, and your blood pressure was lower than what I like to see."

"Ah," she reacted, still frowning, realizing she didn't remember much of the night before.

"Christina, we discussed this," her mother said in her clinical voice, the tone she reserved for her most disobedient patients. "You don't eat much, these photo shoots are a resource drain, so you *have* to pace yourself. You'll burn out. *Vogue* won't go bankrupt if you take a day off every once in a while."

It was the eternal conflict between the two of them. Her mother meant well but failed to realize a model's career span only lasted a few short years, and she couldn't afford to waste a single day. She was twenty-six years old, already on her way to becoming old news. Soon, the agencies would start sending her templated emails, saying stuff like, "After careful consideration, yadda, yadda, we have decided to proceed with a different candidate who suits our needs better at this time." Free translation? "You're too old for this game, sorry. We've got someone younger; find something else to do with yourself."

But that day hadn't arrived yet; she was still one of the most sought-after models in the industry, and her photo shoots took her around the globe, adorning her in designer clothing that she got to keep after showing on coveted catwalks under the incessant flicker of thousands of flashlights. Dizzy or not, she had a schedule, and she intended to keep it. Her pickup limo was due at nine, and she wasn't going to be ready in time.

She toughed it out and pushed her mother's concerns aside with a beaming smile and a hand gesture.

"I'll be fine, Mom, don't worry. I'll even do some blood tests if you'd like, but not today. Any coffee left for me?"

Her mother gestured toward the Keurig machine. "Got you some vanilla pods, the ones you like."

"Hazelnut too?"

"Hazelnut too, sweetie," she smiled, then placed a smooch on her cheek and rushed out of the house, jingling the car keys in her hand. "Have a safe flight! And get some rest."

"I will," Christina replied to the empty house, suddenly as cold and quiet and scary as her nightmare had been.

Still shivering, she threw the coffee maker a regretful glance as soon as she realized it was a quarter to nine. Not nearly enough time to put on makeup and get dressed. She forced herself to move quickly, although it felt like she moved in slow motion, the air thick as if it were water, opposing too much resistance for her weakened body to overcome.

She entered the bathroom and turned on the vanity lights, then gave her face a critical overview. Dark circles under her eyes that would require concealer, a pallor that asked for more blush than usual and maybe a darker foundation tone. Hollow, haunted eyes that needed a touch of eyeshadow to bring their faded color forward.

She turned on the shower and began undoing her buttons, still examining her face, but her fingers hesitated; she looked in the mirror and her breath caught. Her pajama top was buttoned wrong, the lowest button fastened through the second lowest buttonhole. Trivial.

Then why did she feel her blood turn to ice when she looked at the uneven hems?

She felt a new wave of dizziness wash over her and took a step back. A strangled whimper came out of her mouth as faint memories invaded her mind.

Cold, latex-gloved hands touching her, stripping her naked, manipulating her body. A piercing, evil stare from behind a mask, and a raspy, terrifying laugh, a stranger's snicker, yet eerily familiar. The sound of a camera shutter, over and over, in a familiar rhythm of rapid bursts. Her own skin, turning to goose bumps when those strange hands invaded her. The same hands dressing her, putting on her pajama top, grazing against her breasts while doing the buttons.

She wrapped her arms around her body and took faltering steps back until she ran into the wall, her eyes riveted on the mirror, on the image of her unevenly done buttons.

"Oh, God, please…" she whimpered, as tears rolled down her pale cheeks. "Please don't let it be true."

The nightmare was real.

2

Day Off

Tess ran on the sand at a leisurely pace, enjoying the fresh morning air, the soft colors of the calm ocean, and the warm rays of the sun, all good distractions to keep her from thinking too much of the man running alongside her. She watched their feet hit the ground synchronously, sharing a rhythm, almost like sharing a heartbeat. Then she looked away, over the emerald waters, and let a smile flutter on her lips.

It felt good to share a life moment with someone. She hadn't done that in a long time, and she didn't know what that moment really meant if anything. Maybe just two cops exercising together, two colleagues, nothing more.

Of course, it was nothing more. She was an FBI agent, he was a homicide detective with the Palm Beach County Sheriff's Office. On occasions, they worked cases together, when Palm Beach County had an investigation that required the support of the bureau.

She shot him a quick glance and frowned a little.

"Are you pacing yourself?"

He looked at her and grinned but didn't say a word.

"What, you're taking the fifth now?" she asked, sounding a bit out of breath.

His grin widened.

She made a dismissive gesture with her hand. "Okay... Change of topic. Why isn't Michowsky sweating it with us?"

"He's taking his kids fishing," he replied. "We just closed a tough case. He needed a break."

"And you?"

"Me? I'm fine, I guess, but a break never hurt anyone, so a long weekend plus two more days off sounds great."

He stretched his pace for a few seconds, then turned around, landing in front of her and jogging backward, without skipping a beat.

"Any plans this weekend, Special Agent Winnett?"

She hesitated before replying. It didn't take twelve years as a federal agent to know where the conversation was headed. Did she want to go out on a date with Detective Fradella? Maybe it wasn't the smartest or most logical thing to do, but the thought of it made her smile.

She shot Fradella a quick, shielded glance. He was a perceptive cop, one curious enough to ask unusual questions and bold enough to formulate intriguing theories. Ambitious and eager to learn, he'd made himself available twenty-four hours a day during their most recent investigations, absorbing profiling techniques and methodologies insatiably, then applying them correctly when the first opportunity presented itself.

But he wasn't running by her side that morning to learn behavioral analysis techniques. He was there as her friend, a friend who was willing to be whatever else she'd allow him to be. That morning it was different; it took willpower, but she decided to turn away from her past, forcing her mind to ignore the wound that would never heal completely, the distant, yet still raw, memory of that terrible night, twelve years ago.

Maybe it was time to move on, even if that meant taking small steps and allowing people a little closer. Maybe it was time to learn to live again; the past had held her captive long enough.

"Um, not sure yet," she eventually replied, veering her eyes sideways. "Nothing popped up on my agenda, but it gets fairly busy on the weekends," she added jokingly.

"Then I better hurry up and ask you to dinner tonight," he said, smiling under a bit of an insecure frown. "And a movie?"

She laughed. "I'll see what I can do. What did you have in mind?"

"Whatever you're in a mood for," he replied quickly, then turned around and resumed running alongside her.

"You didn't really plan this, did you, Detective?" she asked, then clammed up, embarrassed, about to apologize. He didn't deserve the third degree she was giving him.

"No," he replied, raising his arms in the air. "Pure spontaneity, that's me."

"Uh-huh," she replied, then continued to run in silence for a minute or so, her mind completely empty of all thoughts, enjoyably relaxed.

"Hey, do you mind a work question?" he asked after a while.

"Shoot."

"Why did you decline the invitation to join the Behavioral Analysis Unit?"

She looked at him for a moment. "That's not a work question, that's personal."

"Sorry, I didn't mean to pry," he muttered, keeping his eyes trained forward, on the horizon line.

"No, I meant it's a personal question, not a work question, but I'll answer anyway." She paused, not knowing how much she should share. "I didn't feel ready, you know; and Quantico? Not for me."

"Why?"

She slowed her run, coming to a stop, then turned and looked at the ocean that glimmered with a million sparkles in the morning sun. "Would you leave this?" she gestured toward the water.

"For Quantico? In a heartbeat," he replied with a wide grin.

He wasn't even panting after the three-mile run on the soft beach. She felt tired all of a sudden and sat on the sand, tilting her head backward to let the sun warm her face. It felt good, like expert fingers giving her a facial massage, while the wind played with her hair. If she let herself go, she could stay like that forever.

"I don't know who you are, Detective Fradella," she eventually replied, with a tinge of amusement in her voice, then her tone turned all serious. "I thought of Quantico many times, but it just doesn't seem right."

"That BAU guy said he'd help you adjust, right?"

She frowned for a moment, trying to remember. "You mean, Supervisory Special Agent Bill McKenzie?"

Fradella nodded.

"He's the one who nominated me for the position, but it's not an issue of adjusting. I'd be working cases, just like we do here, only chasing the worst possible offenders, closing the most brutal cases, and I'd be nationwide, not regional, like I am right now. That means travel, a lot of time spent away from home."

"In that case, I don't know who *you* are, Special Agent Winnett," Fradella replied, his smile lingering. "I've never seen you shy away from a difficult case, not to mention you don't strike me as particularly attached to your home."

That was the problem with dating a colleague, a good investigator on top of it. She couldn't lie or fudge things up, because he'd easily catch on to it and the questions would keep pouring on. He was right to keep asking, because she still hadn't mentioned the main reason she'd turned down Bill's offer, and his instinct was telling him there was more to the story. She took a moment to think about it, although it wasn't the first time.

She didn't feel that sure of herself, not yet, not enough for Quantico, for working on a team alongside the most brilliant investigators in the entire bureau. Whenever she thought her past had been forever locked away, her PTSD would resurface with an unexpected moment of hypervigilance, a snapped response or a startled reaction to the simple event of someone entering the room, reminding her she wasn't ready yet. She couldn't share that with Fradella, not now, not ever. Not without telling him what had happened to her twelve years ago, and that she could never do.

Instead, she decided to deflect. "You see me as a calloused wanderer, huh?"

He shook his head. "No, that's not what I meant. I believe you have an opportunity, and you're letting it slip away. It won't be there forever, Bill or no Bill."

She let a few moments of silence pass by, enjoying the subdued whoosh of the ocean waves brushing against the shore.

"You like sushi?" she asked, not taking her eyes away from the ocean's sparkling surface.

"I love sushi, and know a great place," he replied enthusiastically. "Is 6:00PM okay with you?"

She nodded. She had plenty of time, and nothing to do. Their run was over, and she didn't expect Fradella to hang out by her side much longer. Maybe she could take her car to the car wash, or do some grocery shopping, maybe vacuum the living room? Nah... she'd be better off helping Cat at the bar. She almost burst out laughing when she quietly admitted to herself that outside of her job she didn't have much of a life. Maybe she did belong in Quantico after all.

"Hey, have you climbed the Jupiter Inlet Lighthouse?" Fradella asked. "One hundred and five steps in creaking cast iron. We could grab a snack and go up there." He searched her eyes. "If you'd like."

She didn't get a chance to reply. Fradella's phone rang, and he groaned when he saw the caller's name displayed on the screen. She stared at the ocean some more, ignoring Fradella's phone conversation and taking in the beauty of the endless stretch of water.

"Raincheck?" Fradella asked, crouching next to her. "We're being called in. It's an apparent suicide, so it probably won't take long." He made a gesture with his phone. "I'm guessing we're still good for dinner."

"And Michowsky?"

"He'll meet me at the scene. Doc Rizza's inbound too."

He extended his hand and she took it, letting him help her get up. She brushed off the sand from her capris then turned around, ready to leave.

"Car's over there," Fradella said, his frown still deep. "Come on, I'll drop you off before heading to the scene."

They walked quickly, but as they approached the car they slowed a little. She couldn't say whose fault that was.

"So, it's a suicide, huh?" she asked, unable to stop thinking how she would've loved to climb the 105 steps of the Jupiter Inlet Lighthouse.

"Yep," he replied grimly.

"No need for a federal agent, I guess?"

His frown vanished. "Hey, there's always a need for a federal agent. Us county cops, we might screw things up like we always do."

"Yeah, right," she laughed. "Wait until Michowsky sees me. He'll be thrilled." The sarcasm in her voice was unfiltered.

"Actually, he really would, you know. He thinks the world of you."

3

Suicide

They made quick stops to change clothes on their way to the crime scene. Tess didn't believe showing up in capris and a sports bra was suitable for a law enforcement agent investigating someone's death. They moved quickly, and it didn't add much of a delay to their arrival time.

With Fradella behind the wheel, driving to the North Palm Beach address, Tess reviewed the case details on the laptop, trying not to feel queasy from keeping her eyes locked onto the screen, while he took turn after turn above the speed limit.

"Our vic is Christina Bartlett, twenty-six, single," Tess read from the screen, squinting in the bright sunlight. "She's a model, works with a number of top-shelf fashion publications. Her mother, Iris, is a dentist, and her father, Sidney, an attorney. Clean record, no priors," she added, not even realizing her voice had lost momentum, and her words had turned into barely intelligible mumbles as she typed a new search string into the computer.

Fradella shot her a quick glance as he approached a stop sign. "What's up?"

"There's something about her father, Sidney Bartlett. He seems so familiar; his name resonated in my mind, but I can't place him. I ran his priors; he's clean." She sighed and looked at the street for a moment, absorbing the layout of the neighborhood. Neatly trimmed lawns, tall palm trees with clean trunks and glistening leaves, palmettos and flowering shrubs flanking alleys and driveways. Where did she know Sidney Bartlett from?

A quick internet search returned zero useful results; just corroborated what she'd learned from the database. Sidney was an attorney, a successful one with his own firm in partnership with two other names that came after his. Nothing out of the ordinary. Maybe her mind was playing a trick on her. Or maybe they'd crossed paths during a trial where she was called to testify.

One more turn, and Doc Rizza's van came into sight and backed onto the driveway of a massive, single-story, brick house. Two police cars were still flashing their lights, and another van was parked farther down the street, bearing the insignia of the Crime Scene Unit.

Tess walked slowly toward the entrance, observing every detail. There were modern security cameras monitoring the front door, the sides of the lawn, and the driveway. Probably the back too. An eight-foot masonry fence surrounded the backyard, and beyond that, she could see the roof of a screened pool.

A pat on her shoulder disrupted her scrutiny.

"Special Agent Winnett," Michowsky said, with a grin and a nod, "what an unexpected pleasure. Did Fradella bother to mention it's a suicide?"

She gave him a quick hug. "Yeah, he did. I'm just tagging along, if you don't mind."

"Have at it," he said, making an inviting gesture and letting her lead the way. "The more, the merrier," he added, but a quick rise of his eyebrows said otherwise.

She walked carefully on the shiny marble floor, heading toward the living room, where distant, subdued chatter could be heard. A woman's tearful voice kept saying something repeatedly, something Tess couldn't hear clearly, not from where she was. As she entered the living room, she could understand the woman's words better, but her attention was drawn to a large, framed picture of a young girl. Stunningly beautiful, the girl wore a rhinestone-studded crown over her long, blonde hair, and a white sateen sash across her body with the words *Miss Florida USA* printed in black, cursive letters.

"You have to tell them," Dr. Bartlett was saying, wringing her hands in her lap. She was leaning back and forth, like a child in need of comfort. Tears rolled on her cheeks and stained her blouse, but she didn't seem to mind. Her swollen eyes stared into her husband's, pleading.

"Think about what you're doing," Mr. Bartlett replied. His chin trembled badly, and his voice was choked with tears. "Think about the media and everyone else. We can't do that to her. Not now. Especially not now."

Tess took a step toward them but then stopped. Better give them more time to process; there would be opportunities to ask questions later. She checked the time and calculated it had only been less than two hours since the 911 call was dispatched. Christina's parents were still in shock.

She turned and followed a crime scene technician toward the back of the house. She slid on protective booties over her shoes before entering the bedroom and nodded a quick greeting toward the coroner's assistant.

The bedroom was large and bright, with white furniture and pink bedsheets; a princess setting, most likely reminiscent of Christina's childhood. However, Christina was not a child anymore; she was a grown woman, as proven by scattered lingerie in black lace and a portrait of her, slender and sexy and tan in a minimalistic bikini, beaming in the arms of a dark-haired man. The man had a look of arrogance on his face, expressing pride of ownership rather than love, the way a new owner looks at his brand-new sports car. The same man's photo was framed on the night table, and, for some reason, Tess stared at that photo, postponing the moment she'd have to look at Christina's lifeless body. Even if self-inflicted, death was deeply disturbing, maybe even more.

Doc Rizza bent over Christina's body, probably measuring her liver temperature, then straightened his back with a groan, grabbing his right side with a latex-gloved hand. Then he removed his gloves and ran his hand through the unruly tuft of graying hair that still clung to his balding head.

"Hey, Doc," Tess said, noticing the small sweat beads forming on his forehead. The man was one step away from having a stroke. His clammy skin was stained with blotches of dark red, a clear indicator of hypertension. She thought of mentioning it, but then decided otherwise; after all, he was a doctor; he definitely knew about it. Rumor had it that, since the death of his wife a few years back, the doctor opted more and more in favor of liquid dinners, and that choice of lifestyle was starting to take its toll. Nevertheless, he was still the best coroner Tess had ever worked with.

"Hey," he replied, not taking his eyes off Christina's body. "I'm about to issue a preliminary ruling of suicide. No need for feds this time. You can have your weekend back."

"I'm not here officially, Doc," she replied, almost apologetically. "Suicide, you say?"

He shrugged and gestured toward the scattered empty bottles of prescription pills. "No signs of trauma whatsoever. I'll know more after I finish my exam, but for now the findings are consistent with suicide."

"What did she take?" Michowsky asked.

"Whatever she could find in the house," Doc replied. "Better said, *everything* she found in the house." He slid a fresh glove on his hand and picked up the empty prescription bottles, one by one, reading the labels before letting them drop inside small evidence bags. "Her father's prescriptions of a beta blocker and an ACE inhibitor; that's Inderal and Accupril, respectively. Then her mother's benzodiazepine, or Restoril if you care to know the brand," he added, letting the last of the empty, orange bottles fall into an evidence bag.

"Do you know how many she took?" Michowsky asked.

"All three prescriptions were ninety-day refills," Fradella replied after reading the labels. "The dates on the bottles indicate these were refilled last week, so they should've been nearly full."

"I'll be able to approximate, based on what I find in her stomach and the tox screen," Doc Rizza added. "But I can tell you this much: this girl wanted to die. It wasn't a cry for help gone wrong. She took all the pills, to the last one, and that takes willpower."

"Why is that?" Fradella asked.

"The willpower?" Doc Rizza asked, and Fradella nodded. "The human body protects itself against poisons, inducing defensive vomiting whenever a poison is ingested. After she took the first few pills, she fought one hell of an urge to vomit. That's how determined she was to die."

"Any idea why she killed herself?" Michowsky asked.

"That's your job, Detective," Doc Rizza replied. "I'm ready to move her, if you are."

"Would you give me another minute?" Tess asked.

Doc Rizza moved to the side, making room for Tess to approach the body.

Christina lay on her side, her pale lips slightly parted, as if she slept peacefully, no longer touched by breath. Waves of golden hair surrounded her head like an aura, spread on the pillow, clinging to her shoulders. Her feet touched the floor, as if she'd been too weak to pull them onto the bed. She wore green pajamas with teddy bears, a young girl's PJs. There was no sadness, no depression lingering in the room, in the clothes she wore, in the setting. Whatever pushed Christina to take her own life had been sudden.

Tess could visualize her sitting on the side of the bed, swallowing fistfuls of pills one after another, washing them down with sparkling water. An empty bottle had rolled under the night table, and a half-empty one stood next to the framed photo on the lacquered finish, the cap removed. The water had been cold, fresh out of the fridge; condensation had stained the shiny surface of the night table, leaving a circle of swollen wood, probably permanent damage, a reminder of her demise.

Then she must've grown weak so quickly that she let herself fall onto her side, unable to do more. Had she wanted to scream for help? Had she changed her mind in those final moments?

Tess pulled some gloves on and examined Christina's hands. Perfect manicure, not even a crack in her fingernails. Fresh coat of nail polish, covered by a transparent layer of protective gloss. She examined the cuticles closely and saw no growth between the cuticle and the polish layer. There wasn't any erosion on the tips of her fingernails either. The same woman who killed herself a few hours earlier had applied fresh nail polish the day before.

"Time of death, Doc?" she asked, still studying Christina's hands.

"I'd put it at 3:30AM."

"How did she die, considering what she took?"

"It depends on the number of pills she took from each bottle, but there are only two possible scenarios. If the sedative acted first, she fell asleep, then went into cardiogenic shock. If the Inderal acted first, she could've gone into seizures, then faded away when the Restoril hit."

"How about the third? What was it—"

"Accupril," Doc Rizza replied. "It contributed to the onset of cardiogenic shock."

"Are these drugs common?" Fradella asked.

"They're among the most prescribed drugs in America," Doc replied. "The mother most likely struggles with perimenopausal insomnia, and the father battles hypertension. Nothing out of the ordinary. I don't see anything suspicious here; I'll confirm my findings once I have her on my table."

He beckoned his assistant, who pushed a stretcher through the door, then unzipped a body bag. Tess stepped to the side, watching them load Christina's body and roll it out of the room, but she remained there, staring at the princess bed adorned in pink sheets.

"It's a suicide," Michowsky said, touching her arm in passing. "Come on, let's get going. The unis have the statements."

"I'm staying," she replied. "She killed herself for a reason. I thought you wanted to know why."

4

The Parents

A uniformed cop stood by the living room entrance, notepad in hand, but Tess waved him away with a hand gesture. Most of the Crime Scene Unit had gone already; she, Michowsky, and Fradella were among the last ones left. Doc Rizza's van had pulled away from the driveway, taking Christina Bartlett's body with it and causing her mother to break down in bitter sobs against her husband's chest, as they sat on a sofa in the living room. This time, Sidney Bartlett didn't fight back his tears; he let them fall, squeezing his eyes shut as if rejecting a reality that was too painful to bear.

Tess approached the couple and cleared her throat quietly to get their attention.

"Dr. Bartlett, if I may," she said, speaking softly.

Mr. Bartlett was the first to look at her. "Who are you?"

Forgetting she wasn't there in any official capacity, she pulled out her wallet and showed her ID. "Special Agent Tess Winnett, FBI."

"FBI?" Dr. Bartlett reacted, turning toward her and examining her with swollen, tear-filled eyes. "Why is the FBI looking into a suicide?"

Iris pulled slightly closer to her husband, as if seeking his protection, then grabbed his hand and squeezed it quickly, while both exchanged a quick glance. That was an interesting reaction, definitely something worth exploring. Why would the two be concerned about having the FBI look into their daughter's death?

Tess decided to play down their fears but made a mental note to examine their backgrounds more closely. The two definitely had something to hide.

"The FBI isn't looking into your daughter's death, Doctor. I was working on a case with Palm Beach County Sheriff's Office when the call came in. Since I'm here, I might as well help."

"I see," she replied, unconvinced.

"Please accept my deepest sympathies," Tess added.

"Thank you," she replied, reaching for a Kleenex from the box lying on the coffee table. "Tell me, Agent, what can we do for you?"

"We'd like to understand what drove your daughter's decision to end her life. Are you aware of any—"

"Her death came as a complete surprise to us," Mr. Bartlett said. "It's probably something we'll never comprehend. Such a decision… can't easily be understood."

"Tell me about Christina," Tess said, taking a seat on the opposite sofa, on the edge of the soft leather cushion, and leaning forward toward them, ready to listen.

"She was amazing. Hard-working, dedicated, an overachiever since the first day she set foot in school." Dr. Bartlett patted her eyes with the now-moist tissue, then took another one from the box. "She… didn't deserve this," she added, sending her husband a furtive glance.

Fradella walked the room slowly along the walls, inspecting every window and making notes of the locations of all surveillance cameras. There were plenty of those; Mr. Bartlett didn't cut any corners on his home security. He beckoned Michowsky and the two of them whispered something in a quick exchange, pointing at the back door and the two security cameras that monitored that particular point of access.

"Has anything happened to her recently?" Tess asked, not taking her eyes off the mother's face.

Based on what Tess had overheard earlier, Christina's mother wanted to share something with the investigators, but her husband opposed the idea. She could try to separate the two and question Dr. Bartlett in private but, judging by the way she squeezed her husband's hand, that could prove difficult.

Dr. Bartlett lowered her head.

"Nothing happened," Mr. Bartlett replied in her stead. "She traveled a lot, worked long hours."

"How about a boyfriend?" Tess asked, remembering the photos in Christina's bedroom.

"Pat," Dr. Bartlett replied. "An ambitious young man," she added, then closed her eyes briefly. "They were engaged to be married. He doesn't know yet."

"Pat?" Michowsky asked, notepad in hand, as he walked toward them.

"Pat Gallagher," Mr. Bartlett replied. "He's a Realtor, commercial real estate, high-value properties."

"Anyone else in your daughter's life?" Michowsky asked, approaching the Bartletts. "Anyone who was close enough to either cause this or know what did?"

The Bartletts looked briefly at each other.

"She was close friends with a male model, a colleague of hers, Santiago Flores," Dr. Bartlett replied. "Santiago is in love with my daughter, but her heart belongs to Pat." Dr. Bartlett covered her mouth with her hand to stifle a renewed sob. "Was… I—I can't speak of her in past tense… I just can't."

"It's all right," Tess replied. An unwanted thought crossed through her mind, as she said the words meant to bring comfort. Nothing was ever going to be all right for the Bartletts again, no matter what she said. "Is it possible Santiago was jealous? Felt rejected?"

"No, he's nothing like that," Dr. Bartlett whispered, then stared pleadingly into her husband's eyes. Mr. Bartlett stood and turned toward the window, avoiding her glance. She lowered her head, defeated again in whatever silent battle the two were fighting.

"Why are you looking for suspects when there are none, Agent, um, what was it?"

"Winnett, sir," Tess replied, surprised by the force in the man's pushback. "And while there might not be any suspects, I'll be perfectly honest with you and tell you that I'm not seeing what I normally see in suicide cases."

Bartlett frowned and approached her. "What do you mean?"

"Before someone takes their own life, they go through a period of interiorized struggle. In some cases, there's depression, sadness, the loss of a loved one, or news of a terminal disease. In other cases, there's despair, the inability to live one's life on one's terms. All this interiorized struggle leaves evidence for us to find. I believe that whatever caused your daughter to end her life was sudden and so powerful that her decision came quickly, as if no other alternative was left. I, for one, would like to know what happened, sir, and I hope you'll agree with me."

Tess could read the man's anguish in the way his jaws tensed, tugging at the corners of his tight lips and pulling them down.

"Tell them, Sidney, please," Dr. Bartlett pleaded. "They'll find out anyway."

Tess turned toward her. "Tell us what?"

Sidney Bartlett let out a long, pained sigh, then lowered his eyes. "Last night she received a text message, while we were sitting at the dinner table. Someone had posted on the internet some horrible images of her, taken here, in our house, in her own bedroom."

Without a word, Dr. Bartlett handed Tess an iPhone. The messenger app was already open on the screen. The message contained a link, and Tess tapped on it.

It took effort to control her anger as the first photo loaded on the small screen. Christina, naked and spread-eagled on her princess bed, lay there with her eyes closed and her head in an unnatural position. When that photo was taken, she'd been unconscious. Seeing that beautiful girl violated like that made her blood boil, as if witnessing a crime with her hands tied behind her back.

"I'll need to hold on to this," Tess said, gesturing with the iPhone and avoiding the inquisitive glance Michowsky threw her way.

"In our house... can you believe it?" Bartlett raised his voice to the point of shouting. "I couldn't believe it either, so I accused her of being a part of it." He ran his hand over his face angrily, as if to cleanse himself of what he'd done. "She swore to me she didn't participate in it, but I didn't believe her. Not at first."

"You *never* believed her," Dr. Bartlett said.

"She's a model," Bartlett replied, trying to justify himself. "I thought—
"

"She's a model, not a whore!" Dr. Bartlett snapped. "A hardworking, honest girl. You never saw the difference."

Bartlett's head hung low; he sat back on the sofa, leaving some distance between him and his wife.

"She had no idea when the photos were taken, or how," he added, after a moment of dense silence. "I grilled her last night, asked the same questions over and over again, until I decided that maybe she was telling the truth. Now I know she was, but it's too late."

"What did she do when you were questioning her?" Tess asked, frowning a little. "What did she say?"

"She was unusually calm and silent," Dr. Bartlett replied, before her husband had the chance. "She was pale, white as a sheet of paper. She didn't cry; she just sat there, giving us the same answer to all our questions. She had no idea who did that, when, or why."

"In our house," Bartlett said again, "where my family is supposed to be safe!" He stood and staggered to the back entrance, double French doors that opened onto the back patio leading to the boat ramp. "I have video surveillance everywhere, and an alarm system. How could this happen?"

Tess made a note to check the boat and the backyard. The Bartlett residence was a canal property; the waterway could've been the point of ingress; she'd seen it before. A quiet boat in the middle of the night, a small canoe maybe, could put the perpetrator in someone's backyard bypassing street cameras, neighbors, witnesses, and traffic cops. Completely stealth. Then, what? With the house locked down and the alarm set up, how could he have gained access to Christina? Why didn't anyone see or hear anything?

"We need to bring back the Crime Scene Unit," Tess said to Michowsky. "Check points of entry, her window, backyard, waterway. Get trace to swipe that bedroom inside and out."

Michowsky nodded and pulled out his phone. "I'll get them to look at the alarm code history and download the video surveillance data into our systems."

"Where was her boyfriend last night?" Fradella asked.

"Traveling for business. He's in New York for a land sale, returning today," Dr. Bartlett replied. "He's not... behind this in any way."

"You never know, Iris, stop vouching for people," Bartlett said, without turning away from the French doors. "Who else could've gotten so close to her, here, in this house?"

"Does he normally spend the night?" Tess asked.

"No, never," Dr. Bartlett replied. "Christina didn't want that. She sometimes spent the night at his place, but here... she never had him sleep here."

"Are you always home at night?" Tess asked, looking first at Dr. Bartlett, then at her husband, who walked toward the sofa with an unsteady gait. The man seemed almost ready to collapse.

"Yes," they both replied, almost at the same time.

"We spent a week in the Caribbean last fall," Bartlett said. "Since we came back, we've been home every night."

Tess looked at the photo once again. The frame caught a piece of the window, covered with blue curtains. Not a shred of daylight seemed to come from that window, but she had to enhance the photo to be sure.

Then she shifted screens to the text app. Who sent the troublesome link? It had come from a five-digit numeric sender, not a person saved in her contacts list. The sender had used one of the many online messenger systems available on the internet. Probably untraceable.

"Did she tell you who sent her the link?"

"She didn't recognize the number," Bartlett replied. "I was going to have someone look into it today."

"Someone?" Tess retorted, sounding angrier than she'd wanted. "When exactly were you going to report this crime?"

Bartlett clasped his hands together. "This morning, but we woke up, and she—" He couldn't bring himself to say the words. Instead, he lowered his head again and stared at the floor for a long moment.

Tess wanted to challenge that statement, knowing very well that they were probably going to try to manage the situation quietly, afraid of the ensuing media exposure. She decided to keep that thought to herself, but her loaded gaze expressed it clearly. Silence engulfed the room, heavy and dense.

"You're right, Agent Winnett," Bartlett eventually said. "We wanted to keep this under wraps, because of the media. We were afraid those vultures would have a field day dragging our girl's name through the mud. I thought I'd be able to clean this up, to find who did this, and—"

"Sidney," his wife intervened and stopped him before saying what he was about to say.

The phrase continued in Tess's mind. No doubt, once Sidney Bartlett learned the identity of his daughter's assailant, he'd have found ways to deal with him, also under wraps.

That instant, she remembered where she knew Sidney Bartlett from.

5

Privileged Territory

"What the hell, Winnett? This isn't your case," Michowsky protested, the moment the Bartlett residence front door closed behind the three of them.

Tess didn't reply immediately. She focused on studying the house from the unsub's perspective. How did he enter the premises undetected? Cameras with motion-activated sensors covered the porch from both sides and would've flooded the lawn in bright light the moment he set foot on the property line. Probably the same security system covered the backyard and the dock. Now that she remembered who Sidney Bartlett was, she had no doubt in her mind the house was a fortress.

"Winnett!" Michowsky called, probably irritated with her silence.

Her first thought was to say that she'd felt obligated to step in, seeing how all he could think of was getting the hell out of there, but she decided to keep that thought to herself. Michowsky was a good cop; he'd proven himself time and again, even if he was sometimes prone to jumping to conclusions, to seeking the easiest way out of a case. That probably came with age, with experience, with the accumulation of years of service and countless perps locked up, making it easy for him to assume he had everything figured out already.

"Just think of me as a free upgrade, Gary, the type you get at car rentals after you put in some mileage," she answered, still studying the layout of the security cameras. "It's your case, one hundred percent, I promise."

"It sure as hell don't feel like it, Winnett. What was on that phone, and why didn't you share it with us in there?"

She handed him Christina's phone, sealed in a transparent evidence bag. "Take a look. You'll understand why I didn't share this with two men in the presence of the victim's parents."

Michowsky frowned, then muttered a long, detailed oath as he thumbed through the photos. He handed the phone to Fradella, who glanced at the images and then returned the phone to Tess without another word.

"That's one hell of a nonviolent crime," Michowsky said.

"You think it's nonviolent?" Tess snapped. "Just because there's no blood on the walls? Think again, Gary. The unsub killed her, as clearly and as directly as if he'd shoved those pills down her throat with his own hands."

"Yeah, I guess you're right," Michowsky said. "I've never seen anything like this before. At first glance, it looked more like a party prank gone wrong," he added. "You've seen those on the internet, right? Where the guy wakes up naked and taped to a tree?"

"I've seen them," Fradella answered. "I know a guy who woke up with a butterfly tattoo on his ass and a huge hangover. The photo of his embellished rear end was everywhere for a while, but then the buzz died down. He wasn't too heartbroken about it; he just chose a different crowd to party with."

Then, as if he had just thought of something, Fradella took out his phone and started typing in a browser search window.

Tess reminded them, "It's different for a woman, guys. It's demeaning to a level that can completely ruin one's life. Not to mention it's a crime."

"We're not debating that," Michowsky replied. "We all agree a crime has been committed here. I'm just saying it could've started differently, although she seems really out of it in those photos. Screen's too small to tell though."

"This is worse than we thought," Fradella said. "Whoever released the photos tagged Christina by name and pushed them out through press release channels, making sure they'd flood the net quickly. This wasn't a prank; this was vengeful and targeted."

A moment of silence ensued. The implications of Fradella's statement changed the way Christina's death had to be treated from an investigative perspective, whether a suicide or not.

"There's something else you need to know, guys," Tess said in a low voice, grabbing both their arms and pulling them closer to her. Still on the front porch, she didn't want to be overheard from inside the house.

Fradella shot her an inquisitive look. "Bartlett?"

"Yes. He and I met years ago, when he was a defense attorney in a high-profile case, and I testified for the prosecution."

"I wonder how that one went," Michowsky chortled.

"The case was a RICO prosecution against a Colombian national," Tess added. "Our friend Mr. Bartlett seems to have a penchant for attracting RICO clients, all of South American descent, mostly Colombian. He's since defended quite a few and many of them have walked free. He must be advertising to that market," she continued.

Her sarcasm wasn't lost on the two cops. "You think he's connected?" Michowsky asked.

"Depending on whom you ask, you might hear he's the lead enforcer for a major Colombian drug cartel in his spare time," Tess added, further lowering her voice. "That changes a few things."

"That was never proven, Agent Winnett," Bartlett said calmly behind them, his voice strong, unfaltering.

Tess turned swiftly, startled and irritated that she'd let someone sneak up on them.

"I'm aware it was never proven, Mr. Bartlett, otherwise this conversation wouldn't be taking place on your front porch." She held his gaze firmly, unapologetically. "Do you understand we need to have all the facts if we're to catch whoever hurt your daughter?"

He lowered his gaze after a long moment. "Do what you need to do, Agent Winnett. Ask what you're going to ask."

"Okay," Tess replied, keeping her voice low. "Let's consider this porch privileged territory. Will you trust me on that?"

Michowsky stared at her with raised eyebrows, then looked at Bartlett, who hesitated for a second before saying, "Years ago, when I had you on the stand in cross-examination, you chose to be truthful and forthcoming, even if it wasn't in the prosecution's best interest. Have you changed much since then, Agent Winnett?"

"Not a single bit."

"Still, why should I trust you?"

"You lost your daughter today, Mr. Bartlett, and that's reason enough for me to grant you this privilege. You deserve a break, and we need to be able to do our jobs."

He nodded a few of times. "So be it, Agent Winnett. Ask away."

"Do you know of anyone who could've done this to your daughter to get back at you? Rival cartels, any scumbag you couldn't get to walk?"

"I thought of that, Agent Winnett. I have several names that come to mind, but these men kill to settle scores. They blow up cars and shoot people's kneecaps."

"Maybe someone wanted you discredited, not eliminated? A rival attorney who wants your clientele?"

"There's one aggressive newcomer; he used to practice in Chicago. He's out to build a reputation for himself with the cartels. I'll give you his name, but I need you to promise me something."

"Shoot," she said, frowning a little.

"I'm thinking these people don't know what happened. Maybe not all of them have seen my baby girl like that. Could you please keep it to yourself?" He looked at Michowsky, then at Fradella. "Please, don't let this be the way the world remembers Christina."

"I—we promise, Mr. Bartlett," Tess replied firmly. "We will be investigating your daughter's death as a homicide. You have my word."

She turned to leave, but Bartlett grabbed her arm, then promptly let it go the moment Tess glared at him.

"Agent Winnett, we're still in privileged territory, right?"

She nodded. "Go ahead."

"When you find out who did this to my little girl, could you please let me know?" he asked quietly, his words barely above a whisper. "Just tell me who did this and leave the rest to… God."

6

The Boyfriend

They waited until the Crime Scene Unit returned to the Bartlett residence, and Tess smiled politely as several of them glared in her direction, pretending not to understand the source of their frustration. She instructed them to look for any sign of forced entry, to dust all windowsills for prints and pore over the backyard with a magnifying glass. One of the techs, a young man whose early alopecia cutting into a dark, unruly mane of stiff, curly hair made him look like a cartoon character, showed some real interest.

"You're saying someone broke into *this* house?" the tech asked, pointing at the surveillance camera above their heads.

Tess nodded. "While people were at home, and no one suspected anything."

The tech whistled. "Well, if he left a trace anywhere, we'll find it."

She smiled. She liked seeing that kind of enthusiasm, of professional commitment and curiosity in an investigator. She didn't have much hope for any findings though. Someone so bold, so organized, wouldn't make forensic mistakes.

She gazed quickly in Michowsky's direction. He and Fradella were talking to Bartlett, their heads close together, their voices low. She waited by Michowsky's vehicle, unable to hear a word of what they were saying. Soon enough, the two men shook Bartlett's hand and walked toward the unmarked Ford Explorer.

"What was that about?" Tess asked, as soon as the vehicle set off.

"We asked him if Christina's reaction to the text she received had seemed normal to him," Fradella said.

Tess frowned. It was an interesting thought. Bartlett had described his daughter's demeanor as unusually calm, composed, tearless, and determined. Not really the typical female response to a psychological shock of that magnitude.

"And?"

"I would've expected him to say she cried, screamed, fainted, or, you know, threw a fit," Fradella said, "which would've been totally understandable."

"In retrospect," Michowsky concluded, while taking the interstate ramp,

"Bartlett confirms. Her reaction wasn't normal, but I'm guessing he was too shocked himself to realize it last night."

"You're saying she knew about it?" Tess asked.

"I think it's a possibility," Fradella replied.

"If she knew, she might've told someone," Tess said, "although it's not something she'd want people to know. Maybe people close to her had noticed something was off. When was her boyfriend due back?"

Fradella checked his notes. "They said today, about noon. He should be home by now. He's in West Palm Beach, by CityPlace."

"Gary, will you—"

"Sure," Michowsky interrupted, then took the first exit.

"Don't you want to study the photos first?" Fradella asked. He rode in the back seat and he'd leaned forward between the two front seats, popping his head between the two of them. "We should be able to find out when they were taken."

"I'd rather see his reaction when he finds out about Christina's death," Tess replied. "That window of opportunity is quickly disappearing. With the photos pushed to the media, it's only a matter of minutes, hours at best, before she makes the news."

"Couldn't we get a gag order or something?" Fradella asked, and by the undertones in his voice, Tess sensed how he felt about the entire situation, despite knowing there was little they could do. Bartlett's request to protect the memory of his daughter had resonated with all of them.

"It's a long shot, but we could ask the ADA to look into it," Tess replied. "You can't gag the media about a celebrity's death. You can't gag them, period; it's an infringement on First Amendment rights. The only exceptions, rarely granted, are in matters of national security, and this doesn't qualify."

"But they'd be helping the perp in propagating his crime, wouldn't they?"

"The media won't release the photos, per se, but there's nothing we could do to keep reporters from mentioning them and from speculating about their impact on the victim, or the correlation with her suicide. The people will do the rest, searching for the photos online. It's the world we live in, Todd, but I'll try. No harm in doing that, is there?"

She grabbed the laptop and typed a quick email to the ADA. Her thin fingers hesitated above the keyboard when she realized she didn't have a case number. She wasn't acting in any official capacity, and she needed to fix that quickly before it could become an issue.

They pulled over in front of one of the high-rise buildings on Lakeview Avenue, and moments later they rang the doorbell of a seventeenth-floor apartment.

She recognized Pat Gallagher from the framed photo on Christina's night table, the moment he opened the door. A second later, she didn't recognize him anymore. He was drawn, his eyes hollow, his face pale. A slight tremble reverberated through his fingers as he held the door open. He seemed afraid, not heartbroken; only scared to death. He'd just returned from his travels; a wheelie stood close to the door, untouched, and he'd loosened his tie, but hadn't taken his shoes off yet.

"Pat Gallagher?" Fradella inquired, showing his badge. "Detectives Fradella and Michowsky, Palm Beach County Sheriff's Office. May we come in?"

He stepped out of the way, then closed the door after them. "It's three of you," he said in a hesitant voice. "Usually it's two." He looked at Tess directly. "And you are...?"

She pulled out her ID. "Special Agent Winnett, FBI."

"Oh," he replied, taking a step back. He didn't say anything else, resigned to stand and wait, seemingly too tired or otherwise exhausted to ask any more questions.

"I'm afraid we have some bad news, Mr. Gallagher," Tess said. "Christina Bartlett, your fiancée, died last night."

His jaw dropped, while blood drained from his face. He let himself drop onto a couch and clasped his trembling hands together in his lap. "What happened?" he asked, barely speaking above a whisper.

"She committed suicide, Mr. Gallagher."

"Oh, God..." he said, then covered his mouth with both his hands. "I had no idea... I swear, I didn't know she was..."

He stopped talking mid-phrase and didn't continue. Tess found his choice of words interesting to say the least.

"Has anything happened to her recently that could explain her gesture?" Tess asked, hoping he'd come forward with whatever information he already had.

Gallagher shook his head, still cupping his mouth in his hand. "No... I don't know," he eventually said, then he looked at Tess briefly and rephrased. "Until last night, I had no idea something was wrong."

"What happened last night?" Michowsky asked.

"I was in New York to close a sale. She called me late, after midnight, and told me she..." His voice wavered. "I'm assuming you know about the photos?"

"She told you about them?" Tess asked.

"Yes, last night."

"What exactly did she say, Mr. Gallagher?"

He frowned and looked away, trying to recollect his thoughts.

"She said that someone had sent her a link, and that she didn't know when they were taken. She was... devastated."

"Was she crying?" Fradella asked.

"Not at first, no. She pleaded with me to hop on an earlier flight and come home, to not leave her alone."

"You obviously didn't," Tess replied dryly, aware she sounded cold, judgmental.

"No... I—I broke up with her," he said in stuttered, barely intelligible words.

What an outstanding human being, Tess couldn't help thinking. *That poor girl, she must've been out of her mind with despair.* She breathed and managed to curb her anger enough to trust herself to speak again.

"Why? What happened?" Tess asked innocently.

"You don't know how these things are," Gallagher pleaded, not daring to look at any of them. "Once a photo like that is out there, on the internet, you can't take it back, you can't delete it. It's worse for a celebrity. It's over. Those photos are now on millions of personal computers, and from there they will get uploaded a million more times."

"You wanted to distance yourself, to protect your reputation, your career," Tess said in an understanding tone, encouraging him to spill everything.

"You see, I had no choice," Gallagher replied, sounding relieved. "Even by having been associated with her in the past, my reputation, my career could already be destroyed by now. It broke my heart, but I had to do it."

Tess breathed again, slowly, taking her time. What heart?

"Her call history shows a forty-seven-minute conversation with you sometime after midnight, then a number of calls she made to you after that long conversation, calls you didn't pick up," Fradella said. "Care to explain?"

Gallagher looked briefly in Fradella's direction, then lowered his gaze to the floor. "There was nothing left to say."

"I see," Tess replied, reminding herself how pointless and damaging it would be to tell that man what she thought about him. Instead, she asked, "Do you know of anyone who wanted to hurt Christina? Rival models, angry exes?"

"It's a cutthroat industry," he replied, "but that's why they use agents. The models don't interact much with one another. Of course, there's some jealousy among them, but no one really comes to mind. No exes either; we've been together for three years."

"Who else would she have talked to?" Tess asked. "Any close girlfriends?"

"She didn't have much of a social life; she worked a lot, and when she didn't work or travel, she spent her time with me," he said, sounding more and more sure of himself with every phrase that came out of his mouth. His guilt hadn't lasted long; Tess doubted it was real to begin with. "There's this one girl, Althea Swain, but she's more like a moth."

"A moth?" Michowsky asked, setting down a Realtor of the Year award in heavy crystal he'd picked up from a bookcase shelf.

"You know, someone attracted to the flame of her fame, always willing to go to fashion parties, or wear whatever clothes Christina didn't want," he replied. "Not really that much of a friend. Christina knows who and what Althea is, only she doesn't care. She likes her company. Liked," he corrected himself, without skipping a beat. "But I doubt she would've shared anything with Althea, not about those photos anyway. No one knew, not even Christina."

"She seemed perfectly okay in the recent past?" Fradella asked, slowly walking toward the bookcase, where Michowsky wanted to show him something discreetly, without drawing Gallagher's attention.

"She seemed her usual self," Gallagher replied. "Sometimes tired, but okay. She had a shoot in Tokyo last week that was exhausting, then she flew to Buenos Aires the next day. What a life," he added with a trace of unspoken envy in his voice. "If there's nothing else," he said, standing and showing them to the door.

"We'll be in touch, Mr. Gallagher," Tess replied between clenched jaws.

They were silent the entire time it took the elevator to transport them to the ground floor, but the moment they were in the Explorer, Tess turned to Michowsky with an intrigued expression on her face.

"Okay, spill it. What did you see in there? You two were looking at something."

"His photos," Michowsky replied. "The bastard has photos of himself with a lot of beautiful women, and he keeps them in plain sight. Christina probably *loved* those," he added with a wry grin. "My wife would set on fire any such photo of me with other women."

"Then she'd probably castrate you," Fradella added with a chuckle, "just to be sure."

"She probably would, yeah," Michowsky said. "If Christina weren't dead, I'd say she's better off without that bastard."

"True," Tess replied, "but we still have nothing. I don't believe Gallagher had anything to do with this, no matter how much I'd like to throw his ass in jail. He's selfish and cruel and a jerk, but none of that is a crime."

They drove in silence for a while, headed toward the office. She wasn't paying any attention to the beautiful day, the blue sky, or the warm rays of the spring sun; all she could think of was Christina's killer, and how he'd gain access to the property. Boldest unsub she'd ever seen. Such boldness was never a good sign.

"Doc Rizza confirmed it's a suicide," Fradella announced, going through email on his phone. "No other findings. The tox screen is still pending, though."

"I'm surprised we haven't been pulled off the case yet," Michowsky said. "Because it's not a homicide—"

"The hell it isn't," Tess snapped. "We talked about this."

"Yeah, yeah, we did," Michowsky said, taking his hands off the wheel for a moment and raising them in the air, in a pacifying gesture. "But the coroner's ruling—"

"We can still make the case for homicide, despite the coroner's ruling; you know that. That girl was murdered, just as if someone shot her point blank."

"The DA might disagree."

"And I don't give a rat's ass," Tess replied, raising her voice. "I want this murderer to pay for what he's done."

7

Approvals

The two detectives dropped Tess in front of the FBI headquarters, then drove off, quickly disappearing around the corner. Before entering the building, she stopped for a second and looked up at the gray structure with its tinted windows and many pillars, trying to see if the light was on in her boss's office. As usual, Special Agent in Charge Alan Pearson was there. She couldn't think of a time when he wasn't, from early dawn to late at night.

She went straight upstairs and didn't slow her pace until she rapped her knuckles against his door frame. Then she remained politely outside, waiting to be invited in. He didn't look up at first, engulfed in reading the contents of a file folder. The folder itself was green, a color the bureau rarely used, and it wasn't embossed with the bureau's logo. SAC Pearson seemed absorbed by his reading in an intense way. Whatever he'd found on those pages caused deep ridges on his forehead, a grim expression on his face, underlined by tension around his mouth, and a rarely seen, loosened tie knot. His jacket hung abandoned on the back of his chair, also not something she'd seen that often.

She shifted her weight from one foot to the other, willing herself to wait patiently, although patience wasn't something she could be accused of, regardless of circumstance. SAC Pearson worked his way through another couple of pages before she knocked again.

"I heard you the first time, Winnett," he said, his eyes still riveted on the mysterious file's pages.

"Sir," she acknowledged, remaining just outside the door.

"Come in," he eventually said, closing the folder before she could get close enough to catch the slightest glimpse of its content. "Sit down," he said, then rested his hands on top of the unmarked folder and looked at her inquisitively. "I heard you're working on a case that's not ours," he said, cutting to the point in his typical style.

How the hell did he know already?

She chuckled quietly. "Anything I could help with?" she asked, pointing at the green folder.

"You're on vacation, Winnett. You haven't taken time off in years. Why don't you act like it and give everyone a break?"

He sounded harsh and irritated, but she thought she saw a flicker of amusement in his eyes.

"I stumbled across this case that I wanted to talk to you about, sir. I believe you already know the situation?"

He nodded. "The suicide that you're looking into? Yes, I know some of the details. It's not our case, Winnett. Palm Beach County Sheriff's Office needs to officially request our assistance. We don't just show up and step on people's toes, demonstrating no respect for jurisdiction. I'm surprised complaints haven't started to pour in yet."

A nervous smile touched her lips. "I'm trying my best to avoid complaints, as ordered."

"It's not even an active investigation, Winnett. Coroner ruled it a suicide."

She shook her head. "Some time ago, in the recent past, someone broke into the family's home, while everyone was there, and somehow managed to subdue the victim, strip her naked, and take compromising photos of her, which he then published online with her name attached. The victim killed herself because of that. This is a homicide."

"It's cyberbullying, Winnett, harassment," he said. "If we catch him, we might be able to make a manslaughter charge stick, but not a murder charge. Why the sudden interest in this case? We have more serious cases lined up, if you really can't be persuaded to take a few days off."

She thought for a second before replying. His question made a lot of sense, and she didn't have a rational answer to it; more like a gut feeling, something she'd seen in the unsub's behavior that was troublesome on so many levels.

"This unsub is fearless and extremely organized. I'm guessing you've heard whose home he broke into, right?" A nod from Pearson and she continued. "He's not stopping here. He's a sexual predator who's evolving, who will not stop at taking pictures without leaving a scratch or a bruise on his victims. For now, he's just playing."

Pearson's frown deepened. He rubbed the root of his nose between his thumb and index finger for a moment, but the frown didn't go away.

"What are you saying, Winnett?" His voice sounded tired all of a sudden.

She leaned forward across the desk. "I'm saying this wasn't a one-off, sir. This unsub is just getting started."

"How do you know it's not personal? It seems personal to me. Vengeful. The type of thing someone close to the victim might do, a discarded boyfriend, a rejected fan. Someone who has firsthand knowledge of the home's layout and the family's routines."

"It is vengeful and very personal, I agree," she said. "But I wouldn't write this unsub off just yet. His actions reek of injured narcissism, and his modus operandi is the most efficient I've seen in my entire career. You know, just as well as I do, how this story ends."

Pearson leaned against the back of his chair with a sigh, more like a deep breath loaded with frustration. "What do you need from me?"

She smiled, glad he didn't bring up the cost of such an investigation, all wagered on her hunch. "I'll get the sheriff's office to request us, to make things look good on paper," she said, "but first and foremost, I need Donovan's time approved. He's the best analyst we have, and we can't hope to break this case without someone who can track every bit of the information the unsub has put out there."

"He'll be thrilled," Pearson said, his sarcasm also not something she'd seen before in the contained, always-professional senior investigator. "He's off tomorrow and Tuesday, going to the Keys with friends on a fishing trip for the holiday weekend. I've already approved his request."

"I could still ask him, right?" she asked, her smile waning, replaced by concern.

"Yeah, you could."

"Thank you, sir," she said, then stood, ready to leave.

"One moment," Pearson said, then took a sip of water from an almost empty bottle of Dasani.

She took her seat and waited, watching his fingers dancing nervously on the green folder.

"Off the record, Winnett," he eventually said, "have you ever used FBI resources for your personal interest?"

What the hell is this about, she wondered, feeling a pang of anxiety ripping through her gut. Pearson's question brought back almost forgotten memories, from when she was a rookie agent, trying desperately to find the man who'd assaulted her, who'd left her fighting for her life on the dark streets of the city, only weeks before she'd started training and orientation at Quantico.

"Um," she said, swallowing with difficulty, her throat suddenly dry, "many years ago, I searched for the assailant in an unreported rape case," she eventually said, aware her voice sounded constricted, unnatural. "I'd hoped that if I identified the unsub, then the victim might have the courage to file a formal report." She swallowed again. "Why do you ask?"

"Would you do it again?" Pearson asked, ignoring her question.

She frowned a little, studying him carefully. "Am I digging my own grave right now?"

He looked at her straight, and she couldn't find a single glimmer of deception in his gaze. "No, Winnett, just helping a colleague."

"In that case, hell, yes," she said, feeling the constriction around her throat melt away. "That colleague of mine has friends in the FBI, ready to help. Just keep that in mind."

8

Me: Watching

I watch her sleep.

It's dark in here, only the faint rays of the full moon slicing through the venetian blinds cast faded, diluted lines of silver on the wall. A night light, shaped like a crescent moon and plugged in by the door illuminates the thick carpet at the foot of the bed, where she let her slippers drop from her feet before climbing between the soft sheets.

It's quiet in here, so quiet I can hear her breathe. She seems serene, untroubled by nightly visions of terror. Not everyone has those; only some, those unfortunate people whose past has taught them fear and anguish and sorrow and pain. But her? No, there are no monsters in her dreams. Not yet.

It's peaceful in here; the only movement is her chest rising and falling with every breath she takes, rustling the sheets with a barely audible sound, repetitive and hypnotic like distant ocean waves crashing against the shore. I stand by the wall, engulfed in shadows, and watch every breath of air filling her lungs, then leaving her body after it fulfilled its purpose. There's a melody to her breathing, so soft and gentle that it's barely discernible, yet it's memorable and distinctive, like a signature or a fingerprint. I'd recognize it anywhere.

She feels safe in her sleep. She's pushed the covers off her body and thrown her perfectly shaped leg over them, where cooler air can touch her warm skin. She's perfectly unaware of herself, any trace of the day's self-consciousness now gone. When she sleeps, she's really herself, not who she thinks she needs to be.

I admire her body and almost groan, hating the T-shirt she's wearing, a dark, loose piece of useless cotton that doesn't do her any good. It hides who she is, who she *really* is. Why is it that some parts of our bodies must stay hidden from view, when they're just as beautiful as the rest? Who decided that, and why is everyone rushing to obey? That damn T-shirt conceals her beauty, keeps the world from seeing her how she deserves to be seen. My eyes follow the curves of her body, hating the red bikini she slipped on right after taking a shower, another piece of useless fabric that stands in my way.

Not to worry, my dear, soon the world will see you for who you really are, all that you really are. I will set you free.

9

Date and Time

The conference room at Palm Beach County Sheriff's Office looked just as Tess remembered. Scratched and scuffed walls and furniture that had taken a beating over the years. But a newish, 50-inch TV was mounted on the wall, and a wide whiteboard on wheels, someone had pushed against the wall, was next to the door. A small coffee maker on a side cupboard, and there was a Polycom SoundStation speaker phone at the center of the stained conference table. In short, everything she needed to get started.

Satisfied, she set her laptop bag on the table and unzipped it, Donovan's words still resonating in her ears.

"What do I have to do to get away from you, Winnett?" Donovan had asked, the moment she'd appeared by his desk.

"You could always say no," she offered reluctantly. "But you'd be missing out on an interesting case."

"What case? A suicide? Puh-lease, Winnett. I'm heading out for Key West tonight, trailing a forty-two-foot, Huntress, center console boat, equipped with fourteen-hundred horsepower of pure Mercury thrust, radar, Fishfinder, and a cooler filled to the brim with Bud Light on ice. Hell, if I wanted to, I could run to Havana for Bud Light and be back before supper. It's the last remnant of my racing days, of my long-lost glory before I was turned into a cyborg and chained to a desk. You can't compete with that, sorry."

She had no idea Donovan had been a racer. Who knew? He seemed so docile and coolheaded. She decided to appeal to that side of him, the new Donovan who loved a good challenge.

"I'm offering a sexual predator who's just getting started, and all evidence is digital. Without your help, there is no case."

"Nice buttering up. This so-called case of yours can't wait until next week?"

She hesitated. "Maybe it could, but we can't be sure."

He paused a moment before replying. "Winnett, you're the bane of my existence. All right, I'll give you twenty-four hours of my life. Make the most of them, because come tomorrow at 5:00PM, I'll be gone."

"You're awesome," she said, then kissed a stunned Donovan on the forehead, before he could react, and stormed out of there.

Her next stop had been Captain Cepeda's office, on the second floor at Palm Beach County Sheriff's Office. He listened to her make her case with a doubtful stare and a ridge between his eyebrows, but eventually approved her request reluctantly, saying, "The Sheriff's Office can't afford to keep billing detective time on wild goose chases. If the feds are willing to waste time, I'll take it. I'll give you forty-eight hours, not a moment more."

She'd almost chuckled, thinking Donovan had given her twenty-four. Then a troublesome thought came out of nowhere. SAC Pearson, usually the fiercest of them all, hadn't objected much, nor set a deadline for the investigation. Whatever was in that green folder had knocked him off his game.

She hooked up her laptop to the guest Wi-Fi network and dialed Donovan on the conference phone, just as Michowsky and Fradella walked in. Michowsky's frown still lingered; he probably wanted to be with his family, which is to be expected from happily married people with children on their days off. She felt guilty for a millisecond, wondering if the reason why they were all there on the eve of Memorial Day weekend was personal, driven by the ghosts of her past. Was she raising hell over little more than a suicide? Was she as delusional and as stubborn as some people called her behind her back?

Then she saw the determination on Fradella's face and pushed her guilt aside. Doc Rizza had an innocent girl's body on the cold, stainless steel, exam table down at the morgue, and that wasn't a delusion. She was doing what she had to do, what needed to be done. Her job.

"Shoot," Donovan said in lieu of hello. His voice was neutral, professional, focused.

"Hey, D," Tess said, "we're all here. Let's trace the—"

"Ahead of you already," he replied. "I tried to trace the images posted online and isolate the device or network they were posted from." He paused for a moment, and Tess held her breath. "No such luck," he continued. "However, I've recovered EXIF metadata from the image file."

Michowsky's frown deepened, while he muttered something under his breath.

"In English, please?" Tess asked.

"Digital cameras store all sorts of other data in the image files. These bits of information are called metadata and the format in which metadata is stored in image files is called EXIF, short for exchangeable image file. It stores GPS coordinates, date and time the photo was taken, sometimes the date and time the photo was downloaded or uploaded to social media if that was done straight from the camera, and other technical information about the camera make and model, focal distance, aperture, and so on."

"Don't tell me we've got him already?" Michowsky asked, rubbing his palms together with excitement.

"Whoa, cowboy, hold that horse," Donovan reacted. "We have GPS info that puts the location precisely at the victim's home, but we already knew that, barring some expert Photoshop skills. We have date and time: April 15, at 11:43PM."

"April 15?" Tess reacted. "Why wait until now to tell her?"

"Maybe it wasn't the unsub who sent the text message," Fradella said. "Maybe it went viral and someone else wanted her to find out."

"You're correct," Donovan said. "The photos are now hosted on hundreds of different sites, but I was able to pinpoint when and where it was posted first. On a press release, issued on April 16 at 3:02AM, using a free service operated from Asia."

"He took the pictures, then went straight to distributing them. He wanted her hurt badly," Tess said. "He did everything in his power to ensure maximum damage."

"If we can't track him," Fradella said, "we could ask the press release service provider to share the IP—"

"You'd be wasting your time," Donovan said. "That is, if they even bother to reply."

Tess stood and started to pace the floor without paying much attention to her surroundings. She tried to portray this unsub in her mind. What does someone like that look like? How does he talk, how does he interact with people, with society? Is he married? Does he have a job? Nothing jelled; there were too many unanswered questions to allow her to sketch any hint of a profile yet.

She stopped her pacing and leaned over the table to be closer to the conference phone. "Let's send this case to the Cybercrime Unit," she said, "maybe they can do more."

"You're kidding me, right?" Donovan said, with a bitter chuckle. "Do you have any idea how many leaked celebrity nudes are out there? Gazillions. They'd laugh in your face, Winnett."

"This isn't a leaked, nude selfie, Donovan. This is the only evidence we have in a crime that cost a young girl her life."

"I get that," he replied, sounding a little irritated to be admonished like a child. "Otherwise I'd be halfway to the Keys by now. That said, you have to accept there's a limit to what can be done starting from a photo published all over the internet."

"How fast did the photo turn viral?" she asked, unfazed by his pushback. She was already exploring other avenues.

"Fast. I ran a comparative study with a Kardashian photo that was released last year, and it trickled though media just as fast, if not faster."

"How come? Christina Bartlett wasn't nearly as famous," Fradella said.

"These photos were pushed," Donovan said, "using all the tools out there. Press releases, automated publication on hundreds of channels like blogs and forums, Pinterest, Instagram. Your unsub knows his stuff, I'll give him that."

"But he didn't know to remove that photo metadata, did he?" Tess mumbled. "Maybe he's not that technical."

"Most people don't know that metadata exists," Donovan added. "He used a good camera though, a Nikon DSLR. Top shelf, $1,500 price range, but not something we could trace."

She leaned against the wall and closed her eyes. Who would do something like that to another human being? She hated to admit it, but it sounded more and more like a personal vendetta than a sexual offender in the making. At least the evidence pointed in that direction.

"All right, let's handle this investigation old-school."

"Meaning?" Michowsky asked.

He seemed unusually quiet, preoccupied. What was it with everyone?

"Meaning we have the date she was assaulted. Let's check some alibis, download some home security footage, interview some people."

"How about me?" Donovan asked. Can I go to the marina and hook up my boat trailer?

Tess replied. "Let's dump Christina's phone and see what else was going on in her life. Go over text messages and social media. See if you notice a change in her social media activity after April 15. I'd like to figure out if she knew she'd been assaulted."

"Got it," Donovan said. "I'll check if any of her online friends have posted anything in relation to these photos. If anyone is, say, overly enthusiastic or involved with the events surrounding her death."

"Try to track down the sender of that text message too, will you please?"

"Done and couldn't," Donovan replied. "Another one of those free service sites that doesn't even require a login."

She shook her head, feeling a wave of frustration send a rush of blood to her head. They needed a break and weren't catching any.

She thanked Donovan and hung up, then immediately dialed the Bartletts' residence.

"Mr. Bartlett," she said, the moment she recognized the baritone at the other end of the line, "this is Special Agent Winnett."

"What can I do for you?" he asked, in a voice lacking any intonation.

"On April 15, were you and your wife at home in the evening?"

Several noises indicated he'd set the phone down and switched on the speaker, then they heard Bartlett ask his wife.

"We had a late-night fundraiser, but we were back by one, one-thirty, maybe a bit later. Why?"

"Do you remember noticing anything out of the ordinary that night when you came home?"

"N—no," he replied, and Tess could hear Dr. Bartlett also say no in the background. "That's the day he was here? When we were out?"

"I remember something," Dr. Bartlett intervened, her voice remote at first, but then closer, as she probably approached the phone. "Christina wasn't feeling very well; we were a little worried while we were out."

"Do you recall what was wrong with her?" Tess asked.

"She felt a bit faint, and her blood pressure was low. I gave her a Coke and she felt better, although I had to fight with her to make her drink it."

"Why?"

"The calories," Dr. Bartlett replied. "She counted calories for every bite she put in her mouth. In the morning she was still a bit pale and tired but seemed okay. She left for a photo shoot in Paris right after I'd gone to work."

"How about the alarm system? Do you recall it being off when you came home?"

A moment of silence ensued while the Bartletts tried to remember something that had seemed trivial at the time, more than a month ago.

"Probably, yes," Bartlett replied. "Usually we don't arm it until all of us are home." His voice broke, as if the memory of his daughter knocked the air out of his lungs. "But video was still running, it always is, whether the system is armed or not. You have all the data."

"We do, and we'll go over it in detail," she said, feeling pessimistic without any real cause. Or maybe because she knew that someone so organized wouldn't leave the premises without addressing the security tapes.

"Thank you," Tess said, "that's all for now. We'll be in touch."

"Agent Winnett," Bartlett said, "please keep in mind what we discussed. I'm counting on you."

She hesitated for a split second. There wasn't much she could say.

"Like I said, Mr. Bartlett, I'll be in touch."

Tess ended the call, then dialed Gallagher, reminding herself to be polite and contain her bursting disdain for that heartless jerk.

"Hello," he said, his voice unbelievably cheerful. In the background, the sound of young women laughing came across loudly, together with clinking glasses and some music.

"Agent Winnett, FBI," she introduced herself coldly. "Where were you on April 15?"

"Let me check my calendar," he replied immediately, sounding a little out of breath. Then the background noise subsided with the thump of a door closing. "Um, I took my mother to Jacksonville that weekend. We left on Sunday morning. She had a Monday appointment at the Mayo Clinic, at 6:00AM. Can you believe those people?"

"And you were with her the whole time?"

"Yes. She's suffering from heart failure. I had to wheel her through an entire day of appointments, lab tests, an MRI, and whatnot. We flew back on Tuesday."

"Are you certain about that, Mr. Gallagher? We *will* verify."

"Positive," he replied, sounding very sure of himself. "It's in my Outlook."

"We'll be in touch if we need more information," she said, then promptly ended the call.

Fradella did real-time database searches to validate Gallagher's alibi, using Tess's laptop logged into the FBI systems. He scrolled through Gallagher's credit card charges, highlighting those for airfare and hotel, restaurants, car rental in Jacksonville. Everything checked out.

Without a word, Tess speed-dialed Donovan's number.

"We struck out, D. We have nothing."

A long moment of silence, thick and ominous, while no words were spoken.

"All right, Winnett. I'll tell them to go ahead without me. You owe me one."

10

Assumptions and Scenarios

Tess stared at the clean whiteboard, gnawing on her index fingernail without realizing, focused on the web of thoughts and theories that ran through her mind, trying to disentangle and arrange them into heaps of actionable data. The problem with having too little information is uncannily similar to having too much information; both situations are magnets for speculation and confusion.

Behind her, a coffee maker whistled and dripped into a paper cup, while Fradella and Michowsky chatted casually, venturing hypotheses about the unsub's ability to enter premises without detection, without leaving a single trace of evidence behind. The smell of fresh coffee filled the air, dissipating the gloom brought by the dark windows and flickering fluorescent lights. Sunset had come and gone, hours ago.

She picked up a dry eraser marker and split the whiteboard into three vertical sections, then labeled them, *Victimology, Assumptions,* and *Desired Outcome,* respectively. The victimology section took more than half the space, and she started drawing a table with many columns in the lower half of it.

"You're doing a victimology matrix?" Fradella asked. "With only one victim?"

She threw him a quick glance, and instead of responding, she went over to the assumptions section and wrote, *Personal Vendetta vs. Repeat Offender.*

"We need to get creative and organized," Tess said. "We don't have much else to go on."

"But we've never done a matrix with one vic," he protested, although less energetically than before.

"There's nothing to lose if Christina is the only victim. We'll just have a lot of empty whiteboard space. No harm in that."

She wrote Christina's name as a line header, then labeled columns one by one, with every detail she thought would become relevant if her initial hunch proved correct and the unsub was an evolving serial offender. She grouped physical features together, like race, hair color, eye color, age. Then she added a column labeled *Sexual Assault* and wrote *No* on Christina's line. She hesitated for a moment, then added another column labeled *Famous,* and wrote *Yes* below.

Finally, she wrote *Crime Scene* as the next column title, and marked *Home* below.

"Anything else?" she asked, without turning around. She knew the two detectives were paying attention; their chatter had subsided for a while.

"I'd add something about the security of the home," Michowsky offered. "Maybe with qualifiers, like high, medium, and low. Bartlett's residence is a 'high' in my opinion," he added, making air quotes with his fingers.

"Yup," she said, then added the information as a new column labeled *Home Security.*

"I'd put occupation," Fradella said, "because it ties into the fame part."

Tess frowned a little. "I'm not following."

"People can be famous for a number of reasons, but this girl was highly visible. People saw her on a daily basis, loved her image, her face, the beauty ideal she represented. There are famous scientists or authors out there and no one cares what they look like. Their physical aspect is irrelevant."

"That's an excellent point," Tess replied, adding one more column labeled *Occupation,* and wrote *Model* below.

No other suggestions followed, so she moved over to the assumptions section.

"Let's brainstorm and add pros and cons," she said drawing a large T under the words she'd written here earlier, *Personal Vendetta vs. Repeat Offender.* She waited, but no one offered any inputs. "I'd say *Access* speaks for personal vendetta," she said, writing the word in the left column. "The unsub knew his way quite well around the Bartletts' home security and schedule. He picked the one evening when the Bartletts were out late. Unfortunately, we can't ask Christina if she opened the door for anyone she knew, but there were no signs of forced entry."

"The alternative is stalking," Fradella offered. "If he's not a close relationship, he would've stalked the victim for a while."

She wrote *Stalker* in the right column.

"Why at night?" Michowsky asked. "Did he have to do this at night? The Bartletts are gone all day."

"Maybe Christina was gone too? Most of the time?" Fradella offered.

"Maybe, or access was easier, safer without neighbors and gardeners and delivery drivers dropping by," Tess replied. "This speaks to the repeat offender scenario."

"I think it speaks more to the drugs he used," Michowsky said. "She was definitely subdued with drugs, right? If he assaulted her at night, early night like we know it happened, the victim had enough time to sleep it off undetected. Probably that's why she had no idea she'd been assaulted."

"Right," Tess replied. "Otherwise, if either of the Bartletts would've found her sleeping like a log in the middle of the day, they would've instantly known something was off. Again, speaks to the repeat offender scenario."

"That scenario is gaining steam," Fradella commented, "but the crime *feels* personal. I don't know how to turn that into anything useful though."

She wrote it down. "You don't need to. It feels personal to me too, but

I'm getting the repeat offender vibe at the same time. Oftentimes, a serial offender's first victim is a personal acquaintance."

The room fell silent for a while, and Tess took a few steps to the right.

"I meant to ask," Fradella said, "what do you mean by desired outcome?"

"In a murder, we know what the killer intended; to take a life. In this situation, we're not sure, at least not yet."

Michowsky frowned. "This is assault, followed by cyberbullying, harassment, violation of privacy. What am I missing?"

"What if he wants them dead?" Tess asked. "Or, say, punished for their fame, which he might perceive as arrogant or undeserved."

"Hence the title of this section," Fradella said. "Desired outcome. But how will we know?"

Tess pressed her lips together for a brief moment. There was no easy answer to that question. "We can only speculate, but once we figure that out, we'll know what his MO is, and what his signature looks like, what actions he took, in addition to those required for the perpetration of the actual crime. His ritual, if you prefer. The signature gives a profiler the most insight into an unsub's psychology. Right now, we don't know where that line is drawn."

"What are our options?" Michowsky asked, ruffling his eyebrows even more.

She took a sip of tea from a freshly brewed cup bearing the insignia of the Palm Beach County Sheriff's Office. A small piece had been chipped away from the mug's lip, and she turned the mug to avoid that section.

"I'd say assault is one potential desired outcome. In this scenario, the unsub wanted the victim subdued, naked, and powerless. Like with any form of sexual assault, this is about power. He took photos as keepsakes from his assault, as collectibles, and shared them with the world to show everyone how powerful he is."

"Why wasn't there penetration?" Fradella asked, and Tess could've sworn he blushed a little. "Doc Rizza said she wasn't raped."

"Excellent question," Tess replied. "Impotence could answer that and might also be his motivation for the crime. Maybe he can't be around women anymore, because he knows he can't perform."

"Or maybe he's working up his courage," Michowsky added. "This unsub is definitely smart, and sexual assault is a forensic deathtrap."

She nodded. "Yeah, that could work," she said, then added some notes on the whiteboard. The words *Power, Impotence* with a question mark, *Forensics* and another question mark. "The second option is *Harassment,*" she said, writing the word in block letters. "If his intended outcome was to harass Christina, the assault was just a means to an end. He needed the compromising photos and did whatever he had to do to get them."

"It aligns better with the personal vendetta scenario," Fradella said. "Christina wasn't harmed physically in any way. Well, other than drugged."

"Correct. Then a third possibility is pain. He wanted her to live a life of shame, of suffering, to lose the life she'd made for herself, to be forced into hiding and never see daylight again. That also aligns with personal vendetta."

"You have a fourth potential outcome?" Michowsky asked, a little incredulous.

"Yes, and that's murder. Like I said before, he could want them dead, but not by his own hand. He delivers a devastating blow, then waits and watches until they die."

Michowsky whistled. "It's far-fetched, don't you think?"

"For someone who gets off on people's pain? No, it's not," she replied. "He might watch them, waiting for their despair to run its course. He might continue to stalk them after the assault has happened, to be close to them, to see them agonizing." She took another sip of tea, now cold. "It's the ultimate power trip. No one has more power over something than the one who can destroy it."

"Where are you getting all this from?" Michowsky asked. "All these theories?"

She exhaled sharply. "From years and years of staring into the abyss, Gary."

Fradella chuckled quietly. "Not sure if you've noticed, but you started talking about *them*, when we only have one victim."

Tess shook her head gently, disappointed with her own Freudian slip. "Just a persistent, annoying gut feeling, that's all."

11

Nickname

Tess checked the time, then turned toward the two detectives. It wasn't that late yet, only 9:17PM, and she wanted to interview Christina's friend, Santiago Flores, before the end of the day. The personal vendetta scenario still carried a lot of weight, mostly because of access to the victim's home, and that typically meant someone close to the victim had been invited inside the home, rather than finding a smart way to break in, unseen and undetected by a sophisticated security system.

"Santiago Flores," she said, "what do we know about him?"

"Clean record, no priors," Fradella announced, going through various screens on the laptop. "IRS has him reporting revenue from various 1099s, but I recognize a few names. I see *GQ, InStyle, Vogue,* even *Esquire.* He's doing okay; he pulled in almost five hundred large ones last year."

"Let's pay Mr. Flores a visit, shall we?" she invited, already headed out the door.

They caught up with her by the time she reached Michowsky's Explorer. He unlocked the doors, and she hopped onto the passenger seat, while Fradella took the back seat.

"Where's your car?" she asked Fradella. "Did you leave it at the Bartlett residence?"

"One of the CSU techies drove it back here," he replied, somewhat surprised. "I didn't think you noticed."

She smiled. Of course, she noticed such things. Up until two hours ago, she still hoped they'd be able to make their dinner reservations, but that had dropped off the calendar for the foreseeable future.

Not waiting for Michowsky to start the engine, she dialed Donovan on speaker.

"Hey, D," she said, as soon as he picked up. "Still at it?"

"Yeah, and I've got bad news too, although we were kind of expecting it."

"Shoot."

"An extended portion of the Bartlett home video surveillance data is missing. The deleted chunk starts sometime on April 9 and ends on April 24."

"How the hell did he manage that?"

A moment of silence ensued, the only thing coming across being a frustrated breath of air that Donovan let out between his teeth.

"I'd have to look at the system settings, maybe talk to one of the system experts. I was hoping he'd erased the data up until the moment he left the home and we might still catch a glimpse of him leaving the premises, because this is digital, you know. It's not like you remove the VHS tape from the system and it stops recording until someone notices."

"Would you like to venture an educated guess?" she asked, thinking about Doc Rizza for a moment, and how reluctant the coroner was in making any assumptions. Apparently, people who work with measurable data don't like to speculate much. Just like Doc, Donovan needed some convincing before sharing some useful scenarios.

"Based on the specs I've seen online," he eventually said, "the system records information on one of four hard discs, cycling through them one by one. Each disc holds about two weeks' worth of video; all four discs combined cover about two months of surveillance on multiple channels. My guess is he did something to damage the disc that was in use at the time, without resetting the system or generating an error that would've caused it to switch to the next available disc."

"How the hell did he pull that off?" Michowsky intervened, sounding irritated. Tess threw a quick glance at him, surprised by his emotional outburst.

"There's no way of knowing, not without talking to the manufacturer tomorrow morning," he replied. "But if I were to do it, I'd probably use a strong magnet, or an EM field generator. A more advanced user would be able to download a virus that deletes every bit of information that is stored on that hard disc, moments after it's recorded."

"A virus? Jeez," Michowsky reacted, still angry for some reason.

"What kind of skill level are we talking about, D?" Tess asked.

"Either relatively high, or at least someone smart enough to know what to buy from the street. Keep in mind, the alarm didn't go off to begin with. That part was not tampered with."

"Yeah, I know. The Bartletts said they never arm it when one of them is out."

"Then, you know what that means, right?"

"Yeah, I know what that means. The unsub knew precisely what to expect at the Bartlett residence. No forced entry means Christina invited him in. He is someone she knew well." She paused for a moment; she was about to ask Donovan to work an impossible miracle for her, something so challenging she didn't know if it was even possible, but it was worth a shot to try. "D, I need you to search for other victims. I know this sounds—"

"Crazy? Like you've completely lost your mind?" he reacted, not unlike she'd expected. "What the hell am I supposed to look for? Nude photos with names attached? I'll be buried in internet filth for months to come, and still have nothing to show for it."

"Let's think through this," she pleaded. "You know the drill. Establish search goal, then define parameters, one by one."

"This is insane, Winnett, and you know it."

"Parameters, Donovan, please."

She could visualize him pushing away from his desk, disheartened, almost bitter, then gulping some of that weird water he always had a hefty supply of handy in a transparent travel mug.

"What's in that water of yours, D? I always wanted to ask."

"Jeez, Winnett, how the hell did you know I was drinking that right now? You're scary."

She didn't react in any way, giving him time to stop fighting her idea. Fradella grinned widely, visibly entertained by their exchange.

"It's lemon with rind, a few mint leaves, and a slice of cucumber," he eventually said, seemingly back to being calm, composed.

"Sounds tasty," she replied. "Parameters?"

"Um, yeah. Geography?"

"South Florida for now."

"Age, gender, race?"

"Let's go with sixteen to thirty years of age, female, Caucasian."

"What are you basing these criteria on, Winnett?" Donovan asked, his voice still riddled with doubt.

"This search only makes sense if the unsub is a serial offender, a sexual predator. They rarely cross gender and race lines, and almost always choose either adult or child; never both."

"Okay, what else?"

"Cross-reference with recent suicides or attempted suicides."

"Going back how long?"

"Say, five years."

"Got it. It still comes back in the thousands."

"Can you cross-reference these names against nude photos posted online with names attached?"

"Whoa... That would take some doing. I'd have to write a rather complex piece of code that would crawl the entire internet looking for images, then parse their names, then cross-reference with DIVS search results. It would take weeks. Image search by a parameter such as 'nude photo' is still in its infancy. Artificial intelligence can't tell a cat from a naked woman, you know. Not yet."

She swallowed her frustration and forced herself to think of alternatives. "All right, then, let's attempt to define another parameter: fame. This is what you do best, quantify the unquantifiable, right?"

Fradella chuckled quietly. "I'd like to see that one done," he said in a low voice, meant only for the three of them.

"I bet you would," Donovan replied coldly. "Why do you think your vic's fame is relevant, Winnett? One data point doesn't make a pattern."

"The unsub destroyed her life. He took her life and dragged it through the mud. I'm thinking there must be some rhyme or reason behind this. Her fame can't be a coincidental factor. I'm willing to bet it was a factor, maybe even a trigger."

"Taker of Lives... I like that," he said with a hint of amusement in his voice.

Tess frowned but decided to refrain from scolding him. Pasting nicknames on unsubs was never helpful; it created stereotypes in everyone's thinking.

"So, look for famous people against the database results? We don't capture fame anywhere in our systems, Winnett."

"No worries, I'll give you a way in. What happens when famous people get in trouble, any kind of trouble?"

"All the social media and the tabloids are all over it."

"Because the unsub wants it that way," Tess replied. "I believe the initial press release is part of his signature, or even his MO, if his desired outcome is to harass and cause pain."

"Got it," Donovan replied, then hung up.

They drove in silence for a while, but then Tess decided to ask a question that had been at the forefront of her mind for a while.

"Gary," she said hesitantly, then cleared her throat. "I meant to ask you, is there anything wrong?"

He shot her a quick glance, then turned his attention to the crowded highway. "Why do you ask?"

"You seem to have something weighing on your mind lately, that's all."

"I'm fine," he said, a bit harsher than his usual tone, then he clenched his teeth.

He wasn't fine; that was obvious. Then Tess realized she should've probably asked him that question when Fradella wasn't present. Michowsky might have something to say in private. A brief jolt of self-directed anger coursed through her veins. For someone so adept at psychology, she sometimes was an unbelievable klutz.

"It's this stupid technology," Michowsky suddenly blurted. "I've been on the job for almost thirty years, and now I can't even follow half the conversations. How the hell am I supposed to do my job, and be good at it? Maybe it's time to call it quits."

"You think a Donovan can replace a Michowsky?" Tess asked calmly.

"You bet he could," he replied bitterly, "only the bosses are used to doing the job the old-fashioned way, hence I can still pay my mortgage. Don't you see, we solve our cases from the conference room these days. From the damn computer. No more chasing perps, no more outsmarting scumbags in interrogation."

Tess shifted in her seat, folding her left leg underneath her. "Listen, no amount of database searches can replace a good cop's gut."

He fell silent again, grinding his teeth. His lips moved, as if he were battling words, trying to keep them locked inside his mouth. "You're just saying that to make me feel better," he replied quietly. "No need to sugarcoat it, Winnett."

"I'm not," she replied. "If I were, Donovan would've been a field agent by now, and he's not, no matter how much he wants it, and how many times he tried to get that promotion. He's just not field material. You are. Fradella is too."

"I didn't see what you saw," Michowsky said. "With the Taker of Lives, I mean."

Ah, great… the nickname had stuck.

"I'd've gone home," he continued, his voice riddled with bitterness, "maybe interviewed a few people over the next days, just to satisfy that curiosity I still have, because all this technology? I don't even know where to start with it."

"Maybe at first," Tess replied. "Technology or not, you asked the right questions all along, and that's the core of our job. Why did Christina kill herself? How were those photos taken? How did the unsub—well, you'd probably called him a perp—but either way, how did he gain access to secure premises? Then you would've found the answers. Technology is just a tool, one of many."

She looked at him, realizing how difficult it must've been for him, a seasoned detective only a few years away from retirement, to openly admit he felt inadequate. Somehow, that didn't make him look weak in her eyes; quite the opposite. Detective Gary Michowsky had moral and intestinal fortitude, and he'd just earned more respect from her in those few minutes than in their entire history of solving cases together.

"There isn't a trace of doubt in my mind that you're one of the best cops I've met," she said, as he was pulling in at the curb in front of Santiago Flores' condo high-rise. "Not a single trace."

12

Me: Waiting

I watch her sleep, and I wait.

Her slumber is peaceful, undisturbed, and her breathing is quiet, measured, the steady rhythm of life: perpetual, natural, healing.

I can stop that rhythm. I can make it go away so easily it's deplorable, not worth mentioning. One needle prick, one push on the syringe piston, and the rise and fall of her breasts against the sheets will stop, to never resume again.

The only problem with killing someone is that it's too damn easy.

I struggle with drugs, you know. I'm not a chemist, a pharmacist, or a doctor of any specialty, nor did I ever aspire to be. Everything I know I taught myself; they say in the age of the internet that lack of knowledge is nothing but laziness. Of course, take that with a grain of salt, because not everything they put on the internet is accurate or even real, and not everything you see in movies is either.

Take chloroform, for example. Stupid thing nearly got me busted. Don't you remember how they used to subdue girls, men too, in the movies with a simple handkerchief soaked in chloroform held at their noses? They used that trick on the big screen for decades. Turns out in real life it doesn't exactly work like that. First time I tried, the bitch thrashed around violently for a good couple of minutes until she finally settled somewhat, but she'd already woken the entire house with her bedlam. A moment later, she started throwing up, projectile vomiting aimed at a new Guinness World Record, spraying her puke all over the room. I hated her for it, but that barf attack saved my life. I kicked my bag under her bed and hid inside her closet before she woke up enough to realize I was there. When her parents rushed in, no one remembered to ask what was with the noises they'd heard only moments before.

I had to wait it out, inside the closet, holding my breath, and not daring to move, afraid some garment would become loose and fall from its hanger, drawing everyone's attention. Thankfully, she kept on throwing up, and soon they all left for the hospital, too rushed to set the alarm.

I got away with it. The hospital, in its typical style of providing healthcare in the age of insurance dominance, diagnosed her with food poisoning from some sushi she had for dinner at a nearby restaurant. They didn't bother to run a blood toxicity screen, because the insurance wouldn't cover it. That's how I got away with it.

The next day, a health inspector landed on that restaurant's doorstep with inspection papers in his hand. Why, you might ask yourself? It was just food poisoning, right? Yes, but the bitch was famous, and fame changes things. It's funny how things work in life; if I watched the wrong movie, leaving me with the impression that chloroform could help me do what I wanted to do with that girl, that single event rippled into making an otherwise decent sushi place pay ten grand in Health Department fines. Because, of course, the inspectors found something. They always do.

But I learned my lesson that night. No more movie bullshit; I had to do the hard work. I remember learning about Rohypnol and GHB, how both have the same effect, but Rohypnol comes at a premium with erasing the user's short-term memory around the time of the event. Not to mention GHB induces vomiting. Please, no more of that.

I remember when I first tried Rohypnol on a girl, and it was oh, so, damn easy! She wasn't anyone you'd know; no, just someone I wanted to test my new method on. We got to talking, then drinks, then she would've done anything I wanted, dizzy, confused, malleable. I put her to bed and thanked her for the help with my experiment. I know what you're thinking in your perverted mind, but no, I didn't lay a finger on her; I just ensured she made it safely to her own room. She didn't remember that part though; she didn't remember any of it. The next day she had no idea we'd spent hours together the night before. Perfect!

The following week, I tested it on someone else, and her family too, some unsuspecting folks who asked me for dinner one time. They drank their roofies without the slightest suspicion, then one by one excused themselves and went to bed, leaving me all alone in the house, in complete control of their existence. That night I learned a few more things. That people under the influence of Rohypnol will buy any lie without debate, becoming easy to manipulate and order around. That I needed to learn my way around commonly used alarm systems, and that if I kept the time between my arrival and the actual ingestion of the drug to a minimum, say, under 30 minutes, they would have absolutely no recollection of our encounter the next day. It could prove tricky to do, but not impossible.

Rohypnol wasn't going to do the trick by itself, not for the girl I wanted to work on. It wasn't strong enough. I couldn't give her a double dose, because I was afraid of what might happen. That's why I mentioned earlier I struggle with drugs. Last thing I want is a girl dying on me, for no purpose whatsoever, by accident, in a haphazard act of ignorance and stupidity. No... I want their deaths to mean something, to make a statement, a bold one that people will remember. That meant I needed something else on top of the Rohypnol.

I wanted them willing, unconcerned with appearances, not a shred of self-awareness, so we could create something memorable together. I was getting smarter about things, and I wanted a drug that would wear off quickly and have no lasting effects, that would disappear from the bloodstream quickly, so no one would be able to figure it out. A drug that was safe to use, easy to handle, just like the stuff they use in hospitals for short-term anesthesia. Exactly like that.

It's funny how, once you know precisely what you want, opportunities start presenting themselves. It took me a few minutes to find a supplier and, using an encrypted proxy, I ordered the drugs I was looking for online, together with an assortment of accessories, for which I paid using bitcoin. Untraceable. A few days later, a package arrived at my door. I was ready.

Yeah, I'm smart, aren't I? Too bad studies show absolutely no correlation between intelligence and success, be it either financial or social. Who cares if you're smart? No one does. But if someone has the right shapes, the right skin, the right gender, and the right hair, people will put that someone on a pedestal and swoon over every single, narrow-minded, narcissistic, and self-indulgent word that comes out of their mouths.

Not to worry, I'm going to show you all how misplaced your admiration is. I have the power to destroy all your undeserving idols, although you don't even know I exist.

13

Santiago

When Santiago opened the door, Tess could see he'd been crying. His eyes, swollen and red, were still flooded with tears, although he tried to hide his face from them. He invited them in, and then excused himself for a moment. Tess heard the water running in the bathroom for a minute or two, but when Santiago came back, his eyes were just as red and swollen.

She recognized his face. She'd seen one of his ads recently, most likely an advert for Rolex or Omega, or was it Breitling? No, John Travolta was still the official face of Breitling. It must've been Rolex then. He was handsome, with delicate yet masculine features and thick, raven black hair.

"Mr. Flores," she said, speaking gently, "thank you for seeing us so late in the day. I'm assuming you know what we're here about."

"I've heard about it on TV. No one called me," he said, his voice breaking as he spoke the words. "I had to find out from the news. If she would've called me, I—"

He stopped, then sat on the sofa with urgency and abandonment, as if his knees had buckled and couldn't support his weight any longer. Tess sat across from him, on the edge of an armchair, while Michowsky slowly paced the room, observing every detail of the trendy living room.

"There was nothing you could've done, Mr. Flores," Tess said. "It's my understanding she took her life shortly after she found out about the photos."

The emotions on Santiago's face shifted, from the deepest sorrow to the sharpest anger. "Do you know who did that to her?" he asked.

"Not yet, but we're working diligently to find out," she replied. "What can you tell us about your relationship with Christina?"

His anger vanished, pushed aside by sorrow and despair. "I was in love with her," he said simply, while his chin trembled in an effort to contain his tears. "Hopelessly in love with her since the day we met on *Vogue*'s studio set in New York City two years ago."

"Did she feel the same toward you?"

"No…" he admitted, turning his head away for a moment. "She loved Pat, her boyfriend, but I knew what kind of man he is, and I'd hoped one day she'd see it too. I was going to be there for her when he broke her heart."

"You weren't jealous of Pat?"

"I'd lie if I said I wasn't, but I couldn't do anything to upset Christina. I was resigned to be her best friend, content to share whatever bits of her life I could, and I waited."

"Were you ever angry or upset for being rejected over a lesser man like Pat?"

"Angry? Never," he said. "Lesser man? Maybe, but I didn't think of him that way. Pat was the man she chose, and I respected that."

"Was she happy?" Fradella asked.

"She was, and that made everything acceptable for me, although I knew he'd make her suffer eventually," he replied. "It hurts to admit, but she was happy with him. Her career had taken off too, she was booked everywhere, yes, she was happy."

"Did she mention any issues with her family?" Tess asked, thinking maybe they'd been looking in the wrong place, although the very thought of it made her sick to the stomach.

"What do you mean?" Santiago asked, frowning and looking first at Tess, then at Fradella.

"Did she ever complain about her father, or his friends?"

"Oh, no, definitely not. The Bartletts are respectable, civilized people. She never said anything."

"Any creeps or stalkers she might have mentioned?"

"None," he said, without any hesitation. "We all have fans, but most fans are reasonable. None of hers stood out in any way that she shared with me."

"What other important people were there in her life? Anyone else worth mentioning?"

"There was this girl, Althea," he said, blushing a little. "I did my best to avoid her, because she always seems to want to be alone with me, if you know what I mean, and I'm not interested."

"Were she and Christina close?"

"Not particularly, no," he said. "Sometimes, when Christina was home between location shoots, she'd come by to hang out with her, see what clothes she brought back, talk fashion and stuff."

"Girl stuff?"

He shrugged, then shook his head. "I doubt it. Christina wasn't like that. She didn't care much for gossip."

Tess exchanged a quick glance with Fradella and Michowsky. It seemed they needed to talk with this girlfriend too, just to cover their bases. Maybe she knew something, or maybe Christina had confided in her after April 15, the night she was assaulted.

"We'll need to speak with her," Tess said. "Would you happen to have her phone number?"

"Sure, but you'll probably have to wait a while. She's in Europe, studying."

"When did she leave?" Fradella asked.

"Early April sometime," Santiago replied. "It was before my *InStyle* shoot, and that started on the first weekend in April."

He took out his cellphone and retrieved a number from the phone's memory. He initiated the call on speaker, then set the phone on the table. Three beeps, and an automated voice announced that the number they were calling had been temporarily disconnected. It was another dead end.

Tess studied his attractive face. Not a trace of deception on his features, in his behavior, in the words he chose, or the things he said. If he knew something relevant, he wasn't aware he did. Maybe she could trust him with a little more information.

"Mr. Flores, please keep what I'm about to share in the strictest of confidence," she said, earning herself a long, scrutinizing gaze from Michowsky.

Santiago nodded and clasped his hands together in his lap. "Of course."

"Christina was assaulted in her own home on April 15, about midnight; that's when those photos were taken. We have reasons to believe she was drugged by someone who was comfortable enough with the property and its surroundings to act without fear. Did she mention anything after April 15 that could shed some light on what happened?"

"Nothing," he said, after spending a moment thinking. "I went over there that week when she came back from her Paris location shoot. We had dinner with her parents. Pat was out of town or something."

"And she seemed perfectly normal?"

"Yes, absolutely. A little tired, maybe, but that's to be expected with all the jet lag and the crazy hours."

"Can you think of anyone who could've done this, Mr. Flores?" Michowsky asked.

"No," he answered quickly. "I've spent all day today wondering how it was possible, her photos ending up out there like that. She was a modest girl; she never did naked shoots, no matter what they offered. She turned down *Hustler*, . did you know that?"

No, they didn't know that, and it was a valuable piece of information. It said a lot about Christina's character.

They thanked Santiago and left, then called it a night after wolfing down some burgers and fries under Cat's watchful eyes, at the Media Luna Bar and Grill. Whenever Cat laid eyes on the two detectives, a deep crease appeared between his eyebrows and wouldn't disappear for a moment.

She'd asked him about it, and he'd merely replied, "They're cops, and I don't trust cops." She laughed, because she was also a cop. Since the day Cat had saved her life, almost twelve years ago, he'd watched over her fiercely, ready to do whatever it took to protect her from all harm. His devotion warmed her heart and helped heal her deeply buried wounds that still hurt at times.

She'd only been asleep for a few short hours when a chime woke her, a little before 6:00AM. A text message from Donovan: "Read your email."

She quickly read through the message and the attached files, then texted

Michowsky and Fradella. At 7:25AM she found them already waiting for her in the Palm Beach County Sheriff's Office conference room when she brought in coffee and donuts.

They had another victim.

14

Press Release

"We looked Estelle Kennedy up and there's no report of a suicide or attempted suicide," Fradella said, the moment she stepped through the door.

"Good morning to you too," she replied, offering the coffee cups that were accepted quickly with nods of gratitude, and putting the donut box on the table between them. "That's because Estelle is still alive."

Michowsky shot her an inquisitive look, while taking a careful sip of hot Starbucks latte.

"She fits every other criterion, except for the suicide part," Tess explained, "which leads me to believe she might not know about the photos yet."

"All right, let's see what we've got," Michowsky said, then approached the screen-mounted TV to be able to read the email displayed there.

"Donovan has already analyzed the photos he found online, and they were taken on May 10, with GPS coordinates matching the victim's residence."

"I see a pattern here," Fradella said, then picked up a dry eraser marker and started filling out the second line of the victimology matrix.

"Estelle won on *American Idol* two years ago, and she is one of the few who continued to grow their careers from there," Tess said, reading from Donovan's email. "She isn't a one-hit wonder, but none of her songs made it to Top Ten either; not yet, anyway. This girl is on her way up."

"Age?" Fradella asked, marker in hand, ready to put the number on the whiteboard.

"Twenty-three," Tess replied. "Her parents, Jim and Nadia Kennedy, sold their restaurant and took early retirement. She still lives with them. Add this to our victimology matrix, please."

Todd drew a vertical line at the end of the table and wrote, *Lives w Parents*.

"Do you think living with parents is part of the victim profile?" Michowsky asked. "Why would that matter to the unsub?"

She shrugged. "Not sure. Maybe he's reeling from a traumatic event he's trying to recreate, having to do with successful or famous adult children living with their parents. Or maybe these are the vics he has access to. A girl like that rarely lives alone; typically, there's a romantic relationship going on, and it's more difficult to sneak into a bedroom and subdue two people instead of one."

"A girl like that?" Fradella asked, frowning a little, the way he usually did when he wanted to make sure he grasped everything correctly. She had to give him points for rarely, if ever, making assumptions.

Tess displayed Estelle's *American Idol* photo on the screen. She was stunning, her almost surreal beauty augmented by the glow imparted by the achievement of winning. The photo showed her turning her head to face the camera, while playfully tugging at the strap of her blue, sleeveless top and smiling widely, happy and proud at the same time. Her gaze was showing confidence not debauchery, and her classy clothing made the same statement. Despite the occasion, she wore discreet makeup, nothing vulgar or exaggerated. Estelle was a good girl.

"How about the other photos?" Michowsky asked, then cleared his throat, visibly uncomfortable.

"Donovan's email has them," she replied. "I'm not going to display them on the wall," she added, shooting a quick glance at the glass wall that separated the conference room from the squad room that was already buzzing with activity. "They're worse than before, and Estelle was unconscious, just like Christina was."

"Taken at night?" Fradella asked.

"Yeah, sometime after midnight. Donovan sent the stats in the body of the email."

"Is it just me, or does the timeline of these attacks seem out of whack to you?" Michowsky asked.

"Let's put it on the board," Tess replied, and grabbed the marker from Fradella.

She drew a long, horizontal line above the victimology matrix and marked a point about two thirds to the right with a small vertical line.

"That's today, Friday, May 25," she said, adding the date below that point. "Christina was assaulted on April 15, but didn't hear about the photos until May 24, when she killed herself." She added all those dates as she talked through the timeline. "But the unsub kept busy, because on May 10, he assaulted Estelle."

"Are we sure it's the same guy?" Fradella asked. "We know Christina wouldn't pose nude, but we don't know that much about Estelle."

"That's true," Tess replied, "but we have this," she added, then displayed a press release on the screen. It was written in the modern style, aptly named clickbait, and it reeked of undisguised contempt. "It doesn't take an expert to see it's the same guy. He posted it only a few hours after the photos were taken."

They fell silent, gathered in front of the TV to read the press release.

What Do We Really Know about Estelle Kennedy?

Two years ago, the young Miami resident was just as anonymous as millions of other people, until one day when we all learned to say her name and whistle her tune. Since then, her career has skyrocketed. Apparently, not even Ms. Kennedy's lackluster performance since can keep it from taking off. Was hers the best voice carried on radio waves that year? Not really. Was she backed by one of the notable record labels? Nope. Was she the most talented American Idol *contestant? Not even close.*

However, we could venture a guess or two as to what drives her unlikely success.

She doesn't take chances with her music. *She borrows her sound from established performers like Taylor Swift and Kelly Clarkson, sound we're already used to liking and voting for.*

She looks just right. *Yeah, you heard me. The beautiful, slender, seemingly intangible blonde with long, wavy strands of silky hair, yadda, yadda. You know what I mean. The same type we've been falling over ourselves to fall in love with for generations. If you look the right way, you can't lose. We won't let you.*

She puts out. *Don't let her innocent looks deceive you; Google her name and be shocked at the extent of her depravity. All her secrets will be revealed, and we mean that literally, in high resolution and with amazing detail.*

"Whoa," Michowsky reacted. "This is vicious. Are you telling me the media outlets published this poison?"

"Some did," Tess replied. "Mostly online outlets, the shady ones who operate in the tabloid sphere and aren't overly concerned with lawsuits or with telling the truth. Donovan found this exact release already picked up by 145 different media outlets, verbatim. It's out there."

"But there isn't anything untrue in this release," Fradella said. "You mentioned the concern with the truth, or lack thereof. As far as anyone can tell, all of it is true. I know her music; she does sound a little like Taylor Swift."

"Correct," Tess replied. "However, any respectable publication would hesitate before releasing this story, in the form it was submitted. That's expecting too much from a disappearing breed of journalism. The emerging breed only cares about ratings, and this release is prone to go viral sooner or later."

"What bothers me is the timeline," Michowsky insisted. "He took a new victim before he finished with the first one. We've seen this before in a serial killer case, but it was different. What do you make of it, Winnett?"

"The release is searing and reeks of injured narcissism. These girls make him feel insignificant somehow; I wonder why. Maybe they reject his advances." She stood and paced the room slowly, thinking, visualizing the timeline in her mind, the unsub's actions, his potential triggers, his routine. "The timeline shows he's able to stalk two victims at the same time, which is rare. It takes an organized, methodical, highly intelligent person to pull that off."

"Could it be that he's waiting for them to find out about the photos on their own, and intervenes only when that doesn't happen?" Fradella asked.

"It's a good theory," she said, tilting her head slightly, as she let her mind explore the validity of the idea. It made sense, and, if true, brought some clarification to the unsub's desired outcome: pain. Tremendous psychological suffering, destroyed lives, pain he witnessed and enjoyed, pain from which there was no coming back.

"But how does *that* happen," Michowsky asked, gesturing toward the TV screen where the press release was still displayed, "and Estelle hasn't heard about it yet, after two weeks?"

"Informational overload," Fradella replied. "There's so much stuff online these days that things could go unnoticed for the longest time."

"Correct," Tess replied. "Until someone close to the victim finds out and lets her know. This time we might be ahead of him. Estelle is still alive, as far as we know. Maybe she remembers something from that night." She grabbed her keys. "Are you guys coming?"

15

Another Life

Tess usually delivered bad news to families in the form of next-of-kin death notifications, followed by routine questioning. She couldn't remember a time when she'd talked to a live victim, one who didn't know she'd been victimized.

Her colleagues at Cybercrime encountered, with increased frequency, cases involving the release of explicit imagery with the purpose of harassment or retribution; it was a sad mark of the times. This horrendous, digital crime had its own name; it was called revenge porn. That normally involved one of two possible scenarios: a disgruntled ex who had received an explicit selfie, possibly even recorded a sexual encounter; that was a personal type of revenge. The other scenario involved leaked explicit selfies and sex vids from unsecured mobile devices that fell prey to hackers. In Christina's case, they'd eliminated both scenarios, and they probably would in Estelle's case too. This unsub was different.

She climbed the three wide steps to the front door of the two-story building, but her finger hovered near the doorbell for a moment, undecided. She wasn't prepared to deliver the message; in her rush to catch Estelle before the girl could do anything desperate, she hadn't allowed herself the time to prepare.

Tess heard a young woman's laughter from inside the home. She clenched her jaws and rang the bell, then held her badge in front of an unfrosted section of the front door glass.

Estelle opened the door widely, traces of her earlier laughter waning from her lips, as she studied the three of them with increasing concern. In person, she was even more beautiful. She wore denim shorts with frayed edges, and a yellow T-shirt that fell off her right shoulder.

"May we come in?" Tess asked, after briefly introducing the three of them.

Estelle nodded and led them into the living room. "What is this about?" she asked, her voice trembling a little. She fidgeted with her hands for a moment, then clasped them together in front of her stomach to hide her anxiety.

Tess hesitated a moment, then remembered the Volvo parked in the driveway. That didn't seem the obvious choice for a girl her age; the Volvo more likely belonged to her father or her mother.

"Are Mr. or Mrs. Kennedy home?" she asked.

Estelle didn't reply; she rushed to the bottom of the staircase and shouted, "Dad! The police are here." Then she turned toward them with a nervous smile. "He'll be down in a second."

It actually didn't take more than a second for Mr. Kennedy to show up and rush downstairs with heavy steps, panting slightly from the effort. Following closely right behind him, Mrs. Kennedy, slack-jawed and pale, still dressed in a bathrobe, grasped his arm right above the elbow.

"Can I help you?" Mr. Kennedy asked, moving his scrutinizing glance from Tess to Fradella and then to Michowsky.

"Let's all take a seat, please," she replied, then sat on the sofa, waiting for them to follow suit. "We have reasons to believe someone was in your house on May 10, after midnight."

Mr. Kennedy shook his head vigorously. "That's impossible," he said. "We would've known. Are you sure you have the right address?"

"Unfortunately, we're quite sure," she replied somberly, and her ominous tone brought a visible degree of pallor to Estelle's cheeks. Her pupils dilated, and her hands started trembling.

"Do you remember anything about that night?" Tess asked, looking straight at Estelle. "Anything at all?"

"My parents went to bed early," she said, her voice trembling and weak, "at about ten. I stayed up late, wrote some music, but then I felt weird, nauseated, dizzy. I just... went to bed."

"That's all you remember?" Tess asked.

Estelle fidgeted in place and veered her eyes away for a moment. "Yes, that's it."

She was lying and wasn't very good at it.

"What do you think happened here, Agent Winnett?" Mr. Kennedy asked.

"Where's your bedroom, Miss Kennedy?" Tess asked, dodging her father's question. She wanted to get as much information as possible before all hell broke loose.

"I sleep downstairs," she replied in a choked voice. "I sometimes play music at night or watch MTV."

"Are you going to tell us what this is about?" Mr. Kennedy demanded, standing and approaching Tess, as if to give more weight to his request. "Whatever it is, just say it already."

He tugged spasmodically at the collar of his shirt, then undid the top button. His face had gained a dark red complexion, not unlike Doc Rizza during one of his hypertensive episodes.

"Please sit down, Mr. Kennedy," she said firmly, and he obeyed. "There's no easy way to say this, but your daughter was assaulted on May 10, here, inside your home."

He stared at her for a short moment, in shock, but then shook his head again. "No, you must be mistaken. We have an alarm system, with monitoring and all that." He pointed toward a control panel affixed to the wall next to the door leading to the garage. "There, see for yourself."

"Please, Mr. Kennedy, let me finish," Tess insisted.

He fell instantly silent, gasping, as if a cold bucket of ice had been poured on his head. Blotches of purple spread on his cheeks and his neck.

"During this assault, the perpetrator drugged your daughter and took pictures of her, then posted them online," she continued, as calmly as she could.

"We were here," he reacted vehemently, almost shouting. "There's no way."

"Let me see them," Estelle said calmly, standing next to Tess with her hand extended. "Please."

Tess felt tempted to postpone the moment when she'd have to share those horrible images, but there was no point. The sooner Estelle came to terms with what happened, the sooner they could focus on catching the unsub.

She unlocked her phone and handed it to Estelle. The girl looked at a few images, thumbing through them quickly, and handed her back her phone. Then she let out a heart-wrenching wail, letting herself drop to the floor and hugging her knees, shattered by uncontrollable sobs. Her mother rushed to her, while her father extended a demanding hand for Tess's phone.

"Who would've done this, Mr. Kennedy?" Tess asked, while he looked at the pictures.

He didn't reply; he grabbed at his shirt with his right hand, as if wanting to tear it off, gasping for air in short, pained breaths.

"They have my name," Estelle cried between sobs. "They have my name. Oh, God… I'm finished."

Mr. Kennedy took two steps toward his daughter, his hand still grasping at his collar, but his knees buckled, and he fell to the floor with a loud thump. He convulsed several times, heaving, then fell silently still. For a moment, Estelle's sobs ceased, silenced by unspeakable fear.

"We need a bus at my location right away," she heard Fradella say into his phone. "Possible heart attack. Step on it, already!"

Tess rushed to Mr. Kennedy and felt for a pulse. It was too late.

The killer had taken another life.

16

Arguments

"He died right there, in front of his family, and there wasn't a damn thing we could do!" she shouted, angrily pacing SAC Pearson's office, while he looked at her disapprovingly, a deep frown trenched across his brow. "Jim Kennedy was murdered, and you know that just as well as I do," she stated once more.

"Palm Beach County still hasn't requested our engagement, Winnett," he said, the moment she stopped shouting. "Officially, there's nothing we can do. Jurisdiction is very clear—"

"Argh… screw jurisdiction!"

She stopped in front of his desk with her hands propped firmly on her thighs, leaning over almost menacingly. In passing, she'd noticed the same green folder under her supervisor's clutched hands but dismissed any thought of that and refocused on the issue at hand.

"Sir, they're not equipped to handle this unsub at Palm Beach. They're an inch away from letting the case grow cold and fall through, because this man leaves no evidence behind. None whatsoever. Technically, he doesn't kill."

SAC Pearson stared at her with critical eyes, but she didn't lower her gaze. He sighed, visibly frustrated, and gestured with his hand, pointing at one of the chairs in front of his desk.

"Sit down, Winnett," he ordered, and she obliged after a second's hesitation. She was tense, angry, impatient, and sitting made it worse.

"Sir, this investigation needs a profiler, or the closest thing we have to one: me. That's the only way we'll catch this unsub."

Pearson unscrewed the cap of a bottle of Dasani and took a few swigs, unnervingly slowly. "Argue your case, Winnett. I'm listening."

She took a long breath of air, willing herself to be calm and articulate before opening her mouth. She'd already overstepped her boundaries, and last time she'd shouted at Pearson, it didn't end well. At least this time he was willing to listen. When she spoke, she sounded professional, albeit still a little loud.

"He's a new kind of unsub, bred by these modern times we're living in, by social media turning everyone into instant gratification addicts, by the explosion of malignant narcissism on a wide scale as a direct consequence." She stopped talking and took another deep breath, aware she was still coming across as aggressive, argumentative. "He stalks his prey thoroughly, not shying away from secure properties, even a rumored cartel enforcer's household. He gains access to these properties and subdues the victim while other people sleep in the house. He's incredibly bold; I've never seen anything like it."

"Do you think he's escalating?" Pearson asked, leaning forward. Something had piqued his interest.

"Definitely escalating. He's a sexual predator getting ready to kill."

"He hasn't raped anyone yet, has he?"

"No, but there's sexual viciousness in his crimes. He exposes his victims naked and powerless for the entire world to see. Rape is about power, you know that." She swallowed, aware of how dry her throat suddenly felt. Discreetly, she extracted a mint from a tin of Altoids in her pocket and put it in her mouth. "Although there's no physical penetration during the assault, this unsub does something worse. He takes their lives. He…"

She hesitated, unsure how to best explain what she was thinking. How can anyone describe such atrocity?

"In the typical sexual assault situation, the victim at least has her privacy," she continued, "and that privacy is paramount. It allows victims to heal, to put the assault behind them. That's why many attacks go unreported, because victims value their privacy more than they care for closure or even justice. This unsub makes the assault public, robbing his victims of any chance of living a normal life."

"He tags the photos with their names, right?" Pearson said, and as he spoke, a dark cloud washed over his features, as if he'd remembered something troublesome, something urgent.

"Yes. Can you imagine? Whenever anyone looks them up online, those horrible, explicit photos are the first images that come up, for the rest of those girls' lives and beyond. He takes their lives, takes control of their existence, then squashes them in a public display of power. He reduces their existence to a reprehensible pile of internet smut. He leaves them no way out other than death, or a life worse than death." She watched him closely, expecting a reaction that didn't come. "I promise you he's escalating, and he's going to kill with his own hands."

"Why do you think he hasn't done it already?"

She gave the question a bit more thought, although it had been on her mind for a while. "It's the typical progression, from lust rapist to lust killer, only he doesn't violate their bodies; he pillages their lives. I believe he's trying to figure out how to kill to make an even stronger statement."

"Jeez, Winnett… Statement of what?"

"Of his immense power over any creature that somehow, intentionally or not, takes away from his ego, his self-worth. The assaults are remediation for the narcissistic injury he's experiencing, but there's no blind rage. He's highly intelligent, organized, and knows that revenge is a meal best served cold."

"He's never hurt anyone, has he?" Pearson asked, running his hand over his shiny scalp.

"Physically, no. We believe he has chemically restrained them, but by the time we learned of the assaults we were too late to find any forensic evidence at the crime scenes or in the first victim's blood. Doc Rizza is working with Estelle, his second victim that we know of, to see if he can find any traces of chemicals in her bloodstream, but it's been two weeks," she added, making a gesture of despair with her hands.

"You have no evidence, no crime scene you can work, no leads, nothing but a tentative profile," Pearson said. "How are you planning to catch this man?"

"I know he's escalating, and I know we'll find more victims. We'll work backgrounds, and we'll find out how he chose them. The more information we have, the better we can define the profile and set a trap," she answered, aware she sounded unconvinced that this was the best approach. What she didn't want to say is that she didn't want to wait until more victims showed up. She wanted to lure the unsub, challenge him in his display of power and superiority, and get him to make a mistake, but Pearson didn't like taking such risks, and most definitely didn't endorse what he called, "cat-and-mouse games with serial killers."

She frowned. Was this unsub a serial killer? Technically, no, but practically, yes. She was willing to bet her career on it, the rarely seen, perfect, case-solving score she'd earned and that every single one of her colleagues envied. Somewhere in the deep recesses of the unsub's mind, a fantasy was being created and molded into the perfect shape, into the ideal scenario that would bring the ultimate illusion of power and supremacy to his feeble, shattered ego. What would that kill look like?

"It's interesting, you're foreseeing his escalation, but he's not a violent person, or hasn't been yet, has he?" Pearson asked, but she barely registered his question.

Would it be a public suicide he'd orchestrate somehow? Would it be video streamed on the internet, for the entire world to witness, live, as it happened? She remembered how powerless she felt when Jim Kennedy keeled over and died at her feet. There was nothing she could do, nothing that stood a chance in front of the terrible power of—

"Winnett," Pearson snapped, bringing her into the moment. "Are you still with me? Or just taking space here in my office?"

"Sorry, sir," she replied quickly, while her mind refused to let go of her chain of thought.

Yes, he'd want the entire world to feel just as helpless as she'd felt, witnessing Kennedy's demise. He'd want the entire world to scream, paralyzed and powerless, while their heroines, their role models, their beloved beauty queens and artists and musicians found humiliation and death at the hands of the Taker of Lives.

But she knew how to lure him out.

"Yes, sir?" she said smiling, waiting for Pearson to speak.

"You didn't hear a word I said, did you?" he grumbled, then repeated his question. "How sure are you that he'll escalate, as he's not a violent person?"

She grinned. "For a nonviolent person, he seems to be doing just fine filling Doc Rizza's morgue."

He sighed, leaning back into his chair and folding his arms at his chest. "All right, Winnett, I'll approve the case. I could open a federal case right now, but I'd rather you work with the Palm Beach County Sheriff's Office and get them to file a formal request."

"I will, sir."

"I thought you said you had that covered. What happened?"

"The long weekend, I guess. People are getting distracted. I'll remind Captain Cepeda to do it today."

She stood, ready to leave, feeling a wave of relief washing over her. A formal case meant access to FBI resources, labs, technical experts, the Cybercrime Unit, and last, but never least, Donovan.

"Sit down, Winnett," he said, this time sounding less commanding, almost like a friendly request.

Her eyebrows shot up, as she took her seat. She watched him quietly, waiting for him to speak, but he hesitated, keeping his eyes riveted on the green folder on his desk. He drummed his fingers against it a few times, as if weighing a decision. Then he pushed the folder toward her just a little, maybe an inch or so.

"Is your offer still on the table, Winnett?" he asked in a low, enigmatic voice.

"Absolutely," she replied without any hesitation. "What's this about?"

He didn't reply right away. He seemed uneasy talking about whatever was in there, but eventually he opened the green folder, turned it her way, and pushed it across the desk.

"This man is dating my daughter," he said, tapping his index finger against a young, attractive man's photo, affixed to a standard background printout. "He checks out," he added, sounding doubtful. "Clean record, college grad, good job. He treats my daughter well, and she's happy."

"But?" she asked, already suspecting where that was going.

"When I look at him I get this... uneasy feeling in my gut," he said.

"Say no more," she said, then reached to take the file, but Pearson still kept his hand on it.

"My daughter's falling for this man, Winnett," he added, his voice carrying undertones of parental worry and sadness at the same time. "I can't intervene directly. I can't be involved in this in any way."

"I completely understand, sir." She lowered her gaze and read the man's name from the background printout. "Give me a day or two, and I'll have Mr. Esteban Carrillo all figured out."

17

Dark Web

She checked the time, then walked over to Donovan's desk with a spring in her step. It was already mid-afternoon; although she'd skipped lunch, she didn't feel hungry, only excited at the thought of testing her theory. She could hope to lure the unsub, if Donovan found the way to convey a message to him, a message so public and so demeaning he couldn't afford to ignore.

She stopped in front of Donovan's desk and waited for him to finish typing.

"Ah, it's you," he said, without lifting his eyes from the screen. "The archenemy of fun, my own personal nemesis."

She chuckled. "Don't be so dramatic. I'm giving you an opportunity here to hunt for a criminal like none other I've seen."

He threw her a disappointed gaze, then looked at the screen again.

"What you're giving me is a raincheck for a long weekend in the Keys, all paid for, at a date of my choice. Deal?"

"Sure, in principle, yeah."

He grinned widely, "Really? I didn't think you'd go for it."

"If you can settle for Motel 6 and three fast food meals a day, I can make it happen. I'm afraid that's all I can afford."

"Buzzkill."

She didn't know what to reply, so she didn't. She'd always been a little uncomfortable interacting casually with her colleagues. She felt as if she always said the wrong things, insulted everyone's sensibilities, or made people uncomfortable. She was relentlessly focused on catching her unsubs, and rarely stopped or slowed to mind the needs or wants of other people. Many believed she put her own interests above everyone else's, and Pearson had her on an ultimatum to integrate better with the rest of the agents, to become more of a team player. She had every intention of doing that but no idea how. Fact of the matter remained, she was more comfortable interrogating an uncuffed serial killer than talking nonchalantly with a colleague. Even now, she realized Donovan had been joking about the raincheck, while she took it seriously. She wanted to kick herself.

Instead, she pulled a chair over from a nearby desk and sat, ready to listen.

"I heard you confirmed that potential vic," he said.

"Yeah, your search was spot-on. Any other names that popped up? We can start deep backgrounds already, search for any commonalities."

"Estelle wasn't a one hundred percent match, because there was no suicide or suicide attempt. She's the only one that scored high enough to be a likely match."

Tess had hoped to discover more victims, to help her gain a better understanding into the unsub's motivations, his triggers, and his signature. They were back to having nothing.

"And I have more bad news," Donovan added. "Your unsub went Dark Web on us."

"What exactly does that mean?"

"The latest photos were posted from an encrypted peer-to-peer network, then referenced on the surface Web, to make the content searchable by engines such as Google or Yahoo. We can't locate him using the source of these photos, because we can't trace the source itself."

"How about his email? The one listed on the press releases?"

"It's an encrypted account, hosted online by ProtonMail. It's free, fully encrypted, doesn't ask for any personal information to set up an account, and it's protected by Swiss privacy laws. I'll get one for myself; it's that good."

"What does that mean? Our unsub is learning?"

"He's learning faster than anyone I've seen. The first press release was his most vulnerable, so I went back, trying to trace the ISP where he uploaded the photos. Now we have a warrant pending for that ISP to share the account details for the user."

"How did you get a warrant going without a case number?"

He glared at her for a brief moment. "Winnett, what the hell? Don't ask questions you don't want answered, all right?"

Without blinking, she replied, "You misunderstood. I asked when will the warrant be granted?"

He snickered quietly. "That's better. Probably in the next few hours, but don't hold your breath. This unsub is smart. He probably uploaded from a parked vehicle at the airport, or a Starbucks patio. We talked about this, didn't we?"

She sighed. Yeah, it seemed hopeless. Every way she turned was a dead end. "All right, then, let's set up surveillance for this new account," she said, frowning, thinking how to ask Donovan to do what she really wanted to do— bait a trap.

"Pfft, Winnett," he scoffed, "there's no surveilling the Dark Web. That's exactly the point. Not even the NSA can do that; no one can."

"How the hell does he know about this kind of tech?" she asked. "How difficult is it to figure out?"

"If you ask the right questions online, it's not that difficult. You can easily get set up in less than ten minutes, without having to graduate cum laude from some top-notch computer science program. Anyone can do it, provided they're smart enough and reasonably computer literate."

"Fabulous," she mumbled, then swallowed a long curse. "He's getting smarter by the minute, taking care of every loose end and every angle where we had the tiniest shot."

"Thankfully, he still hasn't figured out the EXIF part yet. If we lose access to time, date, and location where photos are taken, then we'll really have absolutely nothing left to go on."

"How about social media?"

"I'm willing to bet Christina knew about the assault, or sensed something was wrong, because after April 15 she turned quiet on social media. Almost no tweets or Facebook posts. Before April 15, she posted a few times a day, mostly pictures from her travels, some selfies in haute couture attire, that kind of stuff."

"And Estelle?"

"There's no change in her social media after May 10. Estelle didn't know she was assaulted. By the way, how did she take it?"

"Don't ask," Tess replied somberly. "The poor girl is with Doc Rizza, going through lab tests, but he's unofficially evaluating her for suicide risk. On top of everything else, she feels responsible for her father's death."

"Did Crime Scene find anything in the house? I didn't get any surveillance data to pore over."

"They have a simplistic security system, just some sensors and a keypad. The crime scene was cleaned up twice since May 10. A regular cleaning crew comes in every Monday and does the whole house. We don't stand a chance with these aged, trampled crime scenes. We need fresh forensics, solid evidence to track this bastard down."

"And how exactly do you suggest we do that?" he said, pushing back from the desk and crossing his arms at his chest.

She smiled, one of those crooked, mischievous grins that showed her state of mind. She was about to go over her supervisor's standing order, without hesitation and without asking for approval. She only hoped she didn't have to ask for forgiveness at some point in the future.

"I believe you can help me get a message to this unsub," she said, lowering her voice and making her request sound as innocent as possible.

"Are you crazy, Winnett?"

"I'm as sane as they come, but desperate," she admitted, while her smile vanished, replaced by a look of determination.

"How exactly do you want to contact him? By email?"

"No, that's private," she replied, and winked at Donovan, who raised an eyebrow in disbelief. "We want to give him the same privacy he gives his victims. He'll have no choice but to engage."

Donovan leaned his forehead into his left hand and massaged it a little.

"I believe I can pull that off," he said after a little while. "The site where he posted the photos, not the actual press release, has a comments section. Want to use that?"

"Might work," she replied, leaning closer to the monitor. "Show me. How much traffic does it get?"

"It gets tens of views per day, maybe over a hundred," he replied. "I'm talking about Estelle's page, she's the most recent and the most famous. Christina's traffic has dropped; the posting is too old."

"Any other comments already listed there?"

"Yeah, mostly appreciative of his work. The sick bastard has a fan club, can you believe it?"

"Not only do I believe it, but I know for sure that's what he's after."

Donovan opened a new comment on that page, and changed his default screen name to Hornydog17, then waited, his fingers hovering above the keyboard, ready to type.

"Say this: 'If you had real cojones, you'd be streaming live. That girl looks like she's dead. Are you a coward? Or a necrophile?'"

He typed it quickly, then looked at her again before posting it.

"He could flip and go on a killing spree. I hope you know what you're doing, Winnett."

"I hope so too," she said quietly, then pressed the return key on his keyboard.

The message was live.

18

Me: Enraged

"What? No," I bellowed, staring at the comment displayed on the screen. "You don't even know what you're talking about, you stupid piece of human refuse." I slammed my open hand against the desk surface, making everything on it rattle. The idiocy of these morons ticked me off every single time. I bet this one weighs three hundred pounds, sports a Duck Dynasty beard and a pot belly, so large and overflowing he hasn't seen his own dick in a long time, and almost forgotten how minuscule and shriveled it is. Maybe I'll remind him... yeah.

It was one of many comments that I didn't appreciate, but this particular nastygram hurt like hell. That asshole shouldn't be allowed to use a computer. He shouldn't exist and, because he nevertheless exists, should definitely be prohibited from procreating. What does he know, really, to have an opinion? Everyone else seems to understand the value of what I'm doing, except this asinine being who calls himself Hornydog17. What kind of screen name is that, anyway? I'll tell you: a retarded one.

"I thought of live streaming *first*, motherfucker!" I heard my voice reverberate against the windows, echoing back at me in an illustration of how my anger can't reach him, wherever the sorry excuse for a human being might be.

Thankfully, his comment will soon be buried among other, more recent ones, and forever forgotten. No one will remember that he mentioned live streaming before I had the opportunity to announce it to my fans. He won't matter, because what he says doesn't matter. He's a nobody, jerking off when he sees my work, completely missing the point of what I'm doing and why. No, really, how could he not? Ugh... necrophile, my ass.

I stood and angrily paced the room, going over the things I still had to do to start streaming my shows on video. It was *my* idea, not his! He had no right to take it! Rampant thoughts swirled in my mind, making me angrier than I'd been in a long time, and that was not good. What I do doesn't jibe with angry. Getting caught and thrown in jail jibes with angry, or the other way around. Whatever.

I was almost ready, anyway, just as planned. I wanted to schedule a big announcement, to make everyone aware of what's coming, but I'll compensate somehow. I doubt that his comment was read by too many people anyway. He's a nobody, while I'm finally standing on the verge of greatness.

The benefit of greatness is that people quickly learn about it and swarm and follow, because that's what people do. Show people the right stuff, dangle the right kind of lure in front of their primal senses, and they won't stop coming, attracted by the powerful resonance with their deepest, darkest fantasies, their most secret desires, or even their most horrifying nightmares. That's why that piece of shit Hornydog17 is not going to matter. He's a nobody, born that way and destined to die that way. One day soon, I hope.

I looked at the screen, eager to see how deeply the jerk's comment had already been buried. I searched for him in the lower section of the page, even scrolled down a little, but then I had to scroll back up. His comment still ranked first and had three likes! Three other morons, cowards who didn't dare post themselves, gave that idiot a thumbs up because they felt the same. Because Hornydog17 had influenced their limited thinking and entertained them for yet another meaningless moment of their lives. At my expense!

The tiny number three next to the thumbs-up pictorial turned into a four, then into a five, and I heard myself scream with rage. Hornydog17, be thankful I'm not into working on men. If you keep pushing it, I might become interested in experimenting.

If you knew what's coming, you'd choke on your filthy tongue and die.

19

Moonlighting

Tess fired up her engine and set the AC temperature to 68 degrees, enjoying the cool breeze coming from the dashboard vents. It wasn't summer yet, but the South Florida sun shone brightly, heating up her black Suburban to the point where it burned her hand when she touched the steering wheel. She wondered for a moment why fleet managers were so stubborn and so set in their ways. What was the logic of driving black cars in hot climates? For the entire southern United States, black law enforcement vehicles made absolutely no sense; maybe the color choice served a purpose of intimidation, but to the detriment of climate, fuel efficiency, and passenger comfort. She'd seen some county sheriff's offices get white SUVs to replace the old, black ones, but only a few. Miami-Dade County was one of the pioneers. The regional bureau was not.

She drank a few gulps of stale warm water from the bottle lodged in the cup holder between the seats, then opened the green folder that had been at the center of her supervisor's mind. SAC Pearson had been thorough in preparing the file. There was complete background on Carrillo, several photos, including some with Pearson's daughter, Lily, and complete contact information.

She studied Esteban Carrillo's photo first. He was attractive, with high cheekbones and symmetrical features, a pleasant smile that curled his lips nicely, giving him an appearance of sexual allure, of magnetism. Definitely a man Lily could easily fall in love with. He was twenty-eight years old, a business college grad, and well off, judging by his clothes and demeanor.

She set that photo aside, then picked up another, taken when Lily and he were on their way to some event. They were wearing evening attire, Lily charming in a long, beige gown with rhinestones encrusted on the hem and corsage, and Carrillo sure of himself in an impeccable tux. Lily smiled, beaming from her entire being, while she clutched the man's forearm with her right hand.

Lily had Pearson's tall forehead and intelligent eyes, and her mother's predisposition to weight gain. She wasn't overweight yet, but she wasn't too slender either. She was curvaceous and somewhat appealing, beautiful at that age when everything seems possible and everything is.

Tess focused on Carrillo's eyes in that photo. She assumed Pearson had taken the picture, because she recognized the massive stairway and its unique bannister visible in the background. They were inside Pearson's home. Probably Carrillo had picked Lily up before going to a party, a big-ticket event by the looks of it. His eyes weren't as controlled as his overall demeanor. There was something rigid in his gaze, a toughness that didn't match his suit or his smile. There was tension in his jaw and alertness in his upper body, as if he were getting ready to flee or pounce. SAC Pearson's instincts were spot on.

Tess set aside that photo and moved on to the next item in the folder, Carrillo's DMV record. Clean history, and a Lexus RC F convertible registered in his name. If memory still served her, that car went for over sixty grand, just the base model without options. How could a recent college grad working as a sales rep afford it? Or was he one of those ambitious, vain, young men who dwelled in tiny apartments just to be able to afford a life of luxury, well above their means?

Pearson had pulled Carrillo's tax records, and Tess muttered, "Well done, boss," as she turned the page. The previous year he'd declared income from one source, his employer, a reputable pharmaceutical company. His W2 showed almost one hundred thousand dollars in regular income and commission. *Maybe I'm in the wrong line of work*, she thought for a moment, then visualized herself trying to peddle drugs all over town and sighed. "Screw that," she mumbled, "I could never do it." But Carrillo could afford the car, and then some.

The IRS record was the last item in the green folder, and Tess closed the file and set it on the passenger seat. She'd learned everything in there about Carrillo, enough to realize she didn't know nearly enough. Who was that man, and why was he dating Lily?

True love? Maybe, she reflected, almost chuckling at her own pessimism. No wonder Cupid never happened by in her life if that was her attitude. Lily was twenty-two, Carrillo was twenty-eight, so that worked well. He was a stud, sexy, charismatic, with that Latino fire burning in his veins. He probably had girls lined up waiting for one of his heated glances… Then, why Lily? She was a lot of things and had a youthful innocence about her that was part of her appeal, but she wasn't hot. If Tess closed her eyes, she could picture Carrillo with a tall, slender girl with legs up to her neck and a V-cut that reached her belly button, not with someone as nice and amiable as Lily Pearson. Lily was wife material, the good girl men take home to meet the parents, after they'd grown tired of sowing their oats in all four winds. Carrillo didn't seem like the marrying type; didn't appear ready to settle just yet.

Then what was his agenda? Was he looking to get close to Pearson? Was he a spy, working for who knows whom in the drug world? Due to their proximity to Cuba and Mexico, Miami-Dade and Palm Beach Counties are ripe with drug smugglers and their networks of distributors and clients. Maybe Carrillo was on someone's payroll and had a mission involving the FBI. SAC Pearson was the ranking officer in the regional bureau, and that made him a prime target for infiltration.

But with what purpose? She knew Pearson wouldn't open his mouth in front of Carrillo, or anyone else for that matter. His home was treated as a "nonsecure" environment, as he'd advised her on one occasion, when she visited with him and had wanted to discuss a case. Okay, he was cautious, but maybe they, the people who'd sent Carrillo, didn't know that.

Tess gave the green folder a long look, then shifted into gear and rolled out of the parking lot, on her way to Palm Beach County. She frowned and mumbled something unintelligible. She had a big problem. The regional bureau wasn't that large. If Carrillo had an FBI-related agenda, he'd see her coming a mile away.

20

Hair

Tess caught up with the detectives on the way to Doc Rizza's office. He'd texted everyone announcing he had something, and that felt like a miracle. It was about time. Regardless, she chose to hold Michowsky back near the elevators, with a quick touch on the forearm.

"Hey, can I talk to you for a second?" she asked, and Fradella took the hint and walked into the morgue by himself.

"Sure, what's up?" Michowsky replied.

"This," Tess replied, handing him the green folder with Carrillo's information inside. "I can't track down this guy myself; if he's into what I think he is, he'll make me in a minute."

Michowsky grinned, while looking with suspicion at Carrillo's picture. "Who's this street cat?"

"This guy is dating my boss's daughter, and he—we believe he's got an agenda. This is right up your alley, Gary. Old-style detective work, no technology involved. This guy lives completely off the technology grid. The only exception is the phone number he gave the Pearsons; at least that's not a burner. Donovan will locate that for you on a moment's notice."

"What about the Taker of Lives?" Michowsky asked, taking one step toward the elevator, his left hand suspended mid-air, ready to press the call button.

"We'll keep you posted at every juncture. If you need me for this," she gestured toward the green file, "don't hesitate. We need Carrillo figured out just as badly as the Taker. If the top dog of the regional bureau and his family have become someone's targets, I'd say that's damn critical."

"Why not throw the entire wrath of the Federal Almighty Bureau at this loser?"

"Because Pearson's daughter is in love with him, and, so far, he's done nothing wrong. Pearson's in a tight spot as a parent."

Michowsky's index finger completed its journey and landed on the elevator call button. "Got it. I'll handle this with kid gloves."

"Gary," Tess said, "thank you for your help. I know how much you wanted to spend the weekend with your family."

"Ah," he sighed, "don't mention it."

She waited a moment until the elevator doors started to close, then hurried inside Doc Rizza's office. As it normally happened when she visited the morgue, the first breath of air she inhaled stopped her in her tracks. The coldness of the air, the vague scent of disinfectant and formaldehyde, the fluorescent lights reflected in stainless steel exam tables, storage drawers, and shelving, all came together and materialized in shivers sent down her spine.

She could hear Fradella chatting with Doc Rizza near the gas chromatograph, but her eyes stayed riveted on the second exam table, where Christina's body lay under a white sheet. Her long, wavy hair escaped the confines of the exam table and ran down from underneath the sheet, moving almost imperceptibly in the ventilated air. She felt a strange connection to Christina, although they'd never met, and they hardly had anything in common. Anything, except having fallen prey to a predator, a ruthless killer. Tess held her breath, as if afraid she'd wake her from her deep sleep.

Her mind raced back to twelve years ago, to the brutal attack she'd endured. All those years had passed, and she still struggled, but never before had she felt grateful for anything that happened during that assault. It was hard to believe, almost impossible to accept, but she felt thankful her rapist hadn't recorded everything to put it out there, on the internet, and ruin her life forever. At least she'd been able to recover, as slowly and as incompletely as she'd managed, in the sanctity of her privacy, in the anonymity of her secret hell. Only Cat knew what had happened to her, the kind stranger who'd taken her in that night and patched up her wounds with his own hands, respecting her wish to avoid the authorities and the risks that were associated with going to a hospital.

What would her life have been if her turmoil had not stayed private? She would've had no future as an FBI agent; such imagery is one of the first things that pops up in an internet search. All good employers conduct background searches before extending job offers, and that includes an internet and social media search. She would have had no relationships of any kind, because she couldn't've endured having to face people, knowing what they'd seen, how they'd seen her. How everyone would see her. She would've had no life. Nothing but shame.

So much power in the hands of a single man. The power to destroy a life completely, irreparably, permanently.

She approached the exam table and gently touched a rebel strand of Christina's hair.

"I understand why you did this," she heard herself whispering, "and I promise you..." She swallowed with difficulty, fighting back tears. "I promise you I'll get him."

"I talk to them too," Doc Rizza said gently, then patted her on the shoulder. "Are you okay?"

"Yeah, sure," she replied, striving for a normal tone of voice. "What do you have?"

She avoided Fradella's curious glance and kept her eyes on Doc's face, now a more normal complexion, the worrisome redness gone. He'd put on some weight recently, but he'd always been chubby, ever since she could remember him. Chubby and jovial, probably indulging in good foods and the occasional wine, the latter perhaps more often than not. Or was it scotch?

"You've seen my email by now, I assume," Doc said. "This is the least suspicious suicide in my entire career. Official cause of death is cardiogenic shock, as expected. She seized briefly and mildly; I found traces of dried saliva on her lips and cheek, but she hadn't bit her tongue. The body wasn't moved, and no trace evidence found anywhere. Crime Scene came up empty as well; not a single fiber or fingerprint that didn't belong."

She paced the floor angrily. Doc Rizza said he had something; then why the recap of what they didn't have? She knew better than anyone they had absolutely nothing. A five-week-old crime scene, trampled, lived in, and cleaned periodically didn't allow for much relevant evidence to be collected.

"Her blood came back completely clean, except for the pills she took to kill herself. No blood alcohol either, and no other toxicity," Doc Rizza added, then sat on a five-legged stool on casters, the type seen in most labs regardless of specialty. "That's when I thought of her hair."

Tess stopped pacing and looked at Doc Rizza. "What about it?"

"Hair analysis is one of the most disputed areas in forensics, from matching hair types in the absence of DNA, to toxic residue stored in hair fibers. Some believe environmental sources are to blame for infinitesimally small amounts of chemicals found in hair, while other scientists argue that the respective chemicals have to be ingested or inhaled in sufficient quantities or for sufficient periods of time to manifest in a hair strand, weeks after the exposure has ceased."

"Meaning?" Fradella asked, frowning at the coroner.

"Meaning what I'm about to say probably won't hold up in court, but it might still help you."

"Come on, Doc, spill it. What did she take?"

"Christina was exposed briefly to Rohypnol, and the timeline matches the average hair growth rate."

"That's somewhat helpful, but not unexpected," she replied, frowning a little. "Is that it?"

"That's all I could find in Christina's hair, but then I asked Estelle to give a sample. Her hair showed the same chemical signature, albeit a bit more recent."

"Okay, he roofies them, it's part of his MO. We suspected some kind of chemical restraint, didn't we?" Tess asked. "We can't trace roofies; they're everywhere."

"But wait, there's more," Doc Rizza quipped, with a tired smile. "I tested Mr. Kennedy's hair, as he's a guest here, taking cabin number five in my morgue, and he'd been roofied too."

"Now *that's* interesting," Tess said excitedly. "That explains how the unsub entered the premises while the family was at home. He probably drugged them all and waited until they were sound asleep. I'm starting to see it."

"We've got to go back to the Kennedys, ask them about that. Maybe they remember a house guest or something. The Bartletts too."

"Don't forget Rohypnol obliterates short-term memory," Doc Rizza said, just before his phone started to ring. He picked it up on speaker. "County morgue."

"Hey, Doc, Jason Donovan with the FBI. I need you to click 'accept' on your laptop screen. I have something I need you all to see."

"How the hell did you know where we were?" Tess asked, although she knew the answer, while Doc Rizza walked with a slight limp and a hunched back to his desk, where a laptop was powered on.

"So, it's cool for you to know when I drink my fruit water, but I can't know where you are?"

Tess heard him chuckling quietly at the other end of the line, and that sounded strange in the cold morgue, a blasphemy in the presence of Christina's body.

"You're set," Doc Rizza confirmed. "You're on the big screen."

Tess and Fradella turned toward the wall. A browser page opened, and immediately an unfamiliar website loaded on the screen. Tess recognized some of the photos posted on both sides of the interface. They were Christina and Estelle's nude photos, mixed together. At the center of the screen, a message was written in large, bold font.

It read, "Now that the police are watching and the feds too, let's have some real fun."

"No, no, no," she babbled, "how the hell does he know? Donovan, how?" she asked in a raised voice, afraid the unsub might've figured out who was behind the inflammatory comment by Hornydog17.

"Whoa, don't shoot the messenger. I have no idea," he replied. "We'll figure it out."

"How did you find this site?"

"I used the photos and ran an image search, like I did when I tracked the press releases and all the other sites that hosted the photos. The arrogant son of a bitch published these as a portfolio of achievement on this site."

"You can do that?" Fradella asked. "Image searches?"

"Yeah, anyone can."

"Portfolio of achievement," she repeated slowly, trying to understand what that meant. "Did he use those precise words?"

"Yes," Donovan replied, and clicked on one of the photos, opening a gallery page bearing that title, word for word.

"Any traceable intel? IP, ISP, geolocation, anything?"

"No, it's secure and encrypted." Donovan replied. "But I've seen this type of interface before, with the side galleries and the center frame. It's a live streaming site."

21

Clause

Tess rode shotgun in Fradella's SUV, keeping unusually quiet and somber; he respected her need for silence and didn't speak a single word. She welcomed the interlude, because it gave her time to run through scenarios and possibilities, to put her thoughts in order before reaching the Kennedy residence. There was one thought that kept bothering her. A roofie wasn't enough to render the level of unconsciousness she'd seen in the photos. It made people dizzy, tired, and feel as if they were having an out-of-body experience, almost hypnotized, but it didn't make them pass out cold. Well, like with everything else in the world of drugs, it all depended on the dosage. Doc Rizza had said a higher dose of Rohypnol had lasting effects, days of feeling sick, nauseated, like battling the flu. Something people would remember. Now she knew what questions to ask.

She'd called Mr. Bartlett before leaving the coroner's office, but that conversation didn't have the expected results. The Bartletts didn't recall a house guest the evening Christina was assaulted; they were actually sure no one visited. They were adamant they weren't drugged, and with Dr. Bartlett being in the medical profession, Tess had every reason to believe them. Both Bartletts agreed to give hair samples to be tested, but she held little hope. Because the Bartletts were out to that fancy fundraiser that night, the unsub didn't need to drug them; only needed to wait until they left the house. Had they told anyone about the fundraiser? Sure, Mr. Bartlett's assistant knew, because she bought the tickets, and his business partners also knew. The three attorneys rotated through such events, seeking exposure to potential clients of significant means. It was a work function more than anything else, but outside the law firm, he'd told no one. Dr. Bartlett had shared it with her hygienist, in a short-lived bitching session about having to wear high-heeled shoes after a long day at work. None of these people seemed likely to be the unsub, or work with him.

Then, how did the unsub know when they'd be out? Like many other tidbits of information, this question also pointed to one logical answer: the unsub was someone close to the family. To both families. It was a start. Donovan was still digging through both families' activities, social media photos, people they knew, even things they spent money on or liked to do in their spare time, searching for points of commonality. He'd downloaded call histories for everyone's phones, searching for common numbers they might've dialed or received calls from. Desperate but relentless, he'd even compared browsing histories for the two families. Nothing had come up yet. These two families could've just as well lived on two different planets; they had absolutely nothing in common.

Fradella came to a stop in front of the Kennedy residence and cut the engine. He still didn't say a word, but his gaze was heavy with worry when he looked at her. Last thing she needed, an overbearing alpha male who thinks she can't tie her shoelaces without his help. She got out of the car and he followed, while unwanted guilt swirled in her mind, for having thought so little of Fradella. Was it that bad, that unacceptable if someone cared about her?

She pushed the unanswered question to the side and rang the doorbell. It took a few seconds, but eventually Mrs. Kennedy opened the door. She was ghostly pale, and her black attire didn't help with that. She recognized them and invited them in without a word.

"Mrs. Kennedy," Fradella said, "please accept our deepest sympathies."

"Thank you," she whispered.

Tess stepped into the living room, where Estelle was lying on the sofa with her head in a young brunette's lap. The girl caressed Estelle's hair while she sniffled, keeping her eyes shut. Tess frowned, seeing how inert Estelle looked, how completely out of it.

"I'll take care of it," the girl said quietly, looking at Tess, then whispered in Estelle's ear, "The cops are here, sweetie, wake up." Then she patted Estelle gently on the shoulder, gave her another moment, then repeated her request and her pat, a little louder and stronger the second time.

Estelle made a visible effort to pull herself up to a sitting position and opened her eyes. They were bloodshot and swollen, her gaze unfocused, wandering, glassy.

"And you are?" Tess asked, looking at the girl.

"I'm Abby," she said, meeting her gaze without hesitation. "Abby Sharp."

"Friend or family?"

Abby smiled shyly. "Lifelong friend."

Estelle pulled herself up and sat, leaning against the sofa back, her eyes half-closed, clutching Abby's hand.

Tess crouched in front of her. "Miss Kennedy? Thanks for seeing us," she said, looking for a spark of recognition, of awareness in her eyes. There was none. "Let's get her a glass of cold water," she suggested, with a poorly disguised sigh of frustration.

Mrs. Kennedy brought a tall glass of water, and Estelle grabbed it with trembling hands, then reluctantly took a few swigs.

Tess watched her closely. It was a miracle if Estelle remembered her own name.

"What did you give her? What did she take, huh?" Tess asked Abby in an aggressive tone of voice, as if the girl were a drug peddler working a street corner.

Abby's pupils dilated with fear, and she raised her hands in the air, in a pacifying gesture. "Nothing, I swear! Their family doctor prescribed some Xanax, to help her cope. That's all."

"I found it," she heard Fradella say. When she turned around, she saw him counting the pills left in a prescription bottle.

"It was filled today, and two are missing," he announced after he finished counting.

Tess swallowed her anger; it was misplaced, to say the least. She had no right to judge Estelle for taking a couple of pills, after what she'd been through. She crouched in front of Estelle again to bring their eyes on the same level.

"I'm really sorry for what happened to you," she said gently. "I know you prefer to be left alone, but I'd rather catch the man who's responsible for assaulting you and for your father's death."

When she mentioned her father, Estelle had a flicker of recognition in her eyes. She probably mourned his loss rather than her own destroyed life, and that made sense.

"Can you think of any enemies, any creeps or stalkers, anyone who could've done this to you?" Tess asked.

Estelle lowered her head. "No," she whispered.

"Her ex-boyfriend is a real peach," Abby said, her sarcasm unmistakable despite her low tone.

"In what way?" Tess asked, turning her attention to the brunette. She was moderately attractive, overly adorned in jewelry, countless strands of thin, long necklaces paired up with bracelets that jingled with every move she made, and lots of rings on her fingers and toes.

"He always competed with her. Always. Everything was a fucking pissing contest to him," she added, lowering her voice even more when she said the profanity, throwing Mrs. Kennedy a quick, side glance.

"Name?" Fradella asked, approaching the sofa. He'd been slowly pacing the living room, giving her some space.

"Ben... Pagano, I think," Abby replied. "Right, Es?"

"Uh-huh," Estelle replied, without raising her head that hung low, hiding her face behind the curtain of her long, blonde hair. "It wasn't him," she added.

"Do you remember who assaulted you?" Tess asked.

"No... I'm sorry."

"Then we don't know it wasn't him," Tess replied, her pushback as gentle as she could muster. "What else can you tell me about this man?" she asked, turning her attention to Abby. It was better to speak with someone who was clearheaded.

"It was painful to watch," Abby replied, "their interactions. He always wanted to come out on top, and that's hard, being how famous and successful

Estelle is. He's not really anybody, just some guy, but he was jealous of everything she achieved, every piece of fan mail she got, every news article, every show."

"How did it end between them?"

"Es left him one day and moved back in with her parents. Smart girl," she added, then squeezed Estelle's hand.

"When was that?"

"I'd say a few months ago—"

"January 20," Estelle mumbled. "The day I had the Sony appointment."

"Ah, yes," Abby said. "You know what the pissant did? He drugged her, so she'd miss the audition with Sony Music Entertainment. She left him when she woke up and realized it."

Drugged her? Now that sounded interesting. She shot Fradella a quick glance, but he was already typing something on his phone.

Tess turned her attention back to Estelle. She touched her arm gently to get her attention, and the young woman looked at her with hollow eyes.

"I need to ask you again, anything else you remember from May 10? Any soreness on your body, any sickness the morning after the assault?"

Estelle shook her head once, then closed her eyes. Tess took out a business card and put it in Estelle's limp hand. "If you remember anything, please call me, night or day."

"There's nothing to remember," she whispered. "I tried... don't imagine I didn't. All this was my fault." Tears started rolling down her cheeks, and Abby wrapped an arm around her shoulders.

"It's not your fault," Tess said, sounding almost harsh. "None of this—"

"You'll be fine, you'll see. Just trust me on this," Abby said in a soothing tone. "You'll go indie and make a killing. Imagine Dragons is indie, right? And that rock band tops the charts."

Tess frowned, remembering the award she'd seen framed on the wall. It was engraved with the highly recognizable Sony Music logo. "What happened?" she asked.

"There was a morality clause in her contract," Abby said in a low whisper. "Somehow, Sony found out about the, um, photos, and terminated her with prejudice."

How the hell did it find out so fast? Yesterday no one knew, although the photos had been out there for a while. Now, everyone knew? The unsub kept busy at further raping Estelle's life, pushing her to the breaking point. He was killing her, taking her life one slow, pain-ridden moment at a time, and there was nothing Tess could do. She wished she had the bastard in her service weapon's sights—she'd pull that trigger at the slightest twitch.

"One more question," Tess asked. "Do either of you know Christina Bartlett?"

"No," Estelle replied.

"Uh-uh," Abby said, "me neither. Why?"

Fradella gave Tess his phone, and she looked at the screen, then stood and put some distance between her and the two girls.

He'd brought up a database search, and the result showed one Benjamin Pagano, 24, currently doing time in Miami-Dade County jail since late March, on a cocaine possession charge. The jealous, drug-savvy ex-boyfriend was a dead end.

"He's not the Taker of Lives, is he?" she whispered in Fradella's ear, venting her frustration quietly, so only he could hear.

"Nope."

She still held Fradella's phone in her hand on top of her own phone when they climbed in his SUV. Two chimes sounded almost simultaneously from the devices; they both received the same text message. It was from Donovan, and it read, "New activity on the unsub's page."

22

Stakeout

Michowsky abandoned his Ford Explorer in favor of an inconspicuous silver Honda Accord as soon as he left the coroner's office, then stopped for a burrito, anticipating a long evening. It was Friday afternoon, right before Memorial Day weekend, and that meant young people, like that Carrillo character, were just waking up and hitting the streets. He took the burrito to his car and flipped through the green file once more, page by page, then looked attentively at the man's photo. He could recognize him anywhere. The man had to have a serious death wish, playing games with a fed's daughter.

He took another bite of the double meat and cheese burrito, then called Donovan. The analyst picked up with his official greeting, probably not recognizing Gary's caller ID.

"Detective Michowsky here," he said, skipping over the pleasantries. "I need a phone number located, special request from our mutual acquaintance, SA Winnett."

"Shoot," Donovan said.

He gave him the number, then waited, soon taking another mouthful of delectable Mexican fast food.

"No active GPS on this phone," Donovan announced. "Triangulating now… It will be less accurate, but it will give you something."

"What kind of something? How accurate?"

"A few hundred yards, maybe less if you're lucky. I've texted you a map. He's the red dot smack in the middle of it."

"Thanks, Donovan, I owe you one," he said, but the last part of the phrase was spoken to an already disconnected line.

He finished his burrito with one last satisfying mouthful, then wiped his mouth with the wrapper and drove off, in a hurry to get close to Carrillo's location before he vanished from there. As he approached the location shown on the map, he slowed down somewhat, searching for the white Lexus convertible. He zigzagged through a section of about a square mile, centered on that red dot, and finally found the Lexus, parked in front of a doctor's office in downtown Delray Beach.

He rolled past Carrillo's car and parked a few hundred feet away, in the shade of a large magnolia, then watched the silhouettes visible through the partly open window shades inside the doctor's waiting room. Carrillo was talking with another man, showing him documentation and offering demo packages of drugs he was marketing.

Huh… this Carrillo dude was still working, on a Friday night at about 6:00PM. Who would've thought?

Soon he saw the young man leave the doctor's office with a satisfied smile on his lips, then hop into his car. The moment the engine turned, blaring music filled the street—a hot, Latino sound almost hypnotic in its rhythm. Then he pulled out of the parking lot, and Michowsky followed him from a safe distance.

Carrillo took two other sales meetings, one in a small family practice, and another one at a walk-in clinic. By the time he called it quits, it was almost dark. His day was nothing like Michowsky had expected. He thought Carrillo would take Miss Pearson out or do something exciting, when in fact all he'd done thus far was work.

Michowsky realized he wasn't going to yet another sales meeting when the Lexus stopped in front of a house in Kings Point, one of the many, almost identical, crammed-together, two-story brick properties that sell like hotcakes for about half a million dollars. He noted the address, 1105 Mercury Boulevard, then parked his car a few numbers down and waited.

He didn't like stakeouts; when he didn't stay busy, he turned restless and hated the confinement of his vehicle. Keeping one eye on the Lexus and dimming the laptop screen light, he ran a property deed search for 1105 Mercury. It came back in someone else's name, not Carrillo's. He ran priors for that person, also a Latino, judging by his name, but that turned out clean. Just as he was about to start digging deeper into the property owner's background, another Lexus, a burgundy SUV, pulled up at the curb and a couple of African American men in their twenties ambled inside, shuffling their feet and talking loudly in a profanity-ridden jargon Michowsky barely understood.

He waited for a moment until the traffic cleared and snuck out of his car, then returned with the tag number for the SUV. A quick search, and he found the owner was a small-time drug dealer who'd just gotten out of jail after doing time for possession with intent to distribute. It was Miami's influence; even the lampposts had records for possession with intent.

Nothing moved in and out of that property for at least thirty minutes, when another SUV pulled up, this time a black Cadillac Escalade with flashy custom hubcaps that kept spinning after the wheels had come to a stop. A middle-aged man with a nose ring and arms covered in prison ink got out from behind the wheel, then waited for his passengers, three young girls, to catch up with him.

"Move your scrawny ass already," he admonished the girl who'd fallen behind and still fumbled with a transparent, high-heeled shoe that had slipped off her foot. "Ain't gonna make me no cash here, in the damn street."

"Sorry, Pete, I'm coming," the girl whimpered, almost running on the driveway to catch up with the man. She couldn't've been more than nineteen or twenty; Michowsky hoped she was at least legal.

The girls wore minimalistic skirts, ridiculously high heels, and revealing tops, baring as much skin as possible. It didn't take being a cop for almost thirty years to know they were hookers, which most likely made dear old Pete their pimp. So, the party was heating up.

Over the next hour or so, several vehicles arrived and unloaded colorful assortments of men and women; almost all vehicles were registered to people with criminal records, ranging from a variety of drug charges all the way to assault and battery, even manslaughter, some of the most respectable, upstanding citizens the parole system had to offer. Michowsky felt tempted to call for backup and raid the place, slap some collars on those thugs for parole violations if nothing else stuck, shove the losers behind bars where they belonged, but he was on a different mission. It was their lucky night.

After the last bunch made it inside the house, Michowsky dialed the Real Time Crime Center.

"Yeah, this is Detective Michowsky, Palm Beach County Sheriff's Office, badge number 57374."

"Go ahead, Detective," the RTCC operator replied.

"What do you have on 1105 Mercury in Kings Point?"

"Please hold," the operator said, typing quickly on the keyboard. "We show the property flagged as possible brothel or drug hub. No active warrants on the owner or address. Anything else?"

"No, thanks," he replied, then hung up.

He took a few gulps of water from a fresh bottle and sighed; the burrito had left him chronically thirsty and with the makings of a fierce heartburn attack. He let out his belt a few notches, then settled into his seat, grunting and shifting until he found a comfortable position.

It was going to be a long night.

23

Countdown

There was silence again on their drive back to the office; this time Tess was committed to contain her personal feelings and give the one piece of evidence they had some much-needed attention. She'd asked Doc Rizza to evaluate Christina and Estelle's photos, the ones taken and published by the unsub, and write a conclusion. Was the unsub escalating? Was he nearing the moment he'd rape or kill? She'd asked Doc for help because whenever she looked at those images, her blood came to an instant boil and rage clouded her judgment so badly she couldn't organize her thoughts anymore.

She struggled to understand why she had such a strong emotional response to this form of violation, of abuse. To quote from yesterday's conversation, there was no blood on the walls, and at least one victim was still alive. Alive to do what? To hide and suffer in silence? To forfeit her life completely and be resigned to living in shame, withering away, praying to be forgotten? What was one's life but a series of days, inescapably marked by the world's perceptions of one's image, value, emotions, and relationships? Just because the pain was psychological, that didn't make the suffering any less severe. The Taker of Lives knew that perfectly well. Even if Estelle was still alive, she wasn't. She'd died on May 10, soon after midnight, in a stealthy and merciless attack.

She opened the file that Doc Rizza had shoved in her reluctant hand before she left his office and read the handwritten note affixed to the photos.

"There's definite progression in the unsub's repressed violence," the note said. "The way Christina was postured showed care for the victim and for the setting. Her body was attentively positioned, her limbs were posed artistically, her head was propped up on a pillow, her hair arranged neatly around her head. With Estelle, all that care is gone. I guess the main question we need to ask right now is why isn't there penetrative sexual assault? If I were a betting man, I'd say next time there will be. The rest is for you to figure out. Maybe your friend at the BAU can help more than I could."

She put the note aside and looked at the photos, first at Christina's, then at Estelle's, willing herself to stay lucid, analytical. Doc was right; the photos taken of Christina's unconscious body were tasteful, almost classy, her body positioned in ways that led you to think *Playboy* magazine, not gas-station porn. The duvet was neatly folded alongside, the lighting was near-perfect, enhancing the curves of her body with carefully positioned areas of direct light or shadow, hiding some areas, showcasing others.

Estelle's photos leaned more toward the obscene side of the spectrum, with little concern for the layout, for the background or lighting. The images showed escalating contempt for the victim, a stronger drive to depict her in a depreciative manner. He wanted her humiliated on an entirely different level than Christina, exposing her in ways that not only reflected his deep hatred and disdain for the victim, or maybe for all women, but also invited the viewers to look at Estelle as they would look at a piece of worthless trash, to think of her as expendable, inconsequential, and dirty. Not a star, not an idol.

Was that to say the unsub cared more for Christina than Estelle? The first victim of a serial offender is oftentimes the most relevant, the one he is closest to, the one who crosses his path and arouses his sick senses in a way that pushes him to cross the line and attack his first innocent victim.

Or was it because Christina's parents had been gone for the evening and he felt safer, knowing he was alone in the house with the unconscious victim? With Estelle, no matter how bold and organized this unsub was, the close proximity to the victim's parents had to have increased his stress levels; unfortunately, not enough for him to make a mistake that they could find. Not yet.

One thing was certain, and she agreed with Doc Rizza in his assessment. The unsub had escalated rapidly. The next attack would be even more vicious, maybe even homicidal. Then a worrisome thought crossed her mind, right as Fradella pulled to the curb and cut the engine.

"What if he's already done it again?" she asked. "That's part of his signature, assaulting, then waiting for the images to go viral."

"Didn't Donovan look for other victims with those specific parameters?"

"He did, but maybe we're missing something," she replied, climbing the stairs quickly.

As soon as they entered the conference room, she rushed to dial Donovan from the conference phone, while Fradella turned on the wall-mounted screen and fired up the laptop.

"Hey, D," Tess said, as soon as Donovan picked up. "We're here."

"Remember what I asked? Don't kill the messenger, right?"

"Okay, I won't," she replied, some of her irritation with his request seeping into her voice. It wasn't like she'd ever yelled at him or called him names.

As soon as the unsub's website loaded, Tess felt a wave of angst, cold and foreboding, unfurling in her gut and a seeping aversion in her entire body with every beat of her heart. The central portion of the webpage now included a countdown timer showing two hours and forty-seven minutes left, and a statement from the unsub.

It read, "I've decided to up the game a little and do things live. All you need to do is vote. One million votes will pull the curtains open for tonight's live performance."

A gray rectangle with a generic shape of a woman's head and shoulders was centered below the unsub's message, the type of pictogram that online forums and social media platforms display when female users don't upload an avatar. Underneath, a brief description of the targeted victim sent both Fradella and Donovan into a frenzy of database searches.

"Our guest tonight is young and beautiful," the description read, "a tall blonde with long hair and blue eyes, just like your dream girl looks. Trust me, I know."

Her eyes were stuck on the number shown underneath the wide button labeled, "Vote Now," the enormity of the number displayed was stupefying and terrifying at the same time. More than seven hundred thousand people had already voted, and that counter was rapidly growing, click after click.

"This can't be happening," Tess said. "What kind of screwed-up world are we living in?" she raised her voice, but no one replied. She wasn't expecting a response; she wanted to hear herself in an attempt to preserve some decency, some values, some sanity. "Tell me we can track these voters, Donovan," she said angrily. "I'd like nothing more than to give a judge carpal tunnel from signing eight hundred thousand arrest warrants."

"I can't," she heard Donovan's voice over the phone, filled with frustration. For a moment, she couldn't tell if he was frustrated with the case, the unsub, or with her, or maybe with everything lumped together in what he did for a living. "These people know how to protect their privacy. All this traffic is channeled through encrypted browsing, via Tor, which bounces communication around worldwide networks. They're careful, because they know what they're doing is wrong, even if not a chargeable offense."

"You mean to tell me we can't get to any of them?" Fradella asked.

"I see the occasional unencrypted IP," Donovan replied, "but what would you charge them with? They could argue they thought it was a show, not real. No one could prove criminal intent. It's known as the "cannibal cop" defense, based on a New York case that made history by saying the police officer's online chats were all fantasy."

"Since when are you an expert in criminal law?" Tess asked, unable to contain a smile. Donovan never ceased to amaze her.

"Since I've been taking night classes at the University of Virginia," he replied. "I can't stay an analyst for the rest of my life, no matter how much you all need me."

Her smile widened. She felt proud, although Donovan and she weren't exactly close. "Congratulations, D. I know you'll make one hell of a lawyer one day soon, putting many of the scumbags we collar right back on the streets, but let's catch us another unsub before then, all right? Have you tried—"

The screen went dark. The only things left were the countdown timer, the vote button, and the count, now exceeding eight hundred thousand and growing at a faster rate than before. By the looks of it, the unsub had every chance of exceeding one million votes by the set deadline of 12:00AM, and they had nothing to go on.

"Talk to me about these searches. Have you added the physical description parameters?" she asked.

"They were already in, because they fit the other two vics," Fradella replied. "The unsub has a type. He didn't give us anything we weren't already expecting."

"What if you completely remove the suicide attempt or suicide; how many results do you get?"

"Two thousand, eight hundred, and twenty-three," Donovan replied. "Then I thought that fame comes with money, and I filtered out those who reported less than two hundred thousand dollars in income last year. We're down to three hundred forty-seven."

"That's brilliant, counselor," Tess said.

"Still, there's no way we can come up with a way to further quantify fame and run software to data mine it, not until midnight tonight. That software hasn't even been written yet."

"You're telling me we have nothing?" she asked, her voice raised in pitch and volume so high it turned a few heads in the squad room.

"There's nothing we can do, Winnett, I'm sorry," Donovan replied.

She paced the room angrily, watching the counter adding vote after vote with unbelievable speed. "What if it's fake, Donovan?"

"What?"

"The vote counter. What if it's for show? I can't come to terms that so many people could vote to see an assault take place live."

"It's real," Donovan replied quietly. "I tested it myself. It only let me vote once, which is even worse. It means every vote is a different person."

She paced the room some more, then looked over Fradella's shoulder. He was putting Christina and Estelle's addresses on a map.

"Hey, can you map the three hundred forty-seven potential vics?" he asked, and got no response for a while, until a link popped on the screen. He clicked it and saw a view of the entire South Florida area dusted with lots of red dots, mostly clustered in large urban areas and along the eastern seashore. Christina and Estelle's blue dots didn't stand out in any way against the many reds; they just appeared to be entirely random.

"She could be anywhere," Fradella muttered angrily. "Miami, Fort Lauderdale, Palm Beach... We've got nothing."

Tess sighed, a long, frustrated breath of air that scorched her lungs as it left her body and parched her throat dry. A troublesome thought agonized in her mind. What if she'd caused this? What if her message to the unsub only pushed him to be bolder, more aggressive?

Soon she'd know if there was blood on her hands.

24

Me: Working

I'm getting ready to start working. The house is perfectly still and quiet. No one's home except her, and that opens a world of opportunities; the possibilities are endless. She sleeps soundly, overcome by the latest anesthetics that modern pharmacology has to offer for a bitcoin or two. I finish setting up my camera and adjust the lighting. The ceiling light is powerful, too powerful for what I need, but fortunately it's installed on a dimmer. I adjust that and look through the viewfinder again. Better. Then I bring two floor lamps from the immense living room and turn them on, adjusting the cones of light toward the bed, for maximum effect.

I then set some tools nearby on the night table. A couple of syringes already loaded with fluids. One contains a lethal dose of ketamine, in case I decide to go that way. I also brought a handgun and a hunting knife; being home alone with her opens possibilities I don't normally enjoy.

I stop for a moment and look at her beautiful, serene face. What made her better than countless others? What earned her a life of luxury in this 3,000-square-foot waterfront property, when anyone can do what she does, some much better? Who decided she deserves to rise atop us all?

Well, you did. For everything I'm about to do to her and to others, you're the only one to blame, because you wouldn't be bothered to see the truth otherwise.

Have you ever received a nicely wrapped gift and weighed it in your hand before ripping the luscious paper with fingers trembling in anticipation, only to find an empty box inside? Maybe you haven't, but you could easily imagine such disappointment. Only you're not reminding yourself of that when you decide to suspend all cognitive processes inside your head and follow these shallow creatures like sheep, bleating happily all the way to the slaughter of rational thought. Some socialite uses Pink Shadow lipstick; now millions of girls rush to buy it, as if that lipstick could change one's destiny, could shift an unseen railroad switch and take a life destined for mediocrity into much coveted stardom, all for $5.98 plus tax.

Why, you should ask, why do so many people choose to let go of common sense and their own values, trading them for someone else's ideas? Because you imitate; you see success in that socialite, something you covet so dearly you'd be willing to kill for, but shush... don't tell anyone what you'd really be willing to do. You see success and have no idea how to get to it. You have no clue how to get the right combination of factors playing in your favor, especially if you were born the wrong race or ethnic background, or if you indulged in one too many double cheeseburgers. The only thing you can invest, the only thing you can control, is that measly $5.98 plus tax. By rushing to the drugstore to buy one, you can kindle your hope for a better tomorrow. After all, look at that socialite, she uses it too!

The idols you're following are nothing but a meticulously designed exterior packaging, nicely constructed and accessorized to hide the hollow abyss inside. They project an expertly manufactured, idealistic image of a role model we immediately adulate. That's how they manipulate and attract their followers, that's how they become who they become. Not through some merit of lasting value or any contribution to society, but many times only through some game of chance, where dice fall in the right configuration to open the doors of stardom to the unworthy.

What value will survive them into posterity? Have they invented anything of worth? Let me explain to you why they haven't. Because you, yes, you—and please stop looking around to see who else I might be talking to—don't care about value. You care about looks, about packaging. You don't believe me? I'll prove it to you.

Have you heard of Robert Kahn or Vint Cerf? No? You're using the product they invented every single day, more often than probably anything else, maybe even this very second. Those two men invented the internet, among other things. Yet their names don't resonate with anything familiar in your mind, as you rush to use their invention yet again to see if I'm right or wrong. But you could easily name five celebrities, even if you can't think of a single thing of value these social media phenomena with their millions of followers will be leaving behind when they die.

Maybe they should die sooner... even if for no other reason than to test my theory.

You see where I'm going with this? People don't care about value... don't care about anything else but the stupid packaging, the appeal of the perfect shapes and perfect colors, the superficiality of a carefully architected, multicolored wrapper taped around a big chunk of nothing.

If that's the only thing you'll ever respect, if that's the only thing you'll ever admire, I will be forever banished from the limelight of fame and recognition and forced to live a life of mediocrity and rejection, of indifference and anonymity, of forsaking hell. Nothing of value I've done, or I could ever do, would matter to you one single bit. See, I was born with brains, not looks or charisma. No one knows me... no one recognizes me, wherever I go. I simply don't exist.

Well, sorry, but I can't have that; I deserve better. I want my moment of fame, my immortality. Hence, I decided to pry open your mind and force your attention away from Instagram and the latest posting by who knows who that you're the five millionth person to like and follow and tell you this: I had an epiphany. I realized that real power doesn't belong to those false idols, to those girls and boys who live in the limelight projected onto them by the glow of your incessant, obsessive adulation.

The real power belongs to me, the one who can destroy it all. I can smash their lives into infinitesimal shards. I can tear into that wrapper so definitively that no one will be able to tape it back together again, and the hollow inside will be exposed, bare, broken, for the entire world to see how little substance remains once the packaging is gone, pixel by pixel, photo by photo.

You still have doubts? Mark my words: no matter how lucky, talented, or beautiful, how successful or acclaimed they are, I can make it all disappear under a cloud of shame so thick and dark, they'll never want to see the light of day again. They'll know their place. And you'll know my name.

I am the Taker of Lives.

Nice one, Special Agent Winnett, thanks.

25

Initial Profile

The counter had long exceeded three million votes, and more votes were pouring in at such speed that the last two digits of the long string of numbers constantly shifted, unreadable, a blur. Tess stared at the otherwise dark screen, not feeling the tension in her clenched jaws anymore. The tense muscles felt numb yet refused to relax. She racked her brain thinking of something they could do. Maybe there was someone else they could talk to. Maybe some neighbor somewhere has seen something, even though the original canvas had returned exactly zero results in both neighborhoods where he'd struck before.

They had nothing except an endless string of voters, people who knowingly were enabling a serial predator, were cheering eagerly to witness an assault, maybe even a murder take place live, in front of their lustful eyes.

"Let's start sketching a profile," she said, aware she sounded a bit unsure of herself. The quick look from Fradella and the silence on the open line with Donovan confirmed her doubts.

They were still missing critical components for the profile, and the result could prove erroneous, imprecise. They didn't know enough about the unsub's MO. How did he gain access to the premises? How did he surveil his victims, two or more at the same time, without ever being seen? How did he subdue the victims, then disappear without anyone remembering the encounter? How come not the tiniest speck of forensic evidence was found at either scene?

Like everything else in life, Tess decided to focus on the full half of the glass: what they *did* know. She grabbed the marker and took an unused corner of the whiteboard.

"This time we'll profile relying more on probabilities than facts," she said, and Fradella stopped typing, turning his undivided attention to her. "I'm going to go with male, Caucasian, because of the sexual nature of the assaults; a vast percentage of all sexual predators choose victims of their own racial makeup." She wrote the two words as the start of a bulleted list. Then she added "25 to 30" and underlined it. "This is based on the speed at which he's learning; he's tech-savvy. He's highly organized, yet a daring risk-taker. I'd also say college educated, probably technical.

"What about the drugs he uses?" Fradella asked. "Okay, anyone can get Rohypnol these days, but what about the, um, whatever he uses to subdue them for as long as it takes him to do his thing, to photograph them?"

"Good point," Tess said. "Let's add, 'medical knowledge' for now. Anything can be found and bought these days, but he has the medical knowledge to figure out what to use."

She paced the floor a little, going back and forth in front of the whiteboard, not taking her eyes off the list. Then she leaned against the table and closed her eyes for a moment, trying to visualize the unsub. What did he look like? Who would a Christina or an Estelle open the door to? Who would they let inside their homes so late at night?

"He's smart, good-looking, charismatic, probably single," she added, scribbling the words as she spoke them, "based on his ability to gain trust and access with successful, twenty-something years old. Well-integrated in society, probably has a good-paying job. He can easily establish rapport."

"He could hold a position associated with implicit trust," Donovan said, "like a priest, for example."

She frowned for a moment, recalling the visualization she put together in her mind. A priest didn't fit the bill.

"These crimes don't have a religious vibe or message," she said. "But he could be, or pose as, someone anyone would trust, like a cop, perhaps?" She wrote "trustworthy" on the list. "Or he could be quite attractive. Statistics show that women let their guards down in the presence of attractive men."

She took a swig from a stale cup of coffee and wrote another word on the whiteboard, followed by a question mark. "I have to presume he's impotent, until future evidence dictates otherwise," she explained.

"Maybe he has a different motivation," Fradella offered.

"Maybe," she agreed, weighing options in her mind. "I'm puzzled by the absence of violence in these assaults. They're pristine, careful, almost caring, but, as with all sexual assaults, penetrative or not, it's all about power. The extent of the devastation these attacks bring to the victims speaks to an incredible amount of rage, but his actions don't. He's... cold as ice."

"Fame is a factor," Donovan said over the phone. "We've seen envy-motivated attacks against successful or famous people before, right?"

"You're talking about envy or jealousy over a specific concept, not a person?" Fradella asked. "Like that British woman who set her neighbors on fire because they were happy?"

"That was both personal and proximal," Tess replied, "but you're right. Although envy or jealousy as motivators for serial offenders is almost never seen. I'd have to do some research to see if—" She stopped, thinking hard. She'd lost track of an important idea, and she wanted to recall what it was. Yes, the absence of violence. "Jealous rage leads to overkill," she added, "like when we see multiple stab wounds in a single homicide, while this unsub preserves their bodies. It's almost as if he wants to make sure all the victim's suffering is psychological, not physical."

"Does he take souvenirs?" Donovan asked, and Tess could hear him typing at the other end of the line.

"Nothing was missing from either crime scene," she replied, "unless..." She paused, then opened the folder with the photos the unsub had taken and posted everywhere. "Unless the photos are his keepsakes. He might take some he doesn't share with anyone."

"Let's not forget stalker," Fradella offered, and Tess quickly added the word at the bottom of the growing list.

"That he is," she confirmed. "One of the best stalkers I've ever seen. We still don't know how he knew we were onto him or why he called us out on his webpage."

As she said the words, she turned her eyes briefly toward the screen.

"Oh, crap," she said, right after reading the heading now showing at the top of the page. "How the hell does he know?" She pointed angrily at the screen with an accusatory index.

Above the countdown clock, the words, "Taker of Lives" were written in bold, block letters, the type you see on theater marquees.

No one answered. She felt her blood boil in her veins. "How the hell does he know, people?" she asked again, raising her voice. "Either he's surveilling us right here, right now, or one of us spilled."

"No one spilled," Donovan said calmly, "I promise you. What the hell, Winnett? You're not the only one with half a brain in this room."

"He's in control right now," she said, grinding her teeth in anger. "He's the one in control, not us. We played right into his hand and gave him a moniker that feeds his ego. We think we're getting ahead of the game, but he's always the one pulling the strings, and we're only dancing."

A moment of uncomfortable silence engulfed the room.

"Let's go back to his stalking methods," Donovan said calmly. "I need something I can work with. How do you think he's doing it?"

Tess forced herself to breathe slowly, to calm down before she opened her mouth. "He must have the houses under video surveillance," she eventually said, when she felt she could trust her voice again. "Otherwise someone would've seen him lurking. I believe he's continuing to watch after the assault, to see the effects of the damage he's done. This is his reward."

"All right, I'll pull whatever street cam video I can from RTCC and see if I notice any strange patterns, anyone working on the street or installing something around the properties."

"Send a bug-sweeper team to Estelle's tonight," Tess said.

"What, now?" Donovan pushed back. "It's late."

"Yes, now. We need to be sure. If he's still watching, we need him unplugged, blinded, off his game."

"How about the Bartlett residence?"

"That's the weirdest thing," Tess replied. "A man like Bartlett sweeps for bugs every week or so. I'm willing to bet good money on it."

She called Bartlett, who reluctantly confirmed he conducted periodic bug sweeps and had found nothing. He was willing to accept a late call from the FBI's team though, just to be sure.

Then she took a seat in front of her laptop and started typing an email to Bill McKenzie.

"Dear Bill," the message said, "Sorry to have been a stranger for so long; I hope you'll understand. Please take a look," she inserted the link to the unsub's streaming site and a couple of other links to his earlier press releases, "and let me know if you can help me refine an unusual profile. This man is at that point where a serial sex offender is about to commit murder for the first time. He will kill, and when he starts killing, he'll be unstoppable."

26

The Date

It was soon after 9:30PM that Carrillo finally left the house on 1105 Mercury and climbed behind the wheel of his Lexus convertible. Michowsky welcomed his decision, rubbing his thighs vigorously, to reestablish a healthy blood flow after a few hours of immobility.

Carrillo spent some time in his car with the engine turned on and the music playing, engulfed in his phone. The device projected a spectral glow on his face, making him visible from a distance in the darkness of the street, and Michowsky kept his eyes glued on the man's features. Carrillo bounced his head with the rhythm of the music, but rarely lifted his eyes from the glowing screen.

What was he doing?

Michowsky wished he could see in real time what Carrillo's screen showed, but, unfortunately, Winnett didn't think about it too much and forgot to set him up with a clone of the target's phone. It might've come in handy. He snickered to himself… *Look at you,* he thought, *talking phone clones and stuff. You've seen a TV show one time and you think everything is possible.*

In the brief silence between a salsa and a merengue, Michowsky heard a faint chime; Carrillo was texting. He hesitated for a moment, then said to himself, "Screw it," and messaged Donovan.

"Next text activity dump for 305-555-1853, ASAP, please."

Donovan didn't reply to his text; instead, a few moments later, an email with an attachment popped on his screen. He opened the attachment and looked for the most recent message. In passing, he recognized how well-organized and efficient Donovan was; the report emulated a real messaging screen, arranged by conversations and by date.

Other than a few meaningless confirmations and banal exchanges, the main texting conversations took place with Pearson's daughter, Lily. The messages were typical for a young couple in love. Sweet and silly, or at least that's how they seemed to him, who'd never been so extroverted as to put the words *I love you* in writing, not even once.

In the most recent exchange, only a few minutes earlier, Carrillo confirmed he'd finished the day's business and was on his way to pick her up.

She'd replied enthusiastically that she was ready and waiting for him, then added a row of emojis of all sorts and shapes, variations of hearts and smileys.

Pearson must've been thrilled, seeing her get ready to leave the house at ten in the evening.

Carrillo peeled off the curb and Michowsky let him gain some distance before following him. He was comfortable increasing the distance, because he knew where the young man was headed: Pearson's house. A few minutes later, he watched Carrillo pull over in front of Lily's place and wait in the car. He didn't ring the bell or honk; maybe he sensed Pearson's aversion to him, or maybe, being where he'd spent the bulk of his evening, he was a little uncomfortable being around a seasoned cop's nose. His clothes most likely reeked of marijuana and cheap perfume, considering the crowd that populated the den at 1105 Mercury.

The door opened, and Lily stepped out, dressed in a light, summer dress with a yellow floral pattern that made her visible from a distance. There was a happy spring in her step as she leapt over the few steps and almost ran toward Carrillo's car. Watching how happy that girl was made Michowsky think of his own kids and of Pearson's predicament. Most likely Pearson had tried to warn his daughter repeatedly about that man, but had no arguments, no criminal record he could invoke, just his gut. That didn't go far with a young daughter in love with a man from the wrong side of the tracks. What would he have done in Pearson's place? Probably the same thing; call Winnett for help.

He followed them for a while, and then stayed well behind when they pulled over at Baiocco, where Carrillo was a perfect gentleman with Lily. He held the car door for her, offered her his hand, then held the restaurant door open for her with a charming smile. She was walking on a cloud.

Michowsky considered going inside for a moment, but thankfully he didn't need to. The couple was seated by a window, and he could keep his eyes on them from a safe distance. He watched Carrillo continuing to behave impeccably, holding Lily's seat, offering her the menu, topping the wine before the waiter had a chance.

It seemed almost too good to be true, and too damn easy. The easiest stakeout in his entire career. Unconvinced, Michowsky groaned and got out of his car, then opened the trunk and rummaged through the duffel bag he had in there. A few minutes later, he slapped a magnetic GPS tracker underneath the rear fender of the white Lexus.

27

Live Streaming

The countdown showed eleven minutes left, and Tess was so edgy she couldn't settle in one place. She paced the room like a caged animal, furious with her own powerlessness. She was about to witness an assault and all she could do was watch. She couldn't step in and stop the attack, she couldn't draw her weapon and fire the liberating shot.

Doc Rizza knocked twice, then entered the conference room with a tired smile on his lips. A faint smell of stale cigars and yesterday's aftershave came in with him, surrounding him like a cloud.

"Thought I might join you," he said quietly, shooting a side glance at the wall-mounted TV where votes continued to pour in faster and faster, incessantly.

Tess gestured with her hand toward one of the many available seats. "Thanks, Doc, I appreciate it."

"I'm set up on my end," Donovan's voice came to life across the conference line. They'd been keeping him on that open line for six straight hours, but he wasn't complaining. He was an expert multitasker, and Tess could hear him take other calls and handle other things that came his way, while continuing to run searches for the next victim. "I have one station set up to do real-time tracking of the streaming feed," he continued, "although I wouldn't hold my breath. This unsub isn't going to start making mistakes now."

"How will we find her?" Fradella asked. "I have maps pulled up on my end, if that helps."

"It does," Donovan replied. "You do geographic searches starting from the shortlisted names, while I search various databases using all the criteria we can think of, and anything else new we'll find today. If we see her face, I'll capture that screenshot and run a facial recognition against the shortlisted three hundred and forty-seven potential targets."

"Are you recording this?" Tess asked.

"Yes, I've been recording it since the counter passed five million votes. That was twenty minutes ago. Can't believe he's at 5.7 million already. A lot of bored people out there."

"A lot of *sick* people," Doc Rizza intervened. "Bored people get hobbies, read books, walk their dogs. This," he gestured with contempt toward the screen, "doesn't qualify."

No one argued, and for a few moments they waited in silence, watching the countdown clock inch closer to the deadline. Would he prove audacious enough to stream live? Or would he serve the masses a few photos, maybe a short video, and be gone before they could catch him?

A beep on the conference line announced a call waiting. Tess squinted at the LCD screen in the dim light and recognized Bill's number. She patched his call into the open line.

"Bill, thanks for calling in," Tess said. "Fradella's here with Doc Rizza, and we have Donovan on the phone."

"Hello, everyone," Bill said, his voice somber against a background of rustling paper.

The moment the countdown reached three minutes, the screen changed, displaying a message from the unsub.

It said, on two centered lines of white text against a black background, "You've been generous, my dear audience, and so will I. Tonight we're streaming live." Nothing else, but the moniker he'd adopted from them was now embedded with graphics into a header that topped the Web page.

"Taker of Lives," Bill read. "When did he start calling himself that?"

Tess groaned with frustration and closed her eyelids to hide the roll of her eyes. "Immediately after he learned *we* were calling him that."

"How?" Bill asked, the elevated pitch in his voice betraying his unspoken disapproval.

"I'll have to get back to you on that," she replied calmly, although she was nowhere near being calm.

Seconds passed quickly on the timer under their fixed eyes, and as zero approached Tess held her breath, bracing herself, willing herself to not feel any emotion, to be factual and analytical in her deductive reasoning.

A chime marked zero on the timer, and the image changed to a live feed from a lushly decorated bedroom. Window treatments in jacquard silk with long fringes and satin sheets gave the room a luxurious warmth, youthful rather than snobby through the choice of pastel colors.

The video camera was immobile, installed on a tripod by all appearances, and positioned near the foot of the bed. It was elevated to a vantage point similar to that of a standing person, giving the viewers a perspective as if they were standing right there, by the bed, watching what was about to happen.

The girl lying on the pale green sheets was already naked. The duvet had been pulled to the side, and multiple sources of light were trained on the girl's perfect body. Her face, turned slightly to the side, was covered by wavy strands of long, blonde hair. She fought to open her eyelids, but her eyes stayed stubbornly closed; she was probably too drowsy from the chemicals he'd given her. She kept shaking her head slowly, restlessly, as if desperately trying to emerge from the narcotic daze that had rendered her almost unconscious.

"Damn it," Tess muttered, "tell me we have enough for face recog."

"We don't," Donovan replied between clenched teeth. "We need her face clear of all that hair, and at a good angle. All we've got is chin and curls."

Then the unsub partially came into view. His entire body was covered in a black, shiny latex suit, complete with gloves and head mask. The suit was several numbers too large; it didn't stretch tightly over his body; it creased and hung in places, out of shape. They didn't see all of him; only whatever parts of his anatomy came on screen as he moved around the bed, going about his business in a relaxed, methodical manner.

Tess let out a long, muttered oath on a pained breath of air. "That explains the lack of forensics. He's too damn smart. Anything we can get on that suit?"

"Nope," Donovan said. "They're quite popular with folks engaged in cosplay. They go for twenty-five bucks apiece and they're everywhere. No dice."

"I can approximate some body measurements, based on what I see," Doc Rizza said. "I'll know more after I analyze this in detail and compute in the actual dimensions of the furniture, but I can already tell you he's about five-eight to five-ten, not very athletic, a little flabby even."

"How did you come up with his height, Doc?" Tess asked. "On video, it's all relative."

"The door came into view a few moments ago when he opened it," he explained. "The standard height for a bedroom door is six feet, eight inches. He seemed a foot shorter than that, maybe less than a foot."

"He's not big and strong," she muttered, thinking of how that played with the absence of violence. Was that the cause? Was he physically weak, or impaired somehow, so that he chose to chemically restrain his victims, rather than overcome them physically? Most lust predators enjoyed physically overcoming their victims. It was like foreplay in their sick, perverted minds.

The unsub came into view again, this time holding four colorful scarves he might've taken from the victim's dresser drawers while he was off-screen. Slowly, he tied the girl's wrists and ankles to the bedposts, taking his time and never stopping to look at the camera, not even once. Tess watched the gestures, the way his arms moved, the way he walked from one bedpost to the next.

"He seems to have some difficulty walking," she said, "or maybe it's the suit."

"Yeah, I see that," Doc Rizza said. "Might be a lower back injury, which could be accompanied by impotence if there was nerve damage."

The unsub finished tying the girl's limbs to the bed and stopped for a moment, as if admiring his work. Then, as if he'd heard their request earlier, he propped the girl's head higher against two pillows and pulled the strands of hair away from her face.

"Got it!" Donovan announced. "Running face recog now."

"For someone so forensically astute, he shows no interest in deflecting us for a while longer," Fradella said. "He's showing off, completely unafraid."

"That's the scary part," Tess grumbled, playing nervously with her car keys, ready to storm out the door the moment Donovan had a name. "He knows something we don't."

They continued watching the unsub, as he started placing a variety of objects on the night table. Several sex toys, a couple of syringes that appeared to be loaded with serums, and several other smaller objects that Tess couldn't recognize.

"See that? That's an ammonia vial," Doc Rizza said, pointing at one of the smaller objects on the night table.

"What, he's going to wake her up?" Tess asked, cringing inside, remembering what it felt like to wake up and find herself immobilized and vulnerable in the hands of a madman. If what was about to follow couldn't be stopped, she was better off asleep. "Donovan, tell me you've got something. Location, coordinates, a name, anything?"

"Umm, guys?" Donovan said, sounding concerned, tense. "You're not going to like this. She's not among our shortlisted names. I'm expanding the search now, to include all Caucasian females under twenty-seven in this state, but it will take a while."

"How the hell did that happen?" Tess reacted. "Did we exclude too many from that list? Did we apply too many filters?"

"It's possible," Donovan replied. "We'll know more once we ID her."

She looked at the screen again, then looked away, unable to stand it any longer. Seeing those hands touching the girl's body, knowing she should be busting through that door instead of watching it powerlessly on TV, all wrenched her gut and cut her breath short.

"You were right," Bill said, after remaining silent for so long. "He's thinking how to kill her. He might start killing tonight. You see the sports duffel tucked against the wall? See that gun handle, visible right where the zipper starts? Those are potential murder weapons he brought along, and so are some of the items on the night table."

"Precisely. The two syringes," Doc Rizza added, "one is labeled ketamine and the other is labeled propofol. They're powerful anesthetics in large doses."

"What kind of effects are we talking about, Doc?"

"Both doses are lethal, I'm afraid."

28

Two-Time Loser

The romantic, candlelit dinner took forever. From where he was sitting, Michowsky could see in the restaurant's dimly lit window how the two shared loaded looks and yearning smiles, talking and laughing, touching each other's hands over the table every now and then. When they eventually stood to leave, it was past midnight and the restaurant had already closed.

The two took their time walking to the car, and from there, Carrillo drove Lily straight home. He was impressively well-mannered; again, he held the door for her and escorted her to the front door of the Pearson residence. The house was completely engulfed in darkness, except for the porch light above the door and the safety lights that came on automatically when the two approached the driveway. They didn't seem to mind, still holding hands and walking as slowly as possible, further delaying the moment they'd have to say goodbye for the night. It was a little strange; young people these days act immediately on their desires; they don't delay sleeping with their partners the way they used to, back in the good old days of his youth. Michowsky had expected the evening to end in a motel room or at Carrillo's place, not back at Lily's home.

Lily took out her keys from her purse, but before she could unlock the door, Carrillo folded her into his arms and placed a torrid kiss on her lips. She wrapped her arms around his neck and pulled him closer, reaching higher, stretched on her toes, passionately responsive to the man's touch. Michowsky shifted in his seat, uncomfortable, wishing that part of the stakeout was over already before he had to get out of the car and tell the guy to keep his hands to himself or lose them.

What did he have against Carrillo, anyway? He used to be just as passionate some thirty years ago. In the meantime, he'd grown up, got married, and had children—two boys and a teenage daughter. Good thing that wasn't his daughter over there on that doorstep, or the evening would've ended in a completely different setting, most likely a hospital emergency room. He couldn't put his finger on it, but there was definitely something off about Carrillo.

Eventually, Lily unlocked the door and disappeared inside the house, and Carrillo drove away, his charming smile gone the moment the girl closed the door behind her. Michowsky followed him from a generous distance, keeping an eye on the GPS tracking app on his phone. Carrillo wasn't going back to 1105 Mercury; he didn't take that exit off of I-95. He continued north, not exceeding the posted speed limit, and took the highway 704 exit, heading to the Palm Harbor Marina. Michowsky closed the distance slightly, careful not to lose sight of him.

The white Lexus turned into the parking lot next to the marina, and Michowsky swallowed a curse, seeing how he couldn't pull too close without drawing attention. Another vehicle, a red Chevy Silverado, was stopped in the middle of the lot, probably waiting for Carrillo. The Silverado's driver, a tall, scrawny guy, leaned casually against the truck's hood and smoked, the orange tip of his cigarette visible from a distance every time he inhaled.

Out of options, Michowsky pulled into the City Hall parking lot across the street. He crossed the street on foot, then approached the two men as much as he could, careful not to be seen, hiding behind shrubs and tree trunks. Thankfully, Carrillo didn't seem to care about his surroundings and spoke loudly.

"My boat better be fuckin' ready on Monday, you hear me?" Carrillo was saying. "Gas it up, fill the water tank, throw some bait and some rods onboard, and fill the cooler with the good stuff. Champagne, caviar, the works."

"Got it, boss," the other man replied. "You want the *Hermosa*, right?"

"Right," Carrillo replied and turned to leave. Then he remembered something and stopped. "Lorenzo, I better not find a speck of dust on that boat, *comprendes?*" He didn't wait for an answer; he hopped back in his car and disappeared within seconds, leaving Lorenzo behind in a cloud of parking lot dust.

Michowsky crossed the street back to his car and climbed behind the wheel, hesitating with his hand on the ignition. He could always pick up Carrillo's trail later using the GPS tracker. Maybe Lorenzo would prove a more useful lead.

He followed the red Silverado and, at the first stoplight he caught, read his plate number. He didn't have police equipment installed on that vehicle; it was a civilian car normally used for stakeouts, completely clean of any police paraphernalia except two flashers buried deep in the front grille. Out of options, he called RTCC and dictated the Silverado's plate number to the man at the other end of the line. RTCC was Miami-Dade, but they extended favors to their neighbors without complaining.

"The car belongs to one Lorenzo Herrera, 27, currently on parole," he heard the RTCC rep say.

"What for?"

"Possession, with and without intent. He's a two-time loser, Detective."

That's all Michowsky needed to hear. He turned on the flashers and approached the Silverado, gaining on it. After a few seconds, Lorenzo slowed and came to a stop near the curb.

Michowsky checked his weapon, then took a flashlight from the glove compartment and approached the Chevy.

"License, registration, and proof of insurance," he asked, and Lorenzo handed the documents without hesitation, but mumbled Spanish curses under his breath. "Step out of the vehicle," Michowsky ordered, "hands on the hood."

Lorenzo complied, quietly, without muttering another word. He'd turned pale; he had something to hide.

"Am I going to poke myself with a needle if I search you?" Michowsky asked.

"N—no, sir," Lorenzo replied. "But I ain't got nothin', I swear."

"Uh-huh," Michowsky replied, and began patting him down.

He felt for weapons first and found a small nine-mil tucked inside Lorenzo's belt. "That's a parole violation and another three-to-five," he said, putting the gun out of Lorenzo's reach. Then he fished a small packet of white powder out of the man's jeans pocket, cocaine by the looks of it, and held it in the air with two fingers. "And this is seven-to-ten, right there. Maybe I'll find more in the car and up the ante from a dime to a quarter."

"C'mon, man," Lorenzo pleaded, trying to face the detective. Michowsky slammed him against the car and bent him over the low hood.

"Hands on that hood," he ordered. He then grabbed his arm, twisted it behind his back and turned him around, staring at him hard. "Unless you're willing to help me out."

"Anything, man, anything," Lorenzo said, "just say the word. Want more coke? I've got plenty."

"I'm going to pretend I didn't hear that," Michowsky scoffed. "You're an unbelievable idiot."

"Yes, Officer, I'm a big idiot. I didn't mean—"

"Shut your trap already," Michowsky snapped. "What's on Monday, huh?"

Lorenzo frowned, visibly confused. "Whaddya mean by that?"

"The boat you have to get ready for Carrillo on Monday, what's the deal?"

A flicker of fear glinted in his eyes. "I don't know, man, I swear!"

"All right," Michowsky replied, feigning indifference and pulling out a pair of zip-tie handcuffs. Lorenzo turned paler and started shaking. "No, man, please, I'll tell you everything you need to know."

"You're already a two-time loser, and unless you start spilling something of value, you're going down hard, you hear me?"

He nodded violently, his greasy hair bouncing around his head as if he were a puppet with a broken neck.

"But if you talk, you walk."

Lorenzo looked at him with suspicion. "You promise?"

"Start talking," Michowsky said, and Lorenzo nodded some more. "Again, what's happening in two days' time, when Carrillo needs that boat?"

"Memorial Day, I guess," he replied, and flinched when he saw Michowsky's reaction.

"You take me for a fool?" Michowsky growled in his face, grabbing his shirt and slamming him against the car.

"No, I swear," Lorenzo replied. "He's got this hot date he wants to take out on the water. He's been talking about it for a week now."

"Why in two days?" Michowsky insisted, unconvinced. Carrillo didn't seem like the type to sweat a fishing trip that badly, even if it meant taking his girlfriend out.

"Everyone's out on the water for Memorial Day," Lorenzo replied with a shrug. "That's what he said, word for word."

"All right, you're going to jail," Michowsky replied, sliding the zip-tie on one of his wrists. "You're not giving me anything."

"Man, there's nothing, I swear. He's not telling me much. I'm just his errand boy, that's all."

"And the coke?"

"Sometimes I sell that," he said, seemingly flustered, and immediately continued, "but not often. Once a year, tops. Only if they make me, otherwise no, never."

"Okay, let's go," Michowsky said, and grabbed his other wrist.

"Wait," Lorenzo said pleadingly. "I don't know anything, but I know who knows. He and Carrillo are partners, man."

"Name," Michowsky ordered.

"Paco Loco, we call him."

"Name," Michowsky repeated in the same tone as before, only a little louder.

Lorenzo threw scared glances left and right and lowered his voice, "Pedro Ramon," he said, almost whispering. "But you can't get to him."

Michowsky chuckled and pulled the zip-tie tight. "Does he even exist?"

Lorenzo nodded again, just as enthusiastically as before. "On my mother's grave, I swear. You can't get to him, 'cause he lives out on the water, halfway to Grand Bahama."

Michowsky pulled the other zip-tie and tightened it against Lorenzo's wrist.

"But—but his gal comes on dry land every night, to get stuff," he blurted, panic clearly visible in his dilated pupils. "She's a two-time loser, just like me, and she's into heroin."

"Name," Michowsky demanded.

"Lucinda, or Luci," Lorenzo said, without hesitating anymore. Whatever threshold of fear he held inside, he'd already passed that and there was no turning back.

"Where would I find this upstanding citizen?"

"Every night, about midnight or later, she lands at Mojito Frio, that bar near the marina, on the water. She comes in a small, yellow speedboat, real fast. If you hurry up—"

Michowsky nodded once, inviting him to continue. "Keep talking. How will I know her?"

"She's a tall brunette with wide hips, totally oomph, if you know what I mean," he said, with a wink and a lascivious grin that showed some missing premolars and a chipped incisor. "She's got long hair, and a rose tattoo on her neck, right here," he squirmed, probably trying to point at something with his hands cuffed behind his back. "Can't miss her. She loves bling, that woman, she's covered in it. Whatever Carrillo's been up to, she and Paco Loco know about it, man. Now will you let me go?" he asked, offering his hands and waiting for Michowsky to cut the zip-ties.

Instead, the detective took out his cell and called for a backup car at their location.

"What the hell, man? You promised," Lorenzo said bitterly, tears choking him. "I can't go back inside."

"I'll put you in a forty-eight-hour protective hold, not a minute more," Michowsky said, almost smiling. "So you won't get any crazy ideas and start calling people."

"Then, you'll let me go?" Lorenzo asked, shifting his weight nervously from one foot to the other.

"Yeah, yeah, sure."

29

Fame

Tess held her breath while she watched the unsub pick up the ketamine syringe. He sat on the edge of the bed and ran his hand against the girl's cheek, then arranged one of her rebel hair strands, tucking it gently behind her ear. She was still asleep or maybe unconscious, her eyes closed and her naked body completely immobile, vulnerable and powerless. Not once had she'd pulled against the restraints or opened her eyes since it all began.

Then the screen went dark all of a sudden and Tess gasped.

"What? No," she shouted at the TV, wielding her fist in the air. "We need to know... How will we know?" she asked, turning toward Fradella and Doc Rizza.

"We'll know," she heard Bill's voice, as he replied calmly. His words came across in high definition, as if he were sitting right there in the conference room, staring at the same dark TV screen.

As always, Bill was right. If the unsub went forward with his intention to kill the girl, they'd soon find out. She groaned, frustrated with herself; she'd become emotional, hot-headed, and she'd started hating the unsub, having contempt for him instead of trying to understand him. Nothing good ever comes from loathing an unsub, no matter how repulsive or despicable; it was basic. To understand him, to be able to figure out what drove him to do the things he did, how he chose his victims, she had to let all that contempt go and summon her cold, clinical judgment to take over. Easier said than done.

This case upset her on a deep, personal level; she breathed slowly a few times, willing herself to clear her mind of racing thoughts and emotions and try to understand why it meant so much to her. She'd dealt with many prolific serial killers in her twelve years with the bureau and she'd seen much worse, like The Family Man, credited for over 100 killings. She'd stayed cold and rational in front of murderers who rose to the top among the most abhorrent creatures of this earth.

Yet the Taker of Lives was different.

He stood on the edge of an abyss staring down, feeling more and more compelled to take a dive and explore the darkest side of himself. Tess remembered his hands, covered in black, shiny latex, picking up that ketamine syringe. His fingers didn't tremble, didn't hesitate. He was ready to kill, and she was desperate to stop him, to restore whatever was left intact of that girl's life before he could finish the methodical devastation he'd already begun.

She hoped it wasn't already too late. Soon enough they'd know.

The screen shifted to a black background with white text, a new message from the unsub.

It read, "Want more? Sure, you do. Stay tuned for news. The show is just beginning."

The message was displayed for about a minute, then vanished, replaced by an animation of theater curtains closing. Despite her self-imposed calm and coolheadedness, Tess felt a wave of rage surging through her veins.

"We should be busting through that door right now," she said, her voice elevated and teeming with angst, enough to draw attention in the squad room, on the other side of the glass wall. "Donovan, where the hell are we with that facial recognition?"

"At three percent," he replied.

"We need results faster than this," she said, painfully aware she'd been stating the obvious for a while now, and that wasn't helping, only irritating people even more. "Let's start a new database instance with all filters applied and the three hundred forty-seven potentials lined up, then let's remove filters, one by one, and run facial recognition again and again after each filter is removed." She blurted all that on one long breath of air. "Make sense?"

"Perfect sense," Donovan replied, after a split-moment hesitation.

"I'm looking at Donovan's filters," Bill said, "and the biggest opportunity lies with defining fame. I also believe you skipped a few steps, Agent Winnett. Your profile is incomplete; you failed to define the unsub. Is he a lust rapist? Is he a mission offender? Is he motivated by power, by the need to control his victims?"

"There's no time for that now," Tess blurted. "We're already behind this guy, racing to catch up with him and failing."

"That's because you forgot the basics, Tess," Bill said in a gentle, parental tone. "Slow is fast, remember? Your first week of behavioral analysis training?"

She let her head drop and pressed her lips together to keep words inside, words that were better off left unspoken in Bill's presence. He was right. As always, damn it, he was right, and she wasn't ready for the BAU, for Quantico. Not yet. Not by a long shot.

"Okay," she said quietly, repressing a long sigh, "let's start with the basics."

"Why did you exclude the unsub's motivation from your initial profile?" Bill asked.

"Because I'm still struggling with it," she replied, after a short hesitation, her words rushed, and her pitch elevated with frustration.

Fradella looked up from his laptop screen, where he'd been sifting through countless social media profiles.

"Walk me through it," Bill said calmly.

"He's got the sexual component that accompanies the typical lust rapist, but he doesn't complete the act. For a mission offender, he lacks the statement; whatever his mission, he's not advertising. The degree of psychological torture he's devised for his victims indicates a sadist, while the total absence of violence contradicts that argument."

"Please, take a seat," Bill said, and Tess looked around as if to see whether Bill had video cameras installed somewhere in the conference room. Then she realized he must've sensed from her fluctuating voice that she'd been pacing the room, going back and forth between the door and the wall, then over to the TV, then back to the door again.

She pulled back a chair and let herself drop, instantly feeling the tiredness in her bones.

"Now close your eyes and think of the unsub," Bill said, and Fradella looked up from his screen again. "Then think of all the serial killers you know of, dead or alive. If I remember correctly, you studied all the serial killer case files you could get your hands on, correct?"

"Uh-huh," she replied, keeping her eyes closed and trying to clear her mind enough to give Bill's exercise a chance. She understood what he was trying to do: summon her gut, calling on her instincts to lend a hand where logical thought faltered, because this unsub didn't visibly fit any existing profile type.

She thought of the unsub, dressed in the black latex suit, just as they'd witnessed him, but then pushed that image aside and tried to think of the unsub as someone ringing her doorbell, inviting her for dinner, spiking her drink without her noticing. Who would she allow to get that close? What would that man look like? She breathed, pushing aside the repulsion she felt unfurling in her gut, and tried to "match" a serial killer face to go with the unknown subject in her imaginary dinner setting. One by one, she saw them all in her mind, like browsing through the pages of a catalog filled with humankind's most despicable creatures, and none seemed to fit, not until a particularly haunting image came to her memory.

"Ted Bundy," she said, opening her eyes. "That's who I see. He was power motivated though."

"But he was a necrophile," Bill said, "just like you had the instinct to call this unsub in your online comment, right?"

"Oh… you know about that," she said, and nervously gulped a swig of cold coffee from her almost empty mug.

"Yeah, I know about it, and it was the right call to make," Bill stated. "Scorned, he'll make a mistake, and we'll be waiting."

"But isn't his proclivity for famous victims an indication of a mission-based offender?"

"What is fame, other than power over the masses?" Bill replied. "Think about it."

"Speaking of fame," Fradella said in a hesitant voice, "I hate to interrupt, but I think I have something. An idea."

"Shoot," Tess replied.

"As you know, I've been digging through the social media profiles of the two known victims, looking at how they interact, searching for unusual activities. Stalkers, inappropriate comments, stuff like that. The two profiles have numerous friend or follower accounts in common, but that's not that unusual. They're all local, here, in Miami metro. We could investigate all these common accounts, and that would take us weeks at best, or we could, with Donovan's help, try to quantify fame, put a number to it."

"I thought of that," Donovan replied. "I tried to build working models, then tested them against both victims, but all my models failed."

"Oh, then maybe it's not going to work…" Fradella pulled back, unsure.

"No, no, just walk me through what you've got," Donovan replied.

"How did you go about it?" Fradella asked instead.

"Public relations agencies and advertising firms use software and tools to measure what they call online sentiment for a target person or brand. I used that and artificial intelligence-powered social listening tools, to try to quantify how prevalent the two victims were in online conversations, posts, engagements, comments, videos, tags, and so on. What did you have in mind?"

"Something much more basic," Fradella replied. "If we consider fame to be directly correlated with the number of followers—"

"Yeah, okay," Donovan interrupted, "but some might favor Facebook, while others favor Twitter."

"Correct, that's why I thought of adding them," Fradella replied.

"Adding what?"

"The number of followers on all the social media channels that represent 90 percent of the market, like Facebook, Twitter, YouTube, Instagram, and LinkedIn."

"Why LinkedIn?" Tess asked. "It's not where I'd expect celebrities—"

"Christina used it," Fradella replied. "That makes it relevant, even if we don't really understand why. Maybe she used it as a professional tool. Maybe others do too."

"I get it," Tess replied. "What next?"

"Next, I need Donovan's help," Fradella said, sounding a little embarrassed. "That's as far as I went with this."

"We should be pulling numbers from all platforms, compile, compare against known celebrity baselines, and rework the list," Tess said. "If number of people is what he cares about, then the names of the social media platforms are irrelevant."

"This is great," Donovan replied, typing quickly and loudly on his keyboard. "It's simple, so simple it might actually work."

"I also noticed another thing while digging through all this mess," Fradella gestured toward his laptop. "Fame doesn't necessarily mean wealth. Some people are desperate to have a following, the illusion of fame, and they rake in people and do all sorts of stuff to please them, but they're flat out broke."

"Crap," Donovan muttered, typing crazy fast. "I'm removing the declared revenue filter, and we're back to two thousand, eight hundred, and twenty-three. Running facial recognition against these records now."

"How long do you think?" Tess asked, tapping her foot impatiently. The wall-mounted TV screen had turned dark almost an hour ago.

"It's going fast," Donovan replied. "We're at twenty-two percent already."

Thick silence engulfed the room, while Tess and Fradella stared at the conference phone, waiting, holding their breaths.

A chime sounded, quiet, yet almost startling in its meaning.

"We have a positive ID," Donovan said, and Tess jumped to her feet, ready to storm out the door. "Deanna Harper, twenty-one. Blogger, socialite, fashion trendsetter. The big names paid her just to wear their stuff at parties." His voice was slow and sad, not conveying the urgency she would've expected.

She felt a chill. "What's wrong, D? What aren't you telling us?"

"She's the subject of an active homicide investigation," Donovan said. "Deanna Harper was killed ten days ago."

30

Hell Hath No Fury

The Mojito Frio was an open-air pub with extra-long hours and its own boating dock extending far into the intracoastal water. Loud Latino music blared, covered at times by roars of laughter and lively chatter, the pub's patrons many and enthusiastic, despite the late hour.

Michowsky walked briskly the entire length of the dock, searching for the yellow speedboat mentioned by Lorenzo. He'd said Lucinda came about midnight to get whatever it was that she was getting from that place, probably food and drink, maybe some smokes too. It was almost one-thirty in the morning; probably she'd already come and gone.

He saw a street bum going methodically through garbage cans, fishing for empty cans he could recycle and collecting his find into a squeaky shopping cart lifted from a nearby grocery store. Michowsky took a twenty-dollar bill from his wallet and approached the man, holding it in plain sight.

The man grinned, but took a step back, putting the shopping cart between himself and Michowsky.

"You know Lucinda?" Michowsky asked, extending his arm halfway over the cart and holding the bill with two fingers.

"Yeah, I know that bitch," the man replied, then spat some chewing tobacco right next to Michowsky's shoe. "She ain't kind, that one."

"Describe her to me," he asked, not believing a word the man said.

"*Alta morena puta,*" he replied, then spat again. "A tall, dark-haired whore. Comes in a yellow boat." He reached to grab the twenty from Michowsky's hand, but Gary withdrew it a few inches.

"She been here tonight?"

"Ain't seen her, no," the man said, then reached for the twenty again. This time, Michowsky let him have the money. He took it, looked at both sides of the bill, as if checking to see if it was real, then folded it and slid it inside his chest pocket. "For another one of these I'll—"

But Michowsky was already gone, trotting quickly toward the parking lot. He climbed inside his car and moved it close to the dock, so he could see the yellow boat if it came in, then called RTCC again.

"Hey, what do we have on a Pedro Ramon, aka Paco Loco?" he asked as soon as the call was picked up.

"One moment, Detective," the analyst replied, then whistled quietly in short bursts, impatient, while searching for information. "He's got a long rap sheet; I can push it to your phone."

"Have we been looking at him recently? Any street intel, any leverage I could use with his missus?"

The analyst whistled again, then chuckled. "His missus, you're saying? I bet she'll be thrilled to see these. Sending them to your inbox."

He put the phone on speaker and opened his email. Several photos depicted Ramon, a thirty-something, covered in prison ink and ripped to the extreme, with several young women wrapped around his body like boa constrictors in heat. Another picture showed him and Lucinda walking on that same dock he was now watching. Lorenzo had done an excellent job describing her.

He hung up and went inside the pub, where he climbed on a tacky barstool and ordered tacos and a cold Dos Equis. He was halfway through his second taco when Lucinda strolled into the place, throwing arrogant glances at any patron who stood in her way or eyed her body for too long. She wore tight, ripped jeans and a short leather top, exposing her midsection and showing off a navel piercing with a sizeable diamond, two carat at least, sending fiery sparkles in the dim light.

"*Hola*, Mateo," she greeted the bartender, who managed an unconvincing smile that quickly went away.

"The usual?" he asked, putting a cold Bud Light on a coaster in front of Lucinda.

She gulped a few thirsty swigs, then wiped her mouth with the back of her hand, not letting go of the bottle. "The usual, *primo*."

Then she took a small packet of white powder out of her jeans pocket and palmed it discreetly. There must have been at least 20 grams; two, maybe three thousand dollars street value if that was heroin. When the bartender brought a paper bag filled with supplies, she reached out and swiftly deposited the packet in his hand with a smooth, well-practiced gesture. He took it without hesitation and quickly made it disappear under his apron, then continued hauling stuff for Lucinda, already packaged in brown paper bags.

Michowsky moved a few barstools closer to her, apparently focused on the TV above the bartender's head and sipping his Dos Equis. He kept Lucinda in his peripheral vision, but didn't look at her directly, not even once. With some effort, he could make out what she was saying to the bartender; it wasn't anything important; just small talk.

She finished her beer, then high-fived the bartender before picking up two of the paper bags and heading for the door. Quick on his feet, Michowsky grabbed the third bag, filled with beer and a bottle of tequila, and opened the door for her.

She glared at him.

"Allow me," he said with a smile.

"Don't get any ideas, *guapo*, I'm not interested."

She walked ahead of him with her head held high, swinging her hips and bouncing her hair with every step.

He stopped when she reached her boat. One look at it and Michowsky understood how she managed to come all the way from the sea in the dead of the night. It was a jet-powered speedboat, equipped with radar, proximity sensors, GPS, and everything else invented in navigation electronics. It probably did sixty miles per hour, while she didn't break a sweat.

He tapped her shoulder twice with his wallet, open to show his badge.

"Yes, but I am," he said, with a smile in his voice, "very interested."

She froze and turned, as if she'd seen a snake.

"I ain't done nothing wrong, pig," she said, not bothering to keep her voice low. "*Vete a la mierda!*"

"Let's say I believe you this time," he replied calmly, then offered her his cell phone with one of the photos displayed, showing Ramon with an almost-naked blonde, barely seventeen. "I bet he has done something wrong though."

"*Oh, Dio mio*," she replied, dropping the paper bags and grabbing the phone with both hands. "*Lo mataré*," she mumbled, then continued cussing while tears pooled in her eyes. "I'll kill him."

"Rumor's got it you're getting a little old for the man, if you know what I mean," he said, putting the paper bag on the dock with a heavy sigh.

Her eyes shot arrows through a blur of tears. Remembering how Ramon looked in those photos, it was difficult for Michowsky to imagine someone could love him that passionately.

"You want him dead?" he eventually asked, seeing how Lucinda stood frozen, staring into emptiness and not saying another word.

She stared at him intently, a million emotions reflected in her blue irises.

"Y—yes," she eventually said. "But not fast," she added, her voice peppered with venom. "If I wanted fast, I could go out there and kill him myself," she added, gesturing angrily at the water. "No one would ever know."

"I didn't hear you say that, Luci," Michowsky said in a somber tone. "But I can make him pay, the legal way. The right way."

Fear flickered briefly in her eyes, replacing for a short moment the homicidal rage he'd noticed before.

"What's going on in two days?" he asked, lowering his voice even more.

"No," she whispered, pulling away from him. "They'll kill me."

"They won't know," Michowsky said. "I swear they won't."

"And I'm supposed to trust a cop?" she asked, back to being snotty again. "Really? What, do I look like I was born yesterday, *cabron*?"

"If I search you, I'll find heroin on you. I've witnessed your little transaction with, what was his name, Mateo, right? That puts your ass in jail for twenty years." He paused, searching her eyes and finding the rage he was looking for, intact once again, untainted by fear. "Or it could be his ass in jail, and yours in the Bahamas somewhere with all his money, roasting in the sun, and screwing much younger men than him. Your choice."

"There's a shipment coming in on Monday," she eventually said, her voice low to a barely intelligible whisper. "By water."

"Where's it coming from?"

"Colombia," she replied, lowering her voice even more.

"Who's bringing it?"

"Pedro, on his boat. He's going to meet them out at sea tomorrow night and transfer the load onto his boat."

"What's the name of his boat?"

She bit her lip nervously before replying. "*Reina del Mar*."

"What about, um, *Hermosa*?"

"Nah, that's a small one. The shipment won't fit on that."

"What kind of shipment are we talking about?"

Lucinda veered her eyes sideways and fell silent. Michowsky grabbed her elbow firmly.

"Too late to stop now, Luci. He didn't stop when he had the chance to screw that girl," he added, showing her the cell phone screen with Pedro's photo with the young blonde.

"Twenty-five hundred pounds," she whispered. "First grade, uncut cocaine." Then she turned toward Michowsky and grabbed his sleeve. "Promise me you'll make the bastard pay. Make him suffer." A flicker of raw, undiluted rage glinted in her eyes.

"Oh, I promise," Michowsky said. "Don't you worry about that. But why does Carrillo need the *Hermosa* on Memorial Day? How come he's not helping Pedro?"

"I don't know..." she replied, lowering her heated gaze. "I heard them talking about it, and they kept saying the *Hermosa* is for *seguro*, for, um, insurance."

"In case the *Reina* breaks down?"

"No," she said, shaking her head so vigorously her long earrings jingled. "The *Hermosa* is small, just a thirty-four-foot center console boat. Won't take that much load."

"A thirty-four-foot can take at least ten people," Michowsky pushed back. "That's precisely twenty-five hundred pounds." He baited her, knowing what the issue was, but looking to test her, to see if she was telling the truth.

"The volume, *hombre*. It won't fit. Have you even seen what a hundred million dollars' worth of cocaine looks like? It's a mountain of dope. You think it fits in the trunk of your car?"

He didn't bother to reply. The entire arrangement made sense. While Pedro was out at sea transferring the dope on the *Reina del Mar* and taking it to shore on the busiest boating day of the year, Carrillo, coincidentally, was going to take SAC Pearson's daughter out to sea for a day of fishing and indulging. They were smart, those guys, very smart. If all went well with the dope transfer, Carrillo would bring Lily home without incident. If not... who knows what the heck they were planning, but it sure as hell wasn't good.

"Now what?" Lucinda snapped, yanking her elbow out of his grip.

"Now you be on your way, and keep your mouth closed. If you warn them, I'll know it was you, and I'll come for you, no matter where you'll be."

"I won't warn the son of a bitch, *lo juro*. Let his sorry ass die in prison." She kicked one of the paper bags into the water with the tip of her shoe. "I think it's time I took off to see my mother in LA. She's dying… I just found out. I can leave tonight."

"Excellent decision," Michowsky said. "Won't Pedro be suspicious of your sudden disappearance?"

"I'll call him from the cab and explain. He won't see it coming, just like I didn't see his cheating until it hit me in the face."

She kicked the second bag off the dock and it disappeared in less than a second, going straight to the bottom. She secured the bow and stern mooring lines, then turned to leave. "I'm ready."

Michowsky took out his wallet. "Do you need cash for your plane ticket or anything?"

Lucinda laughed, the loud, raspy laugh of someone who drank and smoked her way through life without holding back. Then she patted her jeans pocket with an almost obscene gesture, while thrusting her hip forward. "*Gracias, cariño*, but I've got more in here than you make in a year."

He watched her walk away with a determined gait, throwing her hair over her shoulder and straightening her back, the gesture itself making the slender woman seem stronger, unafraid. She headed for North Flagler Drive, where she hailed a cab while talking on the phone.

Within a minute, she was gone.

31

Lies and Truth

"He lied!" Tess shouted, pushing her chair away from the table and springing to her feet. "The damn son of a bitch lied! This wasn't live... He's playing us."

She went to the TV and stopped right in front of it, her face so close to the screen she could see the pixels forming the dark image. "Spineless, gutless, piece of shit," she muttered at the TV, as if the unsub could hear her somehow.

An unwanted thought came to her weary mind. Why did she believe he'd be truthful and broadcast live, when he'd never done that before? He'd always attacked in anonymity, stealth, then waited until the crime scenes would be trampled and the damage he'd done gone viral, spread all around the world on millions of computers, before announcing what he'd done. Why would tonight have been any different? Just because she'd prodded him with that online comment? Apparently, that wasn't enough to compel him to change his signature or make a mistake.

Yet tonight was his first kill, at least by all appearances; the crime scene fresh and his signature different. But different, how? He still opted for delayed gratification, waiting ten days before putting that so-called live streaming video out there. He'd still played it safe, going for ketamine as a murder weapon, and deploying countless forensic countermeasures. He'd still showed no sign of violence... Who kills without any rage, and what were his motivations? A cold-blooded psychopath, someone who would score top points on the Hare Psychopathy Checklist. That's who kills without any rage, in ice-cold blood.

She mumbled another curse, then turned to Fradella with an apologetic expression on her face. Fradella had closed the lid on his laptop and sat defeated, staring into thin air.

"He's playing us," she repeated, but in a different tone, cold, determined. "We need to reverse that; we need to play him." Then she reached for the car keys. "Hey D, shoot me Deanna Harper's address and her file, and go get some shut-eye, all right? I'll run over there to see the crime scene."

"The scene has been released back to the family," Donovan announced. "The autopsy results are in, from the Miami-Dade coroner's office. It *was* ketamine," he added, then cleared his voice quietly. "But they also found Rohypnol in her bloodstream and an inhalational anesthetic, sevoflurane."

"Any trauma or sexual assault?" Tess asked.

"Nothing."

She didn't bother to ask about trace evidence; it was pointless, after having seen the extent of the forensic countermeasures the unsub took.

"How about fingerprints?" she asked.

"With that latex suit?" Donovan asked. "I doubt it, but give me a second, I'll check all outstanding labwork on the case."

"I promise you the unsub didn't show up on Deanna's doorstep looking like that. She would've never opened that door, let alone invite him in and drink whatever he offered her."

For a moment, all they could hear was Donovan's typing on the other end of the line.

"They've got nothing," he eventually said with a long sigh. "Some areas were wiped clean, others left untouched."

"What areas were wiped?"

"Kitchen mostly, the dining room table, coffee table in the living room, some door handles."

"Any trace elements, hair, or fibers found near those locations?" she asked, already knowing the answer.

"Nothing that didn't belong," he replied. "Sorry, Winnett. He got out clean. Again."

She groaned and leaned back against the chair, then closed her eyes. She could visualize him coming inside the house, visiting the kitchen, maybe fixing drinks or food with the host, sitting at the coffee table for a drink, or at the dining table. The typical movements of someone who was a close friend or relative, someone the families were comfortable with. That someone must have left a fingerprint, a hair somewhere. That someone must've visited the families at least once before the night of the attack.

"We need to get Crime Scene into these homes again," Tess said, "and lift evidence from underneath the sofas, the creases of the pillows, the edges of the upholstered chairs, or anywhere hair fibers and epithelial cells might survive a few rounds of cleaning. Then we need to compare everything we find across all crime scenes. One of the donors will be common to all scenes, and that's our unsub."

"You know this will take weeks of processing time, right?" Fradella said.

"I'll pull some strings to prioritize it as much as I can," she replied. "We don't have those weeks. His next victim might already be dead by now."

At least she could understand his MO better. Once he gave them a roofie and they were subdued, he had them inhale the anesthetic and kept them under for as long as it took.

"Sevoflurane... That's a fast-acting, fast-clearing gas, right?"

She heard Donovan type fast. "Yes, the fastest one on the market."

"As soon as he's done, he leaves," she mumbled, staring at the stained ceiling tiles, "and they wake up on their own if they ever wake up. But not anymore, they don't. He's brilliant."

She grabbed her car keys from the table and gave Fradella a determined look. "And we're going to catch him."

"Signing off, then," Donovan said.

"Before you do, please send the bug-sweeper team to the new crime scene. I want to make sure he's not watching us still."

It was barely dawn when they pulled up at the curb in front of the Harper residence. A CSI tech was waiting for them, reading something in the dim light of his van's ceiling light. She recognized him; she'd seen him working at the Bartlett crime scene. She remembered him clearly, not only his distinctive physiognomy enhanced by hair so curly and stiff it sat upright, but his unusual gumption and intelligence.

The young tech climbed out of his van to greet them.

"It's Javier, right?" Tess smiled, extending a hand. He gave her a short yet strong shake.

"Call me Javi," he said. "I've just finished sweeping the Bartlett place."

"And?"

He opened his left fist to show her a tiny device. "This was mounted inside one of Christina Bartlett's dresser locks. Mr. Bartlett sweeps the house regularly for bugs, but never thought of sweeping his daughter's bedroom."

"Can you trace it?"

"It's not that uncommon, unfortunately," Javier replied. "It's short range and was configured to transmit video and audio in short bursts of information, to save battery life. It's motion-triggered."

"How short range?"

"One hundred yards or so, not more."

She turned to Fradella. "Let's get some uniforms here to start knocking on doors."

"No need for that," Javier replied. "The receiver is a repeater of higher power and range, just a relay with a five-miles radius. This is how these gizmos work."

"Did you find it?"

"Yeah," he replied with a bit of pride in his smile. "You're not going to believe where he planted it. On top of one of those dock posts, under the edge piling cap. You know, the white cone plastic thingies at the top of the dock posts," he added, seeing the confusion on their faces.

"How on earth did you find it?"

He tapped his tool bag proudly. "It's an active receiver. My device picked it up."

"How long would it take the perp to install one of these?" Fradella asked.

"He obviously knows what he's doing, so not long. Five minutes, tops."

"How about Estelle's home?" Fradella asked.

"We found the same minicam in her bedroom, one in the bathroom, another one in the living room. Even the kitchen had one. The unsub knew the Kennedys would probably never sweep for bugs, so he went crazy."

"And the Kennedy's, um, repeater?"

"The relay? That one I couldn't find in the dead of the night. My device didn't pick it up, and I need to get in the neighbors' yards and stuff. I prefer doing that during the day; I'd rather not get shot," he quipped.

"Agreed," Tess replied. "When you find it, please see if you can download whatever you can. We still don't know how he learned what we call him."

"What, Taker of Lives?" Javi chuckled. "That's out there now, but I'll try to figure it out for you."

They rang the bell and waited a long minute until Mrs. Harper opened the door. She seemed frail and prematurely aged, and walked slowly, shuffling her feet. She invited them in without a word and led them to the living room, where fingerprint dust still stained surfaces, and upturned furniture reminded everyone that the house had recently been the scene of a crime.

Mrs. Harper clutched her trembling hands in her lap. "FBI?" she asked quietly.

"We have reasons to believe what happened to Deanna has happened to other young women," Tess replied to the unspoken question.

A tear rolled down the woman's parchment-like cheek.

"I was home that night," she said in a low whisper. "How could I have slept through it all?" She wrung her hands spasmodically, then clutched them again, tightly, until her knuckles turned white. "They told me I'd been drugged, but I should've known…"

"Do you remember anything about the man who visited the night before?"

She shook her head and stifled a bitter sob.

"Nothing at all," she finally whispered. "I don't remember anyone being here with us. I just remember arguing with Deanna, then feeling very tired while watching TV. Then I went upstairs to bed. The next morning…" she covered her mouth with her hand and didn't continue. Per the case file, she was the one who'd found Deanna's body, still naked and tied to the bedposts, just like they'd seen on video.

"Did you hear anything at all?" Fradella asked.

She shook her head again. "I sleep with a small fan on. The whoosh helps me fall asleep faster."

"What were you and Deanna arguing about?"

"Her so-called career," Mrs. Harper replied, bitterness tinging her voice. "I've been a corporate human resources professional my entire professional life, and I know how careers like hers end up." Another sob shattered her. "I thought that was the biggest risk, her throwing her life away blogging and wearing clothes for a living, instead of college and an internship with a large company."

"Was she successful?" Tess asked.

Mrs. Harper nodded. "She was, and that didn't help me get to her any better. She was making big money, living the life she wanted and didn't care she'd have nothing when it all went away. It went to her head, and we fought about it almost every day. She accused me of never believing in her. Now, all I can think about is the harsh words I said to her the night before she—" Mrs. Harper stopped talking, choked by fresh tears.

"You meant well," Tess said gently, "I'm sure she understood that." She gave the grieving woman a few moments, then asked, "How come she still lived with you?"

"I insisted, knowing her blogging glory would soon end, and she'd be broke and alone, too proud to come back home. Her good-for-nothing boyfriend was no help; he always encouraged her to do whatever she wanted. If you were to ask me, he's behind this somehow. He's so intense, so aggressive, he's almost scary." She wiped a tear off her cheek with her fingers. "She was about to move out to live with him; she was almost finished packing. She told me it was because I drove her crazy."

Tess and Fradella exchanged a quick glance. Miami-Dade had investigated the boyfriend, a day trader by the name of Kurt Briggs, and found nothing suspicious. He had an airtight alibi for the time of the attack, trading live on Asian markets from his own loft, miles away from the victim's residence. Video surveillance in his high-rise condo put him arriving home after nine, and not leaving until the next morning.

Tess breathed deeply, cringing at the thought of what she had to do. She had to tell the grieving mother that a video of her daughter's assault had been released on the internet.

Or did she? What good could ever come out of her knowing that? Maybe the unsub wouldn't publish his typical press release with photos now that Deanna was dead. Maybe that so-called live streaming video was the extent of it, and Mrs. Harper could grieve in peace without ever learning about it.

She stood and thanked Mrs. Harper for her time. Javier stayed behind to finish his sweep; by the time they left, he'd already found a minicam lodged behind a kitchen cabinet door handle.

For a while, she rode quietly in Fradella's SUV, troubled by an uneasy feeling in her gut that they were missing something critical. She asked herself what that was and went over everything she could think of. They had victimology figured out. Financials, family members, friends, and relatives. Places of employment, deep backgrounds too, although Donovan was still digging, trying to find that one individual who all victims had in common.

No, the problem was with the timeline.

"Why now?" she asked, and Fradella shot her a quick glance from underneath a furrowed brow.

"What do you mean?" he asked, keeping his eyes on the road while sipping from an almost finished water bottle.

"The unsub's been doing his thing for the past month and a half, yet now he's stating, 'The show is just beginning,' and he unveils his victims, one after another. I need to understand why now, after spending almost two months stalking, assaulting, and killing. What's so special with this particular moment in time?"

"He's after fame himself," Fradella replied. "He's making quick releases to make sure people don't forget him. That's what he wants, and that's why he hates these girls. Fame."

"Precisely," she said, her voice subdued, almost absent. "Because he's putting up a show. That's the only part he was truthful about."

"Which part?" he asked, with another quick glance thrown her way.

"That he's only just getting started."

32

Me: Unsatisfied

I watched them land on Deanna's doorstep four hours after I'd shown her face on the net. Four hours! Can you believe it? I'm actually impressed with these cops, but not for the reason you might think. No... identifying someone using facial recognition in this day and age, starting from so many already known factors, shouldn't've taken them four damn hours. I'm impressed that none of those cops readily recognized Deanna; that makes them special, not the typical sheep I see every day of my life. These people actually have lives, do work that matters—even if that means they're after catching me—and choose not to waste their time gawking at whatever Deanna did, wore, said, or posted. Hats off to you and yours, Special Agent Winnett!

On second thought, I hope they didn't SWAT the wrong address; it's known to happen. They bust through the wrong door looking for a suspect or a victim, next thing you know, they shoot the family dog and throw a flash bang in the baby's crib, then they apologize and leave. Yup... it's *that* sad. Not everyone's as smart as you are, Agent Winnett, but sometimes, smarts can go against you, and that's why you'll never catch me.

Enough about the cops and feds for now. Let's talk about all of you for a moment. You, all those who follow my streaming site, who decided to embark on a journey of self-discovery that will take you places you never knew existed. You thought people are essentially nice, all emoji hearts and smileys, goodness and empathy and such? In your dreams! People are dark inside, like an Oreo cookie in reverse. The outside looks clean, righteous, while the inside is dark and ready to spill out at the slightest pressure. I'll help you discover who you really are... that's a promise, made solemnly to all five-point-seven million of you. Buckle up; your journey starts with self-awareness.

You don't understand anything about me and what I'm doing, now, do you? You still don't see it. I desperately tried to show you the shallowness of that carefully designed wrapper that constitutes the public image of your idols and demonstrate to you that nothing's left once that wrapper is torn, soiled, and dragged through the mud. Yet, you didn't see any of that. Reading your comments was illuminating from that perspective. Instead of becoming aware of your beloved stars' superficiality, you've grown sympathetic to their ordeals and completely missed the point I was trying to make.

That hurt, you know, and I spent precious time wondering what would rattle you enough to make you see the prejudiced ways of casting fame and granting success in our society. However, you rallied in the millions, attracted to what spoke to your primal instincts: the lure of depravity, of corrupted values and degenerate sex. That's what you want, don't you? Be brave and admit it, safely, to yourself only and to me, by casting your discreet vote from behind a proxy firewall.

While you squirm, figuring yourself out, I'm going through my own personal brand of disquietude.

I took a life. I pushed that ketamine plunger all the way; seconds later, she was gone.

And I felt nothing.

No release, no joy, no exhilaration, no vindication. I felt absolutely nothing, as I felt for her pulse and found nothing.

She felt absolutely nothing, as she slipped into oblivion from her deep, dreamless sleep.

She and I both were robbed of something critical.

I'll explain.

For Deanna, the ending came in an optimal way. After a life of luxury and little meaning, of self-indulgence and endless adulation from the masses, she died in her slumber, not understanding why, not comprehending what was going on with her, not realizing how she'd wasted her life and millions of others'. Just as her life had been, protected by whatever unknown yet fiercely powerful goddess of unadulterated, perpetual good luck, her death was ideal.

For me, her death wasn't liberating. Don't be fooled by my ice-cold mannerism and the ability to control myself; underneath the surface I am screaming with rage for the life I should've had, for the doors that never opened for me, no matter how hard I tried, when for them those doors didn't even exist. For a fleeting moment, I stopped obsessing over having the wrong gender, the wrong body, or the wrong hair color to attain success, and I pushed that plunger, hoping I'd feel vindicated, but she died too soon, without any turmoil, without agonizing fear written in her eyes, without screams that would resound forever in my mind and ease my own personal brand of pain.

Well, that's about to change.

33

A Promise

"I can't catch the Taker of Lives if I can't bring myself to think like he does," Tess said, almost shouting, although Fradella had done nothing to deserve it. He'd just asked if she had any new ideas, but her internal turmoil and self-doubt got the best of her and spilled over in the frustration undertones and the elevated pitch. After all that time, they still had nothing, or almost nothing.

She stopped talking and stared straight ahead at the busy highway, calling on her reasoning to take charge. Once more, she went over what she knew about the unsub, and what she didn't. The profile was incomplete, and she knew better than to leave it like that; after Deanna's death, she had enough information to release a profile, although they still missed an important piece of the puzzle: access. The Taker of Lives moved freely inside the victims' homes, as if he belonged, yet those families had no one in common that the investigators could find: no friends, relatives, or boyfriends; no vendors, no schools, and no patterns of behavior. They didn't eat at the same restaurants or attend the same churches. No one recalled a visitor the night of the attack. It was as if the unsub didn't exist.

Doc Rizza had explained that Rohypnol, especially synergized by sevoflurane, or most anesthetics for that matter, would be responsible for a drug-induced amnesia, executed flawlessly by someone who knew their way around a drugstore. Maybe the unsub was a medical professional; he definitely had access to schedule 1 controlled substances.

There it was, that damn word again: access.

"You'll figure it out," Fradella said in a calm voice, as he took the highway exit.

She shot him a quick glance, grateful for his vote of confidence, a confidence she wasn't feeling. She wasn't used to being uncertain, and that uncertainty made her angry. The Taker of Lives was still ahead of them, leading at an advantage, still pulling the strings, still taking lives, and she couldn't let that happen anymore.

She took a deep breath and closed her eyes for a moment. She knew what she had to do, and normally she wouldn't think twice, forging ahead with little thought given to what could go wrong, because normally she was sure of herself, an experienced profiler with an envied 100 percent success rate in solving cases. However, this unsub was a far cry from normal, even by serial killer standards, and she couldn't afford to make the tiniest mistake. Not when lives were at stake.

With a long sigh, she acknowledged she needed help. She grabbed her phone and typed a quick message to Bill.

"Ready to finalize the profile," she said in the message. "Are you available to assist?"

Just as Fradella pulled in at the curb in front of Kurt Briggs' condo, a chime announced Bill's reply.

"Call when you get started," Bill's text read, short and to the point.

They took a high-speed elevator to the twenty-first floor. It seemed eerily familiar, down to the discreet, pine-scented air freshener, and, for a split second, she wondered if she'd been in that building before.

"It's déjà vu," Fradella said. "It's just like Pat Gallagher's building. These hot shots, they all live the same."

Kurt Briggs had the same athletic, self-assured demeanor they'd seen in Gallagher, but the similarities stopped there. Kurt was visibly devastated by the loss of his girlfriend. He led them into a vast living room that he'd converted into an office, equipped with a huge desk that held a computer and eight monitors arranged in two stacked rows of four, all dark, powered off. On the wall behind the desk, clocks with labels neatly printed underneath showed the time in London, Tokyo, and Shanghai. But Kurt didn't care about any of that. Unshaven, for a few days at least, still in pajama bottoms and a crumpled T-shirt at almost eleven in the morning, he didn't seem to care about anything anymore. The apartment was shrouded in darkness, not a single ray of sunlight making it through the heavy draperies, and the air was stale, reeking of metabolized alcohol.

Kurt examined Tess's badge for a long moment but didn't ask any questions. Instead, he sat at his desk and powered up his computer. The monitors came to life, and, within a minute or two, started displaying charts and graphs of all sorts.

"What can I do for you, Agent, Detective? The other cops have come and gone."

"I'm very sorry for your loss, Mr. Briggs," Tess replied.

He nodded without turning his head away from the browser window he'd opened. Fradella approached slowly, apparently just aimlessly wondering, but squinting a little when he read what Kurt was searching for. Then Tess saw his brow lift, as he shot her a concerned glance. What the hell was Kurt doing?

"I'm hoping you could help us shed some light over the people close to the Harpers," Tess said.

"Have you noticed anyone stalking you two, or has Deanna mentioned anyone?" Fradella asked.

"Stalking us? No."

"Perhaps one of Deanna's fans got carried away?" he insisted.

"No, she never mentioned anyone. All her fans post messages online, and those postings are all over the place, different shades of weird, but no one stands out."

"How about her family? Was everything all right there?" Tess asked, not very convinced the direction was worth pursuing. Her question was intended to jog his memory, to make him go through an inventory of recent events and experiences and uncover a detail that could prove relevant.

"So, you're a profiler, huh?" Kurt replied instead, while one of the monitors displayed Tess's biography. "Is that stuff real? Or it only works in movies?"

Yeah, he's aggressive all right, Tess thought, remembering what Mrs. Harper had said about him, but that didn't make him a killer. In his line of work, people were routinely assertive, driven, and very smart. The decisions they made each day relied on facts and data, and the ability to draw the right conclusions quickly, without emotion or hesitation.

"It works," she replied, curious to see what other search he was conducting now. He typed quickly, and the search result displayed on the screen made Fradella look away from the screen and plunge his hands in his pockets. That wasn't a good sign.

"Really? Why don't you profile me?" Kurt asked, and turned around to face her, while behind him an interface was loading something. She couldn't see what it was; she only saw a status bar progressing quickly.

She smiled, weighing the challenge and holding his scrutinizing gaze. Maybe he needed some convincing before he'd be willing to collaborate.

"Sure, why not," she replied, then took a few seconds to observe the details in Kurt's physical aspect, demeanor, and surroundings.

He crossed his arms at his chest and leaned back in his seat. Behind him, the status bar finished running its course and shifted into an arrow symbol, the type displayed on streaming videos.

"You were an only child, and you lost your father at a young age," Tess said, "not older than seven. You weren't an active child; you chose computers over any form of physical activity but ended up in good shape because you learned to combine the two for optimal performance. You care about performance more than anything else in your work. If it's worth doing, then it's worth doing fast and right."

He nodded a little sideways, and made a gesture with his hand, encouraging her to continue.

"You wear white shirts and charcoal suits but prefer shorts and a T-shirt when you don't have to dress up. You're a bold risk-taker, but always set aside a portion of your gains and invest in a mutual fund or hedge fund, as if making sure you're not overly confident in your abilities. A risk-taker, but one who's smart enough to use a safety net."

"You checked my financials?" he reacted, visibly annoyed.

"No, we didn't," she replied. "You asked me to profile you, and I did."

"Then how the hell did you know what I do with my capital gains?"

She smiled politely but didn't answer. This wasn't the time or the place to train Kurt Briggs in the fundamentals of psychological profiling.

"Better yet, why is an FBI profiler looking into Deanna's death?"

She drew closer to the monitors, enough to see what was displayed on the screen. He'd conducted a search for Deanna by name, and the video that was loaded on the screen, ready for viewing, bore the mark of the killer. Tess recognized the white, cursive font on black, although blurred under the video controls, that read Taker of Lives. It was the same video she and the team had watched a few hours earlier.

She took a deep breath and decided to trust him with more information than she'd normally be willing to share with a witness or a family member.

"The man who murdered your fiancée recorded the assault and streamed it on the internet. Unfortunately, Deanna wasn't his first victim."

Blood drained from his face and his jaw slacked. As if hypnotized, he turned slowly to the computer screen and stared at the video, not daring to click the play arrow.

"You're saying…"

She nodded quietly, then gave him a few moments to process the information.

"This man entered the house, managed to drug both Deanna and her mother, then felt comfortable enough to record video for more than an hour before, um, the recording ends."

"What do you need from me?" he asked in a low voice, grinding the words between his clenched teeth.

"Tell me who would've had the access. Who visited with them?"

He shrugged, staring at the carpet, confused. "No one… She would've told me if anyone was visiting that night. She never had friends over that late. Deanna and I talked at about ten and she was fine. I don't—"

He looked at her, any intensity gone from his eyes; all that was left were sadness and powerlessness. The mark of the Taker of Lives; wherever he went, those were the only things left in his wake: powerlessness and devastation.

"How does one take down such—" he started to say but couldn't bring himself to finish the phrase. Instead, he gestured toward the monitor.

"We can put you in contact with the Cybercrime Unit, and they might be able to assist," Tess replied, but the tone of her voice betrayed her lack of confidence.

"I don't know how I'm going to watch this," he said, thrusting his chin forward with determination, "but I will. Maybe I'll recognize him, or something."

Tess offered her business card and he took it, staring at it for a long moment.

"One more thing," he said with a sad smile, "how did you know I proposed to Deanna? No one else knew but us."

She pointed at a small shopping bag bearing the logo of Barclay's Jewelers, folded neatly on a nearby bookcase shelf.

"I'm really sorry for your loss," she repeated, as she walked toward the exit.

"Catch the son of a bitch," he said, then sprung to his feet and caught up to her just as she opened the front door. There was an intensity in his voice, an urgency she could understand better than anyone. "Promise me you'll catch that sick bastard and make him pay."

She shook Kurt's hand and replied, "I promise."

34

The Profile

Tortilla chips lent a slightly rancid smell to the conference room, but neither Tess nor Fradella seemed to mind. She grabbed a few and munched, not taking her attention from the Harper crime scene photos. She had to admit that photos were still the best way to examine a crime scene after the fact. Video conveyed far more emotion, and its dynamic, fleeting nature led to overseen details, because video focuses the viewer's attention on the big picture, on the message, the action, and the sentiment it shows, not on minutia that could make or break a case.

Why did the unsub bring ammonia, when he never intended to wake her up? Why did he have a gun? Its handle was indeed visible in the duffel bag tucked against the wall. Was he prepared to shoot anyone who might've surprised him? Or had he planned to shoot Deanna instead?

More important, why didn't he stream the actual murder? If he was such a desperate fame seeker, why didn't he release the most explosive part of the video? Something told Tess he'd recorded that part, only he chose not to release it. Just like with the photos he took of Christina and Estelle, Tess suspected he'd kept a few as private keepsakes of his achievement. Maybe the missing scene from the video recording was the same thing: a trophy from his first murder.

And finally, how does one prevent something that had already happened? She took a deep breath and cleared her mind of the last remnants of frustration. The answer came within seconds: one didn't. This unsub was no different than those she'd caught before, whose victims were found buried in the forest or drowned in the ocean. Just like those bodies were discovered at any given time after their deaths, the Taker's victims were exposed after a while, buried in the myriad pages of online content that compose cyberspace. The Taker controlled the moment they were found just as other serial killers before him controlled when their victims were discovered. Some weighed down their bodies with boulders, hoping they'd never again rise from the bottom of the sea. Others traveled to the darkest corners of the Everglades, where wild life was the best forensic countermeasure a murderer could hope for. Still they were found, and still she'd caught those killers and put them where they belonged: sometimes in the ground, other times on death row or behind bars for the rest of their despicable lives.

She took one last look at the Harper crime scene photos, then closed the file folder, arranging its content neatly. She was ready; she knew exactly what the Taker was and how to catch him.

She smiled, a crooked grin that caught Fradella's attention.

"Glad to see the Tess Winnett I used to know is back," he said, shooting her a quick glance over his laptop screen.

"What are you up to?" she asked, taking another crunchy bite from a tortilla chip.

"Donovan and I divided and conquered the searches for social media anomalies and commonalities. He has this amazing piece of software that quantifies the emotional state of the person posting a comment. I'm extracting all those profiles, while he's looking for any other victims we might not know about."

"Got anything?"

"Nothing yet. Since the beginning of the year, we've had one thousand, two hundred, and forty-two violent deaths in Florida, but when he applied the filters, there's no match. Not even one. Maybe he hasn't killed anyone else since Deanna, but Donovan isn't buying it."

"Smart Donovan," Tess replied. "I'm not buying it either. The Taker is escalating; no way he just stopped ten days ago." She drank thirstily all the water she had left in a small bottle of Dasani, then sent it flying across the room, straight into the trash can. "Ready for the profile?"

"Sure," he replied, and the look of excitement in his eyes made her smile. She liked his eagerness to learn, to develop his skills, to become a better crime fighter.

She dialed Bill's number, and he picked up immediately. "Just give me a second, let me get settled in my office," he said, and she could hear him walking quickly through a long corridor filled with loud people chatting. Then she heard a door close and the background noise vanished.

"Okay, I'm set," he said. "You might want to know Donovan set me up with a camera view of your whiteboard."

She looked up and there it was, mounted on top of the ceiling projector, a relic from the olden days before the flat screen had been installed on the adjacent wall.

"The whiteboard is outdated for the most part," she started to explain, looking at her scribblings with an uneasy feeling. If she'd known he was able to see it, she would've taken a few minutes to update all the information written on it. "Everything else except the victimology matrix is—"

"I believe you'll agree the personal vendetta scenario is out," Bill said. "I like your approach to figuring out the unsub's desired outcome. Let's not delay this anymore; let's talk about his motive. Have you decided, Tess? Is he a lust killer? Or power assertive?"

She hesitated a quick moment before replying. If wrong, that apparently simple choice could alter the profile to the point of making it 100 percent incorrect, and lead everyone on a wild goose chase. Yet in her gut, she knew exactly what the Taker wanted.

"Stripping his victims naked and posting their photos online threw me off in the beginning; I believed he was a lust offender evolving to a murderer, probably fueled by impotence and some other stressors in his life. Not anymore," she added, feeling more confident with each word she spoke. "He's a malignant narcissist, lusting for power and recognition, who is enraged by anyone getting the public's attention more than he does."

"You speak of rage, but he's calm, organized, thorough, and an effective stalker with unlimited and quick access," Bill said.

"He is all those things, but he's also enraged," Tess replied. "Only he's figured out that rage won't work, if he wants to inflict maximum damage. He's a cold-blooded psychopath, a sadist, although he doesn't come across as one; his crimes aren't violent; there hasn't been a single drop of blood spilled, but there will be, I promise you. Rage is one hell of an emotion to control at length, no matter how organized you might be."

"You say he's a sadist," Fradella intervened, "are you saying there have been other nonviolent sadists?"

"I'm saying this one thrives on his victims' psychological pain. The agony he inflicts is prolonged, refined. He's almost… feeding off it somehow. Probably that's why he maintained active video surveillance in Christina and Estelle's homes, to witness their pain."

"Then why kill Deanna?" Fradella asked. "How does that play with his need to cause long-term psychological pain?"

"He's escalating," she replied with a slight shrug. "He's discovering who he is, and in that process, his taste evolves; his rage is nearing the surface, ready to explode in violent bloodshed."

"I don't see it," Fradella said, lowering his gaze for a moment, "I'm sorry. I thought he could very well be a lust offender, one with excellent understanding of forensics, and the self-control to refrain from raping the victims, concerned with a higher risk of getting caught."

"Have you seen his latex suit?" Tess asked. "Penetration could happen with such a suit; that's how they're used in some forms of sexual cosplay. But he's not touching those girls; that's not what he's after."

"Could he be homosexual?" Fradella asked. "The only time I've seen body latex like his was in a gay magazine," he said, veering his eyes sideways, seemingly uncomfortable with his statement.

"That's a possibility, yes," Tess said, and for a moment she explored the thought, trying to ascertain how plausible that scenario was. "It would explain the lack of sexual interest in the victims, his disdain for these young women, his need to diminish their value, his sense of being in competition with them for the love and attention of other men."

"What is he after, Tess?" Bill asked, and she could hear a hint of pride, of satisfaction in his voice. "What does he really want?"

"He's out to prove to anyone who will listen how these girls are unworthy of their fame, and he's the only one who should be followed and adored. There's something to be said about exposing them for the world to see. It's almost like he offers them naked for anyone to abuse, at least with their eyes, if not in their minds."

"Keep going," Bill said. "You're on to something."

"Fame is the key component in this profile. He's an authentic taker of lives; he seizes their lives and destroys them, even when he allows the victims to survive. He destroys them from all perspectives, so thoroughly and so completely that not even after death they can't be respected or cherished." She stopped for a moment, waiting for questions, but none came. "He deserves his moniker."

"He's got a well-defined type," Fradella said. "If he's choosing them because of their fame, how do you explain that narrow victimology?"

She grinned. "I don't explain it; we all do," she said, and Fradella's eyebrows shot up. "When we choose the people we like, the actors we love the most, the singers, the models, what do we normally see?"

"You mean, it's because of the type of people who become famous?"

"I'm saying, if you were to put all famous female entertainers on a matrix, what would be the most common traits?"

"Caucasian, young, fair-skinned, light-colored hair, almost always long and wavy," Fradella replied. "It kind of makes sense, because white Americans are the racial majority, at more than 73 percent, if I remember correctly."

"It goes deeper than that," Tess replied. "The population in the twenty-two or so northern states and Florida can be traced back to German ancestry. It's possible that with that ancestry, the preference for a certain physiognomy has become engrained in our culture, leading to a higher likelihood of Caucasian blondes to attain social acceptance and professional success, especially in socially driven entertainment like *American Idol* or beauty pageants."

"You'd expect more of a Latin influence here, in Florida," Fradella replied.

"You would, and that influence is starting to show as our society becomes more open to diversity, and so does our culture. It's a process of transformation."

"But you still believe the unsub is white?" Fradella asked.

"Most offenders are active within their own racial group; we rarely see cross-racial attacks, so, yes, I believe he is white, despite the fact that white serial killers haven't been the majority since the eighties. For our current decade, African Americans hold the pole position, with almost sixty percent of all offenders caught."

"Let's finalize the profile," Bill said. "We brought up impotence a number of times, as a potential explanation for the lack of penetration. Do you believe he's impotent?"

"N—no," she replied. "In lust-motivated, impotent offenders we see symbolic penetration, most often stabbing of the victim. Stabbing is a penetration substitute, but I thought we agreed he's not lust-motivated."

"We agreed," Bill said, and she heard that smile in his voice again. "I'm going over every aspect of his MO and signature; call it an inventory, if you'd like. I want to make sure these characteristics fit within our categorization as a power-assertive killer."

"Fair enough," she replied.

"Do you think he's jealous of his victims?"

"He might be," Tess replied, after giving the question a moment of thought. "But I believe he's after fame himself. In the new world, people will do anything."

"What do you mean?" Fradella asked.

She stood and grabbed a new bottle of water from the table. She would've loved another cup of coffee, but she didn't have the patience to wait for it to brew. She had a bitter taste in her mouth, leftover from the tortilla chips.

"Let's face it, crime isn't what it used to be only a decade or two ago. Crime used to make more sense, used to be personal, primal, and basic. A crime of passion was an easy solve: almost always a rejected lover or spouse. People killed other people for clear, strong motives, not out of boredom or to prove themselves. Random killings have ruined crime-solving rates in the past twenty years. Drive-by shootings, dares between teenagers, gang initiation rites, we've all seen those."

"Yes, but I don't see how that ties in to serial homicide," Bill said, and this time Tess was the one to smile. He was testing her thought processes, while providing a sounding board for her theories.

"We've seen people do crazy things to gain followers on social media, regardless of channel. Some injure themselves in the process, or even die. As the devastating effects of social media continue to shape our psychology, we see others try it every day, more and more desperate to gain access to the apparently endless, internet-provided, narcissistic supply of adulation. That's why I believe the unsub isn't necessarily jealous of anyone in particular; he just uses these high-profile targets to assert himself, to prove they weren't worthy, but he is."

A long moment of silence filled the room.

"I believe you're ready to release the profile," Bill said. "Before you call everyone in, tell me, how do we catch someone like that?"

"Donovan is working on the fame aspect of his victims, trying to narrow down a target pool with enough precision to allow us to prevent his next attack and catch him in the act. That won't be easy though, seeing how effective his surveillance has been thus far. Fradella is working the social media angle, looking for any shred of evidence that could help us explain the access he gains to the victims and their families. Somewhere, someone posted something mentioning a man who appeared in their lives and the ruse he used. As for me, I'll prod him into making a mistake."

"How, exactly?"

"I'll try to jeopardize the one thing he's killing for: his fame."

35

Tactical Plans

The conference room was full of people, standing room only, and more had dialed in on the open conference line. Captain Cepeda had spoken with SAC Pearson earlier and took the seasoned FBI investigator's recommendation to expand the profile release to Broward, Miami-Dade, and even Monroe Counties. The conference line chimed whenever someone new dialed in, and they kept joining. There were a few more minutes until the announced starting time.

Tess gathered her notes and prepared a quick list of items she wanted to cover and a few action points she wanted clearly communicated and thoroughly understood. The Taker of Lives wasn't an unsub who would let a mistake slide. One screw up, one tiny mishap, and he'd disappear, never to resurface again in their area, or with that same MO.

Right on the hour, Tess cleared her throat discreetly and leaned forward a bit, to be closer to the conference phone.

"Thanks for calling in or attending," she said. "For those of you who don't know us, I'm Special Agent Tess Winnett with the FBI, and we have Supervisory Special Agent Bill McKenzie on the line with us from Quantico." She paused for a moment, allowing Bill to take over.

"Hello," Bill said. "It's late, so we'll get right into it. We believe we have a serial killer currently operating in South Florida."

Tess let the subsequent wave of whispers and comments subside. "We're looking at a highly intelligent, organized, and tech-savvy Caucasian male, five-eight to five-ten. He's well-integrated into society, holds a good job, is well-liked and respected."

Another wave of rumblings from the room. Everyone expected serial killers to be long-bearded, one-eyed loners who wore rags and lived deep inside the Everglades somewhere, or on a remote mountain. No one could really stomach the idea of integrated psychopaths walking undetected among church-going folk or drinking water from the banal office cooler, so people, and that included cops, did what people do best when they can't handle something: they pretend it didn't happen.

"This unsub gains immediate, unrestricted access to properties occupied by relatively famous young women. He most likely is using an effective ruse and, based on his ability to gain immediate trust and access, must be above-average good-looking. He's twenty-five to thirty, maybe a little older, but not by much. He's overly concerned with the image he projects, so his clothes are impeccable, and his vehicle clean, accessorized, new."

She watched the cops in the room, as they scribbled notes quickly and glanced in her direction every now and then. "There's a relatively low likelihood this man is a homosexual, but it could happen to be the case."

A young cop raised his hand, and she nodded in his direction.

"How many women has he killed?"

"Only one that we know of—"

Another wave of murmurs grew, and one woman's voice rose above it. "Isn't a serial killer supposed to have killed at least three people before we can call him that?"

"Our latest guidelines allow us to categorize an unsub as a serial killer if we detect certain behavioral clues in his MO and signature. Additionally, this unsub has assaulted two other victims, one of which consequently took her own life. We believe that was his intention with both his earlier victims, to murder them indirectly."

The room suddenly fell quiet.

"We are confident he will escalate," Bill's voice came across the conference system. "He's a fame-seeker and will stop at nothing to garner the attention he obsessively craves. He's posting photos or video of his crimes online, and he's got millions of Dark Web followers."

"He's sophisticated and incredibly bold," Tess added. "He assaults and kills his victims while other family members are sleeping in the house, probably chemically subdued with something as superficial as Rohypnol. After he leaves, no one remembers he's been there."

"And how do you suppose we'll catch this guy?" an older detective from Broward County asked. "You're describing an everyday, middle-class, white guy who drives a nice car."

"We won't catch him by the way he looks; that information is more for elimination purposes," Tess replied. "We will catch him by organizing the force into ready-to-act groups, located in certain areas of the city, and encrypting communications he's most likely listening to."

"Not sure I follow," a Miami-Dade County sergeant said, tentatively raising her hand at the same time.

"Our analyst is working with Palm Beach County Detective Fradella in identifying a small pool of highly probable subjects who might be the unsub's next target. We will share those names with you, and to each name we will assign a number. As soon as we have confirmation of a target, we'll communicate with you by radio, and the respective team will go in."

"Our main objective is to ensure reduced response time," Captain Cepeda intervened. "We'll have teams conducting speed enforcement in the proximity of all the target addresses, all shifts. We will use coded communication, announcing a chemical spill with potentially explosive risk at the TGV chemical plant across town, then we will follow that with a reservoir number. That number corresponds to a name on your list, and that's where the assigned team will respond."

"What if TGV really blows up, and none of us respond?" a young uniform asked, grinning crookedly like a real smartass.

"If TGV really blows up," Cepeda replied, with a deep furrow of his brow, visibly irritated by the man's insolence, "you won't hear a reservoir number; instead you'll hear us say, 'this is not a drill.' Got it?"

"Yes, sir," the young man replied, his grin still lingering.

Another hand in the air, and Tess invited the middle-aged detective to speak.

"How many potential victims are on that list, and when do we start executing this tactical plan?"

"We don't know yet," she replied, after a brief hesitation. "Our analyst is still working to refine it. We don't want the list to be too long, but we don't want to omit any potential target either."

"How would you know who he's after next?"

"The unsub has a well-defined type, young Caucasian women under the age of twenty-seven, who are famous in some way."

A few subdued comments of disbelief circled the room.

"There are three kinds of people living in Florida," a Miami-Dade County detective said with a patronizing tone he was trying to pass as humorous. "Drug dealers, famous people, and retirees."

"Yeah," a few others interjected, sprinkling bits of laughter here and there.

"As soon as they can afford to live in paradise, they all come here," another uniform added.

"Yes, the Sunshine State has the highest prevalence of famous people, right after California," Tess replied calmly. "We're well aware of that, but we have methods to filter and identify those most likely to pop on our unsub's radar. As soon as we have the final list of names, we'll release it."

"Is this the Taker of Lives we're talking about?" came a question from the far side of the room.

Tess frowned, searching for the man who'd asked the question. He was in his late twenties, with a goatee and a bit of an attitude written all over his face. How did he know about the killer's moniker unless he'd been on his website?

"And you are...?"

"Officer Delacruz, Palm Beach County Sheriff's Office," he replied hesitantly, looking sideways.

"Where have you heard that moniker, Officer?"

"Um, I don't know," he replied, then touched his ear in passing. "Around, I guess." A moment later, he scratched his nose.

The man was lying.

"I hope I don't have to tell you how important it is to keep this quiet.

Don't speak to anyone about this case," Tess said. "Don't post anything online, don't tell friends or family, don't speak with the press."

She looked at a few of them and liked the determination she saw in their eyes. If they kept their mouths shut, they had a decent chance of pulling it off.

That, and if she managed to scorn the Taker so badly he'd come out of the shadows and attack his next victim in real time.

She thanked everyone for attending, ended the conference call, then closed the door behind the last one to leave and sat down with a long sigh. Her phone rang before she could decide whether to eat a few more chips, or just get another cup of coffee going.

She frowned a little when she saw SAC Pearson's name on the screen.

"Sir," she said, as soon as she took the call.

"Great job on the profile, Winnett," he said. "Let's hope it won't be a waste of resources and time. I've read the file; it's a long shot at best."

"Nothing else we can do, sir, but try to catch that son of a bitch," she replied, a little concerned with his lack of confidence in the outcome of the case. He was an experienced investigator, and his assessment carried weight in her eyes. "We'll catch him, sir; I made a promise I intend to keep."

There was a moment of silence in the air.

"Speaking of cases, any news on that file we discussed?"

"You were right to give that one to me," she replied, keeping all specifics to a minimum while on the phone. She didn't want to take any risks, especially when anyone could intercept cell phone conversations with ease and a small investment in spyware.

"Do I need to step in?" he asked, and she could hear worry in his voice.

"No, not yet."

"I can't stand the thought of her being alone with that man," he blurted in a low, subdued voice.

Argh… So much for keeping specifics out of the phone conversation, she thought, hoping no one was listening in.

"She's not, sir, not for a second," she replied. "Give me another day or two. We need to find out the what and the why."

He thanked her and hung up in his typical, immediate style. She didn't get the chance to put the phone back in her pocket before it rang again. This time, she took the call on speaker; it was Donovan.

"Hey, guys," he said, sounding cheerful for a change. "We caught a break. Christina and Deanna used the same agent."

36

The Agent

The tactical response team took positions around the small house. Two approached the front door, weapons drawn, while Tess and Fradella followed closely behind them. Another two carried a ram and stood right in front of the door, ready to bust it open. Four others hurried around back, keeping their heads down, so as to not be visible from inside the house.

A short crackle in a radio, then the tactical team's commander ordered, "Breach. Breach. Breach."

The two officers slammed the ram against the door, sending wood shards into the air, then rushed to the side, making room for the other two to enter the property. They walked in, carefully checking every corner of every room before moving on to the next one.

"Clear," one of them announced, after checking the kitchen.

Tess took the dining room, then headed to the back of the house when she heard another officer's voice.

"Hands where I can see them," he ordered, and Tess followed the sound of his voice to the master bedroom.

The man held trembling hands up, seemingly shocked by what was going on. He wore off-white boxer shorts and a dirty undershirt, stained primarily in the abdomen area, where he must've wiped his hands against it repeatedly. He was forty-two per his file, earning an inconsistent living from a one-man talent agency named after himself, Koester Stars.

Tess looked at him intently, trying to pinpoint what exactly made the man seem so slimy. Was it his oily, unkempt hair, or his splotchy goatee? Or was it the state of his abode, in terrible need of a thorough cleaning, much as his clothing? This man didn't fit the profile, not one iota.

The photos pasted on the walls told a different story. Above his antiquated, scratched desk, he'd hung professional head and body shots for Christina and Deanna, and several other girls Tess didn't recognize. On the back wall, printed in full color and high-res format, she recognized the most indecent photos of Christina and Estelle, and a few screenshots extracted from Deanna's video.

"Haul this piece of trash out of here," Tess grunted, curling her lip in disgust.

"I didn't do anything," Koester said in a pleading, almost whimpering voice. "I swear I didn't!" Then he turned his head quickly toward the back wall, following Tess's gaze. "Those are legal, you know. All those women are adults."

One of the officers finished cuffing him and was about to drag him out of there, when Tess stopped him.

"Did you represent Estelle Kennedy?"

"No," he blurted right away, "she rejected my contract terms and went with someone else."

"Smart girl," Tess said, deep in thought. He didn't seem to be the right guy. The unsub they were looking for was younger, smart, organized, good-looking, obsessed with projecting an appearance of control, of power and of status. While Koester was nothing but a slimy little parasite.

Tactical found a couple of cameras in the house. She examined them curiously, after sliding on a pair of gloves, but they were the wrong brand; neither camera was the Nikon DSLR used to take Christina's photos. She sighed with frustration; they were wasting their time, but she signaled one of the officers to pack up Koester's computer anyway. She wasn't hoping to find any evidence confirming him as the Taker of Lives, but maybe they'd get lucky and find some child porn on it and put that piece of slime where it belonged. She doubted any of his clients would've wanted to have anything to do with him if they knew what he kept for wall décor.

She went outside, grateful for the fresh air she was able to breathe after the filthy staleness of that place. She suddenly felt tired and sat on the cement steps, lowering her head in her hands.

"Are you okay?" she heard Fradella ask.

"Yeah," she replied, unconvinced. What did okay mean, anyway? Not bone tired and hungry? Or having the real Taker of Lives cuffed and locked in the back of a police car? She would've taken the latter any time of day, but they had nothing.

Just another dead end.

37

Me: Planning

I don't waste time hating people. It's a meaningless, time-consuming activity that leaves me with zero gratification. It's true I believe some people should die, slowly and screaming and at my hand preferably, but I still don't hate them. They simply exist, and I respect that; how very zen of me.

Yes, they simply exist. They're as meaningless to hate as it would be to despise the fly that's buzzing circles around your head, keeping you from reaching that deep state of relaxation your entire body craves. Would hating that fly make it go away? Would it make all flies go away? No... not in the least. Flies, just as superficial, spoiled, and irritating as certain humans, wouldn't care.

Then how does someone like me get rid of those pesky insects? Not without a good swat, you'll have to agree. Hit her hard, when she least expects it, leaving her dizzy, unable to pick herself up and fly again, incapable of standing in my way, ever again.

That's why it's pointless to hate anyone, especially people, regardless of how completely detestable they are.

That's what I've been telling myself, over and over again, trying to regain the calm I need for tonight's performance. Only this time, it doesn't really work. My heated blood is rushing to my head, I constantly feel the urge to punch yet another hole in the wall, and I can't stop bellowing, even if there's no one here to yell at.

I have to admit it... I really hate that FBI agent, Tess Winnett.

I know what you're about to say; I started it, I prodded her by calling her out by name on my website, and now she's coming after me with a vengeance. Okay, I'll give you that. I confess, guilty as sin of the supreme arrogance of telling the world about her. I didn't think she'd care that much; she must be just like me, tired of being ignored, of working herself to the bone with little or no recognition.

Because otherwise, none of this makes any sense.

You know what she did? Do you have any idea what she had the audacity of perpetrating?

Not only did she strip my video cameras from every place she could find them, leaving me blind and ravenous, but she blatantly lied to everyone, posting on my feed that the FBI is tracking all users who visit or vote my streaming site. I lost almost three million users in a matter of minutes. Argh... people are so damn stupid!

It took me hours to post replies, quoting from experts and Dark Web users, even quoting the NSA, believe you me, to calm people's fears down from boiling hot. No one can trace you on the Dark Web, if you take simple precautions. No one! Just get it into your thick skulls already and come back, join the party that's about to start. She can't reach you, people, don't be so shortsighted. You think I'd be doing this if I were in any real danger?

Yes, I'm willing to put in some effort to show you all how ill-directed your admiration is, but you're not that important to me to be risking my own freedom. You're the loser, if you don't get the message; it's you who will be wasting the rest of *your* life, not mine, fawning over inconsequential words and actions spouted by trivial, self-centered people on their social media channels and calling it entertainment.

I found different, more interesting things to do, like experiment on *you*.

I hope you won't mind it much, but with every experiment there's a little blood to be spilled. It's all in the name of science, you know. Not wasted but studied. Not taken for granted but researched, accepted for what it is, and made worthwhile. Well-documented for the future generations to understand why humankind, who was doing oh-so-well in the age of technology, suddenly decided to take a nosedive and sink into a bottomless abyss of ignorance and complacency so gloomy and hopeless it will make the Dark Ages seem like a Broadway show.

Because I know just who you are. You're one of those people who gasp at the profanities spray-painted on the public restroom wall and swear they'll never use that particular stop again, while obsessively reading the filthy words again, and again, and again, while going through the catharsis of relieving yourself. You grew up in a God-fearing household but pored over every page of *National Geographic* you could find, not because you were drawn to the science, but because, at times, you could gawk at bare breasts depicted in a full-color, high-resolution photo printed on quality paper, something to feed your fantasies for years to come. Now you're self-righteous by day, taking the kids to soccer practice while your wife's baking cookies for the church sale, and slaving twelve-hour days all week in your mid-level job from which there can be no escape. But at night, you tiptoe down the basement stairs and turn on the old laptop, the one everyone believes is broken, and visit with me, eager to see what I have got in store for you.

Don't worry, I've got you covered. We're going to explore a new side of you tonight, one you didn't know existed. I'll plant such a delicious memory inside your brain that you'll be forever in my debt, because whenever you think you won't be able to take another minute of kid talk, of soccer practice, or stupid-as-shit sales meeting, all you have to do is close your eyes and remember tonight's show. You'll be free again.

As for Special Agent Tess Winnett, let's just say I'm allowed to fantasize too. She's a bit older than what I like, and not really that relevant to you, which makes her inherently uninteresting, but she's outdone herself and become too relevant for me to ignore any longer. I've started spending way too much time planning the seduction and submission of an armed federal agent to not doubt my own sanity, especially since she triggers in me the absurd, yet intense, all-consuming feeling of hate. For now, I've just sent her a very personal message. Because, you see, I also know who she really is, behind her tough-cop wrapper accessorized with gun, Kevlar vest, and two spare mags of ammo.

But before we get to have some fun with dear old Tess, let's focus on tonight's performance. Let's focus on you.

It will be unique. You'll get to choose what happens.

38

Dinner Plans

Tess breathed in the grill smoke in the air outside of Media Luna, and a familiar rumbling resonated in her empty stomach. The smell of Cat's burgers was mouthwatering, and she hurried toward the entrance, eagerly anticipating the first bite of hot food she'd had in more than a day.

The bar was not that busy for a weekend; probably most patrons were out on the water somewhere, fishing, drinking, or just hanging out. Others chose to travel on Memorial Day weekend and visited family or friends or locked themselves in the house with a pet project to tinker on.

She smiled widely when she caught Cat's glance, and he returned the smile with a quick nod and two fingers raised at his temple in a sketched salute. He finished wiping a glass with a white napkin, then set it in front of a pot-bellied customer and poured whiskey, double on the rocks. He put the bottle back on the shelf, wiped his hands on his apron, and started her way, his grin widening with every step he took. Then he froze in place, hands firmly on his hips, while his grin was quickly replaced by a grimace complemented by a frown.

Fradella had walked through the door.

Oblivious to the reaction his arrival had caused, or maybe just choosing to ignore it, Fradella approached Cat with an extended hand and a polite demeanor. Cat hesitated and gave him a long, loaded glare, then shook his hand. By the time he let go of his hand, Fradella wasn't smiling anymore. Cat crossed his arms at his chest and pursed his lips, while Fradella thrust his chin forward with a gesture that said, "I ain't going anywhere."

Tess barely refrained from chuckling and continued watching the two in their intricate and lengthy alpha male posturing game.

"Isn't it funny how those two are almost identical?" Michowsky whispered, appearing out of nowhere while she'd been watching the interaction. "They could be father and son, if you didn't know any different."

She snickered quietly but studied the two men from Michowsky's perspective. He was right, yet she'd never noticed it before. Both men had the same bony structure, tall, with long hair that would've looked awful on anyone else but looked just fine on the two of them. Cat's was more salt-and-pepper, with a distinctive prevalence for salt, but he had an ageless, timeless air about him, reminding her of Willie Nelson. If any man could sport long, gray hair and still look distinguished and charming, that was Willie. And Cat.

The two men were saying something to each other, each leaning toward the other as they spoke, then pulling away and straightening their backs. Cat eventually unfolded his arms from his chest, and the familiar tattoo that had earned him his name became visible; a tiger inked in tribal pattern, its hypnotizing eyes showing where his Hawaiian shirt's top buttons were undone. Fradella plunged his hands into his pockets and started moving away from Cat, conceding defeat in that apparent confrontation, but reluctant to turn his back to the older man.

She had to agree; they could've been family. Maybe they were and didn't know about it. She knew Cat had some indigenous blood coursing through his veins, Seminole, if she remembered correctly; she made a mental note to ask Fradella if he had any Native American ancestry.

Fradella approached them and took a seat next to Tess at the bar, but Cat returned to the serving station and shot her an apologetic glance. She stood and walked to him, smiling, then she went behind the counter and gave him a hug.

"Hey, kid," he said, looking at her. "Good to see you."

"Maybe," she quipped, "but you're not that thrilled to see those two."

"Them?" he gestured with his chin, not bothering to look their way. "They're cops, and you know how I feel about cops."

She bit her lip, unwilling to remind him she was a cop too. "Fradella and I, well, we've been hanging out," she said.

"You're not getting enough of him at work?" he said, then laughed. "I'm yapping like a teenager's dad," he added. "It's great you're going out a little, even if it's with a cop."

She looked up and he placed a kiss on her forehead; the gesture warmed her inside, awakening feelings of family and belonging she hadn't felt in ages.

"Thanks," she said, then hugged him again. Moments like those were so precious, and she couldn't understand why she didn't visit more often. Cat was pushing seventy; soon she wouldn't find him behind that bar counter, no matter how hard she looked.

She breathed, forcing down the knot in her throat and clearing her eyes of the unexpected mist, while promising herself she'd come at least once every few days. Then she pulled back and tilted her head a little. "Are you willing to feed us cops, or not?"

"Coming right up," he said. "Now get out of my way, or it'll take twice the time."

Michowsky and Fradella had moved from the bar to take seats at a table in the corner, away from unwanted ears. They both looked grim as Tess joined them.

"What's up?" she asked, looking first at Michowsky, then at Fradella.

Michowsky started sharing what he'd found, what Carrillo was up to, and his confirmed suspicion that Lily Pearson was to be used as insurance, in case the Coast Guard or the DEA stumbled across the drug shipment.

"Where is he now?" Tess asked, concern ruffling her brow.

"I have GPS on his car," Michowsky replied.

"We should seize this shipment," Fradella said.

"Yeah, no kidding," Tess replied. "All right, we have enough for warrants, phone surveillance, the works. I'll bring Donovan in on this and have him set the wheels in motion."

Cat brought burgers and fries, laid out expertly with all the trimmings on heated plates. He set them on the table, then came back with a club soda pitcher and a mint lemonade for Tess. The two men thanked him, and he mumbled something in response, the friendliest he'd ever been with the two cops. Tess swallowed a chuckle and bit into the burger with a healthy appetite.

"Oh, this is good," Michowsky said, taking another huge bite. "Your friend will have to deal with the fact I'm about to become a regular in this place," he added, chewing with his mouth open.

She smiled absentmindedly, thinking of Carrillo and his plan to use Lily Pearson as leverage. She had to brief SAC Pearson, even if it was almost nine. It was his daughter, and that made everything they did next his call. Nevertheless, did they know everything there was to know about the incoming shipment and the smugglers' plan? It seemed too simple, too easy, but once the Colombians set their eyes on a fed's family, nothing was simple anymore.

"Can you stay on Carrillo a while longer?" she asked Michowsky, shooting him a critical gaze, observing how tired he looked in yesterday's wrinkled and smelly clothes. He'd been at it for almost forty-eight hours, and she was asking him for more.

"I'll take the night shift," Fradella offered, "and you'll get some shuteye," he added, looking at Michowsky. "You do what you've got to do," he then said, looking at Tess.

"Uh-huh," she acknowledged, wolfing down the rest of the fries on her plate. "I'll get things moving on the shipment issue, then go back to the precinct. The night's still young, and something tells me the Taker of Lives isn't taking the day off today."

Her phone rang, and she looked at the caller ID with a sense of foreboding. "It's Donovan," she announced, then took the call on speaker. "Hey, D, what have you got?"

"They're releasing Koester," he announced impassibly. "He's alibied out, rock solid, for the night Estelle was attacked. There wasn't any trace of high-tech stuff on his computer."

"Yeah, I expected that. What else?"

"The streaming site just went live again," D said, exasperation seeping in his voice. "He's announcing the show will start shortly."

"What's it saying, exactly?" she asked.

"It says, 'We're about to begin, with you in charge. Get ready to vote for your favorite means of entertainment.' That's it."

"Okay, call me the moment that changes. We need to know what the hell he's planning to do this time."

"Or what he's already done," Fradella added.

"Yeah, you're right," she replied, frowning. "Where are we with creating the short list of potential targets?"

"Almost there," Donovan replied. "For every iteration of the model I'm building, I run simulations, and I expect it to return the victims he's already attacked at the top of the list. That's how I validate the model. I believe we're close, but I still need a little more time."

"We don't have a little more time, Donovan," she snapped, turning heads in the bar and earning herself a disapproving glance from Cat. "We need to know who he'll attack next."

Silence ensued, the air dead, as if the conversation had ended.

"I'm sorry, D," she said, lowering her voice. "I know how hard you're trying."

"Yeah," he eventually replied dryly, "or so you say."

"No, I mean it. You deserve better."

He just hung up, leaving her frustrated and ashamed. They were all tired, but that was no excuse. She drank some lemonade to quench her thirst and barely felt its taste.

Michowsky and Fradella stood, ready to go. Fradella handed her his car keys.

"We'll swing by the precinct and get another car," he said, then squeezed her shoulder briefly. "Take care, all right?"

The moment they were gone, Cat took Fradella's seat across the table from her.

"What's on your mind?" he asked in a low, understanding voice.

She sighed, looking at his creased face, at the kindness in his eyes. There wasn't enough time to explain everything that was wrong in her life, no matter how much she wished she could take that time and just unload her burden for a while.

"I don't know how he's doing it," she said instead. "This... bad guy I'm trying to catch, he seems to always know ahead of time what people will do, with precision."

Cat grinned. "Sounds familiar, doesn't it?"

"What do you mean?"

"Isn't that what you do? Know ahead of time what people will do? Anticipate the scumbag's next move?"

"Yeah, but he's not like me," she replied. "He's playing everyone; he organizes these votes but knows ahead of time what people will vote for and how many."

"What's so unexpected about that?" he asked, leaning closer to her across the table. "If I'd have these folks here, in the bar, vote for their favorite beer, do you think the result would be a surprise for me? I see what they drink every day. It's right there, in front of me."

She tilted her head, looking at Cat, while an uneven smile stretched the corner of her lips. Could it be that simple?

She stood and put a smooch on the man's cheek. "Cat, you're amazing."

39

Scenarios

Tess drove up and down the street, slowly, observing, then pulled in at the curb in front of SAC Pearson's house and looked around one more time. No one seemed to have the house under surveillance. She couldn't see any parked vehicles with the driver waiting inside, anywhere on the entire street.

Then she looked at the Pearson residence windows, all shrouded in darkness, trying to ascertain whether everyone had already gone to bed, or if the windows were covered with completely opaque draperies. After her eyes adjusted to the darkness, she noticed a TV flicker coming from one of the lower-level windows, just a sliver of it, barely visible along the center of the window, where the curtain panels should've overlapped.

She texted Pearson and he appeared within moments, tying a colorful bathrobe with a double knot and walking briskly toward the Explorer in oversized house slippers. Then he opened the passenger door but didn't climb inside.

"Come on in, Winnett, what the hell."

"No, sir, I don't think that's wise," she replied, barely above a whisper.

Maybe it was her imagination or the dim ceiling light in the SUV, but it seemed Pearson turned paler. He climbed inside and closed the door, then turned to her with a stern look on his face. "I'm listening."

"There's a shipment of Colombian drugs heading into port on Monday," she said, continuing to keep her voice down, just in case. "About a hundred million dollars' worth of the stuff."

He nodded once, slowly, while a deep frown ridged his forehead. "Is this the case you're working on, the evolving serial killer? I'm not sure I follow."

"No, sir, this is the other case... the green folder."

His jaw slacked for a brief moment. "Carrillo?"

"Yes."

"And how's my daughter connected to all this?"

"She's their insurance policy, in case they get heat from anyone."

His chin trembled in anger; he pressed his lips together and clenched his fists, then appeared to make an effort to control himself. "This is ridiculous.

What do they think I could do if the Coast Guard inspects their cargo?"

"Make calls, invent some undercover operation that supersedes their seizure, that kind of thing."

"It doesn't work that way," he replied, raising his voice a little.

She nodded once. "They don't know that. They watch a few episodes of *Narcos* and believe they're smart."

"Do you have all the information?"

"We have the date and the approximate time the coke will be transferred on a Miami-registered boat, the name of that boat, and the names of several players. We need to seize that shipment, sir."

He shot her an angry glare that softened within a moment. "He's going to have my daughter... Do you realize that? Jeez, Winnett, what the hell are we doing?"

"You taught me, sir," she replied calmly, "many years ago, when I was a rookie. You said, 'Keep your cool and go over the scenarios, one by one. Use the one you hate the least.' That's what we're going to do." She paused for a moment, letting it sink in. "There are two boats in play. The *Hermosa*, a thirty-four-foot center console, reserved for Carrillo's fishing trip with Lily." As she spoke, she showed him the images attached to an email sent by Michowsky earlier. "Then there's the *Reina del Mar*, a forty-three-foot, high-speed, fishing yacht equipped with five, four-hundred, horsepower engines. This boat will take over the drugs somewhere at sea from a Colombian vessel and head into port with the crowds returning from Memorial Day activities on the water. That's their plan."

"It pains me to say it, but it isn't half bad," Pearson muttered. "Coast Guard won't know what to inspect first in so much traffic. Nevertheless, I can't leave my daughter in their hands, Winnett, you know I can't."

"If something happens, and she can't board the *Hermosa* as planned, they'll know something's off and they'll disappear, make plans for another day, another way. We won't be able to make the bust."

"No, Winnett, no. I can't," he muttered, lowering his head. "There's a line I'll never cross."

"What if we trail the *Hermosa* from a distance? Put satellite eyes on them?"

"How long does it take to put a bullet through someone's head?" he snapped, and his raised voice resonated powerfully in the closed confinement of the vehicle.

She waited for a moment, thinking the question might be rhetorical, an opening of a statement he needed to make. He looked at her intently, waiting for an answer.

"Seconds," she replied calmly. "Even less."

"Can you be on that boat within seconds, to stop the bullet from Carrillo's weapon?"

She sighed, a long breath loaded with frustration. He was right, except for one detail.

"Why would he keep her at gunpoint?" she asked. "He's got her as leverage, ready to use however many different times they want to do this."

"Do you actually believe this could work?" Pearson asked. "Do you think it's a risk worth taking?"

"No… just going through the scenarios I really hate," she admitted after a while. No one had the right to ask the man to put his daughter's life on the line for a drug bust. "The people on the *Reina* might call Carrillo by sat phone the moment Coast Guard approaches it, and then it would be too late to hope we get to Lily on time. He wouldn't immediately shoot her, because he needs the leverage, but hostage situations at sea are very difficult to control."

He didn't take his eyes off hers but didn't argue anymore. There was no need; she was arguing his point for him. She hated to admit it, but leaving Lily in Carrillo's hands for the Monday fishing trip was not an option. She couldn't think of one single scenario that ended well.

"Now give me an alternative that you hate less, Winnett. One that keeps my daughter out of harm's way, but still gets us those damn drugs."

"Could you tell Lily what's going on? Could she handle it?"

"She's desperately in love with Carrillo and trusts me less and less since she sensed I'm against their relationship. I was quite vocal expressing my opinion of him; I didn't pull any punches." He ran his hand over his shiny scalp once or twice, troubled. "If I were to bring her in on this, the first thing she'd do is call Carrillo to confront him."

"And we lose the shipment, everything. We won't have a single piece of evidence, just hearsay."

"Right," he agreed. "I hate this scenario way too much to use it. What else have you got?"

She started thinking about different things she could do, some of them really outside the procedural box, not necessarily easy to share or explain to a ranking federal agent like Pearson. Then she had an interesting idea, more like a hunch, and a tiny smile fluttered on her lips.

"What if Carrillo were to cancel the fishing trip, be otherwise engaged the day after tomorrow?"

Pearson's eyes lit up. "That would work, admitting you can pull that off from the inside of the drug-smuggling organization."

Tess's smile bloomed into a full grin. "I'll get busy then."

"Do I need to know?" Pearson asked, his hand on the door handle.

"It's better if you don't, sir," Tess replied. "Have a good night."

She drove off, leaving Pearson at the curb looking at her with a dazzled yet hopeful expression on his face. She floored it as soon as she exited the residential neighborhood and went straight for the interstate.

When her phone rang, she expected to see Michowsky or Fradella's number on the car display, or Donovan's, given the late hour, but it was a number she didn't recognize.

"Winnett," she said, as soon as she accepted the call.

"This is Kurt Briggs, Deanna's fiancé," the man said.

"Ah, yes, Mr. Briggs. What can I do for you?"

"I... managed to watch that video," Kurt said, his voice breaking under the load of pain and anger. "The man's gait, the way he handled himself, I believe I've seen that exact gait before. It seems very familiar."

"Who did you recognize?" Tess asked.

"That's exactly the damn problem, Agent Winnett," he said, sounding upset with himself. "I can't remember. All I know is that I've seen that gait before, and that means I know what to do."

"This is very helpful," Tess replied. "It confirms the killer was part of Deanna's entourage. I strongly suggest you don't get involved in any way beyond this point."

"I will invite all the people Deanna and I knew, one by one without exceptions, to dinner, lunch, drinks, or whatever they'll accept, and when I see that gait again, I'll know."

"Mr. Briggs, why don't you let us do our job? Approaching the killer can be dangerous. He won't hesitate, while you might tip your hand. You might make him disappear."

"Agent Winnett, I gamble with millions of dollars every day and I don't break a sweat. I can hold my own."

"Money doesn't want to kill you, Mr. Briggs, nor did it murder your fiancée."

"I'll be fine, ma'am, I promise you that. I won't do a thing; just buy him lunch, let him express his sympathies, then once I know who it was, I'll walk away and call you."

"All right, but promise me this: before you start inviting people, make a list of everyone you and Deanna both knew, and share that with me. As soon as you can, please."

He hesitated for a long moment, then replied dryly. "Okay, I will." Then he hung up, leaving Tess to wonder if it could be that simple.

40

A Favor

Tess pulled over at the curb in front of the Bartlett residence, making the bodyguard standing in front of the door straighten his posture. He was a tall guy, probably six-three, all muscle and attitude. He wore a jacket at least two numbers too large, to accommodate the size of his biceps and the double harness holster he was wearing nonchalantly. His bare scalp shone in the moonlight, and Tess wondered if he shaved his head every morning, or if he was already bald at his young age.

She approached, showing her badge. "Special Agent Tess Winnett to see Mr. Bartlett, please."

"Do you have an appointment? It's late."

"Now, please," she said firmly.

He spoke briefly into the radio, not taking his eyes off her, as if she were the enemy. A moment later, the door opened, and Sidney Bartlett walked outside.

"Agent Winnett," he greeted her, "I've been expecting your call for a while."

She looked intently at the bodyguard, then at Bartlett, but Bartlett didn't react. She shrugged and turned to leave. "Too bad the condition of your porch has changed so much since we last spoke."

Bartlett turned toward the bodyguard and made a quick dismissive gesture with his head. The muscle obeyed promptly, disappearing inside the house without a single word.

"Better," Tess said, "thank you."

"Okay, let's hear it," Bartlett said. "Who killed my daughter?"

"I promise you'll be the first to know when we know, and we are getting close to finding out," she said, raising her hands to pacify Bartlett, whose expression had swiftly turned to intense disappointment. "I'm here to ask for your assistance to make that happen sooner."

"Anything," he replied coldly.

"There's a certain man who, um, should be assigned to take care of some other business over the next few days," she said, pretending she didn't notice Bartlett's raised eyebrow. "We keep stumbling into him and he's slowing our investigation."

"Is he related to the investigation? A suspect?"

"Oh, no, absolutely not," she replied, underlining her response with a hand gesture. "Only he keeps some of our key people busy with his antics, instead of letting me have full access to the team and get them to focus entirely on your daughter's case."

Bartlett frowned. "What exactly would you like me to do, Agent Winnett?"

"If he could be taken out of the picture for a couple of days, say... reassigned, maybe, that would work perfectly for me. I don't believe the investigation will take more than that. We're close."

"And when exactly would you like this man to be busy elsewhere?" Bartlett asked calmly, and Tess felt a cold shiver down her spine. Was she putting out a contract on Carrillo? She definitely hoped not; she'd better make damn sure she wasn't.

She hesitated one more moment, thinking hard. Would telling Bartlett about Carrillo jeopardize the drug bust? She didn't believe so... Law enforcement didn't ask for smugglers to be reassigned if they were under suspicion; they just busted them or hung a tail on them until the bust could happen. She was ninety-nine percent sure the drug delivery would go as planned, only without Carrillo in play.

"Tomorrow he can still do whatever he wants, but Monday morning he should already be out of our way, if you get my drift. On Monday, I need that team to be laser-focused, Mr. Bartlett."

"Absolutely," Bartlett replied. "Consider him reassigned."

"Just to be clear, I only need him reassigned for a few days, not... permanently."

"Understood, Agent Winnett. What's his name?"

She looked straight into Bartlett's eyes as she said his name, ready to catch any flicker of recognition. "Esteban Carrillo, twenty-eight years old, from Miami."

There was a tiny flinch in his eyelids, and probably his pupils dilated too, but it was hard to see in the moonlight. Tess had no doubt; Bartlett knew Carrillo.

"I'll make sure Mr. Carrillo isn't distracting your team any longer, Agent Winnett."

"Thank you," she said, shaking the hand he had extended, then turning to leave. As she did, she caught a glimpse of reflected light coming from the tree across the driveway, next to the street. She froze, then moved her head slowly back and forth, trying to capture that flicker of reflected moonlight again.

"What is it?" Bartlett asked, to her dismay holding a nine mil Sig in his hand.

"Jeez, put that gun away," she urged him. "Now," she insisted, seeing his hesitation.

He complied, shoving the gun in his belt and pulling his shirt over it.

"My apologies, Agent Winnett. After everything that's happened, we're all a little jumpy. What did you see?"

"There," she pointed at the tree. "See it? Something is reflecting the light. Maybe your bodyguard could check it out, and whatever he finds, he should remove with gloves on," she added, offering a pair of blue latex gloves she fished out of her pocket.

Bartlett knocked on the door twice, and the bodyguard appeared instantly. A moment later, he recovered a small camera from the tree, and Tess held out an evidence bag to collect it.

"It was still working," the guard said. "I turned it off."

Bartlett grabbed the guard by his lapel and shoved him against the wall. "How the hell was this possible? Find out."

"My guess is that's been sitting up there for a while, probably since before April 15," Tess intervened, and Bartlett let go of the man's lapel. "Our technicians will look into it."

She turned to leave again, and this time almost made it to the Explorer when her phone rang, displaying Donovan's name on the screen.

"Better get in front of an internet-connected device pronto," he said. "The unsub's site is up, and you won't believe what he's asking viewers to vote for."

41

Time Gap

Tess rushed through the doors and up the stairs to the precinct conference room, then hooked up the laptop to the TV screen and powered everything up, out of breath and feeling a sense of doom, cringing in dread of what she was about to discover on that screen.

She clicked on the link Donovan had placed in her messenger and the Taker's site filled the screen. She dialed Donovan and put him on speaker.

"Tell me we're set up to control this," she said, grinding the words angrily between her teeth.

"To some extent we are," he replied. "The short list model isn't finalized yet; I'm still not close enough when running simulations against the already known victims. This new case will bring more information and it will help, but—"

"But she'll have to die to make that happen," Tess snapped.

A long moment of silence filled the air. "Most likely she's already dead, Winnett, whoever *she* might be."

She wanted to scream at Donovan, but she knew better; he wasn't the one to blame, nor was it his job to make her feel better. Not to mention she'd recently apologized for her bad temper already, and that was enough.

"We're set up with several identities who can post on the Taker's site, under a number of profiles. I've started poking at him, but for now he won't engage. I have a truck driver from Louisiana, a self-proclaimed, antisocial SOB; some other guy calling himself the midnight rapist, and so on. I'll send you the list, if you'd like, but you catch my drift."

She scrolled through the list of comments and found the accounts Donovan was referencing. So far, he'd been moderate in his comments; he'd challenged the veridity of the streamed materials, asked the Taker to show some courage and identify himself, show his real face, stuff like that.

The Taker of Lives was too smart for that; it was never going to work.

She needed to pour gasoline on the fire of his bleeding ego.

"Cat told me something today," Tess said. "He—"

"That hippie bartender from... what's that place?" Donovan asked.

"Since when is he an expert?"

"Since he's been staring at people for decades, while they drink themselves under the table, foregoing their frontal lobe function on a regular basis."

"Ah, interesting," he replied, no longer sounding dismissive of Cat's input. She could hear the smile and the curiosity in his voice.

"Cat said he'd have no problem figuring out what his drunks would vote for, if they were asked to pick their favorite booze. He stares at that data every day, and it never changes."

"You're saying…?"

"The unsub has a background in psychology or sociology. It's possible he worked with inmates, or studied the behaviors of social groups, entities, or representative segments of the population, the type who would most likely troll the Dark Web for sites like his. Does that help narrow it down?"

She could hear Donovan typing fast, and she held her breath.

"No, nothing really pops up," he replied.

She turned her attention to the screen. "Then let's work with what we have."

She scrolled back up, from the comment list into the streaming frame of the site, taking in every detail.

"What the hell?" she muttered. "He can't possibly have known this."

The screen displayed a quick invitation to vote, displayed in the same white font on black background, followed by three buttons. The invitation read, "Our guest star is guilty of condescending arrogance. How would you like her punished tonight?"

The three buttons were clipart images with a text label. The first option showed a symbolic photograph, the kind of pictogram used by online photo sharing sites, and the label read, "Expose Her Secrets." The second option showed the sketched contour of a female head, the kind that social media platforms use as a default avatar until people customize their profiles, but the Taker had crossed it with two diagonal lines. The label read, "Destroy Her Image." Finally, the third one showed the pictogram of a handgun, and the label read, "Take Her Life."

She felt a rush of heated blood course through her veins, as she processed all the information. Could he have known that his sick viewers would want that girl dead? How could he? What kind of world is that, where people can vote in the millions to end an innocent girl's life?

The Taker asked for five million votes to support whatever choice the public wanted, but the third option had already collected well over seven million votes, and the counter was moving so fast that the last two digits were illegible. The first two options hadn't reached a million votes each; apparently, humans had turned into a bloodthirsty, violent species; at least a significant percentage of them.

Tess forced air into her lungs, then let it out sharply. "Okay, let's work this. Can a viewer vote for more than one option?"

Donovan took a second, then replied, "No. Only the first vote is recorded."

"That means each of these votes are distinct individuals?"

"Precisely. Just like yesterday."

She swallowed a curse and stared at the screen, observing, analyzing, playing with scenarios in her mind.

"And we can't track down these bastards, you said."

"No," Donovan replied. "The vast majority of them are visiting the site via encrypted browsing, and even if you could, filing millions of lawsuits just isn't feasible. Not all are American, you know. Not to mention, most of them probably think this is just a weird, perverted show."

"Just like herds," she muttered, and at that moment, Fradella rushed through the door. "Didn't expect to see you back so soon," she said. "What happened?"

"Nothing. Michowsky said he's fine on his own, and I'm needed here."

"What do you mean, just like herds?" Donovan asked.

"The larger the herd, the smaller the individual's probability of being attacked by a predator," she explained. "That means, the more votes the unsub collects, the more likely are the reluctant viewers to vote, believing they're safe. Unfortunately, they really are safe from prosecution."

"What do you want to do?" Fradella asked.

She hesitated for a moment, then replied, her voice filled with fierce determination. "I'm going to make this sick son of a bitch regret the day he was born. D, why don't you write a comment, saying, 'Ha, ha, we know you're a fake. You ain't streaming live. Yesterday's guest star was killed ten days ago. No balls on you.' Got that?"

"You sure about this?" Donovan asked.

"As I'll ever be," she replied, feeling nervous tension grab her shoulders in a vise and squeezing.

A moment later, the unsub had replied. "Real art is ageless and timeless, my friend."

"He doesn't care," Fradella said.

"He does," Tess said, "otherwise, he wouldn't've responded at all. Say this, 'So you say, but your sack's empty. Got guts? Stream live!'"

Fradella whistled. "Where did that come from?"

She threw a quick smile his way, a little embarrassed. "Now use your other identities to vote for this statement, D. Vote it up as high as you can." She saw a bunch of votes appear, endorsing the challenge, but she still wanted more. "Doesn't the FBI have a click farm of sorts somewhere?"

"They do?" Fradella asked.

"Don't think so," Donovan replied. "But I'll add more accounts if you need me to."

"Yup, add them. Now post another comment, saying, 'Show us proof it's live. We're not idiots.'"

Within moments, the message collected about twenty thumbs up.

"I'm not doing this," Donovan said. "I'm doing part of it, but I'm not the only one voting."

"Excellent, they're starting to follow," Tess replied, keeping her eyes riveted to the screen. "Now say in a new comment, 'Right. If you're really live, you should take requests for action,' then add a winking smiley."

A few seconds later, the unsub replied, "Great idea. How many votes can I get for that? Show me what you can do!" The speed at which the votes collected increased visibly.

"Damn," Tess muttered. Nothing seemed to faze the unsub. He kept on being calm, rational, organized, and every word he typed and every action he took confirmed the profile of a deadly, cold-blooded psychopath. One who was almost as good as she was at profiling people, at understanding the drivers of human behavior.

"Do you think we're reaching him?" Fradella asked, powering up his own laptop.

"We should be," Tess replied. "By all the rules in the book, we should be. For all we know, he could be punching a wall right now, screaming in anger." She paced the room restlessly. "Or he could be lying back, relaxed, getting ready to stream the video of something he's done who knows when, and we don't even know about it. We need to close the gap, guys. Any ideas welcome."

"What gap?" Donovan asked.

"Between the time of the assault and the time of the streaming. Maybe that's what this weekend is all about. Have you noticed how the time gap is narrowing? The first victim, Christina Bartlett, was assaulted on April 15, yet he didn't tell her about the photos online until three days ago; that's almost six weeks. Then Estelle, assaulted on May 10, was notified of the exposure two days ago. Only two weeks after Christina, not even that. Yesterday, we had Deanna, and the video of her murder was released only ten days after the fact. Now we have—" she gestured toward the TV.

"You think this one's been attacked more recently?" Fradella said.

"Definitely so," Tess said. She sighed, sending her frustration away on a long breath of air. "Let's talk short list. What's going on there, Donovan? What's the holdup?"

"I've managed to create a model for his victim selection, but when I run it, I only achieve sixty-seven percent accuracy."

"What do you mean?"

"I mean, I can make the model give me Christina and Deanna, but not Estelle, and I can't understand why. I've added the respective social media following numbers for the individuals, and filtered out duplicates, as much as I could identify them. Most people don't know, or don't care about protecting their privacy."

"Just a second," Fradella intervened, "you said you've eliminated duplicates? Why? How?"

"Let's say Jane Doe follows Deanna on Facebook, on Twitter, and on Instagram. I've only counted her once. If people are what the unsub is after, fame, as the profile indicates, that's what he'd do."

"Um, nope," Tess replied. "He only cares about perceptions, not reality. People don't mean anything to him. The more *perceived* fame the victims have, the more pissed off the unsub is, motivated to destroy their lives. Ego doesn't have that much logic; a bruised ego is nothing but raw, raging emotion."

Donovan typed fast, and Tess could've sworn she'd heard him cuss under his breath, an absolute first for the brilliant analyst. A minute or two later, he stopped clacking on the keyboard. "It will take some doing, to revert the duplicates removal from the profile analyzer, but I'll do it ASAP. You might be on to something, Winnett."

"Okay," she replied. "Let's post another message and raise more hell. Say this: 'What a cowardly way to act, with the women drugged, subdued. Are you that powerless? Afraid of a woman's scream? Or are you really into corpses?'"

"All right," Donovan said, then typed the message that immediately posted online. "Are we the least bit concerned we might be pushing him into becoming more violent?"

"We are, and we aren't," Tess replied, watching the thumbs up accumulate on the newly posted prod. "So far, he's streamed crimes that had already been committed; there's no risk with those. How else are we going to catch him, unless we enrage him into making a mistake?"

"Are we?" Fradella asked.

She sighed, a bitter exhalation matching a growing frown on her brow. "Don't ask."

The screen shifted to a quick animation of theater curtains being pulled, and a video streaming frame came into sight. Tess and Fradella huddled closer to the TV screen, trying to make out the victim's face.

The setting showed the same kind of layout as before: a young woman, naked on her bed, unconscious. The room was relatively large and neat, decorated with taste, with Italian furniture and fixtures in modern style, bright colors, glossy finishes, and brushed metal. The space was artificially lit, with projectors that sent light from behind the camera to focus on certain areas of her body. It was almost artistic, although Tess hated to admit it. No trace of daylight came into the room, as attested by the window covered with modern, remote-controlled treatments.

"Guys, we have a problem," Tess groaned. "She's a brunette. That simple fact expands our victimology threefold."

"I saw that," Donovan replied. "I've removed the blonde hair as a physical feature and our list of potentials is up to almost eight thousand names."

They watched as the unsub's silhouette, clad in black, shiny latex, positioned the victim on the bed, then stood to the side, as if admiring his handiwork. He then took a handgun from his duffel bag and checked the magazine, removed and inserted it with expert movements, then pulled the slide back and immediately released it. The weapon was ready to fire.

"Talk to me, guys," she said, already knowing there was nothing much they could do.

"The gun is a Smith and Wesson M2.0 nine mil, equipped with a silencer," Fradella said. "Maybe if we enhance some of this video, we could grab a serial number."

"On it," Donovan confirmed.

Then the unsub put the gun aside and grabbed one of the vials he'd placed on the night table, just as he'd done in Deanna's case. Doc Rizza had told them that the vial contained ammonia inhalants, or smelling salts, meant to revive the victim quickly. He approached the girl and covered her mouth with one hand, running the vial under her nose. She gasped and flailed her arms, trying to grab on to something, but the unsub's grip was strong. She stared at the killer with eyes open wide in terror, and he slowly removed his hand from her mouth.

That was the first time they'd had the opportunity to see her face.

"Got the screenshot," Donovan announced, "running facial recognition now."

Then the unsub took his gun and pointed it at the victim, while placing his left index finger at his mouth, urging her to stay silent. She nodded once or twice, her eyes rounded in fear, pleading.

"Please," she must have whispered, based on the movement of her lips, but the audio didn't catch much of her voice.

The unsub took aim at her head and stretched his arms in a firing stance, supporting his weapon with both hands.

"Please, I'll do anything," she said, now audible on the video, while tears streamed down her cheeks.

The screen went dark just as the weapon fired, the sound of the silenced shot seeming so loud it made Tess jump out of her skin.

"I can't take this anymore!" Tess shouted, pushing aside a chair so forcefully it slammed into the wall where it left a mark. "We sit here and watch the damn TV, eat whatever he's feeding us. Don't tell me he gets away with it again."

"Maybe he didn't kill her," Fradella offered. "We would've known about it. The video cut before we could see for sure. Maybe she's still alive."

"We don't know that," she replied, a dark shade of frustration seeping into her voice. "We don't know a damn thing!"

42

Haley

Exhaustion was starting to show its effects, clouding Tess's judgment and fueling her anger. Since Christina's suicide, she'd caught little shuteye and even less sustenance. She'd pushed herself, thinking one more hour, one more suspect interview, and she'd catch the perp and be able to resume her planned vacation.

Nothing of that mattered anymore; she barely felt the hunger, just a light tremor in her muscles. As for fatigue, it had become her second nature. She started a new coffee cup in the machine and closed her eyes for a moment, blocking the image of that dark TV screen that was bound to haunt her for a while.

What was she missing? Never before had she felt so helpless in chasing a suspect. She'd never felt like the unsub could continue killing for as long as he pleased, and still get away with it. All the time she'd spent investigating the Taker of Lives, he'd always been the one in control.

What was she missing?

A bothersome feeling tugged at the edges of her tired mind, telling her she'd overlooked one critical detail. Okay, she was willing to accept that, but what was it? Had they rushed to any of the profile conclusions? The victimology was proven wrong, just that night, by the latest victim's hair color. What if she'd made other mistakes, other assumptions that were wrong? Two data points don't make a trend, she knew. Apparently, neither do three. Then, how many do make a trend, really? How many victims did they need to be positively sure of their profile?

A knock sounded on the conference room glass wall, and she opened her eyes. Captain Cepeda stood outside the room with a gloomy expression on his face. She checked the time; it was after two in the morning. What was Cepeda still doing here?

She opened the conference room door. "Come on in," she invited the captain.

"No need. You have another victim," he announced.

"Where? Who?" her mind jumped straight to the brunette they just saw on TV. Maybe the transmission had been live after all, and the time gap had closed.

"Downstairs, in the lobby interview room."

She rushed downstairs and Fradella followed. She opened the door expecting to see that young, dark-haired beauty. Instead, a man in full military garb stood when they walked in and extended his hand. Another man, someone she recognized as a Miami-Dade detective, remained seated but waved in their direction, then flashed his badge.

"I'm Detective Decker, Miami-Dade, and this is Jorje Estrada," he said, pushing a file across the table in her direction. The file bore the stamp of Miami-Dade County Sheriff's Department. "His sister was shot two days ago, in their home, while she slept."

Tess looked at the young man, whose windburned skin and calloused hands told her he was active military, probably just returned from deployment overseas. He wore Army colors and insignia, and she could still see the fine grains of desert sand clinging to his uniform and filling the room with an unfamiliar smell of dry, barren lands.

His eyes were hollow and bloodshot, and his cheeks stained where tears had rolled until recently. He struggled speaking, his mouth gaped open in an attempt to articulate words.

She opened the file and looked at the crime scene photo attached to the report. It matched the young brunette they'd seen on the streaming video. A bullet had entered her forehead dead center.

"What was her name?" Tess asked, looking at Jorje.

"Haley," he replied. "She was twenty-two years old." He clenched his fists. "I... raised her," he added, choked with tears. "Our parents died when she was little, and Grandpa took us in, but I raised her. Now she's gone, and Grandpa too. I came back as soon as they told me."

Tess frowned and looked at the Miami-Dade detective.

"The grandfather found her in the morning and called 911. Then he stroked out before anyone could get there. Massive brain aneurism, the report said."

"I'm very sorry for your loss," Tess said, watching Jorje intently. "Do you know of anyone who would've had a reason to—"

"No one," he interrupted. "Everyone loved Haley."

"What did she do for a living?" Fradella asked.

"She had her own reality TV show on cable," Jorje replied. "I wasn't much of a fan, but it made her happy. That's the only thing that mattered."

"Who would've had access to the property that late at night?" Tess asked. "Who would she have opened the door for?"

He shook his head, then riveted his eyes to the floor and didn't say a word.

She exchanged a quick glance with Fradella. There wasn't much they could learn from Jorje Estrada. His sister was nothing but one of a serial killer's victims, no rhyme or reason.

"Thank you for coming in, Mr. Estrada."

"Why?" he asked, looking straight at Tess. "Why does someone do that?" he looked briefly in Decker's direction. "He told me something about a serial killer. Is that true?"

Tess knew better than to confirm that fact to a grief-stricken brother and grandson.

"We will investigate and let you know as soon as we learn something."

She shook the young man's hand and left the room after thanking Decker for the late-night visit and for sharing the file. Then she rushed upstairs, eager to dive into the information found in that file.

She set the file on the table, ready to plunge in, but then a thought crossed through her mind. Whether mission oriented or power assertive, the unsub wanted to be known, respected, understood. He wanted his voice heard and remembered, with accuracy, for the right reasons. A crooked smile stretched her lips. Someone as rational, intellectual, and controlled as the unsub would balk and shudder with disgust at the thought of being mistaken for a banal lust killer, an animal, a garden-variety pervert who has issues controlling his sexual urges.

She typed a new comment on the Taker's website.

"Why are you doing this?" her entry read. "I don't get it. You can't get off without killing women? That's fucking lame, brah."

She stared at the screen for several long minutes, but the unsub didn't respond.

43

Baiting the Trap

Tess entered the morgue with a spring in her step, so focused on Haley and her file that she didn't react to the cold air and the faint smell of disinfectant in Doc Rizza's fiefdom. She made eye contact with Doc and headed over to his desk. Through the window behind him, the early morning sunlight was beginning to throw darts of light, carrying hues of red and purple. A new day, the same old killer.

"I have Donovan patched in," Doc Rizza said. His voice sounded just as terrible and tired as he looked. He hadn't shaved in a couple of days, and his stubble was gray for the most part, underlining the wrinkled chubbiness of his jowls.

"Fradella too," she heard the cop's voice on the speakerphone.

"Good," she said, then took a deep breath. "I want to know why we didn't hear about Haley the moment her body was found. Didn't we have an alert on murders in Florida, with her parameters?"

"Yes, her parameters," Donovan replied, "only she was excluded because of hair color."

"You've got to be kidding me!" Tess snapped.

"Computers are dumb like that, you know. They do what you *tell* them to do, not what you want them to do. We had confirmed victimology and we used that."

"Then I want us to be notified of any murder that takes place in Florida, regardless of parameters, the moment a body is found."

"Last year we had about twelve hundred murders in Florida," Donovan announced.

"That's three per day. Let's have everything hit our inbox. I don't want to make the same mistake again."

"Speaking of inbox, you have an interesting email I think you should read," Donovan said, and Tess thought she heard Fradella chuckle.

"You've been poking around again, D?"

"Just being of assistance."

"Yeah, right," she mumbled, then took out her phone and checked the latest messages.

An email from Kurt Briggs, Deanna's fiancé, read, "Agent Winnett, these are all the names I could think of, and any information I have about them. These people knew both Deanna and me and have interacted with us in the past year. Forgive me if I won't sit idle waiting for you; I'll start meeting with them today."

The email was dated that morning, Sunday, May 27, at 4:27AM, and it had an attachment, a spreadsheet with names. She remembered most of the names; they'd conducted background checks for some of them, interviewed others, but found nothing suspicious.

"Take the list and run it," Tess said, "full background, financials, whereabouts on the date and time of Deanna's murder, the works. Track vehicle GPS where you can, cell phones too."

"Already on it," Fradella confirmed.

She ran both hands through her shoulder-length hair, moving it off her face and, for a moment, was tempted to grab a few strands and pull. Time was running out; it wouldn't be long before the Taker of Lives would announce yet another so-called "live" performance, and they still had nothing.

Michowsky's concerns came to her mind; what happened to good, old-fashioned police work, and murders that made sense? They were forever gone, a phase in humankind's evolution toward depravity that would never return. Just like him, she'd rather be barging through doors and interrogating suspects, than dealing in statistics and analysis and waiting in front of the TV for the Taker to strike again. The reality show from hell was about to start.

"Doc, run us through the autopsy findings," she said, forcing a breath of cool, morgue air into her lungs and pushing Haley's file toward him.

He pushed the file back toward her; most likely he had his own copy by now. "Single gunshot wound to the head, nine-millimeter, bullet intact and ready for ballistics match. I estimate the weapon was fired from about four feet away." He looked at his notes, flipping through several pages. "The same mix of chemical restraints: Rohypnol to start, then the inhalant, followed by an anesthetic shot, and finally, the ammonia to wake her up. No signs of trauma, but this time there's some evidence of sexual assault."

"*Some* evidence?" Tess asked.

"There's perimortem inflammation and light bruising consistent with vigorous sexual activity around the time of death, but there's no vaginal tearing; that could be explained by the drugs in her system. The findings are inconclusive, but if I were a betting man, I'd say she was raped, and she didn't fight back the assault; she wasn't awake for it."

The Taker was escalating on a path she had not anticipated. "TOD?"

"Time of death was May 26, at 3:30AM."

"How about the grandfather?"

"Frank Cantrell, seventy-two," Doc read from his copy of the file. "Traces of Rohypnol in his system, and a ruptured brain aneurism in the left temporal lobe. No other relevant findings."

She opened the file and read Detective Decker's report. Miami-Dade County Crime Scene Unit had gone over the scene in detail, pored over every fiber, every particle, and found nothing that didn't belong. Just like before, some areas had been wiped clean of fingerprints, but Tess stopped short before requesting CSU to get back in there, searching for residual trace evidence in the areas that had been swiped clean. There wasn't enough time; the Taker of Lives was already on the prowl, about to end another innocent life. Or worse; maybe that had already happened.

"Please pull all the murders that took place since Haley's time of death, see if there's a match, another victim we don't know about."

"Already thought of that, and there's no one who fits," Donovan replied. "In the past two days, we had a couple of gang shootings involving drug dealers, an eighty-year-old male bludgeoned to death in his home for a bunch of trinkets, another burglary gone wrong that ended up killing a family of four, and an infant accidentally killed by a reckless nanny. Nothing fits."

"Crap..." she muttered. What was the Taker of Lives planning? Since he'd started his online perverted show, he'd had one performance per night, every night at midnight. He was going to have one tonight; she was sure of it. She glanced quickly at the wall clock hanging above the lab table, an old, black-and-white radio clock dating back at least thirty years. It was almost seven, and that meant they had only a few hours left before the nightmare started again.

"I posted a comment a few hours ago," Tess said. "Has he replied or engaged in any way?"

"No," Donovan replied. "I endorsed your message but saw nothing since."

"Let's continue along the same lines, as insulting as possible."

"And say what?"

"How about, 'I know why you're not showing the whole thing live. You're into screwing corpses, aren't you? You want your private time with those chicks.' Then like and support these comments with others like it."

"Okay, you got it," Donovan replied, with only a trace of hesitation in his voice.

"What are you expecting he'll do next, Tess?" Doc Rizza asked.

"Escalate," she replied. "Every night he's grown angrier, deadlier, more determined, more violent. Sometimes, unsubs want to get caught, but this one doesn't. He's building toward something; a certain event, or maybe a specific victim, for whom he wants millions to pay attention. When he reaches what he's after, he'll disappear to never be heard from again, and we'll have nothing."

"He killed Haley yesterday," Fradella said. "That's already escalated. How often can he kill?"

"Keep in mind we're not talking about a lust killer; he doesn't need to build up sexual energy to strike again."

"Okay, but he needs to stalk, figure out access, layouts, home alarm systems, install surveillance, you name it," Fradella said.

"Something tells me his homework is already done, for all the targeted victims. He's too organized."

"Speaking of surveillance," Donovan said, "we heard back from Perez, the technician who screened and removed surveillance equipment from the crime scenes."

"Yeah? What did he find?"

"Two things. One confirms your theory; all installed equipment had been running since mid-April."

"Okay, good to know," Tess replied, frowning slightly. "Go on."

"You're not going to like this. The person who leaked the Taker of Lives moniker was you."

"What?" she said, her voice high-pitched under the shock. "I never told anyone."

"You discussed the Taker by name with Fradella, and the cameras in Estelle Kennedy's home picked it up."

"Argh…" she reacted, then started to pace the cement floor angrily. "Goes to say we shouldn't use these nicknames, period. Not even among ourselves."

She stopped pacing and stared absently at the floor pattern, thinking. The Taker knew she was the investigator on the case. He'd seen her on camera; he'd called her out by name on his site, but what did it mean to him that she'd been the one to name him? The moniker had since become his brand; he was invested in it. He liked it; it was almost like he was proud of it.

"D, please post another comment, this time under my own full name and title."

"Shoot."

"Say this: 'I was wrong to name you the Taker of Lives. I thought you had the courage to do things live, but I was sadly mistaken. You don't deserve it.'"

"Are you sure about this?" Fradella asked. "He might—"

"Come after me? We should be so lucky."

44

Marla's Song

The music blared, and the people who were gathered around the immense pool clapped rhythmically, cheering, dancing, and singing along. Marla walked to the beat, swinging her hips and clacking her four-inch stilettos on the marble tiles, heading toward the gate. She pretended the cameras weren't there; it was easier for her to play her part that way. She waited for her cue, a specific word in the song's lyrics, when she froze in place, hands on her hips, then turned her head to look over her shoulder with an abrupt, exaggerated gesture, throwing her long, blonde hair into the air, a shiny wave of silk that moved on its own, as if it were alive.

Then her husband caught up with her, and, on the beat, grabbed her elbow and turned her around, then leaned over her and kissed her lips. The music stopped, and the crowd erupted in deafening cheers. The camera still rolled, approaching them on sliders, then revolving around the two of them as they were lost in their fiery embrace.

"Cut!" she heard the familiar voice, but instead of letting go, she wrapped her arms tighter around Adam's neck and kissed him again. He responded with torrid urgency, and for a moment she thought of leaving their guests alone for an hour or two and taking her man upstairs for a much-deserved celebration, just the two of them.

"And it's a wrap, you two," someone else said, and several people hollered excitedly. "Whoa, you guys... Get a room!"

She pulled away from Adam, regret for doing so lingering with the taste of his lips on hers, but they had work to do. They always had work to do.

"Thank you, baby," Adam whispered in her ear, "you were awesome."

She didn't particularly enjoy shooting music videos with her husband, but her annoyance with the director's arrogance and the producer's constant nagging were nothing compared with the all-consuming jealousy she'd feel over whatever girl they'd cast in her place. Just imagining his hands on some model or wannabe actress made her blood boil. Hence, she replied with a smile and a quick peck on Adam's lips, and decided to do as many of those videos as they'd want her to.

The video they'd shot tonight was just bonus, a private performance set to reward and entertain their guests, but the cameras were always rolling, here, on stage, everywhere, and the nineteen-year-old was only starting to get used to it. She liked the glamour and the attention though; she relished the compliments and the envy written in women's eyes over her haute couture attire and assorted jewelry, not to mention the man on her arm, voted sexiest man alive only last year. Life was good. No… life was awesome.

She held Adam's hand as they approached the table, set lavishly by the pool and lit by countless candles in sterling silver holders. The crowd continued to cheer, while caterers walked all over carrying trays with glasses of Dom Perignon Brut 1999, bought in bulk for about $400 a bottle. She grabbed a glass and sipped a tiny bit, not crazy for the slightly bitter taste, but wearing a dazzling smile nevertheless.

After all, Adam had won not one, but two Billboard Music Awards: one as a rock artist, the second for his latest album, named *Marla*. She smiled at the thought that Adam had poured all his love for her into those songs, and his public heard it and loved him back. The best-selling song on that album, titled, "The Day You Leave," was thought of by many friends as "Marla's Song," because of how Adam referred to it. He'd written that song in one inspired night by the firepit in their backyard, and he'd proposed to her the same night.

She smiled and waved, then danced a few moments in place, on the rhythm of another favorite song of hers. She clinked glasses and chatted and mingled, more and more aware of the tiredness in her bones, dreaming of the moment she'd kick her shoes off and lay on the bed by her husband's side. She grinned at a wicked thought. Yeah, it felt good to know she was the one to take that sexy guy upstairs, when so many women here were drooling all over themselves whenever he looked their way. *Get lost, bitches! This hunk's mine, all mine.*

Not a moment too soon, they were finally gone, or almost, as the last of them said their goodbyes and waited for their cars to be retrieved by the valet. She walked slowly to the DJ's station and gestured with her long, thin fingers, run across her throat, to cut the music volume. He obliged in some measure, but she repeated the gesture and he cut it to normal listening levels. The party was over.

She kicked off her shoes, glad to feel the cold marble under her feet, and trotted to the caterer's station, waving her empty glass. One of the caterers, a broad-shouldered man wearing a black name tag pinned on the lapel of his white jacket, rushed to open a fresh bottle of Dom.

Marla looked around for Adam, but he was near the front gate, saying goodbye to the film crew, and she knew from experience that could take a while. Many times, what started as casual conversation with those guys ended in a full-blown strategy session for the script and release of the next music video.

She heard the champagne bottle pop and that caught her attention. She turned to look at the caterers, two of them now that the girl who'd been serving drinks all night was also behind that counter. She smiled awkwardly as the girl offered her the chilled glass. She still looked sharp in her starched uniform; after an entire evening of making her way among people while serving food and drinks, not a single stain soiled her white jacket. Impressive.

"Um, Jeff, Angie, thank you both for tonight, you were awesome," she said, reading the names written on their tags. "But you're not going to believe this," Marla added, blushing a little while she pushed the glass away. "I know Dom's supposed to be the best, and all that, but my favorite is that cheap, Italian champagne, Martini Asti."

Jeff looked at her with undisguised surprise. "I don't believe we—"

"You know the one I'm talking about, right?" Marla continued. "They carry it everywhere, even at Walmart."

The two caterers exchanged a quick glance, then Jeff nodded once, and Angie took off, car keys jiggling in her hand.

"It will only take a minute or two, ma'am," Jeff said. "May I offer you something else while you wait?"

She inspected the counter with critical eyes, then she glanced at the devastated buffet. Not much was left.

"Would you happen to have any more of those tiny, little pastries? I know I'm not supposed to touch those, carbs and everything, but I deserve one of those."

Jeff produced promptly a small plate with several small pastries arranged in a half-circle on a paper napkin.

"Or six," she said giggling, taking a pastry and savoring it with her eyes half closed. "This stuff is to die for, Jeff."

The caterer smiled, while sizing her up. His eyes lingered on her body a little longer than she would've wanted, but she was used to that. She wasn't getting the creep vibe from him, so she relaxed a little. What was not to like about that tight, little body of hers?

"If I may ask, ma'am," Jeff said, "how does it feel to have people all over you like that?"

"You mean, like this?" she asked, gesturing to the now empty yard, littered with glasses and plates that the cleaning crew was rushing to collect.

"Yes, ma'am, precisely. How does it feel to be famous?"

She looked at him intently, but he held her gaze while maintaining a polite smile.

"It's cool, I guess. There are times when I wish no one knew me, or both of us, for that matter. Everywhere we go people are like, 'Wow, do you know who that is?' Then they rush to us, tug at our clothes, holler after us, take pictures. Hundreds and hundreds of pictures," she laughed with a tinge of bitterness in her voice.

"I can only imagine how tough it can be, ma'am. I was never famous in any way, and I'll probably never be."

"Trust me, fame is overrated," Marla replied, then took the last pastry from her plate and chewed it for a long moment, savoring its taste. It would probably be months before she dared indulge in another.

She looked for Adam again, still leaning against the counter at the caterer's station, and saw he was chatting away with the film crew. Yeah... that was going to take a while.

Then Marla heard another champagne bottle pop.

"Here you go, ma'am," Jeff said, and she turned to look at him just when he was pushing a new glass of champagne her way. The glass was well-frosted, and Angie smiled neatly, seeming a little out of breath. The poor girl must've run all the way to get that bottle so quickly.

"If you could have it differently, ma'am," Jeff asked, "would you give up all the attention?"

She frowned a little, irritated by the caterer's insistence. She understood a couple of questions, okay, but what the hell.

"Thank you both for this," she said, gesturing with the glass. Then she reached over the counter and grabbed the bottle of Martini Asti. "You were supercool. I'll make sure you're happy with tonight's gratuity."

Then she turned away before they could thank her and walked to the far end of the pool, where the hammocks were lined up. She put the bottle carefully on a small wicker table and let herself fall onto the mesh of knotted rope. What a feeling... yeah. She took another sip of champagne and felt it travel to her weary bones, relaxing every muscle fiber and relieving all her tension.

"Come with me," Adam said, startling her from her sleep a few moments later. She'd dozed off, glass empty in her hand. The cleaning crew had finished and gone, and the caterers were nowhere to be seen.

"Um, where?" she asked, struggling to keep her eyes open. She felt dizzy, confused.

"Los Angeles, for the Capitol Records meeting," he said, seeming a little saddened that she'd forgotten. "The jet's ready."

"Oh, I'm sorry, it completely slipped my mind. You're leaving now? It's Memorial Day tomorrow; don't those people take time off?"

"Entertainment never takes time off. I'm hot as coals right now, babe; I'm it. They want me in that office first thing tomorrow. I get new terms, new contract, we're rocking this deal. Come with me," he said, making small dance moves with his arms, excited like a teenager.

"I'm dead tired," she replied, aware she was mumbling, slurring her words, despite the effort she was putting into speaking. "Why don't you stay..."

"I can't," he replied, then stood, ready to leave. He leaned over her and kissed her lips once again. "Let me get you inside."

"Uh-uh, just go," she mumbled, already falling asleep again. "I'll be fine."

45

Waiting Game

The hours rushed by in a frenzy of searches and interviews. They'd brought in several people whose names were provided by Kurt Briggs, including Deanna's estranged father, Rod Harper. Based on the background information Fradella had dug up, he'd been behaving strangely as of late, moving large amounts of money between accounts, liquidating assets, not leaving the house much. Tess cringed at the thought that a father could kill his daughter, and the man didn't fit the profile one iota, but she interviewed him nevertheless. A wasted hour later, she'd uncovered the man was dying of cancer and keeping things quiet while putting his affairs in order, unwilling to put his family through hell.

When she returned to the conference room, the air was stale to the point of being nauseating; she left the door open and asked a uniformed cop to crank up the AC, to get some fresh air flowing. Fradella joined her moments later, after finishing his interview with Deanna's former agent, another dead end.

Tess looked at the dark TV screen and reluctantly turned on her laptop, then hooked it up. She dreaded what she was about to see, yet headed there implacably, as if hypnotized by the eyes of a snake. There was no other choice; if she was ever going to catch the Taker of Lives, she had to learn to live in his world, understand him better than he understood himself, even if her skin crawled at the thought of that.

Why was the Taker so different than all the other unsubs she'd understood and caught? Her gut was trying to tell her something, but she couldn't read the information clearly. It was as if she were still missing a critical piece of information, something that was right in front of her, only she couldn't see it. There was something in the organization, the coolheadedness of this killer that made him stand out from the rest of her contributions to Florida's death-row inmate collection. The level of planning he'd demonstrated, the way he'd orchestrated his shows, and the reason, as far she could understand it, for his actions, sent shivers down her spine.

Even a serial killer like The Family Man, the murderer of families credited with over 100 deaths, had some hint of an excuse for his actions. He'd struggled as a young boy, was severely and repeatedly abused by his parents. It was a big stretch, yet Tess could push herself to almost understand his motives. But the Taker? Hell, no. He seemed to be jealous of other people's fame, their success. In what demented world did that make any sense?

But she knew the answer already; it was part of the profile she had already released. The world of a malignant narcissist, injured in his ego beyond the point where he could control his urge for deathly revenge. That was the nature of the animal dubbed the Taker of Lives.

The laptop chimed as it powered up, and she opened a browser window and found the Taker's site. She expected it to be idle, considering Donovan hadn't called yet, but it wasn't.

Slack-jawed, she approached the screen and her hand went to her mouth without her realizing it. The site announced in bold letters, "Per FBI Special Agent Tess Winnett's personal request, today we transmit live! You, my dear fans, get to choose the weapon. I'll only be the hand that wields it. Ten million votes to start streaming."

Then three buttons with vote counts were displayed underneath. One showed the pictogram of a rope and had collected over four million votes. The second one showed a handgun and had amassed almost nine million votes. The third one showed a knife and had already reached twelve million votes.

She dialed Donovan without taking her eyes off the screen, using her phone's voice command to call the number.

He picked up after a few rings, in a sleep-loaded voice. "Yeah?"

"What the hell, Donovan," she said, but her urge to scold him vanished, as she realized he'd been at it for more than forty-eight hours without a break. She, too, had dozed off earlier that morning, when she lost the fight to keep her eyelids open, and Doc Rizza's leather couch happened to be nearby, not to mention his medical advice, coupled with some very direct threats.

"Don't tell me," he mumbled, "damn son of a bitch is at it again."

She heard him type, then mumbled again.

"Tell me you've got something," she said. "It's almost eleven; we still have time to stop him, if your software's giving us targets."

"If he's telling the truth," Fradella chimed in.

"Yeah, it's funny how our fierce Agent Winnett always believes this schmuck when he says his shows are live. You fall for it every time, don't you, Winnett?"

She groaned in frustration but realized there was little she could say in her defense. Yes, she chose to believe the Taker every time, because she couldn't bring herself to accept she had no control whatsoever and no hope to save those girls. That meant she'd already lost and the Taker of Lives had already won, and he could keep on killing for as long as he damn well pleased.

"Where are we with that software?" she asked, instead of saying what she was going to say in reaction to his comment.

"We have a working model," Fradella announced excitedly. "Well, Donovan has," he quickly added apologetically, "I was only manual backup for on-the-spot verifications."

"Walk me through it," she requested, her voice much harsher than she'd wanted. "Please," she added.

"Simply put, we've built a system of points," Donovan said, and Tess chuckled softly. Nothing that brainiac ever did was simple.

"For each follower, regardless of social media platform, the woman gets one point," Fradella explained. "No more elimination of duplicates; just simple arithmetic."

"Then why don't we have results yet?" Tess asked, trying and failing to hide her impatience. She understood what she was asking for wasn't easy.

Donovan scoffed. "Seriously? Because there are two-point-five million Caucasian women in Florida between the ages of sixteen and thirty years old, that's why. Because we had to restart the engine once we removed the blonde hair filter, and that added almost two million people, and because we couldn't get a single, damn social media platform to cooperate and give us database downloads with the numbers we're looking for; not a single one. All of them have lawyers and promised they'd fight our court orders to the full extent of the law."

"They wouldn't share the info? It's public, it's displayed in plain view on those profiles," Tess reacted. "Did you tell them what it's for?"

"No, 'cause I'm an idiot who can't think for himself," he reacted. "Of course, I did," he added, a moment later, probably after taking a sip of fruit water. "They're afraid of being perceived as cooperating with law enforcement at the cost of their users' data privacy. I've built a piece of software that searches and screen-scrapes the information. Only it's not easy for it to run, and it takes a while."

"How sure are we this is it?" Tess asked, shooting a worried glance at the digital clock displayed on the screen. Time was running out.

"All simulations returned the right girls, the existing victims in the right order."

"How far along has it processed, your miracle software? How many of the two-point-five million women?"

"About seventy percent."

She paced the room, thinking what they could do instead of waiting for the clock to strike midnight and the killer to stab the next victim to death. The knife was leading in the vote collection race by several million votes.

Why stab? The majority of people preferred guns for killing; more than fifty percent did, and that included serial killers. All statistics agreed. Why the discrepancy then?

Her eyes stared at the gun pictogram, then at the knife, then back. What was different, in terms of homicidal reward? Stabbing was a metaphor for sexual assault; many times, repeated stabbing in the abdominal area was the preferred MO for impotent lust killers. *For killers who couldn't perform the rape because,* she thought, *because they weren't there in person.* Yes, it had to be. All those millions of voters were murderers by proxy, most of them lust-driven, their homicidal urges carefully nurtured and fueled by the Taker of Lives, who took them with him in his journey of self-discovery, of becoming cold-blooded murderers themselves.

The Taker of Lives was giving millions of people a taste of what it meant to kill.

She shuddered, feeling ice shards traveling though her veins.

"I know you can't trace these people, D, but can you at least tell how many are American?"

"Why?" Fradella asked, popping his head up from behind his laptop screen.

"Because some of these people will become addicted to the thrill of killing. After the Taker is done with his charade, they'll come out to hunt on their own."

"I can't estimate that," Donovan said after a few moments, "because almost all the users are browsing via—"

"Yeah, you told me, encrypted browsing and all that."

"But there's the occasional unencrypted IP I can see, and one of those fools is right there with you, in your precinct."

46

Live

Tess turned toward Fradella, fuming with rage. How could a cop, one of the good guys, engage with the Taker of Lives and endorse his action with a vote? "Get IT in here, discreetly."

A moment later, a middle-aged guy with a potbelly and scruffy jeans walked through the door. Fradella closed the door behind him and pointed toward a chair. The man sat, but an expression of wariness lingered on his face. "What's this about?" he asked.

"Please keep your voice down," Tess asked, throwing a concerned glance at the glass wall separating them from the squad room. "Do you have a list of all users in this building and their IPs?"

"Uh-huh," he replied, shooting her an inquisitive look from underneath a furrowed brow.

"Trace this one, please: 24.238.3.142," Fradella said, reading the numbers off a bright yellow sticky note. "Do you know who that is?"

"I'll find out," he replied with a groan, as if searching a database was a terrible effort. He typed something on his iPad and then replied, shooting them each a disgusted look. "Officer Delacruz."

"Where does he sit?" Tess asked, itching to go after Delacruz.

"Over there," Fradella pointed out a man in his late twenties. "The one with the goatee."

"Oh, I know him," Tess replied. "I remember him from the profile delivery. Get his ass in here, now."

Fradella hesitated a little, but then brought Delacruz into the conference room, holding him by his arm, like a perp.

"What is this?" Delacruz protested. "Are you crazy or something?"

"You're fired," Tess said, throwing the man a glare loaded with all the disgust she was feeling.

"You have no right to fire me," Delacruz replied with a quick, defiant laugh. "Who the hell do you think you are?"

"Believe me when I say you're fired, and you won't be able to leave this building until you answer some questions," Tess added, her voice cold as ice.

"You're fucking crazy, bitch!" Delacruz yelled, and yanked his arm out of Fradella's grip.

Captain Cepeda appeared, probably drawn by the commotion. "What's going on here?"

"She can't fire me," Delacruz shouted. "FBI doesn't have the authority."

Cepeda sighed and ran his fingers over his gray moustache, as if to check that it was still in its rightful place on his upper lip, then turned to Tess. "What's he talking about?"

She glared at Delacruz one more time before replying. "He's one of the people voting on the Taker of Lives' website. He wants the victim stabbed; he just expressed his preference."

"I'm only helping with the case," he shouted, but blood drained from his face as he spoke.

"You're not on the case," Cepeda said calmly. "You're right, Agent Winnett can't fire you, but I can." He turned his gaze to Tess. "I'm guessing you want to question him?"

She checked the time, then the TV screen. "Yes, but not now. We don't have time now. Have him wait, please."

Cepeda beckoned a detective and Delacruz was taken away, still shouting senseless excuses and accusations, and some references to his union rep. "Unbelievable," he muttered. "My apologies, Agent Winnett."

"Captain," she said, remembering that her mandate included maintaining excellent relations with local law enforcement, "I understand he could easily claim a justified professional curiosity, and I hope you don't feel I overstepped, but regardless, I'm aware that I did, and I apologize."

"Thank you, Agent Winnett," Cepeda replied. "I probably would've lost it too if I were in your shoes. Strange place we find ourselves in, only two days after this wasn't even a case, huh?"

She'd already turned her attention to the screen, where the timer showed less than twenty minutes until the show would start and another innocent girl would die.

"Donovan, talk to me, man," she pleaded. "Where are we?"

"Almost eighty percent complete," he replied.

"Has your software identified the existing victims yet?"

"Yes, all of them, and in the right order of priority, matching the unsub's chronology."

"Who appears after Haley Estrada on that list?"

"Nora Frye, twenty-seven, but the engine hasn't finished crunching all the data. Nora could be the next one for real, or hundreds more could still be found with higher scores than hers."

"Let's send patrol cars to Nora Frye's place and the next two after her. Maybe we'll get lucky."

Fradella coordinated the action and had dispatch call the respective patrol units by cell phone, after first identifying who was nearest the respective addresses. At two minutes before midnight, all three units had reported back. The Taker of Lives was at none of the addresses.

When the streaming finally started, Tess was out of breath; her heart thumped against her rib cage and her palms were sweating. She approached the TV, taking in all the elements of what she was seeing. This time, the girl, a slender blonde who looked very familiar, was already naked, spread-eagled and immobilized on a wide poolside bed. Like others before her, she seemed unconscious, unable to fight her attacker. Rebel strands of hair covered her face, making facial recognition impossible.

Tess breathed deeply several times, willing herself to stay clinical. The Taker had changed his MO. The set up was outside, by a pool, not in her bedroom like before. What did that mean? A larger property, secluded, where he could have his way with the girl and not be disturbed? The nearby waterfront with boat dock seemed to contradict that theory. Was someone sleeping soundly on some drug in a bedroom nearby?

The Taker went off camera for a moment, then returned with what appeared to be a twelve-inch blade tactical knife in one hand, and an ammonia vial in the other. He was careful; that part of his signature hadn't changed a single bit. Not once did the camera show his face, or any part of him other than his back, his arms, and the back side of his head, all covered in black, shiny latex.

The Taker ran the blade against the girl's pale skin, caressing her thighs with the shiny metal, going up and down against her body as if anticipating, savoring what he was about to do. After a long minute or two, he broke the ammonia vial and put it under the girl's nose. Panicked, the girl rose as much as her restraints allowed, struggling, yanking at them and screaming, bloodcurdling shrieks of pure terror.

The Taker didn't seem to mind the screams, despite the open waterfront only yards away, overlooking nearby properties. He looked at her intently, brushing the hair from her face, and that only fueled her fear. Then, without any hesitation, the knife came down.

"No!" Tess shouted, tears filling her eyes. She lifted her arms in the air, in a gesture of despair, then let them fall under their own weight.

The video feed faded, and the screen turned dark, then the familiar white text appeared. It was a message for her. It read, "How was this for live action, Special Agent Winnett? Are you satisfied now?" Then a close-up portrait of the victim was displayed right under that message.

"Oh, crap," Fradella said, "that's Marla Quinn. You know, Adam Quinn's wife?"

Tess grabbed her keys and ran out the door. "You know where she lives?"

"In Miami Beach," he replied, "on La Gorce Island."

"Shit, that's sixty miles away," she said, her voice showing the despair she was feeling. How could they hope to catch him? "We need to dispatch Miami-Dade units."

Fradella stopped briefly in Cepeda's doorway. "We have a lead, and we need backup. Doc Rizza too. Miami-Dade is closer; it needs to respond." He didn't wait for an answer. A moment later, his SUV burned rubber on its way out of the parking lot, its siren blaring, followed by three other units.

By the time they arrived at the Quinn residence, Miami-Dade cops had finished clearing the property. They'd discovered Marla's body, but the Taker was nowhere to be found, gone without a trace.

Tess entered the property, feeling nothing but dread and a paralyzing sense of déjà vu. How many times were they going to do the same, watch the Taker's crimes on TV, powerless, hopeless, unable to intervene? How much longer was he going to remain at large, free to prey on innocent girls?

Her frustration subsided somewhat under the assault of reason; yes, he was still out there, but the gap had been closed, and the crime scene was fresh, untainted. She focused on the crime scene and the details she was seeing. The house was huge, about six thousand square feet, set on a sprawling property surrounded by tall, thick hedges. That wasn't why he didn't care about the screams, though. Marla's cries for help must've carried over the water and neighbors might've heard something, but between her first scream and the moment the Taker had fled the scene, less than a minute had passed. Impeccable planning, lightning-fast execution.

She looked up and found motion sensors and surveillance cameras were installed everywhere. She beckoned one of the Miami-Dade cops who were swarming around.

"Did anyone check the security system?"

"Yes," the man replied. "I believe they said something was wrong with it. It was stuck, or frozen, or something like that."

Of course, it was.

She approached a group of uniforms huddled together, chatting.

"The party last night. I heard it was huge," a woman was saying.

"What party?" Tess asked.

"Adam Quinn won a Billboard Music Award," she explained, "and they always throw some kind of poolside bash after those kinds of events. We'll see it in the media tomorrow."

Media? That meant social media too, and that had a different dynamic; no need to wait until morning. She called Donovan.

"Hey, D, I'm willing to bet the Taker was at the Quinn party tonight."

She heard him type and waited patiently.

"It was select," Donovan said. "Massive but select. Only big names and close friends. Didn't you posit that the Taker is someone who isn't famous? He's craving fame because he can't have it?"

"Yeah... I'm thinking maybe he wasn't a guest. Perhaps he's someone who works with celebrities, and their fame is in his face all day long, fueling his rage. Look at service personnel, cameramen, crews, staff, including cleaning."

Donovan cleared his throat quietly. "But didn't you say he was gainfully employed, well-educated, making good money?"

"Okay, maybe not cleaning personnel then, but still. Let's start digging.

All those people will post photos online. Let's grab them and identify every single one of the people who were here last night."

"You got it," Donovan replied.

"One more thing," she said, almost afraid to ask the question. "How come Marla, who's obviously the most famous of all the victims so far, didn't rank higher from the Taker's point of view?"

"I wondered that also. The software hasn't even found her yet, but that's because it's still processing. I believe the answer lies with the fact that Marla hated social media and rarely posted anything. Her points are really low, much lower than Haley's or Christina's."

"Okay, that would mean the model we've built is still valuable, but why does someone like the Taker only care about social media following, and chooses to ignore someone like Marla, at least for a while? What are we missing?"

"That's for you to figure out, Winnett. You're the profiler. I'm just a data cruncher." He hung up, leaving her to wonder whether they understood all the facts of the unsub's victimology.

She approached the bed where Marla's body lay, covered by a white sheet some cop had pulled off a nearby bed and covered her with. A large blood stain continued to spread, originating from her abdominal area.

Doc Rizza crouched next to the bed, liver temp probe in hand. "Oh, I wish they'd stop doing this," he gestured at the white sheet covering Marla's body. "I understand why they do it, but I still wish they wouldn't." He lifted the sheet to insert the probe, then waited until the device beeped quietly. "This time he did it live," he said, wiping his sweaty brow with the back of his gloved hand. "Preliminary time of death confirms it."

"Cause of death?" she asked, in barely a whisper.

"Single, sharp-force trauma to the abdomen. By the amount of blood loss, the blade severed one or more critical blood vessels, probably the abdominal aorta or the mesenteric. I'll know more after I've got her on my table."

"Thanks, Doc," she said, then turned to leave, about to walk through the entire crime scene in her protective booties, looking for that specific detail that would change the game in her favor.

"Hey," Fradella said, appearing next to her out of the blue. "We got started on fingerprints and access points. How are you holding up?"

She smiled sadly. "Don't ask."

She stood in silence for a moment, making a mental inventory of things they needed to do. Call the technicians and have them screen the property for the Taker's surveillance equipment, including all the trees or high vantage points. Run a search for images posted online. Talk to family members, to Adam Quinn when he returned, to find out why Marla was home alone that night, and who knew that was going to happen. The detectives had notified him, and he'd turned his jet around, halfway to California; in a couple of hours, she'd know.

"What does he get from calling you by name?" Fradella asked.

"What do you mean?" Her mind was elsewhere.

"The Taker's acknowledgment at the end of the video," he clarified.

"He's taunting me," she replied. "Doing that in front of his fans consolidates his appearance of power and control and feeds his narcissistic ego. An FBI agent has perceived power, lots of it. When he's challenging me openly, he states his superiority."

Fradella nodded once. "I see."

"Don't worry, it won't be for much longer. That hunger for power, for superiority, and for recognition is his Achilles' heel. That's our weapon."

47

Findings

Tess stood by the poolside bed where Marla's body still lay, feeling numb, petrified by a single thought. What if she'd caused this? What if the Taker of Lives was nothing but a cyberbully with a perverted, mean streak, but she'd helped create the serial killer that he'd become? What if Marla's blood, crimson and still glistening against the white sheet, was on her hands?

She remembered reading an article about influencing events by expecting certain outcomes and taking actions based on those expectations, as if the desired result were a certainty. She saw a serial killer in the making, when she analyzed what could've been the deeds of a deranged, vengeful freak, but not a killer. Then she acted as such. Did she create the monster?

Her phone rang, and she picked up without checking the caller ID, her eyes still fixed on the young woman's body.

"Winnett," she said, in lieu of hello.

"Hi, it's Bill," the familiar voice said.

She felt a wave of relief; the call couldn't've come at a better time. He'd understand. Could she really voice her concerns to him, a supervisory special agent? What would be the consequences of that?

"I saw what happened," Bill continued. "Any way I can help?"

"Um, not sure yet," she said. "We're here, at the scene, and the Taker's gone again, without a trace."

"What's on your mind, Tess?"

"I'm just tired, that's all. We all are."

"I hear more than that in your voice," Bill pushed back gently. "Remember what I do for a living?"

"You're scary, Bill; really, you are." She took a deep breath, then spoke quietly, turning her face away from the other cops. "I'm afraid I might have caused this. What if I pushed him too far with my comments, and made him into something he wasn't going to become on his own?"

"Whoa," Bill reacted, "aren't you quick to place blame on yourself for things that happened before you even knew the Taker existed? He killed Deanna long before you posted your first comment."

"But I challenged him to do his freak show live, and now…" Her voice trailed off, strangled by emotion as she looked at Marla's lifeless body.

"You had no choice but to challenge him, and even so I don't believe that's why he did it. Now you have a fresh crime scene, and you're starting to assert some control over his game. Next thing you'll know, he'll make a mistake, and you'll be right there, watching, waiting, rattling the handcuffs."

She snickered involuntarily at the visual he put in her mind, although handcuffs had stopped rattling a long time ago, when they'd replaced the metallic bracelets with plastic zip ties. "Thanks, Bill, I mean it."

"Anytime," he replied. "And please, don't have the chutzpah to imagine you can create serial killers with a simple online comment. You're not that powerful."

"I was being arrogant, wasn't I?" she replied, feeling embarrassed.

"What I believe you are is exhausted and unable to accept it when you have little, if any, control, but you're close, closer than you've ever been to catching this monster." He paused, waiting for her reply, but that didn't come. "I'm here if you need me," he added, then hung up.

She wanted to accept everything he'd said, but there was a part of that she still couldn't bring herself to believe: that she was close to catching the Taker of Lives. Maybe Bill knew better, and all she needed to do was accept the possibility he was right. After all, he was a senior profiler.

Feeling energized for no apparent reason, she called Donovan.

"Hey, D, please coordinate with RTCC and let's track the Taker's steps after he left the property. He tampered with the security system here, but not with every camera on every property from here to wherever the hell he went."

"Already on it," he replied. "Miami-Dade cops are knocking on all doors in the neighborhood asking to see their security videos. The area is strictly residential, so no street cameras or ATMs or anything, but we do have a stoplight camera almost a mile from there."

"That's far," she groaned. "Maybe he didn't even take that route."

"It's a fifty-fifty shot. It's the first traffic light you hit when leaving La Gorce Island heading for the mainland."

"All right, as soon as you have something, let me know. How far along is that software of yours? We need that list, like we need air to breathe."

"Eighty-seven percent done. By morning we'll know, and we'll be ready."

She hung up, then turned to the Miami-Dade crime scene technicians.

"You, please bring 360-degree cameras on tripods and scan every room of this house where the unsub might have been. Any signs of forced entry?"

"Here?" one of the techs gestured to the vast yard, fenced by tall, lush greenery. "How could anyone tell? He could've come from anywhere."

She took a few steps toward them, angry and no longer concerned with hiding it. "That's not a good enough answer. Work on it until you can definitively say yes or no."

The tech scoffed with disdain and turned to his colleague. "Who the hell does she think she is?"

Then he shrugged and went about his business, ignoring her request. The other technician stood in place, looking at her unfazed. For a brief moment, she eyed Tess's FBI badge, displayed on her belt, then looked away.

"How about you?" Tess asked. "Are you also a member of the I-don't-give-a-shit club?"

"Nope, we need this perp caught," she replied. "I'll find out how he got in here and get someone on those 360 scans you need."

"One more thing, please. This unsub usually wipes the areas where he leaves prints before he puts on his suit. In those specific areas where you don't find any prints, please be extra careful with trace evidence collection. Anything would work: epithelials, hair fibers, anything."

"I don't know when we could have the results back to you, ma'am." The tech looked around her briefly, then lowered her voice. "With a property this size, processing the fingerprints and trace evidence will take months."

Tess groaned with frustration and rolled her eyes. She couldn't afford months; not even days. The Taker could be history by then, never to be heard from again, or he could continue killing, taking lives every day with no ending in sight. She felt defeated; the only thing they had to go on was the profile and Donovan's software, based on that profile. *That psychological profile better not be wrong one single bit,* she thought, *or we'll keep doing this until the day we die.*

She returned to the poolside bed, where Doc Rizza's assistant was getting ready to load Marla's body onto the stretcher.

"What else can you tell me, Doc?" she asked, touching the man's arm to get his attention.

"No other signs of trauma, at least at first sight. I'm afraid I've got nothing else to offer. The only change in MO I've noticed so far is the absence of the propofol shot. I couldn't see the puncture mark, but I need strong light and a magnifying glass to confirm."

"So, this unsub just got ten times bolder," she mumbled angrily, "and still got away with it."

"Not for long, if he pissed you off that badly," Michowsky said, with a hint of a smile. "I've seen that look before, only hours before you caught your man," He looked drawn, dark circles around his hollow eyes speaking volumes about how he'd spent his time since they last spoke. What was he doing there, instead of catching some shuteye?

"Hey, Gary, what's going on?"

"Ah," he sighed, "I believe our other objective has been reached," he replied cryptically.

"Really? How come?"

He didn't get a chance to reply, because her phone rang. She frowned when she read Pearson's name on the display, and immediately took the call.

"Sir," she said, wondering what her boss knew about the current crime scene. As usual, he probably knew more than she did.

"How's the case, Winnett?" he asked, sounding tense, worried.

Last time they spoke, he'd just learned he needed to orchestrate a major drug seizure with little time to prepare, while his family was being targeted. Not an easy feat, probably taking all his attention away from her serial killer.

"The case has gone terribly wrong, sir," she replied. "No luck so far, but we're getting closer and he's getting bolder. He's about to make a mistake."

"So far, you've only been cleaning up after this unsub, Winnett. Are you planning on becoming proactive any time soon?"

"We know how he chooses his victims, and we'll be waiting next time he tries."

"When will that be? Do you have any idea?"

"It will be tonight, at midnight. I'm one hundred percent sure."

"Why?" Tess could hear the frown in his voice.

"He's orchestrating a show that will culminate with tonight's performance. Every night, at midnight, he's streamed a part of his masterpiece, if you'd like to call it that. Now he's about to conclude the show and disappear. He won't stop killing, now that he's got a taste for it, but he'll end this particular display of power he's putting out there on the Dark Web."

"How could you possibly know that?"

She hesitated for a moment. "Based on the timing of these attacks, the way he's been scaling up the violence, the engagement with his viewers, and based on the profile."

"On a profile that could be wrong? You know just as well as I do that's little more than a scientific guess, constructed more on statistics than on solid evidence."

"All of the above, sir," she replied calmly, swallowing a long sigh, loaded with unspoken expletives. "We have nothing else. No evidence, no leads, nothing. The man is a ghost."

"Then, if you're so sure he's planning to disappear after tonight, you'd better catch him this time. Will you, Winnett?"

"Yes, sir," she replied, barely containing a smile. That was Pearson's talent; he gave her a hard time, challenging every one of her decisions, but made her feel encouraged and appreciated. "How's your daughter?" she asked, after a brief hesitation at the thought of discussing the green folder over the phone.

"Oh, she's crying, Winnett," he replied calmly. "Turns out her boyfriend was in a car crash earlier today and is in the hospital with a bunch of broken bones. They won't even let her visit. She won't be going boating today, and she's devastated. She had such high hopes for this trip."

Blood rushed to her head. Car accident? That wasn't what she'd asked Bartlett to do. That bastard! Jeez... She took a deep breath of air and let it out slowly, calming her stretched nerves. In retrospect, it was a good thing Bartlett didn't kill Carrillo. At least that wouldn't weigh on her increasingly guilty conscience.

"So sorry to hear that, sir," she mumbled.

"Thank you, Winnett," he replied. "No, I mean, *thank you*."

She swallowed, her throat suddenly constricted at the thought that her boss knew she'd put a contract out on someone, albeit a really nasty, ruthless perp of a someone and only for a few broken bones. "How's the rest of the day's entertainment schedule?" she asked, thinking of the planned seizure of the *Reina del Mar* and the drugs she was about to haul into port.

"The rest will proceed as scheduled, Winnett. I'll call you later to let you know where we'll gather for the picnic."

"Thank you, sir."

"Oh, and Winnett? Catch that son of a bitch already, will you?"

He hung up, and she smiled crookedly, while whispering to herself, "Yes, sir. Working on it."

She grabbed Michowsky by the arm and headed toward the gate. "Let's get you home, Gary." He could barely stand, and he offered little resistance, at least not physically.

"I've got work to do, Winnett. It's almost four, and at six the team is meeting for tactical readiness on the drug bust. I still owe them some info."

"Uh-huh," she said, but still walked him toward the street, where their cars were parked.

"You know, I was thinking," he mumbled, "if we don't catch this Taker of Lives soon, he's going to kill all of us. Have you noticed how he won't let us rest? He kills every day at midnight, then he starts the voting bullshit the next morning, and he keeps on going like he's the Energizer serial bunny from hell."

There was noise and flashes of light coming from the street. She opened the gate and found Fradella, blinded by camera flashes and holding his arm in front of his face to shield his eyes.

"What the hell is this?" she asked, almost shouting in Fradella's ear to cover the media ruckus.

Fradella turned to her and shoved a piece of paper in her hand. "The unsub put out another press release. This time, they all came."

48

Adam

She'd shouted "no comment" about a dozen times from the bottom of her lungs, to no avail. The questions poured incessantly, barely intelligible, cameras flashes were blinding, instilling a sense of panic in her, as the people wielding those devices moved in waves like swarms of locusts, pushing through the police in a determined fashion. The cops had already pulled crime scene tape to block the area, but the mad horde had torn through it twice already, even if that was a felony that could land someone in jail.

For a moment, she thought of pulling out her gun and firing a couple of shots in the air, Western style, just to get their attention, but the paperwork would've been a nightmare, not to mention the aftermath. A suspension would be unavoidable, and she definitely couldn't afford that, not after the recent investigation into her higher-than-average suspect kill ratio.

Then the crowds parted under the slow and steady pressure of a black Suburban approaching while honking its horn in rapid bursts. Right behind the Suburban, a stretch limo with dark-tinted windows followed closely. The media swarm hesitated for a moment, then rushed toward the limo, banging on its windows, shoving camera lenses against every square inch of tinted glass and firing away, shot after shot, in the frantic hope of landing the jackpot photo.

Adam Quinn was back.

The Suburban stopped strategically on the right side of the gate, its front grille almost touching the wall, and four armed goons hopped out, bearing the insignia of one of the most exclusive private security firms in town. They pushed the press away from the street with little concern for their health or the integrity of their equipment, then the large gate pulled open and let the limo in.

"I'll take Quinn," she yelled in Fradella's ear, "you take his staff, okay?"

He gestured in response with a thumbs up.

A Miami-Dade detective rushed to stop the limo. "Hey," he called after the vehicle's driver, "you can't go in there, it's an active crime scene." Then he turned toward the uniformed cops keeping the press at bay and yelled to cover the ruckus. "What the hell are you doing, people? This is a crime scene, for Pete's sake!" He ran after the limo and caught up with it as it pulled to the main door.

What would be the alternative? Refuse him entry under the eyes of so many newspeople, while the Taker of Lives watched from the safety of whatever hole he'd dug himself into, via numerous blogs and online tabloids? It would've been a media feeding frenzy, capitalizing on the man's tragedy. Out of options, she decided to allow him entry to the property but planned to make sure his movements were restricted and he couldn't trample the scene where it would've mattered.

Hard to think of such places though, when only hours ago countless people had touched, sat, stepped, and shed hair and epithelials over every square inch of that house.

She already knew the Taker of Lives had left no evidence for them to find. The timing of the attack couldn't've been a coincidence; nothing the Taker did ever was.

Tess approached the Miami-Dade detective quickly and caught up with him before the limo door opened.

"You've got no options," she said, flashing her badge quickly. "The scene is most likely compromised already, and the media outside doesn't leave us too many alternatives. Whatever we do, the killer is watching if we let him."

"It's procedure, damn it," he said. "I don't care who this guy is or what the killer's seeing."

She pursed her lips, almost ready to tell the man what she thought about his lack of compassion or intelligence. Instead, she decided to strongarm him.

"It's a federal case, which makes this my scene. Thank you for your help, Detective. I'll take it from here."

She'd expected some pushback but got nothing more than an irritated glare and a muttered oath, and the man was gone.

Then the limo door opened.

She wasn't going to forget Adam Quinn's heart-wrenching sobs anytime soon. He got out of the limo and rushed to the backyard, pushing her to the side.

"Mr. Quinn, I'm Special Agent Winnett with the FBI," she started saying, but her words trailed off, because Adam was gone. He ran past her into the backyard; probably he'd heard where his wife had been killed and was looking for her body.

She ran and caught up to him, standing in the middle of the patio, seemingly lost, confused. It was strange to see him like that, after she'd watched his music videos, all full of life and passion and joyful rhythm. It seemed surreal, as if the altitude from which he'd fallen had made the fall so much more devastating.

"Mr. Quinn, the medical examiner's office has your wife's body," she said gently, but he didn't seem to hear her. "Let's go inside. We have a few questions for you."

His shoulders shuddered, and a long wail came out, then turned into uncontrollable sobs. He paced in place, hugging himself, as if unsure where to go and what to do.

"Mr. Quinn, please, let's go inside," she insisted. She didn't want him to lay eyes on that poolside bed, still covered in his wife's blood. From his current vantage point, that was hidden behind the corner of the house. "You could help us catch who did this to your wife, if you could only answer a few questions."

He didn't budge, nor seemed to have heard her.

Another young man approached and whispered quietly, "I'm his assistant. What can I do?"

"Didn't he know what happened?" Tess asked, confused by the visible shock Adam was going through. "I thought he turned his plane around. He must've known why."

"Um, no, he didn't know. I made the decision not to tell him. There was press onboard."

"So, when *did* you tell him?" Tess asked, frowning.

"Just now, after we entered the property."

That explained a lot, the man's raw emotion, his lack of understanding what was going on. It was unbelievable how fame changed things, altering a person's life to the point where it changed reality and the perception of it.

"Listen, I need him to answer some questions, and probably he needs a doctor, to help him with the shock."

"You got it," the assistant replied, then vanished.

As she turned toward Adam, he started pacing the yard like a wounded animal, while tears flowed down his cheeks. He was looking for something, and the moment he saw it, he froze in place: the poolside bed, covered in Marla's blood and surrounded by yellow crime scene tape.

He dropped to his knees and let out a long sob. "No," he cried, reaching toward the bed with his hand, although it was more than twenty feet away. He sobbed convulsively, ignoring her and anyone else who tried to console him.

It took the family doctor almost an hour before Adam could answer some questions. Thankfully, the doctor came quickly, and just as quickly poked him with a needle, then again after thirty minutes or so.

Adam still sat on the marble patio, refusing to take his eyes off the bed and go inside. Tess sat next to him, her eyes on the same level with his.

"Mr. Quinn, I'm terribly sorry for your loss," she whispered, and the man barely nodded in response. His eyes were fixed ahead, his pupils dilated from the effect of the sedative. She looked at him, at how pain oozed from every fiber of his body and felt grateful the technicians had already removed all of the Taker's cameras. At least that bastard wouldn't be able to witness Adam's pain.

"Please, help me catch who did this to your wife," she insisted.

"What do you want to know?" he asked in a raspy, guttural voice.

"How many people were here last night? For the party?"

He finally took his eyes off that poolside bed and looked at her.

"I believe two hundred and forty or about there," he said. "Add catering, cleaning, camera crews, and the DJ. I'll give you the list."

"How about video? Do you have—"

He closed his swollen eyes and swallowed. "You'll get the whole thing, unedited, and my security will help you put names to all the faces."

"Was it normal for your wife to be home alone at night?"

"We never liked help to stay overnight. We liked to have the house to ourselves. When I travel without her..." He choked, still struggling, but his mind was organized and alert, despite the sedatives in his system.

"Who else knew you were going to leave last night?"

He shrugged and let his head hang low, his chin touching his chest. "Everyone knew. I'd announced my upcoming meeting with Capitol Records during my press conference right after the Billboards."

"Who was still here when you left for the airport?"

"No one. I made sure of that. They were all gone, all cars gone from the street, no one left in the house."

Tess raised an eyebrow, surprised at his statement. Adam didn't miss her reaction.

"This is routine for us, after these parties. We check every room. People drink too much, they pass out, or they over—" He stopped in the middle of the phrase, and Tess let that one slide. Of course, there were going to be drugs at such parties, but that didn't make Adam the bad guy.

"Where was Marla when you left?"

"She'd fallen asleep on the hammock, right there," he said, pointing toward the far side of the pool, where three hammocks were lined up.

"And you just left her there, asleep, in the yard?" Tess asked, her voice just a tad too loud.

"I asked her to come with me, but she was too tired..." He stifled a sob, then continued. "She sometimes sleeps outside. She likes the night air and the lights reflected over the water. The lawn is treated for bugs, and we have security." He stopped talking abruptly, as if realizing what he'd just said. "I thought we were safe."

Tess could've envisioned the scene, as if she were there. By the time Adam left, Marla was probably already sedated, the Rohypnol making her dizzy and too tired to move. Sometime before Adam left, the Taker had been there to spike her drink and watch her fall asleep.

"One last thing, Mr. Quinn. Can you think of anyone who could've done this? We have reasons to believe that person attended your party, either as a guest or as hired help."

For a long moment he stayed silent, probably going over names in his mind. "No, I can't think of anyone, but I'll have security go over that video in detail and tell you if there was anyone who didn't belong."

That simple statement was music to her ears. Soon they'd know.

Or would they?

49

Again

Cat's place didn't open before four in the afternoon, but he was always there after two, cleaning, restocking the bar, receiving supplies, and doing everything else he needed to do to keep the place in business. Tess didn't think he'd mind the early call, so she talked Fradella into going there for food. In retrospect, she realized Fradella hadn't put up much of a fight; he loved those burgers almost as much as she did.

Cat unlocked the door with a smile and a hug for her, and a frown, a mumble, and a reluctant handshake for Fradella, then watched them take the booth by the window.

"Burgers and fries?" he asked, tying his apron.

Tess grinned widely, feeling her mouth water at the thought of that feast. "How did you guess?"

He laughed, but that quick laugh didn't touch his eyes. "What am I serving here, breakfast or lunch?" he asked, with a tilt of his head and a bit of a raised eyebrow.

Tess knew what he thought about the long hours she put into her job and decided not to fuel that fire.

"Just a snack—"

"Last night's dinner too," Fradella said at the same time. "We haven't eaten in a while."

She looked away briefly, embarrassed to be caught in a lie, then back at Cat with a guilty smile. "Busted," she said sweetly.

"Damn right," he replied, sounding like a scolding parent, a terribly disappointed one.

He disappeared behind the counter and quickly returned with her favorite mint lemonade and a bottle of Perrier for Fradella, then went back to fix their meals.

"It will be a while," he said. "I haven't started the grill yet."

"Take your time," Tess replied, feeling hunger nibble at her stomach, triggered by the smell coming from the grill he'd fired up. She took a few swigs of lemonade and felt better. She leaned against the backrest and closed her eyes, reliving the early morning events.

By four-thirty, Donovan had called with the results from the door-to-door surveillance video search and the RTCC sweep. One of the nearby homes had caught a jogger on its driveway camera, passing by at the right time, and now they had a grainy image of the suspect, wearing loose track pants and a hoodie, zipped up and covering his face completely in the side view caught on camera. Other video systems had captured the same individual, running his way off the island in a light jog, and then disappearing on the streets of La Gorce. Not once did that hood fall off to show his face. Not once did he take his hands out of his pockets. She'd hoped to see something distinctive on his hands, like a tattoo; that would've been great, but no such luck.

After they lost the jogger, they couldn't pick him up anywhere else; he probably got into his car and drove off, but they couldn't pinpoint a vehicle either. No vehicle came to that camera-fitted stoplight for another hour after the jogger had vanished, and when one did, it traveled in the wrong direction.

When Cat approached the table, carrying the two hot plates topped with burgers and fries, he noticed Tess was asleep, her head leaning against the side of the booth and her mouth slightly open. Her partner was snoozing with his head on the table, resting on his folded arms. He looked at them for a long moment, mumbling something under his breath.

"I hope it's worth it, kid. Out of all the kindred spirits you could've found, you had to choose a cop."

He turned away and put the two plates in the keep-warm oven, then muted the TV. He took a seat in a beat-up, old, leather armchair he kept in the back room and dozed off. There was nothing else he could do without running the risk of making noise and waking Tess up.

A couple of hours later, Tess jumped from her sleep to the startling chime of her phone.

"Winnett," she said, swallowing with difficulty. Her throat was bone-dry, and her mind engulfed in dense fog. She reached for the remnants of lemonade in her glass and drank them to the last drop.

"He's back online," Donovan announced on speaker.

Fradella opened his eyes with a groan and straightened his back.

"So soon?" she asked, then looked at the cell phone's screen and saw the time. "Shit," she mumbled. "Has he posted a message yet? What does it say?"

"It says, 'Do you want another one? Now that you can all admit who you are and what you want, let's celebrate tonight. Let's explore your darkest fantasies together,'" Donovan read. "Then he promises live action on demand and gives them the choice between three victims."

Her brain shifted in full gear under the shot of adrenaline. "That could offer some possibilities," she replied. "We could compare to the top names on that list of yours. How much longer until the list is done?"

"An hour, tops. The progress bar says ninety-eight percent."

Soon they'd know who he had set his eyes on next. "Awesome. How many votes does he want this time?" Tess asked.

"Thirty million votes," Donovan replied.

"What particulars does he give?" Fradella asked, while Tess opened a browser window on her phone and loaded the Taker's site.

"Age, generic descriptions, like stunningly beautiful, young and slim, athletic and feisty. Nothing more."

"Whoa…" she reacted, as soon as the page finished loading. "He's already scored twenty-three million votes for the youngest girl. What the hell is wrong with people?"

"How old is that girl?" Fradella asked, unable to see the phone in Tess's hand.

"Seventeen, Todd," she whispered, lowering her voice, although no one else was around. "The Taker's next victim is only seventeen years old. A kid. Let's hope he hasn't gotten to her yet."

She ended the call and saw Cat bringing the burgers to the table. She stood and met him halfway.

"Get these to go, Cat. The damn son of a bitch is back."

50

Me: Enjoying

Whoa… what a rush! Yeah! Marla's last videoclip is something we'll all remember, you and me, for years to come. As I ran from the Quinn residence, I heard the sirens closing in, but I stayed my course at a casual pace and ducked behind a trash can when the cops drove by. And they drove by without looking, without paying any attention to the security lights that flooded that particular driveway, without giving an ounce of thought to anything other than getting where they were told to, as soon as possible.

Have you noticed how cops always rush to the location of a crime, oblivious of passersby who flee the scene? I've seen it in movies, but, if you recall my early experience with chloroform, I chose not to believe it. But then I saw it happen with my own eyes, when my neighborhood Walmart was hit.

Three young men were hauling a large-screen TV while the alarms blared behind them at the doors. It was after midnight, and I presumed they hadn't exactly paid for that fine piece of Samsung equipment. The three asshats ran to their car, a piece of crap banged up and rusty like it'd seen the Vietnam War era, then realized the TV was too large to fit in their trunk. Yeah, you're right to be chuckling, that wasn't very well planned.

Then the cops came, two SUVs flashing red and blue like Christmas trees on steroids, doing at least forty miles an hour into a parking lot. They passed right by the three youngsters who were too focused on trying to make the TV fit sideways in the back seat of their car to notice the five-oh approaching. The cops drove right past them and headed with screeching tires all the way to the store's front doors. By the time they came back outside, the three dumb-yet-lucky kids were long gone with their stolen TV.

When exactly did humans stop using rational thought in their day-by-day processes? Was it when workloads grew like cancer and the fight to survive dumbed us down to agitated amoeba levels? Was it when the culture we live in no longer respected the individual's right to rest, to think, to create?

In any case, regardless of means, it happened. Nobody pays any attention to you anymore unless you're one of these overrated bitches, and, yes, that will cost you dearly.

And it's happened to you too, Agent Winnett, only you were the culprit, the closed mind refusing to see the truth staring right back at you. Or maybe I'm *that* good.

You're supposed to be this tough-as-nails FBI profiler, or so your online reputation goes, but you looked straight at me and didn't recognize the, whatchamacallit, *unsub* you're hunting. We made eye contact... you even spoke with me and didn't really see me. Was your profile that wrong, Agent Winnett? Are you a victim of the same preconceived notions of how people look and act and talk when they reach certain levels of achievement in crime, hence you generated a false image of who I am?

It seems you're the same as all the others who see me but won't acknowledge me, as if I weren't there, as if I'm made of glass, completely transparent and void of substance. Story of my life... I'm invisible. If my shows so far weren't enough to get your attention and make you see me, what will?

At least one thing I guess you can agree with: I've earned the name you have bestowed on me. I've proven myself, and I will prove myself again.

I am the Taker of Lives, and I'm about to pull the curtains open on my final show.

And people are coming to watch, in the millions, despite the venomous, stupid little comments like those from Hornydog17 and others like him. So, what if an infinitesimal percentage of my audience believes I'm a necrophile? Maybe that's what *you* are, because that's where *your* mind is going every time you look into the mirror I hold high in front of your darkest, innermost self. For me, it's enough to know I'm not one; I've stopped trying to make you pissants understand what I am or allowing you to push my buttons; you're not worthy.

I've stopped worrying about those few who post venom and filth but still stay on for the show, unable to let go, unable to take the easy way out and get lost. You wish you were me so badly, don't you? Well, screw you, you're not me, nor will you ever be.

Finally, a few thoughts for the many millions who chose to share their time and their souls with me.

Thank you all; you humble me, and, in doing so, you restore what should've been mine to begin with, and I will reward you richly in return.

We all understand one another to harmonious perfection. The faint of heart have long since left this party, and now it's just you and me left. You, who want to shed blood just as much as I do, but don't have the courage yet. You, who need to see me doing it to get off. You, who can only dream of doing what I am doing. I promise you a show that will never let you forget me, not ever. I will be the most famous person yet, even if only for a day and from behind the dark veil of encrypted internet, and I will retire at the peak of my glory.

Because, you see, if you still haven't understood what I was trying to show you this whole time, you never will. Not to mention, I'm not about to let myself get caught, only to supply your dirty little fantasies.

But tonight, get ready for a show to remember.

51

The Name

Tess rushed up the stairs at the Palm Beach County Sheriff's Office, holding the two Styrofoam boxes with their lunch. Fradella carried the drinks, climbing the steps two at a time. Once she reached the top of the stairs from where she could see directly into the conference room through the glass wall, she froze in place and Fradella almost ran into her.

SAC Pearson was in there, and Donovan too, a first ever. Captain Cepeda was keeping them company, standing, leaning against the wall by the door.

What the hell was going on?

She frowned and trotted quickly to the door, then walked in, keeping her eyes riveted on Pearson's grim face.

"Sir," she greeted him as she usually did, a bit more formal than most of her FBI colleagues. "D," she acknowledged Donovan, but then turned her eyes to look at Pearson again. "What's going on?"

Instead of replying, Pearson looked at Donovan and made a quick gesture with his hand, inviting him to speak.

"We've got a serious problem, Winnett. The software finished crunching all the names and we have a list of the Taker's next possible targets, in order of priority, based on the criteria we used."

Her frown deepened. "And? Isn't that what we wanted?" she asked impatiently, setting down the Styrofoam boxes on the conference room table. The smell of warm burgers and fries filled the room.

"If we take the top three names on that list, they match the descriptions offered by the unsub as choices for his next kill. They match to perfection, beyond a shred of a doubt."

"Who's the youngest?" she asked, leaning forward toward Donovan, as if a closer proximity could relieve her tension.

"The first on the list and the youngest are one and the same, a seventeen-year-old girl by the name of Brianna Gillespie, Miss Teen USA, currently preparing for Miss World. Ring a bell?"

"No," she replied quickly, then looked at Fradella who seemed just as confused.

"She's Senator Wallace Gillespie's daughter," Pearson said.

"Oh, shit," she reacted before she could stop herself, and sat on a chair, as if all the blood rushing to her brain had taken the strength away from her knees. "I need full background on this girl. Where's the senator now?"

"In DC, where else?" Donovan replied. "We have to call him and brief him ASAP."

Her breath caught, as she processed the implications of making such a call.

"Now wait a second," she said, pushing the chair away from the table and standing across the table from Pearson. "You know damn well what that means. He'll freak out, he'll yank his daughter out of that house in three seconds flat. He'll make one call and he'll have Secret Service take care of things for him. Once he knows, there's no way he'll cooperate with us."

"And do you blame him?" Pearson asked. "It's his daughter."

It was almost like déjà vu, only this time Pearson was no longer the father with dire concern for his daughter; he did empathize with the senator though, and part of that empathy had to have come from his recent experience.

Sometimes the way things lined up was a bitch. She needed Pearson at the top of his killer-hunting game, not overly sensitive, drowning in sympathetic parental concern.

"Let's just think through this for a moment," she said, lowering her voice to make herself appear calmer than she was and sitting back down. Towering over Pearson in a threatening demeanor wasn't the best course of action, regardless of the situation.

"Yeah, let's," Pearson said coldly.

"If we tell the senator, and he yanks Brianna out of here, we'll never catch the Taker of Lives. Never. Poof, he's gone," she said, underlining her words with a gesture of her hands, opening her fists and spreading her fingers widely. "We can't do this, sir, you have to understand. It's a unique opportunity to catch a serial killer that we simply can't afford to miss." Her voice started low-pitched and seemingly calm, then the tone raised to almost forceful, lifted by her frustration, and finally ended in an almost humble plea.

"Let me tell you what we can't afford, Winnett," Pearson said. "We can't afford to have a serial killer on the prowl anywhere near a US senator's home. We can't have a single strand of that girl's hair disturbed by as much as a whiff of air coming from a murderer, when we knew about it ahead of time and we could've stopped it from happening. We can't have any of that, not ever. Our careers, our badges? Poof, gone," Pearson said, imitating her earlier gesture with his hands.

Her frown persisted, laying two deep ridges above her brow, and her jaws clenched as she went through all the arguments she could bring to change his mind. She looked at Donovan, but the bright analyst kept his eyes riveted to the floor. He probably wished more than ever he was boating off Key West somewhere. By all appearances, he wasn't going to let himself get caught in what could well end up being a deadly crossfire between two senior agents.

She took a deep breath, then another, willing herself to be calm. Maybe Donovan didn't feel like getting involved, but he already was.

"There's a new component to the profile," she said, "something we all missed in the model."

Both Pearson and Donovan looked straight at her, surprise clearly written on their faces, and Fradella finally set down the beverages he'd brought from Media Luna.

"Don't tell me, Winnett," Pearson said. "The model Donovan used for his search isn't valid?"

"I believe it still is, only there's a part of it we stumbled on and built in by accident, not really understanding it."

"What the hell are you talking about?" Pearson asked, raising his voice for the first time since their conversation started. "There's one thing worse than not telling a senator that a serial killer's lurking in the neighborhood, and that's telling him and being wrong about it. He'll crucify us."

"I don't believe we're wrong, sir. I struggled to understand why someone as famous and as popular as Marla Quinn was so low on the Taker's list. If it's strictly social media following that he's after, she's not at the top, I agree, but she got the best response in terms of media attention after the attack. Out of all the girls the Taker has attacked, Marla was the most influential."

"What's your point?"

"My point is that the type of attack he conducted on his victims was aligned with their order of fame by social media factors and type of fame, if you will. The shallow attention seekers and social-media hogs were publicly humiliated, while the more influential people, those who get tons of media attention, were scaled up in intensity. Haley was a clean, nonspectacular kill with a ketamine shot. Marla, way more popular, was killed in a daring manner, one that imprints on people's memory. Finally, Brianna opens the door for the Taker's ego to transcend the lines and reach beyond the realm of entertainment, well into politics, prime-time news coverage, the heart of our nation in DC."

"Jeez, Winnett, what the hell are you saying?" Pearson asked, running his hand over his shiny scalp a few times, nervously.

"I'm saying the Taker has something really special in mind for Brianna Gillespie."

Silence engulfed the room and lasted long moments. Tess refrained from adding anything else, afraid she'd dissipate the paper-thin urge she'd managed to arouse in her boss to hunt for the killer.

"Who's got eyes on the senator's residence?" she eventually asked. "You remember the Taker installs cameras everywhere, right?"

"Eat your burger, Winnett," Pearson snapped.

She understood quite well that he wanted her to shut up but couldn't say it to her face. Nevertheless, she used the opportunity to wolf down some food. Fradella followed suit.

"I have SA Patton and Walz on the scene," Pearson replied eventually, refusing her invitation to partake in some fries with a swift gesture of his hand.

"Patton's good, but Walz…" she started, but Pearson glared at her and she clammed up promptly.

The silence lingered on, tugging at her taut nerves. She shot the wall clock a quick glance, then broached the subject again.

"Is the scene compromised, sir? If those two tipped their hand in any way, the Taker knows."

"Winnett!" Pearson bellowed, and she froze, her hand, holding the last remaining fries, stuck in mid-air. "When are you going to stop assuming we're all idiots?"

"I didn't—"

"I'm not done yet," he added, still shouting. "We haven't compromised a single thing yet. Patton and Walz are a nice couple vacationing in the house across the street. They set eyes on Brianna earlier and have deployed surveillance discreetly—cameras, infrared, directional audio, the works."

"When did you have the time to—" she started to ask, then turned to Donovan. "Why didn't you tell me? For how many women down that list did we do this?"

"Five," he replied, after quickly glancing at her. "And sorry, but he's the ranking officer," he added, pointing to his right where Pearson sat.

She turned to Pearson. "Why didn't I know about this, sir?" She felt choked, and her eyes burned under the burden of shame, of feeling distrusted. What did he do, put out a memo, advising all those agents to surveil the targeted locations but not say a word to her?

"Get over it, Winnett," he replied. "It was my call to make, and I made it. Donovan's software was taking too damn long to finish crunching those names. Now let's call the senator; it's getting late."

"Sir, if I may," she said, wiping her mouth with a paper napkin and clearing her throat quietly. "I think someone should explain to the senator what we're trying to do, and how important it is. Brianna won't be in any danger whatsoever; we'll be all over her."

"You can't barge into a senator's house without permission," Pearson replied, seemingly more irritated than before. He'd been constantly checking his watch, every minute or so. "You can't surveil it without a warrant. You can't do anything but tell him."

"Do we have an exact location on him?" she asked, wondering if she could still come up with something.

"He's scheduled to give a speech for Memorial Day at 7:30PM," Donovan replied, after checking something on his phone.

"I'm calling him," Pearson said, and started dialing the number on the conference phone.

Out of options, she dove under the table and yanked the phone's cord from the outlet. "No, sir, I can't let you do that," she said, out of breath when she rose, holding the torn cable in her hand.

"Winnett," he snapped, slamming his hands against the table as he rose to his feet.

"Sir, I'm sorry, but there's no way you'll convince him to cooperate by phone. Let me send Bill to talk to him."

"You'll be asking a father to use his daughter to bait a trap, Winnett," he said in a low, menacing voice. "You know how I feel about that," he added, looking her straight in the eyes, as he made reference to Carrillo.

"And you know I deliver, sir, whatever it damn takes," she replied, matching his tone and his posture.

They stood like that for a long, tense moment, staring intently at each other, clenched in a silent battle of wills.

"You always get what you want, Winnett?" Pearson asked, breaking off eye contact.

"I try, sir."

"Okay, get Bill on this, right this moment. If he drives like a maniac, he'll get to the senator before his speech. I won't even ask why you have a supervisory special agent, the head of the Behavioral Analysis Unit in Quantico, no less, serve at your pleasure; right now, I need to run. In case you forgot, I have a shipment of drugs to seize and the DEA is waiting. And Winnett?" he added, looking over his shoulder from the doorway.

"Sir?"

"Don't screw this up."

52

The Senator

Senator Wallace Gillespie was already seated on the front row of plush seats, among other notable names scheduled to speak at the Memorial Day evening event. The secretary of defense was there, and so was the secretary of state, the two officials flanking Senator Gillespie, as if he were the president, chatting incessantly. Occasionally, a burst of laughter came from the three men.

Bill approached the front row after showing his badge to several law enforcement officers, then stopped in front of Gillespie.

"Senator, Bill McKenzie with the FBI," he said, keeping his voice down and showing his credentials discreetly. "I need to speak with you, sir. It's important."

"Now? I'm about to give a speech in less than ten minutes," the senator replied, then turned away and resumed his earlier conversation with the secretary of defense.

"It's about your daughter, Brianna," Bill said, and the laughter on the senator's lips froze into a grimace.

He stood and approached Bill, getting so close he could feel the scent of the man's aftershave.

"What about Brianna? What happened?"

"Please follow me," Bill said, leading the way to the side of the venue, where they could have a more private conversation.

The senator followed, the furrow on his brow matching the deep ridges around his mouth.

"Say it already," he said, grabbing Bill's sleeve and stopping him in place.

"We have reasons to believe your daughter has been targeted by a serial offender we're pursuing. We have ascertained he will make his move on her tonight. We need your permission to—"

But the senator had stopped listening, as soon as Bill had finished his first phrase; he'd beckoned a Secret Service agent.

"Who do you have in Florida? I need my daughter picked up and taken to a secure location."

"Understood," the agent replied, but froze in place, under Bill's commanding glance.

"Senator, if you're not willing to help us, we lose all hope of catching this killer. He could disappear forever."

"What are you saying? Are you out of your mind?" The senator's face was flushed, crimson and purple starting to tinge his tan skin; he grabbed Bill's lapel, squeezing and turning it in his fist.

"For now, he thinks he's in control," Bill continued unfazed, willing himself to ignore the senator's grip on his jacket. "But if he figures out we're one step ahead of him, he'll vanish and start killing people someplace else, unknown and unseen. Criminals like him never stop."

"I don't care," the senator snapped. "There's no way I'll have my daughter placed in harm's way like that. You must think I'm crazy, three strawberries short of a fruitcake." He let go of Bill's lapel and turned to the Secret Service agent. "What the hell are you still doing here?"

The agent turned to leave, but Bill called out. "Stop right there," he ordered.

"The FBI doesn't outrank the Secret Service, now does it?" the senator asked coldly.

"No, but the alternative isn't valid either," Bill replied calmly. "We're both federal organizations that should cooperate. Sir, I must insist. Your daughter will be safe at all times. We have teams around the house, and the moment the Taker shows up, we'll—"

"That's who's after my daughter? The Taker of Lives?" Gillespie reacted. "I saw it on the news last night, what he did to that poor woman. You're asking me to use my own daughter to lure a monster like that? Get the hell out of here," he added, shoving Bill out of the way.

Bill didn't budge, except for taking a step to the side to be back in the senator's path.

"She'll be perfectly safe, sir. I promise you."

"Move over," he growled between clenched teeth, "I have a speech to give."

"Ah, yes, the speech in which you'll speak about the value of human life, and how our heroes' sacrifice wasn't in vain? That kind of speech?" Bill retorted.

"Agent... whatever your name, I will have your badge as a centerpiece for my fireplace mantle before the end of today," he said, getting into Bill's face so close he could feel the senator's heated breath on his face. "I'm a damn US senator," he added, grabbing Bill with both hands by the collar and trying to move him out of the way.

Several Secret Service agents approached, guns drawn, but Bill didn't take his eyes off the senator's scrunched face.

"Yes, you're an elected official who swore to represent the interests of his constituents," Bill said serenely, speaking as if they were chatting casually over coffee and cookies. "To protect them and their families, to keep them safe from harm. Just imagine what those constituents will think if this got out. They'll be thrilled to hear that you let a serial killer go loose, to kill more of the citizens who voted for you."

"Are you blackmailing me?" the senator's voice climbed to a high, almost strangled pitch riddled with rage and disbelief. Tiny droplets of sweat formed at the roots of his receding hairline. "I'll have you fired before the end of the day, you crazy lunatic."

"Do that if you must, but help us catch this killer," Bill said calmly, his gaze steady and firm.

Gillespie let go of Bill's collar and breathed slowly a few times, pacing in place, as if trapped by an impossible decision. "You're a stubborn son of a bitch," he finally said, then made a hand gesture toward the Secret Service agents who promptly holstered their weapons. "Do you swear, on your life, that she'll be safe?"

"I swear," Bill replied, without skipping a beat. He knew Tess Winnett would rather die herself than let any harm come to Brianna Gillespie.

The senator sized him up, still thinking. Then he let out a loud, loaded breath of air and asked, "What exactly do you want to do?"

53

Seizure

SAC Pearson had boarded one of the Legend-class Coast Guard cutters via helicopter and now watched the radar together with a senior DEA agent. They had the *Reina del Mar* tracked by satellite and radar, clearly visible as it drifted in international waters, probably waiting for the cargo, while Paco Loco and his crew pretended to be fishing. No other vessel had approached the *Reina* since it went to sea that morning, although the shadows grew longer by the minute.

Was their intelligence wrong? Or had the Colombians rescheduled the shipment, because that bastard, Carrillo, couldn't provide the insurance he'd promised? He came close, even from the hospital room. Pearson nearly had to lock his daughter in her bedroom to prevent her from rushing to his bedside. The memory of her sobs and the things she'd said to him that morning were going to be with him for a while. One thing was for sure though; as soon as the cocaine was seized, DEA agents stood by to arrest Carrillo and remove him from his daughter's life forever.

Then he'd explain, and maybe she'd understand and forgive him for not trusting her with the truth about the man she'd fallen in love with.

Static crackled in the encrypted radio terminal.

"Phantom, this is Eye in the Sky, come in."

"Go, Eye, we read you," the operator said.

"We've got movement around the *Reina*, one stealth, go-fast boat, now stationary."

"Copy that, Eye. How close to the target?"

"They are loading the goods."

Pearson clenched his jaws. They were already too late.

The cutter was much slower than the *Reina*, its speed half that of the modern, overpowered fishing yacht. They weren't going to be able to catch up with it. Before he could say anything, he heard the DEA agent call the choppers in.

Impatient, he found the Coast Guard commander at his post. "Let's cut in front of them if we can," he said. "We already know where they're going."

"That's where we're headed," the commander replied calmly. "No one wants a high-speed chase at sea. It takes too damn long to reel them in."

"Right," he acknowledged.

"But you don't want them too close to shore either," the commander continued, just as calm. "In case we start shooting at each other. You don't want civilian casualties."

"Right," he repeated.

They obviously knew what they were doing, but he was increasingly restless. It probably had to do with the burning ire, sometimes even blinding rage, he'd felt ever since he'd learned those guys were planning to use his daughter as leverage and how they manipulated her and broke her heart. This time it was personal; he wanted those bastards to pay. If none of them made it to shore alive, he wouldn't be caught shedding a single tear.

"Where are you planning to stop them?" he asked, throwing a glance at a digital map displayed on a screen.

"Right here," the commander replied, putting his finger on the map, somewhere between Palm Beach Marina and the current location of the *Reina del Mar,* visible on the screen as a red dot. The Coast Guard vessel they were on, shown as a blue dot, was moving northbound along the international waters line, closing in on that position. Several other dots, green and yellow, marked the other resources involved in the operation: two helicopters, a couple of Coast Guard rigid-hulled inflatable boats, and another medium-sized vessel, standing by near the entrance of the marina.

The red dot started to move, slowly at first, but then catching speed. The other vessel, the Colombian stealth go-fast, was nowhere in sight on either radar. Probably it was a low-profile boat, slathered in black, nonreflective paint, almost invisible even to the naked eye from up close.

"We're letting them go?"

The commander briefly sucked his teeth. "Can't do anything about it. Foreign vessel in international waters, and Colombia won't grant us permission to board. We're still waiting to hear back on a request filed last year."

"Can't believe it," Pearson muttered. By the look the commander threw him, he understood the Coast Guard sympathized with his frustrations, and probably would've wanted just as much as he did to blow them out of the water, still there was nothing they could do.

The Coast Guard cutter traveled as fast as it could, but the choppers and the RHIBs were going to reach the *Reina* first.

The radio crackled to life about the time the yellow dots had reached the red one.

"Interceptor One moving in," a voice said.

"Interceptor Two in position," another voice said.

"We're taking fire," the first voice announced, almost screaming against a background of high-caliber shots fired. "We're hit! We're hit!"

Then silence for a split second.

"They've got rocket launchers," the second voice said. "We're breaking off. Eagle One, take over. Fire at will. Fire at will."

The red dot continued to move on the screen, without even slowing a little. One of the yellow dots had disappeared, the other one had veered to the south, putting some distance between the two vessels at the top of its speed.

Suddenly, the red dot turned around, heading back out to sea. Based on its trajectory, it was aiming to reach the Bahamas before the Coast Guard could catch up. By now it must've been clear to those onboard that they weren't going to make it to port with their load.

Eagles One and Two, the two green dots on the screen, approached the *Reina* in formation at high speed, catching up with it fast. Pearson held his breath, watching the green dots closing in, then one disappeared.

"Break off, break off," a voice screamed over the radio. "Eagle Two is down. I repeat, Eagle Two is down."

The sound of machine gun fire subsided, and there was silence over the waves again. They could actually see the *Reina* in their binoculars now, disappearing fast into the horizon.

There was nothing left to do.

The commander had changed course to the site of the helicopter crash, hoping to find survivors. The chopper's remnants still burned on the waves, sending whirls of black smoke into the air. It would be a miracle if anyone had survived what appeared to have been a direct hit from a rocket-propelled grenade, an RPG.

Pearson let himself fall into a nearby chair and crossed his arms at his chest. They were done, and the smugglers who had targeted his family were gone, roaming the waters free with millions of dollars in cocaine.

"Phantom, this is Eye in the Sky, come in."

"Go for Phantom," the operator promptly replied.

"We have a go-fast chasing after *Reina del Mar,* closing in quickly. Single individual onboard."

"Coast Guard?"

"Negative. It's a civilian craft. Has a racing symbol on the top, an infinity loop."

"Eagle One, go for intercept," the operator said, and the commander nodded his approval.

"Copy," Eagle One confirmed.

Pearson stood and stared at the radar, where the civilian craft appeared as an incredibly fast-moving dot.

"How fast is he going?" Pearson asked.

"About eighty, I'd say," the commander offered. "He'll catch up with the *Reina* before it reaches Grand Bahama waters." He compared the two views, the radar and the digital map, then added, "About the same time Eagle One gets to it."

"Eighty knots? Who the hell is this guy?"

No one replied; Pearson held his breath, watching the dots move on the radar. The civilian go-fast had almost reached the *Reina* when it slowed its speed, a few seconds before the *Reina* slowed too.

"Phantom, the civilian vessel opened fire on the *Reina*," Eagle One crackled over the choppy sound of a helicopter rotor. "Some kind of sniper fire, shooting holes in their engines from a mile out."

Cheers erupted in the control room.

"Civilian vessel, this is the United States Coast Guard, please identify yourself," the Eagle One operator called on all frequencies, approaching the go-fast from the west.

There was nothing but static on the air for a long moment.

"This is Gary Michowsky, Palm Beach County Sheriff's Office," a familiar voice announced. "The target vessel is dead in the water. Come pick up this load of trash, Coast Guard."

"Yeah!" Pearson reacted, then reached for the microphone. "Great job, Michowsky! Didn't know you were into speedboating."

"I'm not," Michowsky replied. "I borrowed this from a friend, and I'd better return it without a scratch. Only the sniper rifle's mine."

54

Tactical

Tess watched the Gillespie home through binoculars, hidden behind white sheers, standing at a window on the second floor of the house across the street from the senator's, on Seaspray Avenue. The owners, Dr. Weimer, a plastic surgeon, and his family, had been more than forthcoming and had allowed them unrestricted access to the property, while they withdrew to parts of the lower level, waiting anxiously for the entire thing to be over with. For obvious reasons, Tess didn't feel she could share too much of what they were after with the Weimers, hence they were understandably concerned.

Fradella had reached an agreement with the owner of the property behind the surgeon's house, allowing them access through the backyards into the Weimer's place, after a section of the fence had been temporarily removed. As such, they could go in and out of the Weimer house as frequently as they needed to, using Seabreeze Avenue, the street that ran parallel behind Seaspray Avenue, without the risk of being spotted by the Taker's surveillance.

Tess couldn't see much of the Gillespie frontage; just the main door and the driveway with the three-car garage. The house was a sprawling, single-story, white house with blue storm shutters, sitting on a perfectly green lawn. The rest of the house and the front lawn were obstructed from view by thriving palmettos and impeccably trimmed, eight-foot tall boxwood hedges. Even from her vantage point, she couldn't get an unobstructed view of the entire façade.

Two Palm Beach County Sheriff's Office detectives entered the room, followed by Detective Fradella.

Tess didn't take her eyes off the Gillespie home when Fradella announced, "We're all set."

"Walk me through it," she asked.

"The house is surrounded by patrol cars on speed enforcement, all within a five-minute drive from here," Fradella replied. "The units will respond to the chemical spill alert, as discussed. If the perp hears the dispatch call, he'll believe all units are moving out of the area."

"Okay," she said, refraining from adding that the Taker didn't need five minutes to end a life. Last time he needed less than five seconds. On the other hand, they couldn't risk bringing a single patrol car any closer to the target residence. She didn't want the Taker spooked and vanishing without a trace. "Any activity here, before we arrived?"

"The girl was home alone for a while, then she drove off in a red Beetle convertible with the top down," one of the detectives replied. "She met another girl for coffee at the Starbucks on Atlantic Avenue, then both of them drove back here together. They're inside the house right now."

"Who's the other girl?" she asked, frowning. She didn't like surprises, although she realized she should feel relieved instead. At least Brianna wasn't completely alone in the house.

"We didn't see much of her face to be sure," the detective replied, "and Brianna picked up the tab at Starbucks. She wore a sun hat and shades," he added, "but we ran her age and type against known friends or acquaintances in Brianna's life, and she most likely is Ashely Summers, twenty-six, no priors. She's an event planner who's been working with Brianna for a while."

"Ah, okay," Tess replied, still staring at the front windows. She couldn't see anything, due to sun glare and sheers. "How about the backyard? Do we have eyes there?"

"We do. We're tapped into all neighbors' surveillance, plus we have our own," Fradella replied, switching views on a laptop. The display showed a distant, grainy view of the backyard pool, where two girls lay on lounge chairs with drinks in their hands. The sun was descending quickly, about to set in less than an hour. Whatever visibility they still had in the backyard would soon be gone.

She was still watching the house when a Prius stopped in front of the place and a man dashed to the door in a determined step, almost running.

"I don't like this, people, who is this?" Tess asked.

"We have his plate," Fradella said. "Randall Lathrop, the TV evangelist. He's got priors for battery, disturbing the peace, but nothing major. He's her ex-boyfriend. Do we stop him?"

Tess inhaled quickly, the air burning her lungs after holding her breath for a long moment. "No. He doesn't fit the profile. Let it play out."

The man rang the doorbell, but almost immediately started pounding at the door impatiently.

"Do we have audio on that?" Tess asked.

The detective turned up the volume on the laptop and distant, flaky noises came from the built-in speakers.

Brianna opened the door, wearing a minimalistic bikini, then immediately wanted to push it shut. "Get lost, Randy," she yelled, but Randall had put his foot in the door, preventing her from closing it.

"Intervene now?" the detective asked.

"No, hold still," she replied firmly. "This is not the unsub."

"Lost?" Randall spoke angrily, wielding his fist in the air. "You dare talk to me of being lost? Look at you!" Then he spat on the ground. "You should be ashamed of yourself."

Brianna said something unintelligible, still trying to force the door shut, but then the other girl appeared in the doorway. She wore a one-piece swimsuit, a large, white hat, and Chanel shades, looking like a full-page ad for *Travel and Leisure* magazine. She held her phone in her hand and showed it to the man.

"I already called the cops, you freak," she said. "Get the hell outta here."

"Do we have an active 911 call?" Tess asked. If that was true, the Taker was never going to show.

"Negative, Agent Winnett. Just a girl with a lot of grit," the detective replied.

Tess smiled when she saw Randall turn away and leave, spilling Bible verses and curses in the same, endless rant. "Way to go, Ms. Summers."

Randall climbed behind the wheel of his car and disappeared in a cloud of dust.

"Good riddance," the detective said.

"Not so fast," Tess reacted. "I want this man pulled over and kept busy until we end our operation."

"On what charge?"

"Just say the neighbors complained about his violent behavior, because I just did and right now I'm the neighbor. Have a unit pick him up. Dispatch them by cell phone."

"On it," the detective replied, after glancing at Tess for a quick moment, unable to hide his frustration. He probably didn't take too well to being bossed around by a fed. Tough luck.

Fradella followed the exchange and smiled, visibly amused.

Tess pulled a chair near the window and watched the street, painfully aware of the dimming light. Soon they'd lose all visibility into what was going on. On the laptop monitor, the girls still splashed in the pool, drinking, laughing, turning the music volume higher and higher with each song they loved to hear and belt along with.

It was almost completely dark, when a green Beemer convertible pulled in the driveway. Two young men in white golf shirts and baseball caps hollered loudly a few times, honked twice, then one of them dialed a number from his car's media center.

"Open the gates, girls," the man said, "we come bearing gifts."

One of the garage doors opened, and they drove inside.

"I don't like this," Fradella said. "Not one bit."

"Who are they?" Tess asked calmly. Neither of them was the Taker; he never hunted in pairs; only alone. He would've never tolerated to share his fame with another human being.

"Car plate comes back to Wesley H. Stone, eighteen."

The other detective whistled between his teeth. "Eighteen and a brand new M4 convertible Beemer in his name. What a life."

"He's a student, a colleague of Brianna's. I'll take a leap of faith and assume the other kid is too. You good with that?" Fradella asked.

Tess nodded, absentmindedly. Where was the Taker right now, and what was he doing? Was he bothered by all these people at Brianna's house? Or did he feel challenged by the larger crowd he needed to overpower?

"But why the garage?" the detective asked. "I don't pull into the garage when I visit with friends."

Fradella chuckled and shot Tess an amused look. She barely refrained from groaning.

"That's because they're bringing liquor, and that's illegal at their age, last time I checked," Fradella clarified.

A few moments later, the two boys, wearing colorful swim shorts, splashed in the pool. Brianna came out, carrying bottles of booze, and the other girl followed with glasses and a bucket of ice. The party was just starting.

She watched them for a while, feeling the tension in her body increase with every passing minute. There was still time until midnight, but not a lot more. Every few minutes she checked the Taker's website, and nothing had changed for hours; only the vote counter was constantly increasing, now at over thirty-five million votes in favor of killing Brianna Gillespie tonight.

Several hours later, the party ended; it was about 11:15PM. One of the two boys washed his face repeatedly with cold water at the poolside shower, probably to sober up enough to drive. After a few moments, the garage door opened, and the Beemer reversed. The top was up, and they thought they saw the other girl's large, white hat in the back seat.

"Stop this car on a traffic check?" Fradella asked. "He'll score a DUI for sure."

"Might spook the Taker," Tess replied. "It's too late; it's almost midnight. Let them go."

About ten minutes later, they saw Brianna on video take another splash in the pool, all by herself. She didn't bother to clean up or anything; a maid was probably going to do that the next morning. Ms. Summers was nowhere in sight, confirming the theory that it must've been her in the back seat of the Beemer, hitching a ride with the two boys.

Brianna Gillespie was home alone, just in time for the Taker's midnight call.

Only he wasn't anywhere to be seen.

Frustrated as hell and feeling nervous tension that bore burning holes in her skull, Tess refreshed the Taker's site once more. This time it was live, displaying a new message from the killer.

It read, "Thirty-seven million people have spoken their choice." And a countdown, showing twelve minutes left.

It was precisely 11:48PM.

Cursing out loud, Tess dialed Donovan's cell. He picked up immediately.

"How sure are you it's Brianna he's after?"

"At least ninety-five percent," he said, but she sensed hesitation and self-doubt in his voice.

"Damn it to bloody hell, Donovan!"

55

Exposed

Tess watched the countdown reaching zero while holding her breath. Did they get everything wrong? Was the Taker of Lives about to evade capture yet again, while murdering an innocent girl live on camera, for the gratification of millions of viewers lurking in the blackest recesses of the Dark Web?

Finally, the curtains pulled open on the Taker's streaming site, and the image of a girl's bedroom filled the screen. Tess took the photos shared reluctantly by the senator and compared the images quickly. Yes, it was Brianna's bedroom, and the unconscious girl being stripped naked by hands covered in black latex was the senator's seventeen-year-old daughter they'd sworn to protect from all harm.

She took the radio in her hand while rushing downstairs. "Breach! Breach! Breach!" she ordered, and SWAT swarmed around the house, running from the Weimer's yard in full gear.

They busted the door down and rushed inside, clearing all the rooms one by one. Tess ran in after them with her weapon drawn, headed straight for the girl's bedroom, the home's layout still fresh in her mind after reviewing the blueprints and the senator's notes.

The door to Brianna's bedroom was open; she approached it carefully, gun in hand, ready to fire at the tiniest move. She raised her hand with her fist closed, signaling the SWAT behind her to stop and wait for her signal.

Then she sneaked a peek into the room, her gun aligned with her line of sight, her hand firm and her finger on the trigger.

The girl lay naked and sprawled on the bed, her wrists tied in handcuffs attached to chains mounted on the wall. The Taker had straddled Brianna's body and held a gun to her temple, keeping his eyes on Tess and stretching the shiny latex that covered his mouth into a hint of an arrogant grin.

Tess raised her hands in the air, slowly, removing her finger off the gun's trigger, yet unable to take her eyes off the massive erection apparent through the Taker's latex suit. She waited for the unsub to make his demands, but nothing came; not a single word. Instead, he gestured with his hand and she understood the urgency behind his impatience. She crouched to the floor and placed the gun down, then slowly stood.

"See? I'm unarmed now," she spoke in a reassuring tone of voice. "This can still end well for you."

The Taker shook his head without a word, then grabbed Brianna by the throat with his left hand, while his right shoved the gun barrel in her mouth.

"No," Tess pleaded, feeling her heart thumping against her rib cage. One noise from outside, one random, innocent event could trigger the Taker's reaction. Then she realized the camera was still taking video, transmitting it online, live, just as Tess had dared the Taker to do. As far as the Taker knew, tens of millions of people were watching their confrontation; Donovan had cut that transmission, but the Taker had no idea. Tess had cornered herself into a situation that couldn't end well and had gambled with Brianna's life while at it.

Or maybe not... Maybe she could use who she knew the Taker was, deep inside, where only she could see the monsters dancing.

"We could end this nicely," she pleaded, "for them." She pointed at the camera. "For you." She swallowed, willing herself to be patient, to not overplay her hand. "This is your masterpiece," she said, lowering her voice to almost a whisper. "Brianna... Your final show. Don't let it end with SWAT snipers putting a bullet through your skull when you least expect it."

The Taker shook his head again, gesturing toward the covered window. There was no direct line of sight for any sniper, and he knew it.

"They use radar and infrared technology these days. They no longer need a direct line of sight," Tess said, lying without hesitation. "And you won't see the laser dot lighting up your chest. But your viewers will see your blood splashed all over the walls instead of Brianna's, and will know you failed."

His shoulders raised, a telltale sign of stress, of fear and angst, despite the full body latex suit. She was getting close.

"They'll see your real face, your body naked, exposed, vulnerable, just another perp who got caught by the Feds," she continued. "Is this the way you want to remain in the memory of tens of millions of people around the world?"

"Do you promise?" the Taker spoke, and that voice sent reverberations of surprise through Tess's mind.

It was a woman's voice, a voice she vaguely recognized.

Slack-jawed, Tess couldn't find her words; the Taker was a woman! How could she have not seen that coming?

She frowned, thinking there would probably be a lot of time to analyze that at a later time after the Taker was finally booked and thrown in jail.

She managed to focus and replied. "Yes, I promise, if you put the gun down and step toward me, behind the camera. We'll turn it off, then we'll take you out of here, unseen, shielded."

"And there's no press outside?"

"No," Tess replied. "They aren't allowed anywhere near active breach sites. They won't witness your defeat; no one will."

The Taker stared at Brianna's face for a long moment, removing the gun from her face and letting go of her throat. She touched Brianna's lips, then arranged a few locks of her hair in a caressing, almost tender gesture that made Tess feel bile rising in her throat. Then the Taker let her gun drop to the floor.

She leaped over and grabbed the Taker's arm, while shouting, "Clear!" SWAT officers rushed in, the first two to enter the bedroom grabbing the Taker's arms, while Tess ran past them and felt for Brianna's pulse. It was strong and steady, and the girl shifted in her sleep when she felt Tess's cold fingers touching her neck.

"Get EMS in here," she called. They'd placed an ambulance on standby in the Weimer's boat garage; it was going to take less than a minute to get there.

Then she remembered the camera. Fradella was already dismantling it, getting ready to package it in evidence bags.

She freed Brianna's wrists from the handcuffs, giving the entire setting a disgusted look. "He was going to suspend her on the wall," she said, answering an unspoken question, "like a trophy."

She turned to the Taker and ripped the latex off her face. Then she gasped and took a step back.

"It's you!" she said. "The—"

"Insignificant, totally forgettable girlfriend?" the Taker replied, with a bitter laugh.

She beckoned a uniformed cop to bring the mobile fingerprint scanner. The young cop approached and removed the glove from the Taker's right hand, then scanned her index finger.

"Althea Swain, twenty-seven," he announced. "No priors."

"Then how come she's in the system?" Tess asked, her frown deepening. The name sounded familiar, but something was off, and she couldn't pinpoint what it was.

"Get this: she's a TSA-preapproved traveler. She probably flies a lot."

"Of course, she does," Tess sighed.

She examined the Taker's body, still clad in the latex suit, searching for any indication in its shape that could've pointed to a woman, something they'd missed when watching the prior videos. That massive erection still showed through the thin latex, probably a strap-on of some sort. There wasn't anything to give away the curves of a female body. No breasts pushing through the latex, no waistline, no hips.

Only one thing could explain it, probably the reason why the latex suit seemed to be too large, by at least two sizes.

"Remove this suit and bag it," she said. "It's evidence. Take photos, before and after." She didn't believe the Taker was naked underneath that suit; far from it.

As the suit came off, her suspicions were confirmed. The Taker had wrapped her body with tight stretches of fabric, flattening her breasts and modifying her shapes to match the contour of a slightly overweight man. She'd padded her flat abdomen to hide her waistline and the curves of her hips, and even added some love handles to make the body image seem real. The craftsmanship was impressive, and she wasn't the only one thinking that; she realized it when she heard Fradella's whistle. The padding was sewn onto a makeshift suit with a zipper, easy to put on and remove in seconds. The strap-on was attached over the padding, standing out obscenely purple against the Taker's pale skin.

Tess stretched her lips into a smile, giving the Taker a good look, head to toe. Then she turned to Fradella and asked, "Is that camera still ready to transmit?"

Fradella frowned for a moment, then relaxed when he noticed Tess's wink. "It can be, in a second."

"You promised, bitch!" the Taker reacted, pulling against the two officers holding her by the arms.

Tess's smile died on her lips. "I lied."

EMS barged in through the door and loaded Brianna, still fast asleep, onto a stretcher, then made their way quickly to the bus waiting outside. Tess followed them outside to make sure they moved as fast as they could, considering the potential exposure always associated with everything the Taker did. The streaming site was offline, taken down by Donovan the moment he could lock onto the camera's Wi-Fi connection and run a trace.

A black Chevy Suburban pulled to the curb, and Senator Gillespie hopped out of it before it had reached a complete stop. He rushed to the ambulance, where the techs were reviving Brianna. Turning, he yanked Tess by her arm, probably seeing her FBI badge hanging from a lanyard around her neck.

"You swore to me she'd be safe!" he bellowed.

"She is safe," she replied quietly. "She probably won't remember any of this."

The senator shoved her away with such force that she slammed into the open ambulance door, then he turned to the EMS who was fitting Brianna with a blood pressure cuff.

"Talk to me, damn it, I'm her father."

"She's stable, vitals are strong, and this is more of a precaution," the EMS said, pointing at the stretcher. "She was roofied, nothing more."

"Roofied?" he yelled, turning toward Tess with a death glare. "Does that sound safe to you?"

"Sir, may I suggest you let them do their job and move her away from here? The press will soon roll in, and I'm sure you want nothing of that kind of attention."

He didn't reply, nor did he stop glowering at her for another long moment. Then he climbed in the back of the ambulance and ordered them to drive to a private clinic.

Tess didn't breathe normally until the ambulance disappeared from view. She looked at the street, filled with law enforcement vehicles flashing red and blue, the entire area now cordoned off and restricted to traffic. Still, the media was bound to arrive soon.

She went back inside the house and ran into the two SWAT officers escorting Althea Swain outside. The Taker walked with incredible dignity, her head held up high and her black hair now loose of hairpins and the wig net she'd worn underneath the head mask. She looked left and right, probably searching for the media and their camera flashes.

"No way you're getting any of that, bitch," Tess mumbled between her teeth, realizing that she craved attention more than she feared being exposed in her failure. "Put her in that," she said to the officers, pointing at Fradella's SUV, equipped with deep-tinted windows. "Let's make sure the press doesn't get a hold of her."

"How did you like my message, Agent Winnett?" the Taker asked, as she was being loaded into the back of the SUV.

"What message?" Tess asked, frowning.

"I sent you an email a couple of days ago. Check again."

Tess grunted but checked her phone. Her work inbox didn't have an email from anyone who could've been the Taker of Lives.

"No, there's nothing," she replied, turning to leave.

"Not that inbox, Agent Winnett. Your personal one."

She felt her blood turn to ice. How did the Taker know her personal email address? She opened her Gmail and scrolled through a bunch of unread emails; over the past few days, she hadn't had the time to do anything of that sort.

There it was, and the sender was clearly identified as Taker of Lives in bold lettering, marking the email as new, not previously opened.

The message read, "How would you like your best-kept secrets shared with the world, my dear Tess? I can make all that happen for you. I can bring back memories that have been buried for twelve years. Would you like that?"

Tess felt her blood turn to ice, then to fire, as rage took over. Somehow the Taker of Lives knew about her past, knew about the night she'd been assaulted. What could she really do, though? Was she a real danger? She was going away for a long time. She clenched her jaws, fighting the urge to shoot her where she sat. Instead, she shrugged and put the phone back in her pocket.

"I have no clue what the hell you're talking about. There's no email from you," she said, looking the Taker dead in the eyes. "Tell me, how did you get so close to all those people?"

Althea stared at her for a while, trying to figure out if Tess was telling the truth. Then a crooked smile appeared at the corner of her mouth, curling her lips.

"These bitches, they're so used to having people revolve around them, they don't pay attention anymore. They only think of themselves, and the world doesn't see it, just like the world doesn't see me. You didn't see me either, did you, Agent Winnett?" She stopped talking for a moment, and a wave of sadness washed over her eyes. "Did you know I auditioned for Jane's part in Twilight? They gave it to Dakota Fanning instead. I wasn't a physicality fit, they said."

Tess shrugged again, not giving a damn about the Taker's self-pity, but Althea misunderstood the gesture.

"That meant they wanted an ethereal blonde to play the part, not a strong, tall brunette like me. Same thing happened when I auditioned for the lead role in Fifty Shades. Only for that part, my boobs were too small. They said I wasn't sexy enough, not memorable enough. Can't fight that, especially when everyone seems to think it."

Tess turned to her, starting to feel how tired she was now that the adrenaline of the hunt had washed away. "You mean to say, you did all this out of spite, out of envy over some movie part?"

Althea shook her head and looked at Tess with disappointment. "You think it's pathetic, don't you? We live in a world of superficial fools who choose these empty shells of brainless puppets as their role models, while someone like me doesn't stand a chance. Can you believe it?"

"Yet you'd kill to have the same fools fawn over you?" Tess asked. "Wait a second... you did kill? Yes, you did, and you're going away for good. You'll see how famous you'll be, all that fresh meat entering the prison system for a long, long time." Then she turned to Fradella who'd climbed behind the wheel, ready to drive off. "I want to book her myself."

They drove off and rode in silence for a while. A fleeting, half-baked thought gnawed at Tess's weary mind; there was something she couldn't place, a correlation she was missing.

"What was the name of Christina Bartlett's best friend?" Fradella asked. "The one who went to Europe to study?" He pointed at the notepad he kept between the seats. "It's in there."

She flipped through the pages until she found the scribbled note. "Yeah, you nailed it! Althea Swain, there she is. Great memory." She flipped a few more pages. "But that's not where we met, Miss Abby Sharp, isn't it? You sure like your initials, don't you, Miss Ashely Summers? That's who you were for Brianna."

"Now you understand the depths of my talent, Agent Winnett," the woman replied, smiling, relaxed again as if she were interviewing for *Entertainment Weekly*.

56

Me: Amazing

I am licensed to deceive and manipulate individuals and large groups of people; in other words, I have a degree in public relations with a minor in sociology. If there's anything I understand well in this twisted, nonsensical world, it's people. Their inmost fears, their primal urges, their unspoken secrets, so terrifying they won't even admit them to themselves, in the quiet privacy of their own thoughts.

It doesn't matter who you are, what nationality, what age or gender. It doesn't matter if you're an honest blue-collar worker, a renowned scientist, or a rowdy teenager. I can push your buttons to make you feel what I want, when I want. I can make you tremble in fear or I can make you jump for joy, willing to accept the celebratory glass of roofied alcohol out of my hands, while wishing me all the best there is to wish for a nice girl like me.

Christina was the easiest, but also the most difficult. She and I were good friends since high school, or so I liked to believe. It was she who showed me the most there was to learn about the injustice of this world. She demonstrated the value of certain genetics in opening doors and garnering opportunities. For everything I needed to work hard, she only had to accept. Wherever I had to beg, push, or claw my way, she only had to show up. I know what you're going to say, but it wasn't her father's influence that made it happen. It was her long, blonde locks, her blue eyes, her pale skin, her C cups, and her thin waist.

But not only that.

I dyed my hair and wore contacts for a while, padded my bra, and starved myself into a size four. Nothing happened! Those doors I was hoping to pry open stubbornly refused to cede, remaining forever locked in front of me, no matter how I transformed myself.

Curious, I chose my major with the hope of understanding what made people lay their worlds at the feet of someone like Christina.

I got what I was looking for.

I understood.

I also happened not to like the answer, because there was nothing I could do to transform myself into what I wanted to become.

Yeah, you guessed it.

It's sex.

The answer to all the questions is that simple, three-letter word that opens doors and gilds the paths of certain people, male or female.

To translate the concept into easier to understand words, it's the measure in which people would like to have sex with a certain person. In other words, fuckability.

I know you'll hate the word, but you'll grasp the concept.

No amount of makeup, of hair dye, of skin bleach can improve that factor. It's pheromone driven, and I don't believe science fully understands it yet.

Take Joan of Arc, for instance. She was always described as beautiful, but somehow managed to live among military men, even sleep next to them in barns and such, but never have intercourse with any of them. No one thought of touching her. Why? Simply put, she wasn't desirable. Fuckability score: fail.

Whether I like to admit it or not, I don't pass either.

I'd fallen in love with Santiago Flores, but he only saw Christina, even if she was engaged to another guy. I just didn't exist.

I cried endless nights with my face buried in my pillow, until I understood and accepted my reality.

My face is bland, immemorable. By the time I was sixteen, I was already tired of having people call me by different names, always being the someone who "looks just like," then insert a random name; I've heard it all.

I am common-looking, almost maternal, despite my unsatisfactory body shape. I asked my sociology professor to explain it, and he stared at me for the longest time, evaluating, thinking. Then he said, "You're best friend material, not girlfriend material. I can't place why, but it's there."

And best friend I have become. A serial one, you might add.

All I've got going for me is brains; lots of it. I accepted it, grateful for having even that much.

Then came the anguish, the revolt. My life can't be lived in mediocrity and despair, because my smile isn't loaded with innuendo, or my sweet-sixteen crush was a computer, not some movie star who never knew I existed. I deserve to make the big bucks, just as much as the likes of Christina, maybe even more. I have the brainpower to create, invent, innovate, and better the world we live in.

Does it matter? Unfortunately, no.

Why? Because no one really wants to fuck me or become more like me.

There is no brain envy in the world we live in, only body-plus-pheromone envy, that's it.

Somewhere during the course of evolution, things took a terribly wrong turn. In the animal kingdom, only the smartest individuals gain access to mates and reproduce. They're the fastest predators, the most skilled hunters of the wild, the most ingenuous den builders of the forest that get to continue their genetic material, and that goes for any species above the intellectual level of birds.

We all know the peacock and his fancy tail feathers, his entertaining mating ritual, and yes, you'd have to have the brain of a bird to fall for that and take Mr. Peacock to bed, hence agreeing to have peachicks with no brains, just looks.

Except if you're human.

Then you can choose to procreate based solely on good looks and desirability, with no regard for intellect. Women are still feeling the effects of latent DNA code that triggers desire when they see strong male arms with well-developed muscles; ages ago that was the sign of a good provider. Today? Not necessarily, yet women shiver when they see a cool set of abs to complement nice biceps, and a Beemer key on the man's keychain. Yeah... for the same reason, women are sexually triggered by displays of wealth.

It doesn't matter that in today's world, neither means anything worth transmitting in one's genes. One could be a gym freak, the other an heir of some importance but little personal value who might choose not to provide after all.

Do we care?

No, because intellect doesn't even come into play. No wonder the average intelligence quotient of the world's population is declining.

As soon as I understood that for myself, I wanted the entire world to see it, as clearly as I did.

My immemorable, almost chameleonic face helped me gain access quickly to all those famous bitches who made it on my list.

Yeah, I had a list.

I didn't build it solely on the basis of fame; no, I wanted exposure to the right kind of people, those who least understood what should be most important: intelligence. Those who could drive change, or at least accept it.

Christina was the easiest for me; she and I went back a long time, and I had unrestricted access to her house. Even with her, to ensure the result I was aiming for, I "disappeared" to Europe for a while, then unexpectedly showed up on her doorstep one night with a bottle of expensive wine in my hand, not by any accident her favorite brand.

"I'm getting married!" I announced, the moment the door swung open. Then I showed her a big diamond ring.

Hugs and tears followed, and, yes, she drank from the bottle I'd brought, laced with Rohypnol via a needle through the cork. She didn't pay attention to me enough to notice I wasn't drinking, because, in case you forgot, I'm kind of immemorable, not that interesting to begin with. People forget I'm in the room, moments after I've entered it, even if no one else is there but me.

With Estelle, I was pregnant; that was the announcement. For each one of them, I had a different story, one that resonated the best with their inmost desires. With Deanna, I was getting married, yet again; yeah, I recognize the lack of imagination here, but she was also engaged. It fit.

With Haley, I'd just scored a major role in a movie, and I was going to work under Spielberg himself.

With Marla, I struggled and almost failed. I couldn't get close to her. Security guards everywhere, she was never alone in public, so my spilled Starbucks ruse didn't work.

Oh, I forgot to tell you about that.

For each girl I needed a different, clean identity, in case the cops wanted to check me out. It wasn't that hard; all these girls have a ton of vendors, of people they work with: publicists, event planners, assistants, communication specialists, florists, caterers, you name it. I'd look for someone in a line of work I could function in, someone with my initials preferably, the only anchor to the real me I wanted to preserve.

The plan was simple, perfect, easy to execute and repeat indefinitely. First, identify someone who would fit, a young woman who looked like someone I could transform into; she was the identity I would borrow. Over time, I'd get my hands on some of her personal data and get me a driver's license and a credit card in her name, just in case the cops ever wanted to see those. I'd never misuse that data; I never charged a single dollar on those credit cards. I'm not a thief.

Then I'd approach the target with a simple ruse; run into them and spill their coffee at Starbucks or wherever they went for it. How did I know? Simple; I borrowed a cable installer's truck every now and then and hung cameras in the trees across the street from their houses. Then I'd return the truck to the driveway it came from before the owner would wake up for yet another day, and watch patiently from my car, ready to follow my target the moment she left the house.

Then, with that coffee spilled, I'd bury myself in apologies and insist until they'd let me buy another cup for them. A touch of heroin on the lid of that cup or the tip of that straw would create a powerful association in the target's mind; they felt good in my presence, and they wanted more.

During the ensuing small talk, I'd offer my services for free, to compensate for the stained clothing and the disruption in their day. I'd listen to them yap incessantly about countless, trivial things in their lives, fueling my strategy with each one of them and giving me all the elements to surprise them when the time came.

Then I was in.

In all fairness, with Haley, it didn't go as planned, not at first. Her publicist had been with her for years, and I couldn't get her to replace the guy. The dude had to have a serious slip and fall off a flight of stairs to open that door for me.

With Marla, as I was saying, nothing worked. I couldn't get close enough to her. But I was able to get close enough to her caterer and his assistant. I ran the Starbucks scheme on the caterer, then we went out for dinner and made friends; I was posing as a caterer myself, starting with smaller clients and offering my services to him, in the eventuality he needed more help for bigger venues. Then, what do you know? On the eve of the upcoming Adam Quinn party, his assistant became unavailable. She accidentally sat on a syringe needle at the local movie theater, and she was petrified with fear of AIDS. A nice woman in the public told her how important it was to seek immediate medical attention.

No, she doesn't have AIDS, if that's what you're thinking. It was a perfectly sterile needle; I only gave her a brutal attack of acute fear, to keep her indisposed for a few days, until the test results came back. I really have nothing against hard-working women.

I don't regret anything I've done; they all deserved to die, they all deserved to be exposed for the frauds they were. If there's anything I regret, it is something I didn't do.

This Agent Winnett has skeletons in her closet I would've liked to unearth. I've seen the missed heartbeat in her carotid when she read my email; there's pain buried in there, and I will dig it up somehow and savor its exquisite taste to the last bit.

That's a promise.

She's becoming much too famous for me to tolerate. Did you see all those people taking orders from her? When the media arrived, she was immediately surrounded, but all she did was glare at them and yell, "no comment."

Stupid bitch.

57

Dinner and A Movie

"So, you couldn't take their fame, could you?" Tess asked, turning in her seat and looking at the Taker, who sat calmly as if being driven to a club. "You couldn't deal with the fact that they got all the attention, while you got nothing. You only got to watch. I remember how you sat there on that couch, holding poor Estelle in your arms and feeding off her pain like a parasite, drinking in every teardrop, every sob. How good that must've felt, didn't it?"

"Not nearly as good as it should have," she replied calmly.

"Okay, I feel for you. I believe I understand you now, and I'll help you get the attention you deserve."

Tess smiled when she saw Fradella's surprised glance and winked at him discreetly.

"Detective," Tess asked, "what's the prison with the worst inmate-assault statistics, do you know?"

He didn't get a chance to reply. Althea threw herself against the partition between the front and back seats, slamming her shoulder into the steel mesh. "You can't do this, bitch!"

Tess faced her with a serene smile. "Just watch me."

That had the effect of a bucket of cold water poured on the detainee's head. She clammed up and withdrew in the corner of the back seat as far away from Tess as possible.

They took Althea to booking a few minutes later, and Tess nearly choked with laughter when the woman announced to the booking officer that she was open to discuss book and movie rights, if any inquiries became available. She behaved as if she didn't understand her reality, when, in fact, she was well aware of it and ready to take advantage to the maximum extent possible.

"In her own way, she's fascinating," Tess said to Fradella on their way out of the precinct. "The way she gained access to all those houses, her strategies, her timing."

"Yeah," Fradella replied, "and I'm so glad it's over."

"No kidding," she laughed.

On the front steps they ran into Michowsky, whose five o'clock shadow, dating back at least three days ago, lent him a new look, albeit a little more hobo than macho. Tess swallowed a chuckle and hugged the man, ignoring the smell of sweat and grime put out by the clothes he hadn't changed in more than one stakeout.

"What are you still doing here?" she asked. "Go home, get some rest."

"I caught some sleep in the car, while your perp was gathering votes," he replied. "Nice work, you two."

The sun had completely risen and threw darts of almost unbearable light in their direction. Tess shifted her position to put a palm tree between her tired eyes and the reason for her squinting.

"It's been a few hours since we caught the Taker, Gary. Where in the hell have you been all this time?"

"Definitely not taking a shower," Fradella quipped, and Michowsky quickly elbowed him in the side.

"If you really need to know, I borrowed a speedboat yesterday. I had to return it before, um—"

"Before you got caught?" Fradella laughed.

"Oh, don't tell me," Tess said, putting two and two together. "You didn't..."

"Yeah, I did," he confessed, lowering his gaze and staring at the asphalt for a moment. "I heard on the radio they weren't getting anywhere with seizing that coke, and I knew he already had it near the water, so I made a run for it. The thing was right there, by the ramp, begging me for a good race."

"He's going to kill you," Tess said, only half-jokingly.

"Nah... he won't know. That's what I've been doing all night, wiping the thing dry."

That moment, Michowsky's phone rang. The display showed Donovan's name.

"Uh-oh," Tess said.

Michowsky put the call on speaker. "Go for Michowsky, Fradella, and Winnett," he said, as if it were just another normal day at work.

"Imagine my surprise," Donovan said, in a low voice, "when I watch the news about this major cocaine bust, and I see my damn boat in action!"

"Listen, I can explain," Michowsky said. "I'll never—"

"I don't want to hear a single word, Michowsky. If you ever have to do this again, at least have the courtesy to take me along for the ride, okay? At least that much field action I should get, don't you think?"

"Understood," Michowsky replied quickly, but Donovan had already hung up.

"What? You were on the news?" Fradella asked.

"Yeah, and driving a stolen vessel no less," Tess laughed. "Our very own hero. Fantastic work, Gary." She hugged him again. "Thank you very much for your help."

Then she hugged Fradella. "You too, Todd. You broke the case, you know that."

"Me?" he reacted. "How come?"

"You figured out the mathematical model to replicate the Taker's choice of targets. Donovan went too complicated, but you nailed it. You asked the right questions."

He grinned widely, apparently at a loss for words.

"Now, does anyone want to touch on the fact that our profile was completely wrong?" Tess asked, her laughter replaced with a frown.

"It was spot on, and it worked," Michowsky replied. "You caught the Taker."

"Well, Althea Swain might be Caucasian, but she's definitely not a male."

"Ah, that," he reacted, and the three of them burst into laughter.

"Are female serial killers that common though?" Fradella asked.

"They're not, and that's why we typically jump to concluding the male part of the profile. Women account for ten percent of the perpetrators of all the murders in the United States, but they are responsible for twenty percent of the serial killing victims, and that percentage has been slowly increasing over the years."

"So male, Caucasian is no longer the norm?" Michowsky asked.

"The Caucasian part has definitely gone away; like I mentioned before, beginning with the nineties, the majority of serial killers have been black, and Caucasian whites have dropped to the second spot. The gender majority is still held by men, but even that is shifting."

"How are they different, men versus women, when it comes to serial killing?" Fradella asked.

"Women are less likely to physically torture their victims," Tess replied. "That should've been a warning sign for us that the profile was wrong, combined with the absence of violent sexual assault. We should've seen this, guys; next time we'll be more careful before applying statistics blindly."

"Hey, cut yourself some slack, willya?" Michowsky said, patting her on the shoulder vigorously. "We caught the perp, and that's because of you and what you saw in Christina's suicide."

There was a moment of uncomfortable silence, then Fradella turned around and went back inside. "I'll get us some coffee, okay?" he shouted from the top of the stairs.

She sat on the last step and stretched, drained yet happy, a subdued sense of exhilaration fueling her entire body. Michowsky sat next to her, leaning against the bannister. Then he started laughing softly.

"What?" she asked.

He looked at her with amusement in his eyes. "Have you noticed how his phone's not ringing anymore, not that often?"

She fidgeted a little. "Now that you tell me, yeah. Why?"

"Our boy's off the market," he said, his grin widening.

She didn't get it at first, but as she started to understand what Michowsky was hinting at, she felt her cheeks burning.

"Yeah," Michowsky added, "I believe my partner is totally, head over heels—"

Fradella kicked him playfully with the tip of his shoe. "And desperately interested in joining the FBI," he added, speaking faster than he normally did. "Think you could put in a good word for me, Tess?"

She hid her blooming smile and replied, as professionally as she could muster under the circumstances. "Sure, I can. I think you'd be great. I'll send you a link to fill out some forms." The words came naturally; he had talent for the job and he'd probably make a great career for himself as a federal agent. He made her proud.

She stood and took the paper cup filled to the brim from his hand, then took a sip.

Fradella continued to look at her intently, as if he still wanted to say something. He squinted in the merciless sun and smiled hesitantly.

"Wanna grab some really, really late dinner, then maybe catch a movie?" he asked.

Tess smiled and looked briefly at Michowsky, whose grin hadn't vanished.

"You kids go ahead," Michowsky said, groaning as he stood. "I haven't seen my family in days."

She shook his hand and watched him walk to his car, then disappear after turning the corner. Then she closed her eyes and let the warm rays of the sun caress her skin. She saw herself on the beach, lying on the hot sand next to Fradella, eating grapes and letting the heat wear off the tension in her body. Dozing off. Feeling safe. Somehow, that idyllic image looked like the perfect ending to a long weekend filled with darkness and pain.

"How about the beach instead?" she asked.

He smiled and took her hand. "You got it."

~~ The End ~~

Read on for an excerpt from

Las Vegas Girl

They're two fearless, driven, unrelenting cops. They trust each other with their lives... only not with their darkest secrets.

Thank You!

A big, heartfelt thank you for choosing to read my book. If you enjoyed it, please take a moment to leave me a four- or five-star review; I would be very grateful. It doesn't need to be more than a couple of words, and it makes a huge difference. This is your link: http://bit.ly/TLRev.

Join my mailing list for latest news, sale events, and new releases. Log on to www.WolfeNovels.com to sign up, or email me at LW@WolfeNovels.com.

Did you enjoy Tess Winnett and her team? Would you like to see them again in another Miami crime story? Your thoughts and feedback are very valuable to me. Please contact me directly through one of the channels listed below. Email works best: LW@WolfeNovels.com.

Connect with Me

Email: LW@WolfeNovels.com
Facebook: https://www.facebook.com/wolfenovels
Follow Leslie on Amazon: http://bit.ly/WolfeAuthor
Follow Leslie on BookBub: http://bit.ly/wolfebb
Website: www.WolfeNovels.com
Visit Leslie's Amazon store: http://bit.ly/WolfeAll

Books by Leslie Wolfe

BAXTER & HOLT SERIES

Las Vegas Girl
Casino Girl
Las Vegas Crime

TESS WINNETT SERIES

Dawn Girl
The Watson Girl
Glimpse of Death
Taker of Lives

STANDALONE NOVELS

Stories Untold

ALEX HOFFMANN SERIES

Executive
Devil's Move
The Backup Asset
The Ghost Pattern
Operation Sunset

For the complete list of Leslie Wolfe's novels, visit:
Wolfenovels.com/order

Preview: *Las Vegas Girl*

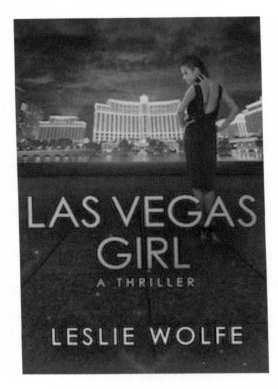

1
Elevator Ride

Her smile waned when the elevator doors slid open and her gaze met the scrutiny of the stranger. She hesitated before stepping in, looked left and right uneasily, hoping there'd be other hotel guests to ride in the elevator, so she wouldn't have to share it alone with that man. No one came.

Her step faltered, and her hand grabbed the doorframe, afraid to let go, still unsure of what to do. The hotel lobby sizzled with life and excitement and sparkled in a million colors, as can only be seen in Vegas. Nearby, clusters of gaming tables and slot machines were surrounded by tourists, and cheers erupted every now and then, almost covering the ringing of bells and the digital sound of tokens overflowing in silver trays, while the actual winnings printed silently on thermal paper in coupons redeemable at the cashier's desk. That was Las Vegas: alive, filled with adrenaline, forever young at heart. Her town.

The elevator had a glass wall, overlooking the sumptuous lobby. As the cage climbed higher and higher, riders could feel the whole world at their feet. She was at home here, amid scores of rowdy tourists and intoxicated hollers, among beautiful young women dressed provocatively, even if only for a weekend.

She loved riding in those elevators. Nothing bad was going to happen, not with so many people watching.

She forced some air into her lungs and stepped in, still hesitant. The doors whooshed to a close, and the elevator set in motion. She willed herself to look through the glass at the effervescent lobby, as the ruckus grew more distant with each floor. She didn't want to look at the man, but she felt his gaze burn into her flesh. She shot a brief glance in his direction, as she casually let her eyes wander toward the elevator's floor display.

The man was tall and well-built, strong, even if a bit hunchbacked. He wore a dark gray hoodie, all zipped up, and faded jeans. He'd pulled his hood up on top of a baseball cap bearing the colors of the New York Mets. A pair of reflective sunglasses completed his attire, and, despite the dim lights in the elevator cabin, he didn't remove them. The rest of his face was covered by the raised collar of his hoodie, leaving just an inch of his face visible, not more.

She registered all the details, and as she did, she desperately tried to ignore the alarm bells going off in her mind. Who was this man, and why was he staring at her? He was as anonymous as someone could be, and even if she'd studied him for a full minute instead of just shooting him a passing glance, she wouldn't be able to describe him to anyone. Just a ghost in a hoodie and a baseball cap.

Then she noticed the command panel near the doors. Only her floor number was lit, eighteen. She remembered pressing the button herself, as soon as she'd climbed inside the cabin. Where was he going? Maybe she should get off that elevator already. Maybe she should've listened to her gut and waited for the next ride up.

A familiar chime, and the elevator stopped on the fifth floor, and a young couple entered the cabin giggling and holding hands, oblivious to anyone else but each other. She breathed and noticed the stranger withdrew a little more toward the side wall. The young girl pressed the number eleven, and the elevator slowly set in motion.

That was fate giving her another chance, she thought, as she decided to get off the elevator with those two, on the eleventh floor. Then she'd go back downstairs, wait for the stranger to get lost somewhere, and not go back upstairs until she found Dan. She'd call him to apologize, invent something that would explain why she'd stood him up. Anything, only not to go back to her room alone, when the creepy stranger knew what floor she was on.

A chime and the elevator came to a gentle stop on the eleventh floor. The young couple, entangled in a breathless kiss, almost missed it but eventually proceeded out of the cabin, and she took one step toward the door.

"This isn't your stop, Miss," the stranger said, and the sound of his voice sent shivers down her spine.

Instead of bursting through that door, she froze in place, petrified as if she'd seen a snake, and then turned to look at him. "Do I know you?"

The stranger shook his head and pointed toward the command panel that showed the number eighteen lit up. Just then, before she could will herself to make it through those doors, they closed, and the cabin started climbing again.

Her breath caught, and she withdrew toward the side wall, putting as much distance between herself and the stranger as she possibly could. She risked throwing the man another glance and thought she saw a hint of a grin, a flicker of tension tugging at the corner of his mouth.

With an abrupt move, she reached out and pressed the lobby button, then resumed leaning against the wall, staring at the floor display.

"I forgot something," she said, trying to sound as casual as possible, "I need to go back down."

On the eighteenth floor, the doors opened with the same light chime and quiet whoosh. The stranger walked past her, then stopped in the doorway and checked the hallway with quick glances.

She was just about to breathe with ease when he turned around and grabbed her arm with a steeled grip, yanking her out of the cabin.

"No, you don't," he mumbled, "you're not going anywhere."

She screamed, a split second of a blood-curdling shrill that echoed in the vast open-ceiling lobby that extended all the way to the top floor. No one paid attention; lost in the general noise coming from downstairs, her scream didn't draw any concern. It didn't last long either. As soon as the man pulled her out of the elevator, he covered her mouth with his other hand, and her cry for help died, stifled.

He shoved her forcefully against the wall next to the elevator call buttons and let go of her arm, pinning her in place under the weight of his body. Then his hands found her throat and started squeezing. She stared at him with wide-open eyes, trying to see anything beyond the reflective lenses of his sunglasses, while her lungs screamed for another gasp of air. She kicked and writhed, desperately clawing at his hands to free herself from his deathly grip.

With each passing second, her strength faded, and her world turned darker, unable to move, to fight anymore. The man finally let go. Her lifeless body fell into a heap at his feet, and he stood there for a brief moment, panting, not taking his eyes off her.

Then he picked her up with ease and carried her to the edge of the corridor that opened to an eighteen-floor drop, all the way to the crowded lobby below. Effortlessly, he threw her body over the rail and watched it fall without a sound.

The noises downstairs continued unabated for a few seconds more, then they stopped for a split moment, when her lifeless body crashed against the luxurious, pearl marble floor. Then the crowd parted, forming a circle around her body, while screams erupted everywhere, filling the vast lobby with waves of horror.

His cue to disappear.

~~~End Preview~~~

Like *Las Vegas Girl*?

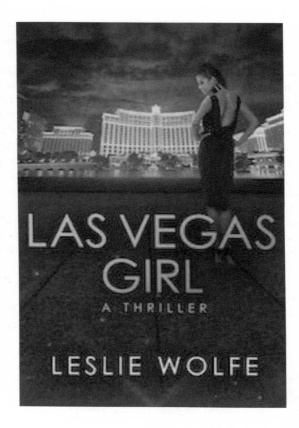

Read it now!

About the Author

Leslie Wolfe is a bestselling author who has been writing all her life, although it took until 2011 for her to publish her first book, *Executive*.

Since then, she has written many more, continuing to break down barriers of traditional thrillers. Her style of fast-paced suspense, backed up by extensive background research in technology and psychology, has made Leslie one of the most read authors in the genre, and she has created an array of unforgettable, brilliant, and strong women heroes along the way.

Reminiscent of the television drama *Criminal Minds*, her series of books featuring the fierce and relentless FBI Agent **Tess Winnett** would be of great interest to readers of James Patterson, Melinda Leigh, and David Baldacci crime thrillers. Fans of Kendra Elliot and Robert Dugoni suspenseful mysteries would love the **Las Vegas Crime** series, featuring the awkward relationship between Baxter and Holt. Finally, her **Alex Hoffmann** series of political and espionage action adventure will enthrall readers of Tom Clancy, Brad Thor, and Lee Child.

Leslie has received much acclaim for her work, including inquiries from Hollywood, and her books offer something that is different and tangible, with readers becoming invested in not only the main characters and plot but also with the ruthless minds of the killers she creates.

A complete list of Leslie's titles is available at https://wolfenovels.com/order.

Leslie enjoys engaging with readers every day and would love to hear from you. Become an insider: gain early access to previews of Leslie's new novels.

- Email: LW@WolfeNovels.com
- Facebook: https://www.facebook.com/wolfenovels
- Follow Leslie on Amazon: http://bit.ly/WolfeAuthor
- Follow Leslie on BookBub: http://bit.ly/wolfebb
- Website: www.WolfeNovels.com
- Visit Leslie's Amazon store: http://bit.ly/WolfeAll

Contents

Acknowledgment..3
Nightmare...5
Day Off...8
Suicide..12
The Parents..17
Privileged Territory..22
The Boyfriend..25
Approvals..30
Me: Watching..33
Date and Time...35
Assumptions and Scenarios..41
Nickname..45
Me: Waiting...50
Santiago..53
Press Release...57
Another Life..61
Arguments...64
Dark Web..68
Me: Enraged..72
Moonlighting...74
Hair...77
Clause...81
Stakeout..86
Countdown..89
Me: Working...93
Initial Profile...96
The Date..100
Live Streaming...102
Two-Time Loser...106
Fame..111

Hell Hath No Fury..116
Lies and Truth...121
Me: Unsatisfied..127
A Promise..129
The Profile..134
Tactical Plans...139
The Agent..143
Me: Planning...145
Dinner Plans...148
Scenarios..153
A Favor..157
Time Gap...160
Haley..166
Baiting the Trap...169
Marla's Song...173
Waiting Game...177
Live...181
Findings...187
Adam...192
Again..196
Me: Enjoying...199
The Name...201
The Senator..206
Seizure..209
Tactical...213
Exposed..217
Me: Amazing..223
Dinner and A Movie...228
Thank You!...232
Connect with Me..232
Books by Leslie Wolfe..233
Preview: *Las Vegas Girl*......................................234
Elevator Ride..235
About the Author...239

43509615R00144

Made in the USA
Middletown, DE
25 April 2019